"WE BELONG; TO THE STORM . . . TO EACH OTHER!"

I plunged through the stubble of rocks and under-growth toward the cliffs and the sea. And then, suddenly, something was in my path—an obstruction I beat against while two arms took me savagely, hold-ing me against a hard male breast. In the brief pale light of the moon, through tossed wild clouds, I saw a lean dark face looking down at me.

I struggled against him, pummeling his chest with my fists, though my heart was pounding with a mounting uncontrollable desire . . .

"Don't!" I screamed shrilly. "Your wife . . ."

He laughed. "My *wife*, indeed. Little you know. My lady wife. Don't speak of her . . ."

Then he said more gently, with one hand sweeping the blown hair from my forehead. "Don't fight me, Carmella . . . my darling love, it's no use. We *belong*; to the storm . . . to each other. . . ."

GYPSY
FIRES

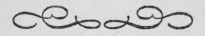

Mary Williams writing as
Marianne Harvey

A DELL BOOK

Published by
Dell Publishing Co., Inc.
1 Dag Hammarskjold Plaza
New York, New York 10017

This work was first published in Great Britain by
William Kimber & Co. Limited as CARNECRANE.

Dell ® TM 681510, Dell Publishing Co., Inc.

ISBN: 0-440-12860-9

Printed in the United States of America

First U.S.A. printing—August 1981

CONTENTS

Introduction

The moon-washed sky was already streaked by intermittent flying clouds as a solitary farm cart labored and lurched along the high moorland road winding northward from Penzance. A freshening wind was rising, and the gaunt coastline loomed black against the turbulent night sea. Huddled among young screaming pigs and straw, a girl sat tense behind the driver's broad back. She had a cardboard crown clutched incongruously in one hand. Her dress, beneath the rough sacking, was thin and gauzy, sewn with paper stars. Her mind, like her body, was still numbed with shock; for an hour ago she had seen her brothers Jasper and Jesse taken by the law for an offense they hadn't committed at the great Autumn Fair. The authorities those days were hard on rioters, who could be transported for making trouble, or even worse, and she feared for their safety.

No one knew how the quarrel had started; only that one moment the three of them were performing *Love Betrayed* on a patch of ground near their wagon. The next there was a fight going on concerning a Bible-thumping preacher, who'd attacked them with others, egged on by the crowd.

Carmella Penvane shivered. Her breath quickened and stomach retched as she recalled the scene—the flying stones and lunging fists, the bawling voices and raucous oaths as their cart was smashed and belongings taken; the stench of beer and sweat and blood—and Jasper! poor Jasper so quiet and friendly despite his immense bulk—with the blood streaming from his face. They'd have had her too, if the farmer hadn't dragged her aside and thrown the sacking around her.

"Keep your mouth shut," he'd said. "Come on now." He'd pulled her away to the outskirts of the crowd where a man stood, dark and broad against the fitful light. He wore a black calf-length coat or frac, a yellow silk waistcoat, and white muslin neck-scarf. His hat was a three-cornered felt, and although Carmella was too frightened to notice details, she was aware he was a man of quality. The peasant stepped forward touching a forelock. There'd been a brief conversation between the two men, a nod from the stranger after one appraising glance in her direction. Then he'd turned abruptly and walked sharply toward the scene of the skirmish.

"Et's settled," Carmella's rescuer said, gripping her arm again. "That theer's William Cremyllas, my landlord and Chairman o' the Bench, an' if you do behave decent an' watches your manners you'dn have a good job with his lady wife. I told 'en what'd happened, an' he'll see your kin's treated just an' proper. 'Tell her that,' 'ee did say. So you do your best. Many'd give all they got an' more for the chance. You should be grateful, girl."

Carmella *was* grateful. Without her brothers there could be no Penvane Theater Company, and she was skilled at nothing else; Jasper and Jesse might be imprisoned for years. She might even never see them again. To one of her looks and profession life could so easily lead to the brothel, and she was too proud for that; neither had she any intention of being publicly auctioned as wife or slave to some bawdy drunkard.

A job: honest work, however poorly paid for—she must have that until the day when her brothers were freed. And if this William Cremyllas was such a man of substance and influence as the farmer said, she'd have to use what assets she possessed to get his sympathy and help. She had looks and manners, and more graces and learning than most "travelers" had, because of her grandfather who'd been a scholar.

Not that learning seemed to matter at that moment.

As the rough cart rattled and heaved upward, she shivered, shuffling away from a young pig thrusting its nose at her face.

The cart gave a sudden lurch to the right, and the driver half turned his head, saying, "That theer's it—that's Carne-crane."

Looking around, Carmella saw the gaunt outlines of a house ahead—standing, it seemed, on the very edge of the cliffs and sea. By the gates of a short drive the man drew up, heaved himself to the ground, and grumbling under his breath went to open them. The mournful scream of a gull rose shrilly on a sudden gust of wind; and as watery cloud dimmed the night sky, the rhythmic sound of horses' hooves echoed from the distance. Instinctively the girl's body tensed. Through her experience as a player she had learned mistrust of solitary riders when most God-fearing folk were abed. In these wild regions of Cornwall reckless acts were committed by smugglers, the Preventative, or thieves who wouldn't stop at murder for a handful of silver in their pockets. And women, she knew, were never safe from marauding hands. So she crouched down again into the shadows of the cart, while the clippetty-clop of galloping hooves intensified and drew nearer every moment.

The driver had returned to the cart and was about to take his seat when the horseman overtook them and dismounted.

"It's all right, Abel," he shouted. "You can go your way, and I'll take the wench."

The girl lifted her head, staring. As the moonlight broke free of cloud, she saw a lean face with narrowed dark eyes staring down at her. For a brief instant the features were clear—strongly carved and arrogant, with dominant chin and nose above a white scarf and black coat.

William Cremyllas.

He waited, holding his horse by the bridle, while she struggled to her feet. With an awkward attempt at dignity she did the best she could to climb gracefully from her undignified posture and position.

The farm man would have pulled her out, but Cremyllas was first. Handing his reins to Abel, he reached up and took her full weight as she jumped lightly down. The contact was brief, but sufficient to start her trembling from a strange unknown apprehension she had no wish or capacity to understand.

A minute later the farm cart was rattling away down a narrow moorland lane, and the two figures of the man and girl were walking with the horse along the windblown drive to the house. The sky had darkened again, for which she was grateful. The smell of animals and straw still lingered in her nostrils; she was uncomfortably aware of her bedraggled appearance and chill in her bones.

No word was spoken between them except by William, who remarked tersely, "You must be tired and hungry. That shall be attended to. Here, put this on."

He took the sacking from her shoulders and replaced it by his own coat. She tried to thank him, but the words somehow wouldn't form, and when they reached Carnecrane he had become his own grim self again.

A light appeared through a half-open door ahead, followed by the figure of a boy from the side of the house. Cremyllas handed the horse to him, then ushered the girl forward. Against the flickering glare their forms appeared dark but briefly distorted, unreal. They could have been two phantoms until the light died, taking them into the shadows of the building.

The high wind moaned and sighed fitfully. There was the click of a door somewhere, followed by the muted murmur of voices. Then silence, except for the creaking and tapping of trees and undergrowth against the walls of Carnecrane.

I

Carmella

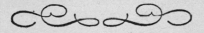

When I first saw the house standing gaunt against the glassy sea, I was suddenly afraid. In the moonlight it loomed prisonlike from the cliffs, waiting, it seemed, to entrap me. Perhaps because I wasn't used to granite walls, or any walls at all for that matter. All my life I had been free, traveling from place to place with my family and friends, sleeping where fancy or opportunity took me, in a barn, empty cottage, maybe huddled together under our cart, or when it was fine, beneath the stars. I'd liked those summer nights, heady with the sweet lush smell of grass, may blossom, and elderflower; and in the autumn too, when woodsmoke curled round the rotting leaves.

We had always been travelers. It was an exciting life; especially when I was old enough to perform with the company. I was ten that first time, and wore a blue dress with a silver crown, because I was the young princess who was persecuted by the three witches of hell. We gave the play on our cart in the village square. It was a large village, and when I was rescued by the noble king and his servant, everyone cheered. My grandfather was the king; he was a very learned man, a rebel, and a bit of a poet who had run away from his father's country rectory as a young man to follow the theater. He taught me how to read and write, and understand good English, because, he said, a time might come when I would want to make myself understood among cultured people. Tessa, his wife and my grandmother, could not write a word. She was of gypsy stock, very beautiful, with a way of dancing I can't describe. Wild; that was it, and her temper was wild too. Sometimes when the crowd didn't like us she would scream and shout so hard in Romany that they'd shamble away like the louts they were, and then we'd pack up and move on again before the law caught up with us.

My mother, who was Tessa's daughter, was gentler and more like her father; but my memories of both parents are dim, because they died of fever when I was nine, followed the next year by Tessa, leaving, except for myself, only my grandfather, my two brothers Jasper and Jesse, and Rebecca my elder sister to continue with our acts. Later our cousins joined us; but when the press-gang took them we carried on alone. Then Rebecca married a gypsy who was later hanged for sheep stealing. We never heard from her again or knew what had happened to her. She had always been wild like Grandmother, and we feared she might be dead too.

I'm sure my grandfather thought so. Sometimes, despite his gaiety, his eyes were sad, making him look more like a preacher than an actor with his fine head and profile. But there was little of the preacher about him.

"Heaven and hell," he said to me once, "do not exist except in the mind. Remember that, Carmella my child. Pious men can be the devil's own. Be free in your heart to love the real things . . . the smell of grass and rush of spring . . . laughter and song, good company and good language. Words can be jewels, child, brighter and more liquid than your own clear eyes. Learn them; learn hard so that you will not forget, so that you can take the stage and have men and women weeping when you speak."

He would talk with me of the great Shakespeare, and taught me many of his lines. I know there was nothing my grandfather would have liked so well as to be able to play Lear. But he realized his own limitations, also the limitations of the audiences we had. And so our performances were mostly of the mummer type of drama, for which we dressed as colorfully as possible, and proclaimed as we appeared.

When I was a small child, I liked most of all to watch my father as Saint George slay the terrifying dragon. After he died, my brother Jesse stepped into his place. At first he was all right, but when the novelty wore off things changed. Jesse was handsome and amiable but not particularly clever, with more of a liking for taverns and women than for us. Jasper resented him. I had a feeling sometimes he resented everything about our life. Jasper was smaller than Jesse, darker, and also harder, with a domineering way that sometimes brought them to fighting.

I used to wonder about Jasper, and could easily picture him as the narrow-minded rector his great-grandfather must have been. Certainly he had little of Tessa in him. My grandfather, I knew, had always found him rather dull as a boy, although he'd never said so, because he was loyal to his family.

Always, when I think back now to those times, it is my grandfather I remember most clearly . . . his largeness of spirit which matched his stature and warmth of heart.

I was thinking of him that night when I entered the great hall of Carnecrane for the first time, longing for his arm around my shoulders, to hear his voice encouraging and giving comfort as it had always done. But I hid such weakness from William Cremyllas, because I had learned early that men were quick to take advantage of a woman's fears. "Let him admire me," I thought, "and desire me from a distance. While he does so, I shall be safe. I will do what he wants and be companion to his lady wife. But my pride and my body will remain my own."

I had no intention of being mistress to any man I did not love, or to any other woman's husband. When I gave myself, it would be to someone tall and young, with eyes only for me: someone just a little older than myself, fair-haired, with a brightness to match my own red gold. I had known from first adolescence just what my lover must be. This man Cremyllas was nothing like him; dark, unsmiling, with stern jaw and smoldering hard eyes under heavy brows. No. Despite my gratitude, I did not even like him. This made it easier. I would tempt him and bewitch him, and so become acceptable in his house until the moment arrived with the opportunity to make my own plans again.

In spite of the sorry state I was in, all this flashed through my mind as I walked obediently beside him along the wide hall which was icy cold, despite the wood fire burning from an immense Italian-looking fireplace, which appeared to me depressing and rather vulgar. The furniture looked French, also the tapestries on the walls. I had seen such furnishings before, in the few rewarding times when, as players, we had been invited to perform for an evening in rich households. I knew too, having traveled the length and width of Cornwall, and heard stories in many inns and kiddleywinks, that such treasures more often than not had been plundered from the Continent, or smuggled from overseas.

This had not bothered me. I knew that to become rich one had to be clever, strong, and daring. But I had resented that so cultured a man as my grandfather had had to struggle hard for a livelihood, and that many of my kin had landed in jail or been taken by the press-gang, when others not a whit more brave, and far less charming, had amassed considerable honors and wealth from dubious undertakings.

"Well?" Cremyllas said, as we came to the foot of some stairs. "What are you shivering for?"

I faced him, throwing my hair from my face. "I'm not shivering."

"Don't lie to me. You're shaking in your shoes and as white as a sheet. You look a mess."

My temper flared, staining my cheeks, so that I had to bite my lip to keep from crying, "A mess, after being abused and jostled and commandeered like any low vagabond to ride with a company of pigs to this cold place? What do you expect?"

But even if I'd spoken, I don't think he'd have heard. His face was away from me as though I didn't exist, and a moment later he shouted, "Thamsin, come here. Where the devil are you? *Thamsin?*"

Seconds later the figure of a broad dark-haired girl wearing a mobcap and apron scurried from the shadows. When she drew nearer, I noticed the sulky furtive look on her face, mixed with fear. No wonder, I told myself. Cremyllas in such a mood was enough to scare a simple creature like herself out of her wits. A very different man indeed from the one I'd thought him when he'd first looked down at me, appearing every inch a gentleman.

"Yes, surr?" I heard the girl ask in a trembling voice. "I was at the back. I thought . . ."

"You're not paid to think," Cremyllas stated brusquely. "God knows why you're paid at all. And where are the others? Penharrick? Tom?"

"I dunno, surr. Tom's somewhere in the yard, but . . ."

"Well, we have a guest . . ." He paused, glancing toward me fleetingly. "A guest who is to help serve in this house; you understand? Take her to Mrs. Thomas so she can be made clean and respectable. Then see she has a room."

The girl came toward me hesitantly, about to touch my arm, but I shook her hand away.

"There may be mud and straw on my dress from the rough ride, Mr. Cremyllas," I said hotly, "but I'm not one of the filthy peasants you may be used to. I come of a clean proud family who needs no woman or man for that matter to see to my respectability."

At first I thought he might strike me. The dark eyes narrowed, becoming slits of fire. Then suddenly he threw back his head and laughed.

"Be off with you," he said then, "and remember . . . respectability you may have, but manners too are needed here. See that you learn them, and how to control that hot temper of yours, or it will be the worse for you."

"I'll do what I can," I replied, knowing that I had got the better of him this time.

"We'll meet in the morning then."

"Very well."

"*Sir.*"

"*Sir,*" I echoed, dropping a curtsey mockingly, that even my grandfather would have approved.

"Thank you."

Before he turned away, I was quick to notice the amusement lurking about his mouth. The eyes had softened, grown warm again, and my anger died as quickly as it had risen. What kind of man was this, I wondered, who could be so hateful one moment and charming the next? Was he to be trusted? Could I believe that my brothers would have justice the next day? There was no answer to the question. I could only hope, and tell myself that a magistrate's word must be his bond. Even so I sensed undercurrents that had disquieting depths. Beneath his controlled exterior was something very different which had showed itself briefly. I would be wary, very wary, while I was under his roof. I, who had longed through adolescence for gentleness such as my grandfather's from a man, knew that I would not find it here. Somewhere, someday, I must meet the lover I had dreamed of . . . fair as a summer's day, tall as a sapling tree, with kindness on his lips and tenderness in his eyes. My body yearned with desire, for perfection of fulfillment, because I was young, and despite the men who would have had me if they could, still a virgin. Virginity was precious, but with the blood of my grandmother rich in my veins, it could also be a torment; and I saw nothing here in the house of Cremyllas to appease my restless sleep; no young hero to ease my body's hunger and give my mind its peace. I had been torn from a hard crowd to a hard and sterile house.

Or so I believed.

How wrong I was.

My thoughts must have wandered longer than I knew, because I heard Thamsin saying anxiously with a touch of irritation, "Are you coming then? The master said to take you to Mrs. Thomas."

"Of course," I answered. I followed her down the hall to the kitchen, which was immense, with several smaller ones leading off . . . a dairy, I discovered later, a scullery, and two pantries. A man was drawing water into a bucket at the sink, and beside the table a woman stood, tall, angular, hard-faced, wearing black, with a frilly apron. The flickering candlelight threw strange shadows around the contours of her cheekbones and eye sockets reminding me of a mummer character representing death.

"And who's this?" she asked in a harsh voice.

"The master said she's to serve here and have a bed," Thamsin replied.

"And what's your name, girl?"

"Carmella," I said.

"Hm. That's no name for a scullery wench; it shall be Nell."

I lifted my head and faced her boldly. "I'm not here as a scullery maid. And Carmella's my name. Mr. Cremyllas has brought me here to be company for his wife."

Mrs. Thomas was about to retort angrily when William Cremyllas himself entered the kitchen. His eyes flickered over my face for an instant; then he said, "How does she strike you, Mrs. Thomas? Think my lady wife will approve?"

"Whether my lady does or does not, sir, the matter seems to have been settled," Mrs. Thomas replied. She paused, adding a second later, "With her hair well hid and in proper sober attire she may not do too badly."

"Then see that she's properly clad in the morning, and give her food now," Cremyllas retorted. "I've had enough of the baggage for the time being. And it's early bed for all of you. Understand?"

I couldn't help noticing the quick almost conspiratorial look flash between the woman's boot-button eyes and the veiled darkness of the man's; but I was too tired and hungry to bother about it, and when Cremyllas had gone I was thankful to be given a warm shawl and a stool at the table.

From a great pan on the stove, Mrs. Thomas ladled me a bowl of hot potato soup, and after that, cut me a hunk of saffron cake. "It's all you'll be getting at this hour," she said. "And in case you don't know it, this isn't my job . . . to wait on a woman like you, or any woman for that matter. It just happens that Lydia the other girl's gone to see her sick aunt over Boseagle way, and Thamsin's having to get your room ready. I'm the housekeeper here, and my word goes over domestic matters."

Smothering the hasty words on my lips, I said meekly, "I'll remember that, Mrs. Thomas. It never crossed my mind you could be an ordinary servant."

"Hm." Her tone was doubtful but from the softening of her mouth I knew she was pleased. That was as it should be. I told myself, remembering what my grandfather had said once when I would have upbraided a domineering member of our company for some paltry meanness. "Never make an enemy where you can win a friend," he'd told me. "Friendship can be a useful commodity, as well as a divine one, and anger only harries the digestion."

So far as I could I'd done my best to follow his sound advice; but there had been many times when I'd failed and given way to hot temper.

"That's your grandmother in you," he had remarked on one occasion. "Just as your green eyes are, and your wild red hair. Ah but what a gift for the stage. You should have been born to wider audiences, child." And I'd known he was thinking of great London and the theaters there where the toasts of the day appeared in fine clothes before the gentry of the land.

But I hadn't wanted that. I had been content with just what I had then . . . the winding lanes between lush green hedges splashed with bluebells and waving foxgloves; small stone-walled fields sloping to the spume-tossed sea, and huddled gray villages of the mining country, where our acts were generally well applauded and paid for, either with food and shelter, or what money was there. Although the tinners had often been bawdy, their generosity had heartened us, and scenes had been colorful when merchantmen with a large company of mules bearing coal to the mines had stopped in their travels to join our revelry. As players we had been well used to improvising, and none more so than Tessa, whose moods had so quickly alternated from joy to despair.

Strange exciting days they had been; but the early mornings best of all when the summer dawn lifted pale above the countryside, and only the cattle and bird sounds to break the quietness.

As I sat in the kitchen of Cremyllas with the bowl of broth before me, these fleeting memories brought a pain stronger even than hunger. I paused before lifting the wooden spoon to my lips, so that Mrs. Thomas said, "Well, isn't it to your liking then? It's good broth, the best."

"I'm sure," I said.

"Then what ails you, girl?"

"Nothing," I answered quickly, tasting the food. "And yes, it is very good. But it's funny sitting here with four walls around . . ."

I could see she did not understand. How could she? Her mouth went round and tight, and her dark brows met over her puzzled small eyes.

"You're a strange one," she said. "I can't for the life of me see what you're doing here, or what's the reason of it."

Neither did I, at that moment. But next morning I did, because it was then that I met Thurston for the first time.

—

2

I was woken that first morning at the great house by Thamsin, who came into the room without knocking and said breathlessly, "Time you was up. Mrs. Thomas gave me these for you last night, and said as how you shud put 'em on and be down ready."

She flung a dark dress on the bed, lit a candle for me, and scurried away banging the door behind her with a rattle.

I sat up in my underclothes. The room was cold and small, furnished only by the bed I had slept in which was a wooden box kind of affair, probably handmade, a rough cupboard, and a bench with a jug and bowl on it. There was no mirror. I determined to ask for one. Even in our poorest times as players we had never been without a mirror of some kind. When I put my feet on the frayed rush floor-covering, a mouse scurried near my toes to a hole under the small window. Delicately bred ladies might have screamed. But I was not that sort, having lived close to the small wild creatures all my life. I took up the dress to examine it, and found a mobcap as well. The gown was of coarse black weave, with a heavy underlining. Well, I thought, if I was to appear as a serving wench I would do so with a difference. By then I felt quite merry, and when I'd got the clothes on I caught up the skirt to my waist in front, and made it secure with a pin from the corsage of my own dress, so it fell with pannier effect on each side. Then I put on the cap, tilting it to the back of my head, letting my red-gold hair tumble free around my shoulders. If I'd had a patch I would have put that on too, and smeared paint on my lips of a geranium shade. That I hadn't was of no consequence, however. I knew the color would be fresh pink in my cheeks, and my mouth had never lacked a rose glow.

Presently I went down. When I managed at last to find the kitchen from the maze of tangled passages leading from the back stairs, Thamsin and Lydia were already at the table eating their breakfast gruel. Lydia was thin-faced, sharp-eyed, but better looking than Thamsin. She poked the other girl meaningfully as I appeared, and a series of giggles followed. I had made my entrance in true theatrical style, and was aware of its impact.

"My dear soul!" Lydia exclaimed. "She's something sure enough."

"Ais," Thamsin agreed.

"You'm better set down and eat before Mrs. Thomas sees," Lydia advised.

I was about to do so when the housekeeper appeared carrying a lantern. She eyed me disapprovingly and re-marked sharply, "Get yourself attired properly, girl, in the manner of respectable serving women or you'll be sent packing by the master himself."

I doubted it, but with downcast head unpinned the dress and pulled the mobcap right down over my ears, pushing every lock of hair under it.

"That's better," Mrs. Thomas said. "Now look sharp, eat your food, and when you've done you shall watch Lydia prepare my lady's tray; it will be your job in future to see it's taken up."

The breakfast gruel was tasteless, and I did not fancy the soused conger, which despite its vinegar smell was also strongly fishy, barely warm, and was the remnant, I guessed, from previous meals.

Later, when Mrs. Thomas had cast a critical eye on the tray for Lady Cremyllas, I was given it and told to follow her upstairs. At the top of the first flight leading from the kitchens, we turned along a narrow landing that curved sharply into a much wider corridor. By then no candles were needed, and in the pale early light I noted the rich tapestries on the walls interspersed with imposing ancestral portraits hanging in ornate gilded frames.

The handrails now were intricately designed, indicating the French influence which my grandfather had pointed out to me in other great houses on our rare visits with the company. Indeed, there was little he had not taught me about the fashions of cultured folk.

As we passed the wide staircase leading to the ground floor, the housekeeper said, "You must *never* on any account use these stairs. They are for the family and guests only."

"I'll remember," I said demurely. "There's so much you can teach me, Mrs. Thomas."

She eyed me suspiciously, but I sensed she was pleased.

I was shortly shown into a vast room which took my breath away at first glance by its elegance, its painted wall panels of Chinese design, graceful rosewood furniture which I later learned had been designed by a member of the Chippendale family, famous cabinetmakers of their time. The great canopied bed, though, appeared French, with its rich gold satin curtaining.

Such details registered in a flash, perhaps because of my inherent gift for quick observation . . . a quality I had acquired from my gypsy grandmother, who had been skilled not only at fortune-telling and mumming, but at assessing the possibilities of any likely client. A moment later I heard a querulous voice from the bed saying, "What is it? Have you my tray? I've been waiting for it since dawn."

Mrs. Thomas beckoned me forward sharply, curtseyed to the figure lying against the pillows, and introduced me, remarking, "This is a new serving maid for you, my lady. She says her name is . . ."

"Carmella," I interrupted, as I laid the tray on the coverlet.

"Oh?" Blue eyes regarded me from a thin face still beautiful though utterly weary and without vestige of color.

"I said Nell was more appropriate," the housekeeper said smugly.

"Carmella it shall be," Lady Cremyllas said. "Go now, Mrs. Thomas, and leave the girl with me."

Though I could she didn't like it, Mrs. Thomas left the room grudgingly, and when the door had closed, my new mistress said without a smile, "Who engaged you? I was not aware we were understaffed?"

"Mr. Cremyllas, your husband," I answered.

"Indeed!" She poured her tea absently, and continued, "How? and where from?"

I hesitated, doubtfully wondering if the truth would displease her, then sensing her annoyance when I did not answer immediately, gave her the facts as simply as I could. I waited for a burst of indignation, but it did not come. Instead a faint smile twitched her lips. "Really? Do you mean to say you are an *actress*?"

"Yes, my lady. I hope so."

"How very odd. You don't look it. My husband has a natural weakness for a pretty face, but you look hardly the type to capture a man's fancy on a dark night."

"The night was not dark, my lady, it was a bawdy one filled with lights and noise, and I was not dark either, as you may well see when I remove this cap. I was also in great distress over my brothers."

I tore the ugly cap from my head and let my hair loose over my shoulders, and as she stared, also tore open the neck of the tight black dress.

"So you see, I am not quite the plain Jane I appeared, and if you will allow me to be myself, lady, no doubt I will be able to amuse you better."

I waited, wondering and half fearing the effect my words would have.

I need not have feared. She was clearly intrigued.

"You speak truly. You are quite a beauty. The question is . . . are you also virtuous?"

"I can assure you that I am. My grandfather taught me that virtue was not only a precious gift to a young girl, but also a fine weapon."

"Your grandfather was a wise man," she commented.

"Wise, and also a gentleman," I told her.

"What was a gentleman doing with a group of players?" she asked.

"He always said the stage was the most cultured profession of all," I replied. "And he was a fine actor. If he had had the money he could have made a great name at Drury Lane, I am sure."

"Like Garrick?" she suggested with faint irony.

"Perhaps."

"But then David Garrick also produces and writes, and studied under the great Samuel Johnson. Did you know that?"

I shook my head. "We never knew London, and though my grandfather taught me what knowledge I have, mostly it was to know good English, and that was only when we had time. It was a busy life going from place to place, and there were other things too . . ."

"What things, Carmella?"

"The country," I said. "Nature. Learning the habits of wild things and when the rain was coming. How to cure with herbs, and mend broken limbs . . ."

"I thought that was gypsy stuff, except from proper doctors."

"My grandmother was herself gypsy," I answered, "and no worse for it; once when we were at a fair an artist wanted to paint her."

"I don't doubt it," Lady Cremyllas said dryly. "Well, Carmella, you can go now. I'm tired. My illness fatigues me when I talk. But maybe you'll bring a little amusement into my dull life. Never appear in that hideous cap again though. I realize it was Mrs. Thomas's idea . . . She's a worthy soul, but hardly colorful or versed in fashion. I'll speak with her, and see you have other clothes to wear. When I want you again you'll know. In the meantime interest yourself how you can. You may like to take a walk. And if you see my husband, tell him I wish to see him before he goes to court."

I gave a brief curtsey and left the room. Only a few yards along the landing I saw William Cremyllas himself turn by the top of the stairs.

"Ha!" he said, stopping me and looking down from his great height. "So it's the wild one I rescued last night?" His voice was mocking, and his eyes were bold. I did not like him, but a fire ran through me because I knew this was a man I would be fighting in many ways.

"It is," I said. "*Sir,* I have been with your lady wife who wishes to see you before you attend the court."

"I'm aware of that," he snapped.

"If the court is not a long one, will I soon know about the fate of my brothers?" I said.

His eyes narrowed to dark slits. "A magistrate is not in the habit of breaking his word," he said shortly. "And don't plague me with questions or I'll send you packing . . ." But his look wavered, as his voice quietened. I knew that look, and replied boldly:

"I don't think you will, sir."

"What?"

"Send me packing," I said, adding before he could speak again, "You see, sir, I shall serve you well, and do my best to amuse your lady. I think she already likes me."

"Hm. We'll see about that." He turned abruptly on his heel, and walked away without another word. But I knew I was there to stay.

I went down to the kitchens. Lydia was sweeping the floor, and Thamsin at the sink washing up. "What's happened to the cap?" Lydia inquired sharply.

"I left it in my lady's room," I said triumphantly. "No

doubt she'll see one of you has it. She likes me better as I am. So do I."

Both girls stopped and gaped at me as I went to the side door.

"Where be you off to now?" Lydia said.

"I'm going to look around. Lady Cremyllas said I could."

"Then keep to path," Lydia told me, "or 'ee'll be in purty trouble with maister."

When I got to the back of Carnecrane, I saw a wide patch of lawn with steps running down the center in a number of terraces which eventually came to an abrupt end. The path ran at the side, beyond which were a series of outbuildings, obviously stables and ox-stalls. The man Penharrick and a youth who was probably a groom were busy there with buckets and hay. Penharrick glanced at me as I passed, but that was all. He was a broad-shouldered short man with bushy black hair falling over heavy brows.

I walked sharply, half running, in case Lady Cremyllas wanted me before I got back. Suddenly the path ended, becoming a mere track dropping steeply between great rocky cliffs to a cove below. There was a gully on my right which cut deep into the land, forming a kind of creek. A drift of cool salty air brushed my face and the sky above became alive with the shrill wild cry of gulls. Something in me responded exultantly to the elements. I lifted my head high, and savored the touch of brine on my lips. Then, holding my heavy skirts with both hands, I carefully made my way between the stones toward the beach below.

The descent was a challenge that pleased and warmed me. When I reached the cove, I was glowing as though rich wine flooded my blood; and the beauty of the place filled me with heady excitement. Such a setting, I thought, would well have suited William Shakespeare's *Tempest*. Strange tall rock shapes loomed against the pale sand, grouped witchlike in a thin sea mist which wreathed and curled above the breaking waves. Involuntarily Ariel's song came to my lips . . .

Come unto these yellow sands,
And then take hands.
Curtsied when you have and kiss'd,
The wild waves whist,
Foot it featly here and there;
And sweet sprites, the burden bear.
Hark, hark!

I wanted to take off the heavy stockings I had been given,
wanted to let the damp sand touch my toes . . . to dance
as I had so often in my grandfather's time, freely and gaily
in my own wild way. So it was not surprising that when
one of the stones took shape and moved toward me, I felt
no shock, except of joy. Here was Ariel himself or some
young Ferdinand come to meet me; a man tall and fair,
with the pale hair blown from his fine wide forehead, his
smile witching and welcoming.

I waited until he stood before me, a gallant figure in
pale gray, with silver buttons and braid diamonded in the
mist. His voice, when he spoke, was low and cultured.

"If it isn't Miranda herself," he said.

I nearly replied, "And you are Ferdinand surely? The
one I've dreamed of for so long." But instead I remarked,
"I would have liked to play Miranda, but I never did. And
now I am servant to the lady at the great house."

"Servant?" He sounded amazed.

"That is so." And I went on to explain how I had come
to Carnecrane.

When I had finished, he took off his frac and put it
around my shoulders.

"Though your hair may hold the glory of the sunlight
and the fire of autumn," he said, with his lips close to my
cheek, "it is cold. So we will go back together."

"Back? You?"

He bowed. "Thurston Cremyllas at your service, Miranda."

As I stared at him I could not speak for the emotion

which swept through me like a glowing wind. I knew that my wild dream had materialized at last. This would be no passing meeting, but one which could endure and be enriched by time.

He took my hand and helped me step by step up the steep track to the top of the cliffs. When we stood on the short turf with the sea far below and only the gulls wheeling against the gray sky, I asked him when he'd come, and from where, his relationship to William Cremyllas and his wife.

"I am the only one and errant son," he said with a touch of irony, "and arrived last night from Oxford where I was studying."

"At university?"

"True. But owing to a distressing scandal, I have suffered the ignominy of being sent down. And that means expelled for a considerable length of time."

From the mockery in his voice I knew that however distressing the scandal might have been, it did not really perturb him.

I couldn't help inquiring, "What was the nature of the scandal, sir? Or shouldn't I ask?"

"No, you shouldn't. But you may be sure it was no woman."

We walked on, silence between us until he continued, "I slept last night in the loft above the harness room, and came down to the cove for a refresher before facing my irate parent."

"Oh."

"Now from what you've told me, he will be away."

"Yes. He has gone to see my brothers are freed," I told him. "The ones I was with when the law took us. I hope he finds them innocent. They certainly were."

"Oh, he'll do that," Thurston replied. "Innocent or not it won't matter to him so long as he gets his price." His eyes were on me meaningfully.

"What do you mean?" I asked sharply.

"Just that my father's conscience can be elastic when a pretty face is involved."

"I don't think you should speak that way," I said primly. "Mr. Cremyllas has been considerate and generous to me in every way."

"Oh, he would be. He would be. He's clever. He was clever when he married Mama, the only child and daughter of Lord Pengalva, who has invested enough in Carnecrane projects to make Penbrecn and Wheal Gulvas the richest tin mines in West Cornwall. However, not quite so clever perhaps in assessing her character. For that I mildly pity him. The connubial bed has been empty for many years, which you will discover for yourself quite soon. . . . I tell you this because it is no secret. So you see, Miranda, there is much to explain his unpredictable behavior in bringing you to Carnecrane. Take care therefore. You're far too lovely to be used as he's doubtless used many women."

I lifted my head. "I don't believe it. And you needn't fear on my account. I know how to look after myself."

"Do you?" His hand touched my waist lightly, but the brief contact inflamed my whole body so that I shivered while the hot color flooded my face.

"Here," I said, taking the frac from my shoulders. "I don't need it anymore. I'm quite warm. And you should look respectable for your homecoming."

He slipped it on, and a moment later we were by the terraces of the garden. He insisted that I accompany him through the wide doors of the house which Mrs. Thomas had emphasized were only for guests and members of the family. When I mentioned this, Thurston answered, "In my father's absence I am master. I will see that all doors are for your use. In future you will have more than servant status. Indeed, I'm sure you have it already."

The housekeeper was at the far end of the hall when we

entered. She hurried forward and bobbed a curtsey to Thurston, exclaiming,

"Mr. Thurston, sir, I did not know you'd come. If I had . . ." Her voice trailed off as her eyes surveyed me disapprovingly.

"You weren't to know," Thurston Cremyllas said, "neither were you to know that Mama's new companion and I had become acquainted. I have given permission for her to have the use of the house as befitting her position. When my father comes back I'm sure he'll agree."

I could see that Mrs. Thomas did not like it. Her expression was almost hostile as she said to me, "My lady has been talking to me about you. I have some clothes for you to change into. Then later you are to go up to her."

Thurston smiled. "Run away with Mrs. Thomas and change as she says. That gown you are wearing is really a hideous contraption. In the meantime I'll make peace with one parent so we can present a united front to my father. Not that he'll be bothered. There'll be a fog tonight I'm thinking . . . and if so he'll doubtless have other things on his mind."

The housekeeper eyed him warily. He laughed shortly and turned to run lightly up the stairs. If I'd not been so entranced and bemused by him . . . so enthralled by the miracle of our first meeting . . . I might have wondered at his strange allusion to fog and "other things on his mind."

As it was, I had no thought but of Thurston; that, incredible as it seemed, I had found the man who had been in my imagination since early girlhood. We had met in the flesh. One day, I was sure, and not too far off, we would be one in reality. For when he asked me I would go to him joyfully without doubt or reserve. My body and my spirit would be unified at last. Already, in my mind, his hands were caressing me, my body straining and pulsing to his touch. Oh, I was not Tessa's granddaughter for nothing. I was in love, in love. My senses leaped, my heart sang, and

my blood was fire. I knew then that fate had brought me to
Carnecrane. What I did not know was the strange dark
path it would take me.

That night I dreamed. Yet some of the time I did not know
whether I was dreaming or not. Above the gentle soughing
of the wind I heard in a half-awake state other sounds that
mingled with the sounds and sights of my dream . . .
muffled conversations and shadows that became men.
Many men from whom I fled until I reached a gap in the
darkness where pure light spilled and took me to its heart.
The light was Thurston. But when I touched him, he dis-
solved and left me in a great emptiness. I cried out, and
my own cry woke me. When I jumped from my bed, my
head spun for a moment and I had to steady myself by the
chair. Like someone sleepwalking I stumbled to the window, groping for the curtain. The foggy air pressed against
the glass. For some reason I was afraid. I stood quite still,
waiting for what I did not know. Then, as the mist wavered, thickened, and cleared again, I saw the blurred glim-
mer of a light. It could have been the moon. But I knew it
wasn't. This light was not static. It moved and faded intermittently, disappearing at last into darkness. By then I was
properly awake, and curious about what was going on.

Presently I lit my candle and opening my door softly
went out into the corridor. I crept along to the top of the
stairs and paused with my ears alert. From the landing below I heard the steady tick-tock, tick-tock of the grandfather clock, followed by the furtive sound of footsteps
climbing. I stared, rooted to the spot. The shadows took
form and a man's face lit pale in the candlelight, emerged
disclike and ravaged, jaw set hard below the stern mouth
and bold nose; eyes burning and unwavering, holding mine
unblinkingly. How long I stood there I do not know, but at
last I turned and rushed to my room, spilling the candle
grease as I went. I locked the door with hands that trembled, and stood with my back against it until I'd recovered

some composure. There was no more sound. Presently I went back to bed, and dozed fitfully until morning.

When I went downstairs William Cremyllas was waiting for me. His stare was impersonal, betraying no knowledge of the night's encounter. I wondered indeed if the whole episode had been no more than a trick of my imagination, an extended dream which had driven me to sleepwalking.

"I was later back yesterday than I thought to be," he said in an aloof voice. "But you will be pleased to hear no doubt that your kinsmen were acquitted."

"Thank you," I answered.

"They sent their greetings and also told me they were off up country where they were thinking to join another company."

So they had gone. Just for a moment I felt deserted and terribly alone. Then I remembered Thurston, and knew with the irrational certainty of youth that I would never be really alone again.

3

As the days passed, my life at Carnecrane settled into a routine of mornings when I prepared the tray for Lady Cremyllas and took it up to her, followed an hour later by a session when I read to her, merely chatted, or gave excerpts from lines I had learned from my grandfather. There were times when she did not need me at all, but relapsed into long silences of melancholia from which nothing seemed to rouse her but continual tots from the brandy bottle she kept in her bedside cupboard. In the usual way my afternoons were free, and I was not required again until the evening following dinner. It was in my leisure hours that I saw Thurston, and walked with him very often across the moors or along the seashore. He told me of his Oxford experiences, of his ambitions as a poet, sometimes taking my hand lightly in his, and gently kissing me, gazing down at me with an ardent expression that quickened my heart and never failed to fill me with inexpressible joy. I wondered about women, but he spoke of none, and I didn't press the subject, because if he'd had a mistress or anyone he minded about in such a way I knew I would have been wildly jealous and unable to conceal it. Besides, Thurston was not the kind of a man to play with a girl; in many ways, by looks and deeds, he showed he cared for me. I soon discovered that he and his father lived in different worlds. Although William Cremyllas had had to accept the fact of his suspension from university, it was obvious that he had not forgiven him. At dinner, which I now

shared with them, sitting at the side of the long table with
Cremyllas at one end and his son at the other, I was con-
stantly aware of veiled hostility. They spoke very little, and
in the flickering candlelight Thurston's lips showed a con-
temputous twist, under the hard stare and uncompromising set of William's jaw. William, who had at first mildly
irritated me, now filled me with hot resentment because of
his hurtful attitude to his son. He treated him almost as
though he was a weakling.

One evening when Thurston spoke to him and he did not
reply, my temper got the better of me, though I'd tried
hard for control. I was wearing green satin that night; I
remember the dress because of the occasion, and because
Lady Cremyllas had given it to me the day before. I had
felt so pleased with myself going downstairs, knowing that
the shade and the low-cut bodice went well with my cream
skin, red hair, and slender figure, which though small-
waisted was yet well covered and feminine. "Tonight," I had
thought, "will be different. We will be friendly with a little
conversation perhaps."

But it was not to be. Cremyllas appeared not to notice
when I took my place at the table, and his churlishness to
Thurston made me exclaim quickly with the hot color
flooding my face, "My grandfather always said that polite-
ness was a worthy virtue!"

Both men turned quickly, as I looked down to my plate
of beef.

There was silence for some seconds until William Cremyllas said in tones of ice, "Are you complaining at not
being toasted, Madame Carmella? If so a thousand apolo-
gies. Drink, son, drink to the noble virtue of the tinker's
wench picked from the rabble on a drunken night at the
fair."

I just sat there, with both hands clenched, frozen with
shame, as William continued, "Well . . . do as I say,
damn you. Drink! Your mother surely has taught you how
to do that."

Whether Thurston obeyed or not I didn't wait to hear. I got up and rushed from the room; then, pulling the shawl tightly about my breasts and shoulders, ran out of the wide front doors into the cool calm of the late autumn night. I ran and ran until I reached the great iron gates opening to the moorland road. It was quiet there. Heady still from the scent of woodsmoke and the rich tang of fallen leaves, I rested my head against the rough bark of a tree while the tears welled from my eyes, trickling over my cheeks and hands in a release of emotion and longing. Longing for Thurston. I wanted him so I could cradle him against my breast; wanted, too, his arms about me, and the thudding of his heart pressed against mine. My fever for him was so intense that I was not surprised in the least when I heard him saying gently, "Carmella . . ." because there is a language of the heart surely between people who love each other, and Thurston must have sensed my desire.

I looked around, and he was there. "I'm so sorry," he continued, lifting my hand in his, "that my father should have spoken so grossly to you. You . . . who are the most beautiful and gentlest of creatures . . ."

"No," I cried. "I'm not gentle, but I love you . . . oh, I love you so much. I don't expect anything from you . . . not marriage or anything like that . . . but just . . ." I broke off, adding after a faint awkward pause, "I shouldn't have said that, should I? I'm sorry . . ."

"But my darling Miranda, I'm honored. I didn't realize you could feel so deeply. I'm not worth it though. What my father thinks of me is true in a way; I'm a failure and a bit of a dilettante. He lost patience long ago. I don't really blame him, and you shouldn't take it to heart."

"But I do. I can't help it. When you suffer *I* suffer. Don't you see, Thurston?"

"Yes. I understand now. But you mustn't . . . you mustn't think too highly of me. Or expect too much . . ."

"What do you mean?"

"We met in a dream," he said half-sadly, "when you were Miranda and I was . . ."

"Ariel?"

"Perhaps. But Ariel was never real, Carmella. You must remember that."

"*I'm* real," I cried fiercely. "Look at me. I'm *me;* Carmella. And we love each other, don't we? Don't we?"

His face became enigmatic. A shaft of moonlight caught it and his mouth was strained under the veiled look of his eyes. "Of course," he said.

"Do you mean it?"

"Why should I lie?"

"And we shall be together always? Somehow, somewhere? . . . We can say boo to your father and go away . . . I don't mind how poor I am, I could make money for us both in so many ways. I am very good at dancing, and I know how to tell fortunes. This may not be lady's work . . . but it pays when the fairs are on the roads . . ." I broke off, disturbed by his silence, the lack of response as his arms fell away. "What is it?" I said. "Have I spoken too freely? If . . . I will do just what *you* want, Thurston. Only tell me what it is."

The moon slipped behind the clouds again. His voice held a chill when he answered, "I don't know what I want, Carmella. Oh yes, I love you; how could I help it? But life must have a plan to it . . ."

"I know," I broke in. "That's what I meant. A plan. Something to work on so nothing can ever part us, so we can be together."

I waited, shivering slightly in the cold night air. He slipped an arm around me. "Come along; you're cold. I'll think things out. In the meantime we're together at Carne-crane. That's something, isn't it?"

"Yes," I said. But my heart was heavy. As we walked back to the house, it seemed to me that our love was defeated before it had ever been fulfilled.

Later, when I thought things over I realized that I had probably been too eager and that my enthusiasm had taken Thurston aback. But he would recover, I told myself stubbornly. He loved me; he had said so. It was just that he was shy of making hasty decisions. I made up my mind then to let the future alone for the moment, and enjoy the present.

I did not see William Cremyllas until the following morning, when he told me he would be away for some days in Penzance attending to business matters.

"My wife will need your full attention," he said. "She had an attack during the night. I shall trust to your judgment in looking after her."

"I don't understand her kind of sickness," I said. "Except that she seems unhappy."

"She has everything she wants, I can assure you. Anything money can buy. She has only to ask."

"Money isn't everything," I said boldly.

"No," he said, looking me very straight in the face. "Neither is a woman's foolish pride. There are many things here you don't know, and have no business to be knowing. Your duty is to Lady Cremyllas, and to me."

"You, sir?"

"Yes. You would do well to remember that and keep your scheming mind from my son."

I was not quick enough to find a tart answer. Before turning abruptly and going to the door, he said, "I don't wish him involved in any way with you. You can never be anything to each other. You would do well not to forget it."

Five minutes later as I went up to see Lady Cremyllas I was still quivering with anger. But when I saw her face bluish-white against the pillows, all other thoughts fled. Her eyes looked vacant; her mouth was slightly open, and the candlelight fell cruelly on the sagging sinews of her neck. There was a brandy bottle near the bed, but it was empty. Her hand lay lifeless over the quilt, as though she was reaching for something.

I went toward her. "Lady Cremyllas . . ."

Her head turned slightly. "Carmella?" she said in a tremulous voice.

"Yes, it's me. Can I get you anything? . . . You didn't want your breakfast. Mrs. Thomas said .. . ."

"No. I want nothing. I just want to die."

I laid my hand over hers. "You mustn't say that. Your husband, Mr. Cremyllas, was very worried about you."

A dry sound that might have been a laugh came from her throat. "You surely don't believe that? He wants it too. My death. Just as he wanted my money and my father's estate. That's all he ever did want."

"But, my lady . . ."

With a sudden flush of color and renewed vitality she sat up, with her thin fingers clawing my wrist. "When I have an attack he goes off," she said. "Take that in, will you? He goes off hoping that when he returns I shall no longer encumber him."

"I can't believe that's true," I said, doing my best not to.

"Just as you like. It's no matter. But one day you may be sure under a mask of kindliness he will bring me a dish of foxglove tea, and that will be the end."

I was horrified, speechless at the implication of her words. I did not like William Cremyllas, who had the knack of riling me as no man ever had before, but I had never pictured him in the role of murderer, and could not do so now. I did not want to hear any more, and after adjusting her pillows and smoothing her forehead with eau de cologne was about to leave the room when she said, "Come back, Carmella. Come here."

Reluctantly I turned and went toward her.

"If anything happens to me . . . anything unpredictable," she said in a weak voice, "I want you to remember what I've just told you. Oh, I know you think Mr. Cremyllas a wise and just man because among other things he is Chairman of the Bench and champion of worthy causes. But just men have been known to do strange deeds. The

gales around here are high sometimes, and the nights are
dark when no moon lights the sky. Sometimes there are
wrecks; and sometimes . . ." Her voice trembled.". . .
sometimes cellars are replenished that were empty before;
pockets bursting with gold and silver. I've known for a long
time that Carnecrane had evil roots." There was a silence
until she resumed again, in a dull singsong way, "I should
never have married him. But I was besotted by his force
and strength. I thought him such a gentleman." A harsh
dry cough rattled against her chest. "Yes," she echoed,
"imagine it. *Gentleman*. Why . . . his strength was nothing but brutality. And it is killing me . . . *killing* me . . ."

"You don't know what you're saying," I insisted, realizing that she did not.

"I know." Despite her wanderings and befuddled state,
there was finality in that brief statement; something that
would accept no denial. I was suddenly deeply sorry for
her. She was a poor thing, I thought, with her reason half
gone, and no physical powers left to help her through the
days that were left. But once she must have been beautiful,
a gentle highborn girl with grace and pretty ways to com-
mend her when William Cremyllas took her to his bed.
What had gone wrong? They had loved and bred a son of
their union, a man with the looks of some bright young god
who was my own love. Thinking of Thurston made me long
to comfort her.

"Oh, my dear lady . . ." I said, reaching toward her,
"don't have such thoughts . . ."

My words had a curious effect. From self-pity her manner became violent, as she said in a voice contorted with
rage. "Get out. Get out. Speaking like that to a Pengalva.
You . . . a scheming lowborn gypsy. Go, go, before I
. . . before I . . " She clutched the bedlothes to her chin
while a spasm of coughing seized her. I stood watching,
afraid, and unable to help, thinking this might be the end
she had predicted. But after a time she recovered suffi-

ciently to ask for a glass of water, which I fetched and held
while the liquid trickled down her throat. Soon a little color
returned to her pale lips. Her eyes opened.

"Is there anything else I can do for you?" I asked.

"No. Just go. Send Mrs. Thomas to me."

Thankful to escape I ran downstairs and told the housekeeper, who immediately stopped what she was doing and
hurried to her mistress.

Thurston was in the hall when I went through. "What's
the matter?" he asked. "You look as though you'd seen a
ghost."

"I feel like it," I answered, and told him about his
mother.

He did not seem concerned. "It's all in the pattern," he
said. "She has these attacks from time to time. They always
pass. Then she will be the gracious lady again, until her
next time with the bottle."

I stared at him, because the heartless statement seemed
at variance with his character. "Don't look like that," he
said. "Remember I've known my mother for a very long
time. Twenty years to be precise. It's no good fussing when
she goes queer. And another thing . . ."

"Yes?"

"Take everything she says with a pinch of salt."

"All right."

"Of course I'm not saying my revered father isn't capable of a trick or two if it's to his advantage. But then, he's
not the only one. The Cornish heritage, I suppose."

"What do you mean?"

He laughed. "Never mind. Come on, Carmella . . .
what about a walk? You've not seen Castle Tol yet . . . or
have you?"

"I don't think so."

"Only a mile over the moors. Splendid view, and quite
an atmosphere."

I was doubtful. "But if Lady Cremyllas . . ."

"She's banished you. She'll only send you away with a

flea in your ear if you appear before she's ready to receive." His voice was mocking, but his eyes held a light I couldn't resist. So presently we set off toward the high moors where the wind was freshening, whipping our faces with the tangy scent of turf and damp heather, reminding me of days long past, when as players we'd camped in lonely clearings and at nights listened to the silence which was never really quiet, but filled with the murmurings and stirrings of nature. My grandmother Tessa had taught me early the note and song of each bird, how to know when an adder was near, and then speak to it in friendship so it would quieten and watch, and eventually slither away.

"What are you thinking about?" I heard Thurston say suddenly.

"Why?"

"Because we're almost at the top, and you've said nothing for quite five minutes."

I gave him my hand. "I was remembering my grandmother. She was a gypsy."

"So are you. And here we are at a true wild gypsy place if ever there was one, though folks say it was once a place for sacrifice."

He pulled me over a boulder, and there before me just over the summit was Castle Tol, a strange erection of stones, including a cromlech with others grouped around it. The wind was stronger there, whining and singing through the undergrowth, blowing my hair free and billowing my skirts so I wanted to dance in the wild way I knew, dance until I was exhausted and there was nothing in the world anymore but Thurston's arm around me and his eyes burning into mine. I turned to him, lifting my face. "Kiss me, Thurston," I cried. "Kiss me, kiss me."

I waited. He took my hand gently. "Not here," he said. "The shadows are more comfortable." He guided me behind one of the great stones, looked down upon me intently with a long penetrating gaze. Then his lips were tenderly on my forehead, and my cheek. I put my arms to his neck, but he disengaged my hands and said quietly, "Carmella, I would not treat you as a gypsy, even though you might be one. And I don't think you are, entirely."

Sick with frustration and humiliation I retorted, "Does it matter what I am? Or what I was born? Besides my grandfather was a . . . "

"A gentleman. I know, and you are a witch. Come along. We're going back."

"You go," I said hotly. "I'll stay here awhile."

He shrugged, and I watched him, half blinded by unshed tears, until his figure had vanished beyond a ridge of the moor.

Presently I forced myself to move and follow. When I got back to Carnecrane, there was no one about but Lydia, who told me Lady Cremyllas was worse, and that if the master did not return soon, he would more likely than not never see his wife alive again. That might be as well, I thought; I could see no future for them together, and it would at least spare him from any suspicions roused by her drunken allusions to foxglove tea.

By the time William Cremyllas returned, however, a week later, she had improved slightly, and in the meantime something else had happened. Thurston's friend from Oxford, Richard Coppinger, arrived.

He was tall, dark good-looking, utterly charming, but I did not like him. I sensed with the intuition bred in me that he was a threat to any love Thurston had for me. And it appeared quite soon that I was right, for after the first night at dinner together, I was told the next day by Mrs. Thomas that in future my meal would be taken in the kitchen before the other servants had theirs.

"Men like to be alone," she said primly with a certain satisfaction. "The young gentlemen have much to discuss, and it is only proper they are left to themselves."

"But Thurston . . . Mr. Thurston . . ." I began quickly, "I'm sure he wouldn't want it . . ."

"Oh, but it was on Mr. Thurston's instructions the arrangement was made," the housekeeper told me, adding sharply, "You have had considerable privileges since you came here; it's time you became more aware of your true position in the house which is one of service."

Her smugness angered me, but there was nothing I could do about it, as what she said was true.

Misery and resentment filled me, making the hours almost unbearable. I wondered what the friends discussed when they were alone together. Learned subjects I had no knowledge of, no doubt; great literature and matters concerning Doctor Johnson. The theater, but the theater I'd never known . . . where David Garrick performed, and fine actresses in silks and satins were toasted after each performance by gallants who crowded the stage doors.

And I looked back, remembering again our own audiences of tinners and miners and Fair people. I was very lonely then. Even the company of Lady Cremyllas was better than none.

"I have given you a bad time, child," she said one day from her bed. "Try and forget it. I never mean to be unkind. It's the sickness and the despair, as I've told you many times."

"I understand," I told her.

With one of her rare fits of acute observation she asked sharply, "You're not happy anymore, are you?"

"Oh . . . not too bad, my lady," I answered. "No one is gay forever."

"Hm." Her fingers tapped nervously on the bedspread. Then she remarked, "Is it that son of mine?"

Because of the hot blood flaming my cheeks I could not immediately reply. "So that's it," she said. "Well, forget him. Apart from social differences it would never do. He's not your kind, and believe me would certainly not contemplate marriage . . . even if you had the impertinence to think of such a thing."

"Marriage was not in my mind," I said coldly.

"Now don't be annoyed." Her hand reached out to me.

"What I said was for your good as much as his. Don't look like that. I dislike dismal faces. Get me the brandy . . . from the dressing table, first drawer down, under the petticoats . . ."

I hesitated. "Go on, go on," she said with irritation in her voice. "You know I drink, so don't try and stop me. And a tot or two would do you a world of good, too."

So we sat and drank together, as I had never drunk before. When we stopped I felt better, more confident of myself, as though the world was a tremendous joke which I held in my two hands. When I went downstairs toward the kitchens, Richard Coppinger was in the hall. He must have noticed my exhilaration because in the evening when I was out for a breath of air to refresh my aching head, Thurston caught me up as I took the path toward the cliffs.

"Carmella," he said.

I turned and we faced each other in the cold light of the stars.

"Yes?"

"Why do you avoid me?"

With my heart beating unevenly I replied, "I think it is you who do that."

"That's unjust. I've merely been more occupied than usual. I can't be with Richard and you at the same time. He's only here for a fortnight at the most. After that things will be the same as always."

"I'm not sure I want things to be the same," I said with a flash of temper. "You say you love me, but as Lady Cremyllas pointed out, we are very different. We don't mean the same thing by love, do we?"

"I don't know what you're talking about," he said shortly.

"No? Well I'm not going to explain. I'm not going to humiliate myself a second time."

"If you go on in this way your humiliation will be complete," Thurston said. "Mama will see to that. Do you want to grow like her? A slave to the bottle? . . . If you do, you'll end up in a ditch or in jail. Mama can afford her vices. You can't. It saddened me that Dick should see you as you were. He admired you before, my dearest Miranda, don't do it, I beg of you."

He turned and walked away. Presently I, too, went back to the house. What he said had been perfectly true. In any case I had not the will to refuse his plea. I decided that in future I would be obdurate when Lady Cremyllas suggested a drinking session; and if she became too difficult I would leave Carnecrane, even if it meant leaving Thurston for a time. We would meet again, I would see to that. So would he. There were other places than Cornwall. There was nothing to stop me making my way to Oxford when his supension was done; once there we would find no obstacle to our love. In the meantime I would study as much as possible, make myself familiar with the poetry of Thomas Gray and other writers whose work appeared in a little book Thurston had given me. There was also a writer Samuel Richardson I had heard Richard and Thurston discussing. His *Virtue Rewarded* had caused quite a stir, and although I had no taste for preaching and moralizing, my knowledge of such work would surely make me more important in Thurston's eyes.

William Cremyllas returned the following Thursday. I was aware of his presence even before I knew he was back; the very air seemed different; charged with vitality . . . something electric that conveyed itself to my nerves like the approach of thunder.

He was coming from his wife's bedroom when I reached the landing with her tray of tea. His stay in Penzance appeared to have refreshed him. He looked younger, a man of true quality, in a bottle-green frac with crimson silk waistcoat and white muslin scarf.

"I'm sorry my lady wife had the megrims whilst I was on business," he said. "You must have had a good deal on your hands."

"Oh no," I replied, "sir. Lady Cremyllas wanted to be

alone most of the time. She was so ill I thought she might die."

"We must all die sometime," he remarked. "It is the living who matter, as I'm sure you appreciate."

Avoiding his gaze, which seemed to assess me from head to foot, I turned from him, saying, "Excuse me, sir, I have tea for my lady."

"Of course." His voice was dry. "I would take it in myself, but she would accuse me no doubt of some foxglove concoction which is one of her obsessions these days."

Without looking at him I went to the bedroom, hearing his footsteps receding downstairs. For the first time I felt a stab of sympathy. Obviously the accusations of Lady Cremyllas had hurt him, and had no foundations whatsoever.

That night Mrs. Thomas informed me when I went for my meal to the kitchen that the master had told her I was to eat with the family in the dining room. I was grateful to Cremyllas, and dressed to please him, not in the low-cut green, but a silver gray, also a gift from Lady Cremyllas, which I knew made an impression of subdued ladylike taste, giving additional color and luster, however, to my hair and green eyes. For our meal we had broth followed by sea-lark pie and taties, a dish of clotted cream and baked apple, with cheese afterward, brandy, and hot toddy.

I was once more reigning in feminine glory at the table, and I was vain enough to relish it. The three men did not speak much, and when they did it was about things I had little knowledge of: politics; references to the fall of Walpole and rise of William Pitt . . . matters which had I understood, would only have irritated me, because they concerned the rich and the powerful, giving no place to the poor or the appalling conditions under which they worked and lived. I *knew*. I had seen, and I did not wish to be reminded of the gross injustices of society. So instead I let my mind wander to other things . . . fanning myself under the admiring eyes of William Cremyllas, which however veiled were often my way, glancing occasionally from under my lashes at Thurston, lifting my chin an inch higher when Richard Coppinger's gaze was upon me. Oh, I played that night, and I played well. My grandfather, I felt, would have commended me; and when, after the toddy, I excused myself for bed, it was William's eyes I felt burning my back, stirring emotions in me that were like dark flame to my body, shaming the purity of my love for Thurston.

In my room later I battled with myself as I had never battled before, because of conflicting passions in me I did not understand. If only I could find peace, I thought, and wondered if the preacher John Wesley could have helped me as he had helped so many Cornish folk, through salvation.

I knew he could not, and dispelled the idea immediately. I did not believe human beings came to God through self-denial and exhortations to a harsh deity. I believe, as my grandfather had believed, that heaven was on earth, where the soul pulsed and the grass grew green. In the autumn and winter too, when the winds blews fresh and keen from the sea. Most of all perhaps in the spring, as the young shoots speared the ground with the promise of blossom ahead. Spring. I was eighteen, and my spring was with me . . . a confusion of desiring and awakening to undreamed of fulfillment. Thurston.

Yet it was not Thurston I dreamed of that night, but a dark face filled with dark demands. I would not admit the image, but in the morning thrust it deeply to the back of my mind, where daylight obscured it, at least for the time being.

4

On the night before Richard Coppinger left Carnecrane, a great gale blew up from the sea, lashing in a fury of wind and rain against the house. I tried to sleep, but it was as though the very elements had me possessed.

I tossed restlessly from side to side, and at last decided that the dark hours would be better spent in trying to assimilate some of the poetic works I had heard being discussed by Thurston and his friends, than in lying useless in my bed. So I lit my candle and very quietly went downstairs, being careful to avoid the particular steps which I had learned made a loud creak when trodden on. The library was next to the dining room, further down the hall, and I was surprised when I reached the door to see a rich glow spreading beneath the crack across the floor. Usually the fire was allowed to die by eleven, and it was now past one. I turned the knob gently, so quietly a mouse might not have heard, and looked in. That was all I did; I took no step inside, but just stood there, with my spine frozen, absorbing at a glance the scene which was all too clear in the leaping flames of the newly stacked log fire. There was a rich warmth in the air, heady with the scent of wood, and except for the occasional crack, a deep silence.

Two figures were silhouetted against the glow. Richard Coppinger was leaning back in an armchair, his hand gently stroking Thurston's fair hair. Thurston! The man I had loved at first sight and whom I thought loved me was half-reclining on the floor, with his head on the other man's knee, his face upturned, in an adoration, I sensed, he had never held for me.

I was so shocked, I wanted to vomit. For seconds I could not move; then suddenly, stifling a cry verging on hysteria, I turned and rushed away, slamming the door behind me. They must have heard me, but as I ran down the hall to the kitchens no one followed. I picked up a coat wildly from a peg, threw it over my shoulders, unlocked the side door, hardly knowing what I was doing, and ran out into the rain and the bitter salty wind, my heart choking me in my throat, so that I had to stand by a tree until the breath came back to my lungs. Then I went on again, on and on, not caring whether I lived or died, longing indeed for the darkness of death though my body resisted it.

I plunged through the stubble of rocks and undergrowth toward the cliffs and sea. And then, suddenly, something was in my path; an obstruction I beat against while two arms took me savagely, holding me against a hard male breast. My fists were clenched. My feet kicked until the strength went out of me. I looked up, and in the brief pale light of the moon, through the tossed wild clouds, I saw a lean dark face looking down at me. Cremyllas.

He held me until the frenzy was done, but his grasp was still tense and tight.

"What are you doing out here?" he demanded.

The wind tore my words away as I answered incoherently. "It was Thurston. He . . . he . . ."

William picked me up in his arms and carried me to a shelter of stones grouped in a semicircle, beneath a ridge of ground where the furze was thick, impeding the lash of the elements.

He stood me on my feet then, saying harshly, *"Thurston . . . That* pretty boy. Forget him. He's nothing to you or ever could be, and you know it. You're mine . . . *mine.* My God, Carmella. Why do you think I took you in? . . . Philanthropy? To be *kind?"* His arms were around me, again his breath hot against my cheek through the cold air.

I struggled against him, pummeling his chest with my fists, though my heart was pounding with a mounting uncontrollable desire . . . something that must have lain dormant since my arrival at Carnecrane.

"*Don't!*" I screamed shrilly. "Your wife . . ."

He laughed. "My *wife*, indeed. Little you know. My lady wife! Don't speak of her . . ."

"I will," I shouted above the moaning wind. "I will . . . I will . . ." My teeth fastened on his wrist. I think he swore. He released me momentarily, and I made a wild bid to get away; but a second later my body was hard against his, the thudding of our two hearts urgent and close. I knew I was crying; great shuddering sobs that tore my lungs with a sense of betrayal, shock, and an unutterable longing I could not control.

Then he said more gently, with one hand sweeping the blown hair from my forehead, "Don't fight me. Carmella . . . my darling love, it's no use. We *belong*; to the storm . . . each other . . ."

I stared at him, with my head fallen back, and knew, with a flash of clarity, that he spoke the truth; knew too, that I could no longer resist, or wanted to. His eyes, burning down into mine, were darker than the darkest night, yet lit by a fire which obscured all else . . . everything in the world except our two selves, hungry in our need of each other. As he laid me down, undoing my cape and gown, it seemed the very earth trembled, until my body pulsed wildly to his, and searing pain brought a climax of joy and fulfillment. When at last my senses quietened under his touch, I knew only utter completeness. His lips still caressed my breasts and thighs, but gently now, as though in adoration. There was no wind, no rain, no world anymore . . . only the two of us, at one in our mating, with the source and meaning of life itself.

When we turned later to go back together to the house, the gale was peace, and the rain a benediction. The thing I had searched for was mine, and nothing would ever be the same again.

Following Richard Coppinger's departure the next morning, I could feel only pity for Thurston, who wandered aimlessly about the house, with loneliness in his eyes. I had been a girl yesterday, and woken a woman, knowing that my Ariel . . . the fey spirit I had first met on the seashore, had nothing of consequence to give anyone of my sex.

I did not blame him, or feel repulsion anymore. Love was love. Just as a flower could grow bent in its search for light, so, my instinct told me, could a youth lose his sense of direction. And although Thurston was two years my senior, I realized now that in experience he was little more than a child. This made me sensitive toward him, and whenever I could I talked with him and discussed as adequately as possible the subjects, such as poetry and the arts, which he enjoyed, being careful to avoid any personal relationship. Whether he knew I had seen him with his friend I did not know for certain, but he probably guessed because he alluded no more to affection for me, neither did he take my hand or by a flicker of his eyes betray interest.

I did not see William for two days after our passionate interlude on the cliffs. Mrs. Thomas informed me he had left early for Bodmin on a "case," and I did not worry. I knew he would appreciate time to himself just as I would. Besides that, Lady Cremyllas had become troublesome again, tirading against me when I would not share her brandy; eventually she resorted to insults. "You have exceeding high and mighty airs for one so lowborn as yourself," she remarked. "And it would be as well for you to remember that you are here only on sufferance, and to obey my wishes. If I choose, you can be out on the roads again this very day."

"I think not, my lady," I retorted defiantly. "I was engaged by Mr. Cremyllas, and it is for him to dismiss me."

"Indeed." Her lip curled derisively, and after a further nip from the bottle she added, "You no doubt serve my husband well, as he does you. Have no illusions, however, it is no uncommon experience with him. He has indulged himself with many women, and when I have insisted he has been forced to obey. Scandal would not suit his aspirations in society. The Pengalvas have influence without which he would be nothing."

I said no word; but the flush on my face did not escape her, for she said with a malicious gleam in her eyes, "Ah. So you have had a little frolic. I thought so. There was a different look on your face when you came in, a boldness to your step which is unmistakable. Just see to it that no bastard is delivered in this house or likely to be; I would not tolerate that. I would see you branded as a witch first."

Her venom was frightening. But because of it I did not believe half she said, and when I left a little later she had reverted to her self-pitying mood, wailing, "I shall soon be dead. So take notice of me. I am a poor weak creature, with a husband who has no liking for me. If he so much as glanced my way I would be content." She fell back against the pillow, and I thought I had never seen so pathetic and deplorable-looking a woman.

The next day the winds died down, and the weather became warmer, with a creeping mist which had thickened into thin fog by afternoon. A sense of brooding expectancy seemed to hang over the house, felt also by Thurston, who remarked, "This is the weather to avoid, Carmella. Stay indoors lest the ghosts have you."

"What ghosts, Thurston?" I asked.

His eyebrows shot up. "Ah. You do not know? There are many ghosts at Carnecrane which you will discover if you stay long enough."

His words disturbed me, because behind the playacting was something I could not fathom, a warning which how-

ever fantastic and elusive might have its roots, I guessed, in
something more tangible.

I wondered if William would return in the evening. But
at eleven o'clock when there was no sign of him, I went to
bed.

That night will be in my mind always as the end of an
illusion and an awakening to reality; a time of fear and
anguish not unmixed with excitement which was to prove a
landmark in my life.

For some time I lay awake, listening to each creak of the
old house, wondering if William had returned. Then at last
I slipped into a light and fitful sleep. What woke me I never
knew; at first I thought it the crying of seabirds disturbed.
But presently my senses were alerted to a confusion of
muffled shouting from the distance; sounds followed presently by the unmistakable noise of shots. I got up and went
to my window. There was nothing to be seen. Away to the
right, the creek was thick in fog. Then, glimmering for a
second and fading again I saw the blur of a light, and as
the fog thinned briefly, caught the hazy outline of a horse.
I sensed danger with the instinct of my kind, just as Tessa
would have done. I closed the curtain of my window, put
on my heavy cape and shoes, and, without a light, went
downstairs. It seemed strange to me that no one else was
aware of anything amiss. All the doors were closed, even
Mrs. Thomas must have been sleeping. I hurried, light-
footed, to the kitchens, and stood listening at the side door.
There was nothing. No sound but a distant murmur which
would have been that of horses' hooves or the sea breaking.
But it was a quiet night; the sea would only be a gentle lap
on the sands and there was no wind to carry it to the
house. Then what was afoot?

Puzzled, I closed the door, wondering what I should do,
whether to venture out or wait downstairs for a time. Matters were solved for me by a thud and dragging sound, not
from outside, but from somewhere below. The cellars
surely.

These were reached from the dairy down a dank dark flight of steep stone steps which I had avoided because of the rats. Liquor was kept there, under the care of Penharrick, the man. I fumbled around for the lantern and matches kept on the dairy shelf, lit it, and went down. Dark shadows leaped and filled the dark place as my intrusion sent a patter of wild feet scurrying around the kegs. There was nothing to be seen, though, but the humped barrel shapes and a few bottles in one corner. Then, suddenly, it came again, a dragging and a groan. With the lantern held before me I searched the unpleasant place and was about to turn and go back to the kitchens when I saw in one corner what appeared to be an incision in the stone floor. I bent down, pushing the dust away and found a trap door with an iron ring rusted from time. As I pulled, unavailing, because it was heavy, I heard the low tones of a man's voice saying urgently, "Pull . . . pull, for God's sake."

I tugged, and must have been helped from below, because the door opened, and there, staring up at me with greenish-white face smeared with blood from one temple was William Cremyllas.

How I helped him through and eventually got him to his room I never knew. He was badly wounded in one foot, and a bullet had also grazed one temple. But I had knowledge of curing and binding injuries, and compassion maybe gave me strength. He lay on his great bed motionless for some time while I bathed and bandaged him. I was frightened for fear the household heard, because I knew that Cremyllas had been engaged in unlawful things that night. I need not have worried. On such occasions, he told me later, everyone was careful to keep to their beds.

"You see, Carmella," he said, when the brandy I fed him had revived him somewhat, "smuggling is my hobby. It has been these many years. How else would a man exist, with a wife who denies him his pleasure?"

"I don't blame you," I said. "Why should I? I have a liking for excitement myself."

"Ah yes. Well, there was plenty this day," he said. "More than I'd bargained for, and nothing for it. The cargo should have been a large one . . . two thousand half-ankers of spirits brought cross-Channel to the creek. It would have been a good haul, profitable too, for I go shares with those who use my land for disposal of the contraband." He paused, while I wiped the sweat from his brow. "But this time, the Preventative must have been tipped off. There was shooting. Much of the stuff was taken, but the vessel and hands, thank God, got away. I also."

"You are hurt though," I said.

"Yes. And in the morning we will send for Dr. Maddern, who is a good friend of mine and will not ask questions."

"What about the law? Will it take you, William?" It was the first time I had used his name, and the sound of it somehow was comforting.

In spite of his pain he laughed. "My dear love, my dear sweet wild Carmella, the law does not take magistrates, neither has it knowledge of my escape route from the cove. Cornwall is a handy place for passages, and the coast is rich with them."

He closed his eyes, and my lips went to his brow, then his mouth. Last night he had woken passion in me and tumultuous desire. Now it was love I felt and the sweetness of love, its compassion and giving; the desire to be of service always, through sickness and experience and whatever the future might hold. When it was light, William told me to find Penharrick and send him to Penzance for Dr. Maddern. The man did not ask questions. I guessed he had full knowledge of the night's events, and had probably been concerned in them. He rode off on one of the horses from the stables and returned an hour later with the doctor, who was a stocky genial-looking elderly gentleman with the speculative dark eyes of the Cornish, dressed in the old-fashioned manner of black waisted coat, black breeches and silk stockings, with a lace jabot at the neck. Whilst he was examining William, I attended to breakfast for Lady Cremyllas, and took it up to her. She looked wasted and bitter, her glance curious and suspicious.

"That was the doctor's voice, was it not?" she inquired.

"Yes," I replied. "The master's had an accident."

"What sort of accident? And why wasn't I informed?"

"No one wanted to worry you, my lady," I replied, "especially as you were sleeping."

"How do you know I was sleeping?" she said peevishly. "I had hardly a wink last night." She paused, adding after a moment, "I asked you a question. What *sort* of accident?"

I was trying to think of an evasive answer when she remarked irritably, "No matter. See the doctor comes in before he goes. I need a potion, and he no doubt will give a straightforward reply to a straightforward request. Another thing. Find my son if you can. Now Dick Coppinger has gone he will maybe have a little time for me."

"I'll do what I can," I said.

"I'm sure you will," he observed dryly, "and whatever your antics with my husband may have been, I am equally confident that your charms have failed to impress Thurston. He is a Pengalva, possessing a morsel of pride. That, of course, you may find difficult to understand."

I was so angered I stopped at the door, turned, and said, "I am proud too. Too proud to indulge myself in the way you seem to enjoy. And if being a Pengalva meant so much I would certainly not drag it down as you do every time you fill yourself with spirits."

She must have been too shocked and surprised at first to reply immediately, but as I went out, slamming the door behind me, I put my hands to my ears to deaden the shrill abuse which followed.

I knew then that I could no longer stay at Carnecrane.

William knew it too. The doctor had been gone only five minutes when Mrs. Thomas told me with a certain smug satisfaction that the master wished to see me in his room. I went up quickly. William was smiling from his bed, but I could see from his pallor and the tight lines of strain about his face that he was still in pain.

"Well, that's that," he said. "The temple is nothing . . . a mere scratch, but the foot I'm afraid may plague me for some time."

I knelt down and took his hands in mine. "Oh, William . . . is it very bad?"

"Sufficient to keep me from my little games for many a day," he answered. "However, I shall sit on the bench and be able to administer justice." The mockery of his smile faded as his eyes searched mine. "Oh, Carmella," he continued, "how you must condemn me, a man who serves the law to serve as well such lawbreakers."

I laughed, because the law did not matter a jot to me so long as William was safe. "I've seen much lawbreaking in my time," I told him, "and sometimes for good ends. Isn't that what matters, William? That the ends should be good?"

He shook his head. "No, my love, it is not. The law is the law, and must be remote from ideology."

On matters of ideology and philosophy I was not well versed, so I simply said, "Then you can be an honest citizen in future, can't you, William? And that will make you the finest lawyer in the land . . . surely . . . because it is a very great thing indeed to be able to resist temptation."

He seemed amused. "What do you know of temptation? You a mere girl."

"A great deal," I told him. "I have wanted all kinds of things I could never have. Once when we took our performance to Truro there was a fine lady watching us with the most beautiful jewels on her breast and in her hair. I wondered about following her in the crowd when the show was over, and slipping a ruby pin from her bodice, I wanted it so much. I imagined what it would be like to wear diamonds and fine silks and attend balls with the richest people in the land."

"I hope you didn't," William said.

"What?"

"Steal."

"Oh no. How could I? It would have shamed my grandfather. But I told him about what I felt, and do you know what he said?"

"Tell me."

"He said the finest diamonds of all were hung on bushes from the morning dew, that I had no need of rubies when my lips were a richer red, and that the music from our own fiddles was sweeter and wilder than that played for the grand minuets. Of course he was a rare character."

"He must have been," Cremyllas agreed.

I was about to leave the room when he said in a different tone of voice, "Carmella . . ."

"Yes?"

"I have been thinking; it's not seemly anymore, after what's happened, that you should stay at Carnecrane. I know too that my wife has made life intolerable for you lately. Therefore I shall make other arrangements. I shall write to a good friend of mine, a landlord of an inn for whom I was once able to do a service, and see to it that you are housed there until such time that I can make other plans. The inn is in mining country not far from Falmouth, and you will be there ostensibly to await the return of your brother from overseas. There will be no difficulties at all. No questions will be asked. Joe Trevargass will accept my word that you are a kinswoman of mine requiring the best service."

"But, William . . . sir . . ." I began, dismayed at the thought of being parted from him. "I shall be alone there, I shan't know what to do with myself . . ." I broke off, confused by the warmth and ardor of his eyes.

"My dear love, you will see me frequently. Have no fear. On the first available opportunity when this wretched foot permits, I shall be off to the Indian Queen and you."

And so it was arranged.

The following week Penharrick drove me by chaise to the Indian Queen, and a period of waiting began for me. A period of joy intermingled with doubt and dread, because quite soon I knew that I was with child.

5

The inn stood on the high moors some miles out of Falmouth, near rows of gray stone cottages built by men who worked in the tin mines of the vicinity.

The landscape was desolate, gray and brown with windblown bushes humped and tired looking, as the men who toiled daily early and late for a paltry living that made the landowners and squires rich.

The interior of the inn, however, was sociable and warm, and the landlord Joe Trevargass very welcoming. I was shown a small parlor which was to be mine while I stayed there, and a bedroom, which though not large, was superior to the cramped quarters at Carnecrane. Dolly Trevargass, Joe's wife, was a spreading, dark-haired, black-eyed creature who proved to be a good cook, and whenever the opportunity arose, a lengthy conversationalist. She boasted a great deal about her husband's prowess and adventures at sea. He had served with the navy in their intermittent skirmishes with the French, and had a wooden leg as souvenir. Joe himself never questioned me about my supposed brother's impending return from overseas, but Dolly was obviously curious.

"Your brother?" she said once. "Bin in they foreign parts long? India was et?" Her eyes were shrewd and questioning under her heavy brows, and in spite of her casual manner I knew she was agog for information.

"Many places," I answered vaguely.

"Oh. I see. The vessel he's sailing . . . d'ye know which?"

"He didn't say," I replied, hoping to end the matter.

"Hm. Men be strange critters," she observed. "To have a young lady like you waiting and not knowing when to see you."

"That's the way of the sea, isn't it?" I remarked. "So much depends on storms and . . . and other things."

"My grandfather, he was a seaman," Dolly went on a little smugly. "A brave man sure 'nuff. Taken by Spanish pirates he wuz, and carved all up in little pieces. And I did hear the Turks was wuss. But the pirates don't exist no more like that, do they? . . . So you've no fear for your brother on that score."

"No," I said.

I knew she was not satisfied, and that she was more than a little intrigued by the evasive figure of my nonexistent brother. On William's advice I had dressed soberly in quiet clothes he had given me, because, he said, it was more befitting a respectable girl of decent family. I kept my bright hair as well concealed as possible, but this did not keep men's eyes from following me if I went through the taproom, an experience I was careful to avoid after the first two occasions.

Once, when Dolly on some trumped up excuse came to my bedroom at night, I was sitting on the bed, brushing my hair. She stopped, staring.

"Yes?" I said.

"Oh, nothing, Miss . . . ma'am. I was just wondering 'bout a hot drink. 'That young lady,' I thought, 'she might be thirsty' . . ." Her voice trailed off into confusion as though shocked by my appearance. All too plainly her glance said, "This is the wildest unlikeliest kinswoman I ever thought such a gentleman as Mr. Cremyllas to have."

I smiled. "No, thank you, Mrs. Trevargass. You feed me too well as it is."

She withdrew then, leaving me to wonder fretfully how

long it would be before William came to see me, and what
my future was to be. When a week had passed with no
word or news from Carnecrane, I went out rebelliously one
afternoon though it was raining, because I could no longer
confine myself to the stuffy atmosphere of the inn. The
comfort which had appealed to me at first now only irritated and set my nerves on edge. I who had been free all
my life had no intention to be deprived of it in solitude. I
was as well overanxious about William's foot. The wound
had been bad. Supposing it had gone wrong and I was
never to see him again? . . . The mere suggestion of such
a thing filled me with anguish. It was no use trying to be
calm. I couldn't dispel the tormenting vision of William left
to die at the great house, alone and needing comfort; *mine*.
But of course he wouldn't be alone. There would be Thurston, his son. Thurston . . . the dreamlike figure who had
once captured my imagination so vividly, and was now no
more than a shadow; a mirror merely that had reflected
my own passionate desire to love and be loved . . .
something fulfilled only by William.

Desperate with loneliness, I walked, half running, along
the ribbon of road leading northwest between the rain-
lashed moors toward the far coast and Carnecrane. I knew
the way was long and I might never reach the house, but
my mood was beyond reason, and fighting the elements
released some of my tension.

I was nearing the top of the hill when a blurred broad
figure astride a horse appeared against the gray skyline.
When he drew close, he halted and dismounted. It was
Penharrick. Holding the horse by its bridle, he handed me
a small parcel. "For you," he said. "From the maister. He
said I was to say his foot had been bad but was now healing, and there wuz no need for ye to worry. Next week,
things permitting, he'll be over."

I took the parcel, which appeared to be a small box,
looking questioningly at the man. His eyes were closed and
secretive as ever in the rain, his brief glance completely

emotionless. There was no knowing what he thought; he would give nothing away either to me or anyone else. His loyalty was to William Cremyllas. For him, I knew, he would die if necessary, and for that I was grateful.

"Well then," he said, raising his hand briefly, "I'll be off back." He mounted, adding before he rode away, "Get you back, girl. 'Tes no day for any woman to be walking the roads."

A minute later he had disappeared over the rim of the hill. With some of my anxiety appeased, I knew he was right, and clasping the little parcel tight against my cape, I turned and went back to the Indian Queen.

Joe Trevargass was going to the taproom from the kitchens when I went in. He glanced at me speculatively, and said, "You shud be gettin' them things off, missie. What would I be saying to Maister Cremyllas if his kinswoman took sick with fever?"

"I know. It was raining more heavily than I thought," I agreed. "Don't worry though, I'm used to all weathers, and I'll certainly take care of myself."

I wondered if I had said too much. For what well-bred young woman would know about storms and rain and cold? However, William had said the landlord would ask no questions, and he had certainly not been one to pry yet. So I ran up to my room and changed as quickly as possible, but not before I had opened William's parcel. It was the ring he wore on the little finger of his left hand . . . a gold ring set with a single large ruby. There was no note. But then William was a lawyer; he would not put words to paper when there was even a remote chance of any message falling into wrong hands. I understood. I knew what the gift meant. It was a token of the bond between us. A bond that no one would ever have the power to break.

I somehow got through the following week. At the end of it William arrived in his own chaise, because his foot still pained him and did not allow him to ride his horse. I knew from his expression that something had happened; sensed intuitively that it was something which could reshape our lives. I was right.

"My wife died three days ago," he said, when he had held me in his arms for a few brief seconds. "She had a stroke which left her in a coma for some hours. The end came quickly then."

I did not say I was sorry, did not express sympathy, because with Cremyllas I could never lie.

"I see," I said, after a long pause. "It must have been distressing."

"Death is never pleasant," William agreed. "But inevitable nevertheless, and in her case one would have expected it earlier."

"When is she to be buried?" I asked.

"Tomorrow. In the meantime, Carmella, it would be as well for you to content yourself here if you can . . ."

"Oh, but . . ."

"Not for long," he interrupted me, with his old air of authority. "Just long enough to observe the proprieties. Then my dear . . . my lovely wild one, I will return and carry you home. We will be married just as soon as it can be decently arranged."

I smiled at him and said softly, "Then it had better be as early as possible, William. For the sake of our child."

I watched his face anxiously, with my breath tight in my chest, half-dreading his reaction, because I knew my news must have been a shock. I needn't have worried. Slowly a fine color mounted his face. His great height seemed to assume added inches, and the years leave him so that he looked a young man again, a man with his deepest hopes suddenly fulfilled.

"Carmella," he cried, and drew me to him with hard strong arms that crushed me as though they would never let go.

And so it was that a month later I was married quietly to William Cremyllas.

* * *

Our first child, a boy, was born in the August of 1749. He was a strong baby with a thatch of black hair and greenish-brown eyes, who from his earliest days laughed joyously when he was content, and cried lustily for anything he was denied. We called him William Laurence, after my husband and grandfather. Our joy in him was complete. But a shadow hovered over our lives . . . the shadow of whispering . . . "Foxglove tea . . . foxglove tea . . ." started by Lady Cremyllas, and echoed through the servants' quarters until at last the echo became a rumor reaching further afield. Because of it William retired from the bench, on the excuse that his foot did not permit such frequent traveling about. I was wildly upset, and if I'd had my way would have taken court action for slander. But William said the source of such gossip would be hard to prove and would only make much out of what was in reality nothing.

In the end I made myself believe what he told me, that it was all for the best. We had much time together, and William had many matters of the estate to attend to, including regular inspection of the two mines. That year was also memorable for two other family events. Thurston's grandfather, who had been an invalid in seclusion for many years, died; which meant that Thurston inherited the title, becoming Lord of Pengalva Court, the gracious family home situated in the most verdant part of the locality.

The other event was small in comparison, but was important to me, because William desired it. A young portrait painter called Joshua Reynolds, who lived in Devon, was commissioned by my husband to paint my picture in a green dress. The young man flattered me by praising my hair and coloring, and although I found the sittings physically tedious, he interested me by his descriptions of Italy where he was going to live, accompanied by a friend with the odd-sounding name of Keppel.

William had great faith in Mr. Reynolds, and believed

he would be famous one day, because his manner of painting was more colorful and less dull than that of most painters at that time.

I didn't care whether he became famous or not. It was enough for me that I was made to look more beautiful, I'm sure, than I really was, and that William approved.

"It is the living image of you, Carmella, love," he said, when the portrait was done. "When we are old together I will be able to show it to our friends and say, 'See how beautiful my wife was when she was young. And tell me . . . don't you think the years have only added to it?' "

But that day never came.

Shortly after our second child, a boy, was born, when Laurence was three years old, William died from an infection of his lame foot, which had turned gangrenous.

I wished it had been me.

"You have your children," people said. As if I cared.

"How like your husband Laurence is," one kindly visitor remarked.

I ordered her out. What I said I didn't even know, except that it was harsh and insulting and intended to hurt. When she rushed out of the room I laughed. I laughed with the scorn and derision of Tessa, and with hatred for the human race. It was only when I glanced at the baby Jasper that a kind of shame stirred in me, because his wondering clear eyes were the eyes of my grandfather.

6

My grief when William died was at first so acute I wouldn't even admit it, or accept his death. I was like stone. I could not even weep. Our brief years together, though stormy sometimes because we were both tempestuous people, had been passionate with love and delight in each other. The twenty-two years difference in our ages had been a comfort rather than a hindrance. He had been a rock to defend me, a refuge physically and mentally through which I could find peace. Each time he took me to him was a reblossoming of body and spirit.

Then, suddenly, except for the children, I was alone.

My bed was cold; I reached out for him in the night and found nothing but illusion. When I spoke his name, there was no answer but from my own lips.

I walked the moors and held out my hand hoping for a ghost pulse against my palm. There was no response there, nothing but the cold air and empty sky.

It had to end somehow, and there was no way to end it, except to be nothing, feel nothing, and become hard as the granite coast. In reasoning moments I realized that I had known with the queer intuition of my blood that something of the kind might happen to William one day. The bullet in his foot had been deeply seated, and although Dr. Maddern had done what he could to cleanse the wound, it had not been enough. I had begged for further consultations with more qualified surgeons, but William had laughed the suggestion aside. "It will get right," he'd said. "These things take a plaguey time to heal. A touch of gout . . . what's that to a healthy man?"

I hadn't argued anymore, for fear of angering him. He had a swift temper which would not brook being thwarted.

A fall from a horse had hastened his end. I was not entirely surprised. The very night before I had dreamed of black dogs chasing across the moor under a pale moon; and although my grandfather had said when I was a girl, "Remember, Carmella, charms and forebodings only work if you believe in them," I had a sense he didn't have; my grandmother Tessa's heritage which had been her people's for thousands of years.

What I felt for the children at first was a sense of duty. They were there, they were mine. I had a responsibility to them, which during the first days following William's death I would rather have done without. If I could, I would have walked away from Carnecrane, and taken to wandering. What use were children without the man I loved? Children could not hold you and sustain you and turn the body's hunger to music. They could not worship a woman's nakedness as a pale blazing fire. I found, in truth, more comfort from the small wild creatures of the moors . . . the fox and badger, and the adders coiled by the stones. In those first agonized days of loss I had a queer kinship with the snakes, which were relentless and cold with my impersonal coldness. Because I no longer felt human, without fear of any kind, they never slithered away or sought to strike, but would sit watching as though spellbound by my own contempt of living.

Life, however, will not admit contempt forever. One day when Laurence was four, I went to wipe his nose, which was snivelly after a brief cold. His face was suddenly contorted. He punched me, screamed, and kicked my thighs with the frenzy of a wild thing. "Go 'way," he shrieked. "I hate you . . . go 'way."

Shocked, I put him down. Jasper was sitting on the

floor. He too had started to cry, but quietly; his gray eyes wide and imploring.

Something thawed in me and turned to compassion. They had known, especially Laurence, that in my heart I had rejected them. But it was not Laurence's anger that changed me. His rage had been there since he was born; it would be short and pass. It was the look on Jasper's face; tender, loving, hurt. No condemnation; only my grandfather's eyes scanning the years.

I lifted him and cradled him to my breast. "It's all right, darling," I said, with my own tears falling at last. "I love you; I love you both. It's all right."

And so the agony passed to resignation.

I determined to mold my future life as William would have wished, and to see to it that his children had the chance he would have given them.

During the next few years I tried.

I turned my attention to business matters which Thurston had undertaken completely before. I had no worries financially. The house, estate, and large interests in the mines were in my name, although Thurston, who was a rich man through the Pengalvas, had considerable shareholdings.

I decided I would interest myself in the tinners and their families; find out how they lived, the conditions of work, which I knew very well were not good. Laurence, who was so obviously a Cremyllas, would inherit one day. I wanted to know the nature of his inheritance, and made my intentions clear to Thurston when he rode over one spring afternoon from Pengalva Court.

He looked astonished. "But my dear Carmella, women don't bother themselves with such things," he retorted. "You have me, two good managers . . . it would do no good . . ."

"Poking my nose in," I interrupted.

The old charming smile flashed across his face. "I was not going to say that."

"You meant it though," I told him bluntly.

"Perhaps."

"I don't see why. I'm concerned after all. I want to meet the miners, and see what goes on."

"You wouldn't enjoy it," Thurston said flatly. "They can be a tough lot; hardheaded, uneducated, resentful of foreigners, and even violent when provoked. Friendliness on your part would be misunderstood and only bring you hurt."

"Nothing can hurt me anymore," I said. "And I'm used to the tough uneducated as you call them. It's a world I well know. Or had you forgotten?"

Thurston eyed me speculatively a moment before he said grudgingly, "Very well. You're a stubborn woman, Carmella, but if you insist I'll arrange something."

"What?" I demanded, refusing to be put off by ambiguous prevarications.

"There's an account house dinner in a fortnight's time," Thurston replied. "In the normal way I would be your representative as well as for myself. But legally you are entitled to attend, though I'm sure it's an unheard of thing."

"It was unheard of when William married a woman of my kind," I said a little tartly. "So we needn't worry about that. But this dinner . . . what's it for?"

"For business discussions concerning management, profits, expenditure, dull-as-ditch-water affairs which will bore you profoundly. Accounts are read by the purser, and the dinner following is a kind of celebration, or tonic to stimulate optimism should the financial situation need it."

"I see. So only the privileged attend?"

"What do you mean?"

"The men who do the work don't share the celebration."

"With so many workers it wouldn't be possible. But you'll meet one or two miners who have a share, however minute, in the company. In any case . . ." He broke off impatiently. "I just can't understand you . . ."

"You never did," I reminded him, "not even when I was Miranda."

He flushed. "Let's not go back to the past. It never pays."

I laughed shortly. "You need have no fear. I have only one past, Thurston, and that is William's. Any feeling I could ever have for you now is because you are his son. Somewhere there must be a spark of him in you, though for the life of me I can't see it."

"I'm not going to quarrel or argue with you," Thurston remarked, turning away. "I realize how you miss my father; I know you were deeply fond of him, and this may account for your strange determination to busy yourself with men's affairs. However, I'll put no obstacles in your way. Come to the dinner; meet the manager of Wheal Gulvas. No doubt he'll be flattered by the questions of a pretty woman . . . although he's a rough diamond, and certainly won't go out of his way to charm you."

And so, on a spring evening as the dying sunlight faded into the first pale violet over the moors, I rode horseback with Thurston to the count house of the largest mine of the estate, Wheal Gulvas, which was a stone building adjoining the mine itself, larger than I'd anticipated, with savory smells already issuing from the kitchen. What I learned at the meeting, which was attended by a dozen or so men of varying status, was negligible, except that the miners themselves were grossly underpaid in comparison with the profits. I heard allusions to Bal Maidens, whom I gathered were young girls employed at the surface of the workings, and even to children assisting, although the full extent of child labor under deplorable conditions was naturally withheld. Of this I only learned later from personal contact with families.

At dinner I sat between Thurston and Joe Cadmin, the manager of Gulvas. Joe, as Thurston had described, was a blunt man, broad, dark, middle-aged, with narrow eyes, almost black, which had a shrewd speculative look in them.

"Funny you should interest yourself in business," he said. "Or is it just the food? Well, it's no fancy spread as you'll see for yourself."

I had already seen; watched the count house woman dip the bowls into the immense caldron of simmering beef and vegetables before she brought them to the table. "I have a good appetite," I told him. "I can appreciate plain food properly cooked."

"Hm. Well, that's no reason for the widow of William Cremyllas to come riding so far on a chilly night," he remarked. "And I'll wager you've no knowledge of engines either, or the cost of them. Nor what it took to have the Newcombe-type installed."

"No," I agreed. "Engines don't interest me."

"Then what?"

"Just people, and the worth of what they do."

He was surprised, I could sense that, although his glance did not betray it, revealing only a kind of contempt intermixed with something I had grown to recognize quite well . . . admiration and a grudging assessment of what feminine attributes I possessed. I was wearing plain clothes that day, but his gaze penetrated through the fabric to my breasts; I knew that in his mind I was already the seductress and the seduced, and the knowledge filled me with intense hatred, bred in me although I did not recognize it, an instantaneous determination to pay him out sometime for daring to covet what was still completely William's.

I did not allow my dislike to show, however, for I knew I might have to use him one day in my schemes for the mines and those who worked them. I remained as aloof as possible, trying to disassociate myself from the overpowering "maleness" of the dinner, which was increased by the amount of punch, ale, and brandy consumed. Talk and tempers became heightened to ribaldry. The whole atmosphere was male and covetous in an almost animal way which made me realize Thurston had been right when he had tried to dissuade me from attending. And yet I did not entirely regret it. The first step into mining knowledge had been taken. I could not determine its worth yet, but every experience had its value at some future time; this was only the start.

Thurston and I were the first to leave. I knew he had enjoyed it as little as I had, and that he had found me an embarrassment.

"Well?" he said, as we rode away. "Was it worth it, Carmella?"

"Yes," I said, "if only for this. Look at the moon, Thurston, and the wild fiery stars. And the wind. It's a sweet spring wind . . . can't you smell it, the salt and the earth, and the bluebells growing . . . ?" I felt free, released from the smell and stares of men . . . alone at last with the things I loved. But I wasn't alone. Someone rode with me . . . not Thurston, but a ghost who still lived and accompanied me wherever I went . . . William. "William, William . . ." my heart cried, as I forced my horse to a wild gallop. For those brief minutes I was sad no more, but filled with exhilaration, oblivious even of Thurston's voice calling my name, thin and reedlike, a puny echo behind me.

My first experience with mining affairs only added to my thirst for practical firsthand knowledge. Driven by the emotional emptiness which my children now could ease but not fill, I visited many poor homes during the following months. Some of them were no more than hovels or huts, housing whole families with children sleeping either under the one bed or on a platform of boards under the roof. Sometimes a pig or a goat dwelt with them. Food was meager, consisting mainly of broth, taties, whey, fish when possible, even seal flesh, which was considered a luxury. To obtain this, miners trained their sons to induce seals to the shore by a particular kind of singing and shouting which the innocent creatures could not resist. Yet the rich thrived on the fat of the land; the rich, who now included me. What could I do about it? I tried taking baskets of goodies to the worst homes; but the poorer they were the more resentfully I was received. I understood. Being proud myself, having known what it was like not to know where the next meal was coming from, I could not blame the tinners for their ingratitude. There was only one way to ensure better conditions, and that was higher wages. I mentioned the matter to Thurston one day. He was sympathetic, but uncooperative.

"One woman can't change a system," he said. "And if you try you will have not only the shareholders against you but the workers as well."

"Why?" I asked stubbornly. "Oh, I can understand the managers and people like them but the miners . . ."

His strange clear eyes held a hint of commiseration before he answered quietly, "Must I spell it out for you, Carmella?"

"What do you mean?"

"They don't like you," Thurston replied. "You are an outsider. You are also someone they cannot trust."

"Why ever not?"

He smiled. "Because you're you," he said, half-dreamily. "A kind of . . . shall we say . . . a 'changeling' girl who appeared mysteriously one day and took William Cremyllas for herself. The Cornish are superstitious." He paused, continuing after a moment, "Let them be, Miranda. It will be better for all of us."

But I could not let it be. There was one family, the Bordes, who had two sons, a boy of seven, the other a year older, down the mines. Their daughter Maria worked at the surface of Wheal Gulvas, cobbing with larger hammers on iron slabs. I did my best to take the boys under my wing, but it was no good. When I suggested they should come to Carnecrane and help in the house or garden, Tom Borde, their father, said, "Don't ye go putten wrong ideas in they heads, ma'am. Mr. Wesley himself said play wasn't fur any

Christian chile. Bible and catechism and plenty of decent hard work, that's what they do need."

I stifled the hot words on my lips, thinking how right my grandfather had been in his attitude to religion, and that Mr. Wesley after all could not be so spiritual a leader as men believed.

With Maria I was luckier. She was a delicate girl, small, slender, beautiful in an elfin way, with large dark eyes and fair hair.

"Let her go to the big house, Tom," her mother pleaded. "She's near thirteen now, and needing more to make her strong than we can give her. Ais. Let her go. 'Tes for her own good."

Tempted by the wage I would pay, more than half of which would go to reimbursing the family, making them considerably better off, Tom Borde eventually agreed, and I left feeling I had achieved something at last.

I had ridden my mare about a mile when I met Joe Cadmin coming from the opposite direction. He halted his horse and touched his hat. "Another tour of inspection, ma'am?" he queried, "or is it something else you're after?"

"Meaning what?" I said, longing to strike him.

He laughed. "A fine woman like you must be lonely abed these summer nights," he remarked insolently. "What more natural than to go searching for company."

Before I spoke I got my thoughts into order. Then I said as haughtily as I could, "You would be well advised to remember who you're speaking to, Mr. Cadmin, and also that I possess the power to dismiss any who don't please me."

He laughed, flinging back his head so that the thickness of his neck showed powerful above his scarf. "Bravely said, ma'am, and well acted. I like a woman of spirit." The tone of his voice changed, became almost menacing. "But don't get in my way, Mistress Cremyllas. And don't try any airs on me. I know my place; see you know yours. Then maybe we can become properly acquainted."

Before I could answer his insult with one of my own, he had ridden away at a gallop, leaving me in a state of fury and humiliation. This man, I knew, was my enemy, and one day we should face each other in open hostility. Until then I would avoid him as much as possible.

The following week Maria Borde came to Carnecrane. From the first day she showed an ability to learn which I found heartening. She was good with the children, and in spare moments I began to teach her how to read and write, so that in a few weeks she could not only put her own name on paper, but could spell simple sentences. She was quick and clean about the house, although at first I could see that Mrs. Thomas did not approve of her presence.

"She's not bred to service in a gentleman's household," she said, still referring to William as though he were alive. "I know the Bordes . . . they're tinners and a primitive lot."

"Were the other girls bred to it?" I asked. "Doesn't Maria compare favorably with Lydia and Thamsin?"

"They work in the way I tell them," the housekeeper replied. "Maria's different. If you don't mind me saying so, you seem to treat her more as an equal than a servant."

"I like her company," I said bluntly. "She's an intelligent girl, and quick to learn."

"Hm."

"Do you realize how lonely I get, Mrs. Thomas? There are times when I feel . . ." I broke off. "But of course you don't. I'm sorry. There's something in what you say. I mustn't make the other girls jealous."

"It isn't only that," Mrs. Thomas said. "Folks are bound to wonder."

"What about?"

"Why you're so bothered about the work people. Your visiting . . . the way you try to change things. Cornish people don't like change. A lot of queer things are said. It's not my place to make suggestions, but once you set tongues wagging there's no knowing where it'll get you."

I didn't reply, and a moment later, shaking her head on a commiserating manner, she left the room. But her words lingered in my mind. There had been truth in them. I could feel resentment everywhere when I went out. I had tried hard to overcome the suspicion concerning my origins, which while William had lived had been suppressed, at least outwardly. Even the whispering concerning foxglove tea following our marriage had been less sinister than the cloud of veiled hosility I felt gathering day by day more ominously about my life and affairs. Maria and the children were my only comfort just then. Socially I belonged nowhere. The gentry ignored me, the poor mistrusted me, and men like Joe Cadmin lusted for me unavailingly, which created a sexual hatred meant to do me mischief. I still attended the count house dinners, much against the wishes of Thurston, who, as Lord Pengalva, would have had me anywhere but at his side. He was not the Thurston I knew anymore; or perhaps I had never really known him. His mind now seemed set on social matters.

In the summer of 1756 he became engaged to Helena, a daughter of Lord Merrick, who supported William Pitt in parliament, and saw future power for the country and himself through war with France. I did not doubt Thurston's affection for her. . . . She was a lily-white beautiful creature with a delicate air and pretty manners. But I did notice that Thurston's former fervor for pure poetry now turned more to political zeal and oratory, which I suspected were meant to impress his future wife's family. I don't know what she thought of me. We met only once before the wedding, which took place in London that same autumn. I was invited, but I couldn't help realizing Thurston was relieved when I declined, on the pretext of not being able to leave the children.

Thurston and his wife did not return to Pengalva Court until the following spring, and shortly afterward I had visitors.

That evening will remain always as a milestone in my life, whether for good or ill, because it meant at last an ending to my long loneliness.

Maria had put the boys to bed, and I had just gone to the drawing room after saying good night to them, when Thamsin knocked at the door, poked her face in which was round-eyed with wonder, and said hesitantly, "There's some folks outside wanting to see ye, ma'am."

"Folks?" I queried. "Who? Did they give names?"

She shook her head. "Not one. There's a big man though . . . in bright clothes, but muddy lookin'. I did ask 'en his business. He just said . . . 'You go tell the missis the compn'ys here.' "

I felt a quickening of my heart. Company? What did that mean? The miners? Or . . . suddenly, with an irrational instinctive joy I had the answer.

"Show them in, Thamsin," I cried. "Don't keep them . . . show them in . . ."

Before I had reached the door myself, they were already halfway there.

I knew him instantly; stouter, more ruddy of face, older, with hair thinning, wig held in his hand ridiculously, shabbily yet gaudily attired . . . smiling amiably, arms extended. I didn't wait. "Jesse," I cried to my brother. "Oh, Jesse, you've come. How I've needed you. I've needed you so much."

As I ran to his arms the years fell away. I was a young girl again in the world I knew, laughing, crying, held close against his coat, with friendly faces around . . . strange most of them, but welcoming, and warm.

"We must celebrate," I said, when the introductions had been made, "and you must stay tonight, all of you . . . and for as long as you wish."

The invitation perhaps was not wise, but I did not care. For years now Carnecrane had been in need of life and laughter. For a brief time then, let the house live.

So it was that on a spring night in 1757 I met the play-wright Hartley Fenton for the first time.

It was a merry occasion. I had the horses and cart put under cover, sent Penharrick for logs to make the fire bright, and for liquor from the cellar. Then I dismissed the servants, and got the food myself . . . pastries and pies which had been made earlier but were still warm from the oven.

We all sat down at the table and through a daze of ex-cited conversation I heard the news . . . how Jasper had left acting and taken himself off to America with a reli-gious group, which didn't surprise me at all; he had always been prone to telling others what to do. There had been bad times after the day at the fair when my brothers had been taken to court; but since then the company had prospered. Jesse introduced me to his wife . . . a comely black-haired woman who had been the widow of a well-established tavern keeper Plymouth way. She had been only too willing to throw in her lot with the players, and I guessed that any loss of financial security had been more than compensated in bed. She looked well content, and had charge of the wardrobe. Besides my brother and his wife there were four newcomers who had joined Jesse after Jas-per's departure . . . a yellow-haired woman with a wide smile, and her daughter, both older than their ways and manner of dress suggested, but I guessed they would look well on the platform from a distance. There was the wom-an's husband, a handsome fellow with a vagabond air and roving eye, a score of years younger than his wife, I judged, and lastly Hartley Fenton. Hartley wrote playlets of a whimsical satirical nature reminiscent of John Gay, which he frequently produced himself for traveling compa-nies. He had even had one included as a short snippet in one of the larger towns up-country, where there was a prop-er theater. I found him stimulating and amusing. He was of average height, slight of build, with expressive features and pointed ears. ~~His~~ eyebrows had a curiously upward slant reminding me of Pan. Indeed, his whole aspect was Pan-ish, and I thought he could well have played Puck in *A Midsummer Night's Dream*. He told me he had traveled with the company for five weeks, but when they moved on, he thought of remaining in the district.

"I need a rest in which to get my thoughts in order for further writing," he told me. "There is an inn not far from here, the Star of Prussia, which looked agreeable and well kept."

I knew the place. "Yes," I said. "And quite costly, I believe. It's not one the tinners use, but mostly travelers."

"I am not without funds," he replied.

"Hartley has got us well equipped with material," Jesse interrupted at that point. "And when we move on in a few days it will be quietly, to quiet small places where the press-gang is not so likely to snatch men to fight the French. We've had success lately in minor towns and large villages, so we can afford to go slow."

"A few days?" I said. "But can't you stay longer?"

"No. We must be away to a country fair where we're expected."

Further memories of that night are hazy in my mind. I do remember that when the gossip was over and as much wine drunk as was wise, I did an excerpt from *The Tempest*, in a way I thought my grandfather would have wished. As I spoke Miranda's words, standing in the candlelight at one end of the room, life flowed from me. The faces before me became mere images and were lost. I became Miranda; Miranda's love and mine were unified, although it was not to Ferdinand I spoke, but to my heart's dream . . .

> I would not wish
> Any companion in the world but you;
> Nor can imagination form a shape,

Besides yourself, to like of. But I prattle
Something too wildly . . .

Like music the well-remembered words stirred the past
to life. My whole being ached, for those brief few minutes,
with the joy and the pain of search, fulfillment, and loss.
When I finished speaking, there was silence until I heard
Jesse murmur, "By God, Carmella, the old man was right.
You have a talent to shame the gods. The only one of us
who has an ounce of it. You're wasted in this great barn of
a place. Leave it, sister. Come with us . . ."

Seeing the expression on my face, he broke off, realizing
I was bound to Carnecrane by roots stronger than any I
could have with the company. He shrugged. "No? . . .
You like it here?"

"It is my home," I told him. "William's. I belong."

"Are you sure? Cremyllas is dead. You can't live with
ghosts forever."

"I know that. I lead a very active life," I said.

"What sort of life?"

"Mine," I said simply.

I knew Jesse did not understand. He had always been a
kindly, uncomplicated man, and I supposed it seemed natural to him that I would want to spend at least a portion of
my time with all that remained of my family. I mentioned
the children, pointed out that I had new responsibilities in-
volving their welfare.

"She's a lady now," Jesse's wife said simply, though
without an ounce of sarcasm. "It would never answer,
Jesse. And 'tisn't as though we'll not be meeting through
the years now, is it? I'm sure we should be grateful for
being able to find such welcome in such a splendid establishment."

Hartley, who had spoken little until then, remarked, "I
should be personally very tardy of leaving a country home
of this splendor for the discomforts of the road. Beautiful
things are so rare these days. And there is much beauty

here." His glance traveled around the tapestries and furnishings appreciatively, coming back to me in a complimentary way which had nothing in it of insolence.

"Thank you," I said.

"Culture. Let's hope it's not a dying art," he went on in his gentle well-modulated voice. "I knew when I stepped into your hall, ma'am, that here was a wealth of it."

I was vain enough to be pleased. "My husband was well versed in taste and good things," I replied. "He was bred to such."

Hartley inclined his head slightly. "There is certainly no need to tell me that."

The playwright left some days later when Jesse and his company took to the road again, saying that after he had properly settled in at the Star of Prussia, he would be over to see me. "We have so much in common," he said. "The theater, a love of fine things, and a mutual kinship with loneliness, I think."

Those last words disturbed me, striking a chord I had not expected, and revealing that he was even more sensitive than I had believed.

During the next few months we met many times, and as full summer brought a flame of gorse to the hills, splashing the undergrowth and lanes with tall blossoming foxgloves and the frail, laced cow parsley, I became aware that his friendship for me was becoming something warmer. Yet he took no advantage of my position, being careful always to address me in the manner of any gentleman used to the company of ladies. This flattered me. I had not been born a lady, but William had raised me in status, and although I had an inherent dislike of class distinctions and the consequent injustices entailed, I still smarted from the hostility of people I would have helped, and from the lascivious familiarity of men like Joe Cadmin, a fact which made me sensitive to courtesy.

Eventually it was a meeting with Joe Cadmin that changed the whole course of my life.

I had been visiting the Bordes one evening, telling them of Maria's progress in the house and with her simple studies, when I decided to ride back by a different route . . . one which took me past a tenant farm on Carnecrane land. The air was windless, filled with the mingled scents of brine, heather, and fine thrusting bracken. A thin crescent moon hung in the translucent glow of the sky above the deeper night-blue of the sea. A magical scene . . . undisturbed by any jarring note, until I drew near a barn, where fitful lighting accompanied by discordant voices and high-pitched squawking told me something was afoot; something more sinister than a farmer and his boy about their work.

Dismounting, I listened a moment, and then walked to the building and pushed the doors wider. What I saw horrified me. There, in leaping candlelight which threw macabre shadows around the stone walls, were half a dozen or so men crouched around a circle of space where two gamecocks battled, their beaks all bloody, and the feathers flying everywhere. One bird was knocked back time after time by the stronger one, torn and wounded mercilessly by the cruel spurs. I was nauseated, too shocked and sickened at first to move or cry. When I did my own voice sounded harsh in my ears: harsh as the death screaming of the dying bird. I ran forward, pushed into the midst of the men who rose as I did so, shouting, "How dare you! What are you doing? Brutes, all of you . . . to do such things on Carnecrane land, *my* land!" The breath was wild in my breast, half choking me. "Get out . . ." I began again. "Go on. Leave this moment, and never dare show your faces here again . . ." I broke off, waiting for movement. But they never stirred, just watched me from hostile faces, eyes veiled and narrowed into mere slits. Then one figure detached itself from the rest and slowly approached.

He stood before me, close enough for me to feel his breath warm against my forehead. Joe Cadmin.

"Maybe we'd better have a little chat, Mistress Cremyllas," he said, taking my arm and pulling me through the door. I shook myself free, and lifted my chin high, facing the square dark bulk of his figure.

"Don't harass me too much," he said then, with menace in his voice which was more intimidating because of its control. "Men don't like a woman who'd interfere with their sport. And in case you don't know it, this barn is not on what you name your property. It belongs to old Jacky Trevose, who owns the Croft farm below that ridge. He has a life lease on it, and its border runs there . . . that path where Cremyllas property ends with its tenant farmhouse. So you'd be well advised not to trespass." He paused, adding after a moment, "Or is that what you want? Are you so short of a man that you have to go looking among the tinners and farmers when daylight's gone?" His arm went around me suddenly, and I felt his hot thick lips on mine, as I struggled wildly, kicking his shins, my hands reaching the thick bristling hair. When he let me go, I was panting and sick with shame. He laughed, and then I struck him, struck him hard against the cheek.

His hand went up to his face. "Don't you ever do that again," he said slowly, "or I'll have you, my fine madam, as sure as my name's Joe Cadmin. Not that you're worth taking. Everyone knows William Cremyllas took tinker's spawn to be wife."

He turned sharply and was gone. My head spun, I thought I would fall where I stood, so deep was my anger and humiliation. Then I started to tremble, and anger gave way to shock and sudden terror. The tears streamed from my eyes. I could not fight him anymore. There was too much against me . . . loneliness, and the united front of those who did not want me, or wanted me in the wrong way.

When I had strength enough, I mounted my horse and rode back to Carnecrane.

Hartley had arrived in my absence and was just preparing to leave. ——

He looked shocked when he saw my face. "Carmella," he said, "what is it? What's happened? You're frightened. Oh, my dear . . ."

I let him help me to the drawing room where the fire was still aglow. I sat down helplessly in a chair and he knelt beside me. "Tell me," he urged.

I shook my head. "I can't, I can't." And I knew I could not. "It's just . . . I can't go on here anymore alone . . ."

My voice faded. He took my hands gently. "There's no need to," he said. "Don't you know that? . . . I'm in love with you. If you'll have me . . . if you think I'm worthy, please marry me. I'll do all I can to make you happy. You need have no fears on that score."

I hadn't. He was gentle, and well versed in the things of my own world. Though I could give him nothing of the passion that had been William's, he would be a refuge, and already had my deep affection.

And so it was that a month later I married Hartley Fenton.

7

Those first autumn months with Hartley were quiet and golden, filled with a peace I had not thought to find in life again. Although his lovemaking failed to stir much response in me physically, he was tender, and knew how to woo. In his life I guessed he must have had other women, but it was a mutual pact between us not to mention the past, and if at times I closed my eyes pretending he was William, he could not have known it, and I never succeeded in really deceiving myself.

The children, who had been too small to have clear memories of their father, accepted him as a distracting and amusing addition to the household. Hartley was fond of reading aloud the scripts he was writing, frequently acting snippers himself with a whimsicality that delighted little Jasper, although Laurence could be critical, wishing for more fights and fewer literary passages. Indeed, Laurence's increasing energy and aggressiveness made me realize that what Thurston said was true. It was time he went away to school. The rector of the parish who had given him lessons in the mornings was growing old, and obviously found him difficult to handle. The thought of parting with the boy for the months of term time made me unhappy, because he was so vitally a part of William, and in many ways so like him. But I knew it would have to be. So I spoke to Thurston on the matter, and it was arranged by him for my eldest son to go to Eton at the beginning of the summer

term during the following year. I had the spring therefore
to have both boys with me, and determined it should be a
happy one. There seemed no reason why it shouldn't be. As
a married woman I was less conscious of the native resentment which had loomed so largely before. I told myself
things had been exaggerated in my mind, and that I had
perhaps been tactless in trying so obviously to play the part
of a man in business matters. So I kept away from count
house meetings, and devoted myself to the house and family, noting with satisfaction that Maria Borde, anyway, had
certainly benefited from my interest in her.

During the two years she had been with me, her childlike delicacy had flowered to ripening adolescence. At fifteen she was a slimly rounded creature with honey-gold
hair, tight high breasts above a waist so small it could be
spanned by two hands, and a way of moving that was a
delight to watch. I could not help indulging her with
clothes that such prettiness deserved, although Mrs.
Thomas did not agree.

"You spoil her, ma'am," she said, shaking her head disapprovingly. "She'll only bring trouble. You just wait."

I laughed the subject off. But as it happened, she was
right.

One day in April I went to Penzance for the day, letting
Penharrick drive the chaise because there were things I
wanted to bring back for the house. I left Hartley writing
in the small room adjoining our bedroom which had been
converted into a study for his use.

"I shall stay away for luncheon," I told him before I
went, "because I want to have a look around for some new
silk for a gown. As you know the Admiral puts on an adequate meal, and it should not be over-full, there being no
market day."

"Is it proper for one of your standing to eat alone?" Hartley inquired dubiously. "I'd offer to accompany you, my
dear, but my play's at a critical point. Still . . ."

"I wouldn't dream of it," I interrupted flatly. "There'll be Penharrick. In any case I'm used to looking after myself." His concern rather amused me.

"Eat with a *manservant?*" Hartley's voice held amazement. "The very idea. No, if you're intent on going I'll drop the work and come with you."

"You will not. I'll take Mrs. Thomas. She'll enjoy an outing, and Lydia and Thamsin are quite capable of carrying on alone for a day, especially with Maria to help prepare the food and look after the boys. Does that satisfy you?"

Without looking up again Hartley answered somewhat absently, "Of course. That's the best arrangement. Enjoy yourself and don't hurry back. The boys and I will indulge ourselves in an all-male session for once."

I kissed him lightly on the cheek, and half an hour later set off in the chaise with Mrs. Thomas attired in her best black silk, looking, I'm sure, far more the aristocrat than myself. The flame of my hair could not help being conspicuous, even under the green sunshade-sized hat which had upturned sides with a flimsy touch of veiling.

The sun was shining as we entered the town; and when Penharrick had put the chaise in the stable yard of the Admiral, and seen to it that the horses were housed with hay in the stalls, Mrs. Thomas and I set off on foot to do our shopping. Finding the silk I needed was quicker than I thought. A large merchant ship had berthed at Newlyn the week before, bringing a quantity of such materials from the East, which provided me with ample choice. Mrs. Thomas was able to purchase the ribbons she needed at the same drapers, where I also obtained hardware. After this we walked back to the inn, and told Penharrick to collect the larger purchases. We then strolled along the harbor front having a good view of the Mount, before making our way again to the Admiral for our meal.

The food was good; broth followed by goose and parsnip

pie, apple tart and clotted cream, or buttermilk cake, and if we wanted it, a taste of cheese with bread freshly baked of wheaten flour.

Mrs. Thomas and I, with our appetites stimulated from the sea winds, had everything except the cheese. Penharrick too must have eaten well. When I sent for him from the kitchen quarters, he looked well satisfied with a fresh color in his usually brownish face.

I settled with the landlord for what we owed, and then, not wanting to waste more time, set off considerably earlier than expected for Carnecrane.

The house was quiet when we got there. Unusually quiet, I thought. But as Mrs. Thomas pointed out, Maria had probably taken the boys for a walk, and Hartley would be busy in his study. I agreed, but still with a disquieting sense that everything was somehow not quite as it should be, and after she'd gone down the hall to the back stairs, I paused a moment, listening, before making my way to the bedroom. When I reached the bend in the front staircase I stood still again, thinking I heard a muffled chuckle. Then there was the uncanny silence. Uncanny because there should have been movement about the house, some sign that the girls or children were on the premises. Fear clutched me, and I didn't know why. The memory of Joe Cadmin's hostile face returned as I had last seen it, intent with malice and the desire to harm. Supposing . . . I did not torment myself anymore, but rushed to Hartley's study and went in. Usually I knocked, because it was his own private domain. But just then all I wanted was the comfort of his arms, his gentle voice soothing my nerves away.

Halfway in the room I stopped, unable to believe my eyes. There, in a confusion of cushions on the floor, was my husband, with Maria Borde pinned beneath him. She was squirming and giggling, her naked thighs entwined in his, their bodies at the peak of sexual excitement. At first they did not even seem to know I was there. Then suddenly, Maria's head turned. She gave a little scream, somehow disengaged herself, and stood up, reaching for her skirt, while Hartley, looking quite ridiculous as all men do when caught in the act of illicit copulation, sought to cover himself in an embarrassment of shame.

I didn't speak at first.

"Carmella . . ." he said. "It's not what you . . . I can explain . . ."

"Oh yes?" I said coldly. "How convenient." I waited a moment, then turning to Maria, said, "Fasten your skirt Maria, and go to your room. Tomorrow you will return to your home. In the meantime I don't want to see your face again."

When the door had closed behind her, I faced Hartley, and saw for the first time not a cultured gentleman who wrote plays, but a weakling philanderer and seducer of young girls. A cheat, who had fooled and shamed me into believing there was some honor in him. During the pause between us his mouth opened as though to speak. But no words came. I saw hope momentarily light his eyes, then die as I said, "And *you*! . . . Get *out*. Go. Take yourself off before I get Penharrick to throw you where you belong."

He must have seen that no plea would soften me. And indeed it would not. I was as cold as ice, hard as rock, bitter with myself that I should ever for one moment have allowed this simpering frightened creature to take William's place as master of the house.

A quarter of an hour later I watched his slight figure half walking half running, disappearing down the drive and through the gates of Carnecrane.

Then I made a vow. "No man shall ever touch me again," I said clearly and loudly to myself. *"Never."*

And no man ever did.

Maria, whom I had grown to love almost as a daughter, was taken back to the Bordes by Mrs. Thomas the next morning. I could not entirely blame her; but any feeling I'd had for her was completely gone, and her presence become nauseating. The family was not having an easy time just then. One of the boys had had an accident down the mine, and their one pig died of a strange sickness. I knew they would miss what Maria had earned at Carnecrane, but for once I steeled my heart against such poverty.

Winter came early, bringing cold and further hardship with it. In late December, shortly before Christmas, Maria died in childbirth, for which I knew Hartley was responsible. By then I was ready to assist the family in some way; but it was already too late, because the whispering had started again. Only this time it was different . . . no longer "Foxglove tea . . . foxglove tea . . ." but rumors of witchcraft and spells; of a woman who laid curses and caused cattle and men to die. In January Tom Borde himself succumbed to a heart attack caused through strain and hard working conditions. I could feel the cloud of menace thickening. Menace to me and mine, stimulated to excess by the hatred of Joe Cadmin.

I could see no end to it. Even Mrs. Thomas was apprehensive. "When times are bad, poor folk get strange ideas," she said. "Why don't you take off to Pengalva for a bit?"

I knew it would have been wise, and a change for the boys. Laurence, at home from school for the holidays, was rebellious and threatened that no one would get him back. But Thurston's delicately bred wife put me under a strain, and I was also too proud to desert the place where I had been so happy with William.

I had never needed him more. In the night hours I lay wakeful, trying to pretend he was at my side; sometimes, in a half-state between consciousness and sleep I almost succeeded, until a rush of despair brought me to myself.

I longed then for Jesse and his kindly wife. If it hadn't been for the boys I would have gone off and found them, left the past, with its joy and dark despair, forever. The countryside, gaunt and gray under cold winter skies, assumed the brooding proportions of some vast threatening power, deriving strength from its own wild acres and massed stones and cromlechs which had once been the scene of barbaric inhuman rites.

But duty to William's children combined with my own stubborn will kept me at Carnecrane.

My love for them, I sensed, might easily be the death of me.

II
Laurence

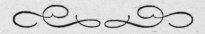

I was in my tenth year when my stepfather Hartley Fenton left home for good. As Maria Borde went at the same time, I guessed what had happened, because despite my youth I had a shrewd knowledge of sex, having watched animals mating. I was, as well, developed for my age. I had liked Maria myself, and had often wondered how she would look without her clothes. My strongest feeling when she'd gone, however, was not caused through her loss, but outrage and resentment on my mother's behalf. I loved her passionately; I always had. Because of her suffering I could have killed Hartley, beaten him about the head with a stick and stamped on him. Mama had tried to curb the wild spirit in me and make me more like my younger brother Jasper, who was fair and gentle, with what she said were "dreams in his eyes." But it was no use.

I had no dreams except for her and what was mine. I could not bear to see her changed. She laughed very little, and though her head after that fateful day was held an inch higher, though she walked with a more determined step, and looked in her pride more handsome than ever, her youth had gone.

She got busy with mining affairs again, and was forever pushing her nose in where she was not wanted. Thurston told me she had become domineering and that none of the men liked her.

"She's fond of you, Laurence," Thurston said, in the

Easter holidays. "You're a big boy now. For heaven's sake, try and make her see sense."

"Have *you* tried?" I asked.

"Yes. But she thinks nothing of me. I've no blood ties with her. No contact but through our father. And I'm more my mother's son."

I could see that well. In the past few years Thurston's hair had thinned. His slight figure already stooped a little through a rheumatic complaint, and he was only three or four inches taller than me. His features had a kind of nobility about them, but I judged him something of a weakling because he had bred no children.

"All right," I said. "I'll tell her what you've said. But she always does what she wants."

Later, when I spoke to her, I saw the temper flash her eyes to bright green. But she did not scold me.

"You mean well," she said. "But you're only a child yet. You don't understand. I'm not going to be beaten by any of them . . . Thurston, Joe Cadmin, or the men; I won't give in, Laurence. Neither would you in my place. Here you have to be master or nothing . . ."

"But you're a woman, Mama. How can you be master?"

"It's nothing to do with sex," she said. "It's temperament. Something in the blood. Look here . . ." She took my hand and pulled me to the window, from where I could see the brown moors stretching to a wild sea, with nothing to break the harsh skyline but lumps of granite and mineworkings. "If you don't fight that," she said in a grim voice, "it will fight you, and win. Do you understand?"

"Yes," I said, and in a way I did. But I thought she must be a little mad.

What happened during the following week was a nightmare I shall remember as long as I live.

My mother had been riding one evening, and returned shortly before seven with the arrogant set look on her face which I had grown to know so well. I guessed she had been in some angry confrontation with Joe Cadmin, which irri-

pearing through the fog, down the path toward the cliffs and cove. I tried to follow, but was pushed aside by Joe Cadmin.

"Get back into the house," he shouted, and to the crowd, "You've done your work, leave it now. No good comes from killing, and the son of William Cremyllas has right to protection."

I didn't move. My legs felt useless and petrified by fear. I watched as the crowd, jerked to some sort of sanity by Cadmin's words, and satisfied perhaps by what they'd already done, gradually quietened and dispersed. Then, turning to me, Cadmin said, "It's not your fault you're her son. But it'll be held against you while you live. If you have any sense, boy, you'll be quite about things and not interfere with folk. Go in now. Your mama will be back . . ."

He turned and strode away, but before he was out of sight I shouted, "If Mama dies you've killed her. . . . If anything's happened I'll kill *you* . . ."

He probably did not hear; I stood for some time while my heart quietened, then ran down the path after my mother, tearing my legs against the prickly undergrowth, rushing almost unseeingly down the rocky incline until I reached the path bordering the gully. At intervals the cold wafts of mist dispersed into clear gray light above the rocks and sea below. I climbed down, and at the bottom I found her.

She was lying near a small pool with her head against a sharp edged rock. Above her the gulls screamed almost as though mourning her. It was not until I examined her more closely that I saw the pool was bright with blood. She was very pale, greenish-pale in the unearthly light. "Mama," I cried, with my face against hers. "Oh, Mama . . . Mama . . ."

She opened her fey eyes once, and gave me a long stare. I could see she didn't recognize me. She just said, "William . . . oh, William, my love." Then everything was quiet. She was still staring at me as I turned and scrambled up the path toward Carnecrane. I had never looked on death before, but had not needed to be told when I saw it.

Penharrick and the rest of the servants were waiting for me at the back of the house when I stumbled exhausted toward the door. Lydia reached forward and clutched me to her. I could hear Thamsin crying, and Penharrick asking something about the mistress. "She's dead," I said in a cold voice as though spoken from other lips, far away. "And they've killed her. You too . . . you never came . . . why didn't you come?"

I was on the brink of tears, but they never fell. I pulled myself from the girl's arms, went in, and upstairs to where my brother Jasper lay sleeping in his bed. The sight of him so youthful and innocent-looking held a strange fascination for me, and I did not move until Mrs. Thomas came from her bedroom and forced me away. "Come," she said in the gentlest tones I'd ever heard from her. "Everything will be all right. They've gone for the mistress. You'll see your mama soon."

"I've seen her," I said mechanically. "She's all covered in blood."

"Sh . . . sh . . ."

"And I don't want to see her again," I stated shrilly. "It was horrible. I hate dead people."

"You should not say that. You should . . ."

I tore myself from the housekeeper's arms. "I shall say what I like," I cried, on the verge of hysteria. "And I shall do what I like. Do you know why? . . . I'm master here. I am William Laurence Cremyllas, the eldest son of my father. You're only servants. You're nothing . . . *nothing . . .*"

I turned and rushed to the small room which had once been my father's study, locked the door, and flung myself on the floor. There at last I could give way to grief, allowing the childish tears to release some of the pent-up emotions of the last hour. How long I lay there I do not know.

Through the heavy sobbing I was aware at times of thumping and banging on the door. At last, with a splintering sound it gave way, and I saw Penharrick looking down at me. His bulky presence brought a reassuring sense of normality with it. My body relaxed into weakness, and when he handed me brandy in a glass I took it without argument. Later, when they'd got me to bed, Dr. Maddern arrived and gave me a potion of something to make me sleep. He stood by me until soothing drifts of darkness claimed me, and I did not wake again until the late morning of the following day.

The inquest on Mama was held that same week. I wanted someone punished for what had happened, but when Thurston rode over to Carnecrane he told me that her injuries could have been caused mostly by her fall, and that her death was due to misadventure. I did not believe it, and said so. "They killed her," I repeated. "They threw stones and killed her. If she fell it was because of what they did."

Thurston did not reply for a moment, then he said quietly, "Try not to believe that, Laurence. Bearing hatred does no good. Your mother was a beautiful but very foolish woman. If she'd not transgressed into men's affairs she'd be alive today."

I did not want to accept what he said, I would rather have gone on hating, because hatred was easier than reason. But the practical side of me knew that he spoke the truth. Women should know their place. Women should be soft and amenable when men wished it. Carmella, my mother, had been amenable to no one, except perhaps my father whom I hardly knew, and to a memory of her romantic grandfather who had taken a gypsy for a wife.

I would never wed a gypsy. When I took a wife it would be someone gracious and highly born who would bring me honor and respect. This was my pledge to myself, which in the unhappy days following Mama's death became my de-

fense, a sword to ward off further grief. And so I bragged
and strutted like a man, while my young brother stared at
me with wondering eyes . . . eyes that had something in
them which shamed me. I could not fathom this shame,
except that he looked to me for guidance that I could not
give. In some ways he was so much wiser than I. Sensitive,
and not afraid of showing it. He grieved for his mother
deeply. Sometimes it angered me because I felt so helpless,
especially when he asked questions like, "Laurence, why do
people have to die? Do you think Mama likes being dead?
Or is being dead just being nothing? Flowers die too, don't
they . . . ?"

"For God's sake stop it," I shouted once. "Who cares
about being dead? What the hell does it matter?"

My brother didn't say anything to that, just turned and
walked out of the house. But I knew I had hurt him.

I found him crouched in his own small garden at the
side of the drive, where his particular pet, a large toad,
lived in the holed crevice of some stones. He had the stout
creature in one hand, and was tickling its head with a finger. He looked up. I tried hard to think of something to
say, but there was no need.

"His name's Moses," he said. "I think that's a good
name for a toad, don't you? And I know you didn't mean it
about the hell. You were just being a man, weren't you?
. . . I wish I was as big as you. I wish . . ."

"Oh, come on," I said. "You wish too much. What's the
good of wishing?"

"There's magic in wishing," my brother answered with a
faint smile touching his lips which just for a moment had a
look of Mama.

"That's it then. It shows it's wrong."

"Why?"

I gave up in despair. For every question answered, Jasper always had another ready; and I wasn't clever in that
way. I had no way of silencing him except by an air of
lofty contempt put on to disguise my own ignorance.

I wondered who he'd manage to plague when I went back to school. By the following week I didn't have to worry. Thurston came over and took us both to Pengalva. "This is to be your home from now on," he said to me. "Penharrick will remain as caretaker at Carnecrane which will be yours when you are of age. Until that time I shall be responsible for both of you. Next year Jasper will join you at school, and in due course you will both go to university at Oxford."

I thought how pedantic and precise he sounded, how strange he should be my brother, when he was so old . . . older surely than my own mother had been. In his way he was a finely bred looking man; but I was glad I didn't resemble him. Mama had always said I was a true Cremyllas, and Thurston a Pengalva. What Jasper was she'd not said, but I had always known that my younger brother had a special place in her heart.

During the holidays, life at Pengalva Court was novel and luxurious enough at first to impress me. The mansion, which had been built in the reign of George I on the site of the earlier Elizabethan home of the family, stood between St. Ives and Penzance, in a fold of hills where the vegetation was lush compared with that of the hardy coast.

Gracious terraces, windows and porches, were hidden from view of the road by trees and rhododendron bushes massed with colorful blooms like immense roses. One of the gardeners told me they had originally been imported from the Alps.

"Foreign," he said, "like them fuchsias and veronica, though I'd not be knowing what parts bred *them*. Fine enough in their way they be. But give me good pink Cornish heather any day."

I was interested in the man's knowledge of plants and land, because one day I meant to improve my own place, Carnecrane.

"Who taught you so much about land and growing things?" I asked one day.

"The old lord and his father had traveled," I was told. "To be rich in those days you had to know about foreign places and how to deal with 'em. And plants is part of the land, edn't en? . . . Same as coke and tin."

"What's coke?" I said.

"A kind of coal used for smelting," the gardener said. "And don't go asking any more deep questions. But let me tell you this, boy . . . ef a man from up north called Darby hadn't discovered how to make coke, the Pengalvas wouldn't be so rich today. The forests were getting used up, see? So there'd be soon no charcoal left for the mines. A few clever ones like the first Lord Pengalva got in with this man Darby at the proper start, and that was it. Understand?"

"Not really," I admitted.

"No. Well, neither do I for that matter," the man said. "Fact is, boy, gettin' rich in them times meant getting away and finding things out. The Cornish were among the first. Off to Americky too. Did 'ee know that? Teachin' 'em how to mine in them wild parts. Ever heard tell of Jonathan Hornblower of Penryn? . . . Built the first steam engine of New Jersey he did. Then there was Samuel Penhallow of St. Mabyn. Went among the American Indians, and taught them religion. Oh, we're a real adventurous lot, us Cornish, and don't go forgettin' et, because et's your birthright. And no more plaguing me with questions. I've work to do."

The gardener's knowledge impressed me. "You're a very learned man I think," I said.

"Facts, boy, facts," the old man replied. "My brother Nicky Tremayne's in Philadelphia this very day, unless the good Lord's thought fit to take him. God rest his soul. Emigrated 1720. Only two letters in all these years. But crammed with facts and cleverness, boy."

I couldn't help pressing the gardener Tremayne further.

"Why didn't *you* go to America?"

He looked up, rubbed his chin thoughtfully, and said.

"*You're* a persistent one, young Cremyllas. Why didn't I go? Well, I'll be tellin' 'ee. I didn't go because like I said . . . us Cornish be adventurous folk, but the roots is here. Like a great tree we are . . . think of et that way. A tree that sends lots of shoots this way and that, spreading underground and over . . . only I be a bit of root that's stuck right here in Cornwall. Satisfied?"

"Yes," I said.

And in a way I was. Jasper, I guessed, might be the "going away" kind, though I didn't know to where. But I belonged where my roots were, at Carnecrane.

After that I had many conversations with Tremayne, and felt happier in his company than with Thurston and his wife Helena. I admired Helena very much; she appeared to me like a lily, a carefully nurtured lily, white and delicate, with all the passion bred out of her. Thurston treated her with deference and respect, but I could not picture them loving or mating as the animals did. There was no fire in her, no warmth, although she was kind. Jasper charmed her, I think. She looked on him sometimes with a kind of longing that was sad. I doubted that she would bear children; doubted too that Thurston really wanted any, because he said to me one day, "If I have no son, you will be Lord Pengalva one day. Would that please you?"

"Yes," I said quickly. "I should like to be a lord." And I was exhilarated by the thought of ruling both Pengalva and Carnecrane, of attending parliament when I had a mind to, and mixing with celebrities like the great Lord Chatham. Power was a torch to me, always culminating, however, in my dreams for my own home. The memory of my mother's terrible death acted as a spur. Although I felt more myself in the company of men like old Tremayne and some of the tinners, I did not mean then to be involved with the poor. Mama, through caring for others, had been destroyed. It should not be so with me. Bitter experience had bred a cynicism in me which was old beyond my years. Power was strength. Power I would have.

Frequently I had to battle with the other side of my nature, and the fight drove me sometimes across the wild moors to Carnecrane, where I'd find Penharrick, talk with him, and wander about the rocky gardens and cliffs.

There I felt free. The air was colder, sharper, and more invigorating than the secluded verdancy of Pengalva. Only five miles divided the estates, but they could have been in different worlds. Even the color of the sky was more blue, the rocks more clearly intensified. "Mine," I thought, "mine." Lustiness was developing in me. Awareness of sex stiffened my youth as the first realization of approaching manhood gave impetus to the future.

After one of my wanderings Thurston regarded me closely and asked. "Why don't you keep away from Carnecrane for a bit, Laurence? It does no good fretting for your mother. It would be better for you to settle down here and try to forget."

"I'm not fretting," I said. "It's no good. She's dead; I don't like dead things."

I knew he didn't understand. Nobody did.

Before I went back to school, Thurston had a friend to stay with him called Richard Coppinger. He dressed in pale colors and smelt scented, like a woman. I preferred the manure smell of the stables; but he was extremely cultured and spent a great deal of time with Thurston discussing works I'd never heard of by a man called Henry Fielding, who had been a playwright as well as barrister. Sometimes when they walked in the gardens I followed on behind, listening intently, because when I went to Oxford I meant to study law like my father, and I was, as well, getting bored by having nothing to do at Pengalva.

Thurston always resented me joining them. "Go off and play," he said quite crossly more than once. I used to make faces and stick my tongue out when they walked away. Helena caught me at it one afternoon. "You shouldn't do that," she said. "It's rude."

"I feel rude," I said. "I don't like that man Coppinger. He stinks."

"You . . ." She shook her head reprovingly, continuing hurriedly, "Even if you don't like a person it's best not to say so."

"Why?"

Helena sighed. "It could make trouble," she said. "And we don't want that, do we?"

I didn't answer, because if I'd told the truth, if I'd said I thought a bit of trouble might liven things up, she'd only have been upset, and I didn't want to hurt her. The fact was that as the days passed, life at Pengalva became more and more oppressive to me, and I was thankful when the holidays were over and it was time to go back to school.

After the first trials at Eton I had become accustomed to the system, and learned to go along with the usual practices of public school including fagging. I had managed early not to show fear even when I felt it, so that when the time came for me to wield seniority I should be respected by my juniors.

Respect was important to me, and I had to work for it. Jasper, I guessed, would be popular without having to assert himself. Two years later, when he joined me, my judgment proved to be correct. Because of his charm and obliging qualities, everyone liked him. He was quick at his studies, especially English and the classics, and had a manner and way with the tongue that set him slightly apart from the rest of the boys. He was bright at mimicry, and proved himself an accomplished actor in school plays. It was clear in those early days where his talents lay. He would be an actor, like the legendary great-grandfather I heard about so often from Carmella, my mother.

I guessed that Thurston would not approve, but when Jasper broached the matter shortly after his fifteenth birthday, I was surprised by Thurston's reply.

"So long as you take your degree first," he said, "I see

no reason against the stage. Great words are spoken in the theater. Shakespeare himself belonged to the profession. Your own mother could have made a name for herself if she'd had influence behind her."

"Shall I have influence, Thurston?" Jasper asked.

"Of course. You are a Cremyllas, and as a Pengalva I shall do what I can for you when the time comes. I know someone in London who is a friend of Mr. Garrick. Don't worry, Jasper. I'm sure you'll have a successful future."

I was sure of it too, because Jasper was the type to be successful. Thinking of the theater set me wondering about my uncle Jesse, whom I'd not heard of for many years.

By a strange coincidence only the week before I went to university, Helena found me in the garden, and told me that Morton had admitted a visitor to the drawing room who insisted she was a relation by marriage.

"What name?" I asked.

"She didn't say except that she was married to an uncle of yours."

"Oh."

"I think you should get the interview over with," Helena continued with a hint of embarrassment. "She's a rather . . . well . . . a little flamboyant."

I wasted no more words but went to the house. I found a large woman waiting for me by the drawing-room window. When she turned I saw that she was also elderly, with a full rather blotchy face under a mass of grayish hair badly tinted to streaky ginger. Her clothes were gaudy but shabby, and from the way her plump small hands fiddled with her skirt I could see she was nervous. She moved toward me heavily and from my full six feet I stared down into her small eyes, which were screwed up pathetically in wrinkles of flesh as though her sight was bad.

"Won't you sit down?" I said.

She shook her head, regarding me wonderingly. "You Carmella's son?" she asked. "My Jesse's nephew?"

"I'm Laurence Cremyllas, yes," I answered. "And do you mean you're really . . . do you mean you're my . . ."

"Aunt Rose by marriage," she said. "But that's of no account now. You don't need folk of my kind as kin. It was just that I had news."

"News?" The woman embarrassed me, made me lost for words.

"About your uncle," she paused and wiped one eye, which was trickling, on a piece of coarse linen. "He was took," she said. "The comp'ny fell on bad times and Jesse got the fever. Now I'm on my way back to Plymouth."

"If I can help . . ."

She gave a toss of her head. "Oh, I'm all right. I didn't come beggin'. I've got my own people to go to. It was for Jesse I came. Real fond of Carmella he was, and it was a shock to me hearin' how she'd gone. That man at the old house sent me here . . . got me a lift in a farm cart, it's waiting and'll take me to Penzance where I've got a cousin, a tavern keeper. He'll see me on my way to Plymouth."

"If I can help you in *any* way," I persisted, "I'd like to. I only met Uncle Jesse once, but I know my mother would want me to."

"No, no. There's no need. It was to tell you of his brother Jasper I came . . . your other uncle, the one who went to America. There was a letter sent but it was lost somehow. It worried Jesse when he was dying. 'You must tell Carmella,' he said, 'let her know how well Jasper's done.' I promised, and so here I am. Jasper's in Philadelphia now . . . leader of some church there . . . and become a judge as well."

She sighed. "They never did hit it off, did they, those two?" She said reminiscently, "That's what Jesse said, anyways. And I can't see that jolly man of mine . . . God rest his soul . . . preachin' to a lot of furriners. But blood's thicker than water as they do say, and I had to tell you, being next of kin, the way things are."

I thanked her, and asked if she'd like a dish of tea but she refused.

"No, thank you. I must be gettin' on my way." As I opened the door for her she said with pride, "A pity my Jesse couldn't've seen you. It'd have eased his departing life, sure 'nuff."

"I'm sorry too," I remarked, realizing, however, that my uncle Jesse would hardly have fitted into the Pengalva household.

The following week I set off for Oxford by post chaise, and a new period in my life began.

2

During my three years at Oxford I studied as much as was necessary to obtain my law degree, although much of it bored me. So many other more exciting things were happening in the world, including the revolution of industry which I realized could make a great difference to Cornish mining. John Wilkinson's tremendous faith in iron was already resulting in the building of railroads for mines. . . . He was immersed in mining, holding interests in the coal mines of the midlands, and the tin mines of Cornwall. Another man was becoming famous through his experiments with steam, James Watt. Together I visualized them as a great force in the land, which could bring increased wealth and power to my own inheritance. I was not so interested in the growth of the country's population, literacy, and consequently its culture, as in practical possibilities. There was nothing brilliant about me. I just wanted to live my own life in my native environment seeing the estate thrive and Cremyllas lands prosper. My possessive instincts were strong. So was my physique. I liked women, and had them. But as my years at Oxford drew to a close, I began to look for a permanent relationship and consciously cast an eye around for a wife. This meant a more discreet code of conduct, and though my self-imposed term of celibacy was frustrating, it proved worthwhile, and gained the esteem of Caroline Weldon, a niece of the dean of my college, whose family were not only cultured but wealthy landowners.

Caroline was tall, fair, and beautiful in a Nordic way, with a small waist, full hips, and bosom that promised well for childbearing. Not that I was conscious of such calculations at the time; her looks alone were enough to stir a man's passion. Her skin, superficially magnolia-white, seemed to radiate warmth from within. At my first meeting I was impressed, at the second desirous. She stood only two inches beneath my six feet, and already I pictured Carnecrane graced by her presence.

I wanted her. Not as I had wanted other girls and taken them, but on a permanent basis as a wife and mother to my sons. I never doubted that she would bear sons, or that she would refuse me. Although she was three years my senior, I knew that my masculinity commanded her respect.

So I took pains to gain favor with her family which was excessively tiring. I had laborious sessions with dowagers and aunts, ingratiating myself in a necessary but odious way. In the meantime I managed to obtain my degree, though without honors. The latter fact did not worry me. I doubted that I would ever bother to practice law. All my ambitions then were for Carnecrane and the estate. Therefore I had to face the fact that bitterness to the tinners and country folk concerning the hurtful manner of my mother's tragic death would have to be put aside. I should get nowhere without their cooperation.

As I had anticipated, Caroline returned my feelings, and when I asked her to marry me, she responded with an eagerness that I found pleasant.

We fixed the date for the end of September of that year, 1770, when I would have passed my twenty-first birthday. In August I took her to Pengalva for a brief visit. Thurston was obviously delighted at my choice of a wife. Jasper, who was back for the holidays, was noncommittal.

"Oh, yes," he said when I questioned him. "I like her very much. She seems very reliable."

"What do you mean by reliable?" I said, slightly irritated. "Don't you admire her looks? Don't you think she's the most beautiful woman you've ever seen?"

Jasper stared at me thoughtfully for a moment, then replied, "No. Mama was the most beautiful."

"Oh, I know. In her way," I agreed. "But . . ."

"It's the way I like," Jasper interrupted. "And if you want to know, Laurence . . ."

"I don't know that I do. All the same, out with it."

"She's rather like a statue, isn't she?" Jasper said. "Caroline, I mean. She rather *looms*."

"Looms? What the hell do you mean?"

"She's big," Jasper stated flatly.

"And what's wrong with that?" I demanded.

"Nothing *wrong*. You're big too. Only I can't see Caroline running along the cliffs or dancing . . ."

"She dances very well." I said stiffly, realizing uncomfortably that there was something in what he said. "And you don't know what you're talking about."

"No," Jasper agreed. "That's true. I really don't know Caroline Weldon sufficiently to judge her. I'm sure you know what you're doing."

The way he spoke discomforted me. In some ways Jasper had insight far beyond his years; for the first time I wondered if I had been too hasty.

Later, however, when I took Caroline over to Carnecrane and showed her the house, my doubts were dispelled.

"It's a wonderful place, Laurence," she said. "I love the tapestries and rugs. We could have a few new pieces perhaps, a little more glass about?"

Her clear blue eyes were wide when she looked at me.

"Of course," I agreed, with my arm tightening about her waist. "You shall choose whatever you want; and before we're married, while I'm up here making what improvements I think necessary, you will do any personal shopping for the house and yourself."

We were standing in the hall, where the stained glass

window from the landing above caught her pale face and
hair, giving her an ethereal yet earthy quality reminiscent
somehow of pictures I'd seen of Joan of Arc. My hand
strayed downward to the firm flesh of her thighs and but-
tocks.

"Caroline . . ." I whispered urgently.

She pulled herself away abruptly. "You mustn't. Don't
do that," she said, looking shocked. "We're not . . . we
. . . we're not even *married* yet."

"But we're going to be," I said with my voice a little
harsh in my ears, thinking, "and when we are, I'll show
you. You just wait, Madame Caroline . . ."

"That's different," she said primly.

Her voice, self-righteous and smug, made me want to
tear the clothes from her body, force her into submission,
proving my mastery, that I was Laurence Cremyllas who
would have any woman he wanted at any time. But I was
wise and strong enough to control myself before commit-
ting or saying anything that would have ended our associa-
tion.

"Come and look at the plants in the conversatory," I said
calmly after a short uncomfortable pause.

She eyed me warily before saying, "Yes, I'd like that. I
do love things that grow."

Still smarting from frustration, I thought how stupid she
sounded.

Afterward I blamed myself for thinking in such a way.
She was finely bred, and virtuous. If she hadn't been I
would not have wanted to marry her, and it was therefore
quite illogical to expect an abandon contrary to her nature
and what I desired in her.

As we walked back together to the Pengalva chaise, my
resentment had already changed back to passionate pride;
the way she walked and held her head, the glow of sunlight
on her bright fair hair and contour of cheek, chin, and
finally rounded throat, gave her the nimbus of a goddess.
The thought that she would be mine in less than two

months inspired patience and gentleness in me, and on the day before her departure to Oxford she said as I took her in my arms, "I shall do my best to be a dutiful wife to you, Laurence. I love you; you are a good man."

I smiled fondly, lapping up the compliments with secret guilt. I knew I was not good at all, just as I knew she had no knowledge of passion or desire. But that was for the future. I would teach her and turn her childish placidity to wild fulfillment; one day, soon, she would know what Laurence Cremyllas demanded of a wife, and what she, in her turn, had to give. I had no doubts of the future; my only problem during the days that followed was how to contain myself in a fitting manner until the wedding.

It was difficult.

During the daytime Penharrick, who was well over sixty now, helped with the cleaning and airing of Carnecrane, showing the new housekeeper where linen, china, and household commodities were kept. Mrs. Mellyn, whom I had employed on the advice of Mrs. Thomas, now retired, was a comely, nice-looking woman of thirty-five, fresh in appearance as a dairy maid, and obviously competent in domestic affairs. The rest of the staff, excluding Caroline's personal maid, were engaged by her, but except for Lucy Trevose, a kitchen girl, were not due to arrive until a week before the wedding.

I had imagined more would be left for me to do about the place until the time came for me to go up to Oxford for the ceremony. But Mrs. Mellyn's competence showed, on the few times I walked or rode over from Pengalva, that any effort on my part to help was superfluous. I was not needed there. I tried forcing my interest once more upon mining business. It was impossible. I could think of nothing and no one but my forthcoming marriage and Caroline.

This made me restless, and as the days passed, bringing a flame of deepening gold and russet to the hills, my restlessness became a fever of torment. I was forever wandering about the countryside, trying to wear off my energy. I slept badly, which was a new experience to me, and when I finally drifted into unconsciousness it was to dream of a woman in my arms . . . a white rose of a woman who flowered in passion at my touch. I never saw her face, but the drift of hair across my lips was Caroline's. When I woke, it was to emptiness and a strain of waiting. I was filled with a dread of losing her. Supposing in my absence she was taken by fever, or stolen by another man? I could hardly contain myself at the thought; and this made me irritable.

One evening Thurston said, "I don't understand you. You're like a bear with a sore head. Can't you find something better to do than snap at Helena? . . . It's not her fault you're being married in a few weeks. I can't help wondering if you're ready for it yet. Married life means a certain amount of discipline, which you obviously don't have at the moment."

Stifling the rude words which came to my lips, I flounced out of the house and strode wildly across the moors toward Carnecrane. It was a fresh night of tossed clouds and slipping moonlight. A night for wrecked ships and plunder perhaps. A magical blood-stirring Cornish night when anything could happen. I recalled ambiguous references to my father's involvements with smuggling, made by servants when I was a child. But all this had been long after his death, and when I'd questioned my mother she had said such talk was just gossip and that my father William Cremyllas had been a just and honorable man.

Now I wondered.

I wondered because of my own wild mood, and because I was supposed to be like him. Without realizing it I had covered the five miles to Carnecrane in less than an hour, and in a sudden brilliant flood of moonlight it rose to meet me, a stark silhouette of towers and chimneys against the sky. Beyond, the gaunt cliff edge was momentarily clearly defined above the glassy sea. Then just as quickly the scud-

ding clouds enveloped the scene into darkness once more,
lit only by a flicker of light from an upstairs window, Mrs.
Mellyn's probably.

I stood watching, not knowing what I waited for, but
sensing like an animal can that something was afoot. How
long I waited I do not know. But presently, with the clearing
of the clouds, I saw a shape dart from the back of the house
where the kitchens were, and cut across to the side, disappearing along a tangled path leading through a few windblown trees and bushes toward the high road over the hills.
I strode quickly forward, and the next moment the figure
reappeared . . . the figure of a woman hurrying furtively
on her way, with something obviously concealed beneath
her cape.

I ran as soundlessly as possible to overtake. But the
crackling of twigs and undergrowth betrayed me. She
stopped, turned, and ran pantherlike toward the shelter of a
ruined barn which was no more now than a conglomeration
of tumbled stone supporting the one remaining wall. I
hesistated, wondering if capture was worth the trouble. Then
curiosity combined with anger at trespassing on my own
land sent me plunging ahead. The fitful light and shade confused me at first. I could see nothing definite until the scene
was suddenly flood-lit by the silver brilliance of a full moon
unharried by mist or cloud; and there she was. A crouched
figure against the wall half hidden behind a rock. Her eyes
were dark and terrified in her face, which appeared whiter
because of the massed black hair around it. She said nothing,
just stared at me with her hands clutched against her, shield-
ing whatever she had found or stolen.

A gypsy.

My first reaction was of anger. I strode toward her and,
with my hands clutching her shoulders, forced her to her
feet. "What are you doing?" I demanded. "What devilment
are you up to? This is *my* land, did you know? Come along.
What are you hiding?"

I must have shaken her hard. Her hands fell to her sides. A thud of vegetables, mostly potatoes, I guessed, tumbled to the ground. After one glance my eyes went back to hers.

"Where did you get this stuff? The house?"

She shook her head.

"The barn then, at the back. That's it, isn't it? Stealing?"

I saw her swallow hard, noticed then for the first time the wild rich bloom of her, which despite her thin unfed look held a provocative and untamed beauty. Involuntarily my hand touched hers, sliding gently up her arm.

"You're a gypsy, aren't you?" I asked.

She nodded.

"Where are your people?"

Her head turned toward the road. "There . . . over the hill. We was . . ."

"Hungry?"

"That's right."

"What's your name?"

"Rosa."

"Rosa. That's a strange name for one who goes stealing and cheating," I said. "And I don't believe you're really hungry. People like you have a way of getting what they want. I think you're just wicked because you enjoy it. Isn't that so, Rosa?"

She tossed her head and laughed, showing a flash of white teeth, as her eyes became dark flame.

"Yes, *yes*," she cried, bursting after that into a flood of Romany which I did not understand. I did not need to. What she said was of no account. I wanted her suddenly, as I had wanted no woman before. Even the memory of Caroline was swamped in the desire and need of this taunting creature whose wildness equaled the wildness in my own blood and heart. And so I took her with an abandon and urgency to which she responded with a passion I had never thought to find.

When it was over and we lay for a brief few moments passively together on the rough ground beneath my coat, I

realized with a touch of compunction how young she was
. . . not more than sixteen or seventeen at the most. I
searched her eyes as my hand stroked her cheek.

"Is this the first time?" I questioned, knowing full well it
was.

She smiled. "Yes."

I was touched with compassion, at the same time realizing that the sooner she was gone the better. I pulled her to
her feet, put on my coat, and felt in my pocket where a
few sovereigns lay. "Here you are," I said, putting them
into her hand, "and now . . . be off with you."

Her eyes widened as she stared at the coins. "For me?"

"And see you behave."

She stood on her toes, pulled my head down, and kissed
me lightly.

"Good-bye, gorgio dear."

Then, as the fitful light darkened, she turned and disappeared with the speed of a young fawn into the gathering
shadows.

I never saw her again.

After that night, time passed more peacefully. It was as
though some dark force in me had been appeased, leaving
me refreshed and free to plan constructively for married
life. I was not troubled by conscience; what Caroline did
not know she would not fret about, and the girl who had so
briefly crossed my path had been well paid for a mutual
pleasure.

On the appointed day the wedding ceremony went according to plan, with Jasper as my best man, and the bride,
on her father's arm, looking every inch the aristocrat as she
came to meet me at the altar. There was the usual fuss and
toasting at the reception later, which I bore politely and
with good grace, I hope, though with an inward feeling of
contempt.

When we set off later in the chaise, for a fortnight's
spell at Bath, I told myself I was the luckiest man in the

world, not realizing how tedious an affair a honeymoon could be.

The truth was that Caroline in bed was a complete disappointment. I discovered quite soon that her stature, the promise of fulfillment in her lovely figure, the radiance of her skin housed a conventional primness which after the first frustration became merely boring. She made a great show of "giving" herself to me, which meant, apparently, we were bound not only for life but for eternity. Her giving, as she called it, was puritanical and reserved. Once the act was completed she relaxed with a sigh as though a tremendous athletic feat had been achieved.

I managed to curb my irritation, telling myself that when we were back at Carnecrane everything would be different.

But it wasn't.

As the months went by, passing from winter into spring, it became worse. I felt cheated and humiliated, and determined to show her who was master. The physical beauty could not all be facade. She was my wife. She owed me something. A son at least.

When an opportune moment arose one morning, I brought the matter up casually, trying to sound gentle and persuasive. She was sitting at her dressing table, brushing the golden flood of her hair which fell below her waist in a cascade of true glory. I was never a poet; but just for a moment I felt poetic. "Caroline," I said softly, touching her gently on the shoulders.

Through the mirror I saw her half turn her head in surprise, and tried my best to dispel the discomforting thought that she looked wary and on the defensive.

"Yes, dear?" she inquired in her usual emotionless, calm way.

"I have been thinking . . ." I began, "it would be nice to . . ."

"Yes, Laurence?"

"It would be nice for us to have a family," I said bluntly. She looked astonished. "Of course."

"Then . . ." My arms went around her, cupping her breasts, which were warm and strong thrusting firmly against the thin wrap she wore before dressing or retiring.

"But not yet, dear," she said, trying to free herself. "We haven't been married long. It isn't usual for people to have children immediately. I want us to be able to enjoy things together. Later perhaps . . ."

I released her, saying coldly, "There is no 'later' about it. I want a son, do you understand?"

She got up and walked to the bed where her maid had already laid out her clothes for that day.

"We've only just had breakfast," Caroline said. "At least, I have. This really isn't the time to discuss such a . . . such a . . ."

"Unpalatable subject?" I interjected harshly. "When do we talk then? A timetable of events for conversation would be exceedingly helpful."

"Now you're being quite ridiculous."

"So I'm ridiculous to expect my wife to be interested in bearing my children. I suppose also I was ridiculous in imagining even for one moment that you had an ounce of passion in you . . . or that you had any intention whatever of being a satisfactory wife? Is that it? You married me because you were at an age when most other women of your social background were already wives or at least betrothed. You wanted to flash your wedding ring before the elderly dowagers and social parasites of your own celebrated family so they could say, 'Caroline has not done badly for herself. We were beginning to wonder if she was on the shelf. But young Cremyllas has quite a large estate and will be able to provide for her well.' That's what you intended wasn't it? To reign over Carnecrane, with Laurence Cremyllas servile to your whims and sterile moods . . . ?"

She drew back, sitting on the bed with both hands supporting her, actual fear obvious for the first time in her eyes.

"No, Laurence . . . no. I didn't . . ."

"You didn't expect a number of things that you're going to get," I said in a temper of passion and frustration. "Such as this . . . madame." I tore the flimsy thing from her shoulders and breasts savagely, "and this . . . !" I pushed her flat on the bed, exposing her complete nakedness, wanting only her humiliation and, through it, conception of my son. I flung myself upon her, stifling her screams with my hand as I took her, not in love, but in despair and hate. When it was all finished I got up and threw the wrap contemptuously at her. "Put it on. You look better covered. You're too large for my taste."

Whether she heard my last insult I did not know. Her sobs, heavy and uncontrolled, left me unmoved except for a feeling of revulsion. I went from the room straight out of the house, sick at heart because the marriage I had hoped would bring unity and fulfillment had turned out to be such a sorry business.

I walked for many hours that day, and eventually arrived at Wheal Gulvas. By then I had recovered a sense of proportion, realizing that my rage at Caroline's inadequacies was also rage at myself, for not having had Jasper's perception in assessing her qualities.

"She's big. She looms," he'd said. How right he'd been.

I could not see our future together except as a tedious affair of compromise. If she bore me a son he might make up for other deficiencies. In the meantime our life would continue under a mask of outward harmony. I would be careful from then on that no word or glance should betray the true state of affairs. Servants were watchful and quick to talk. I had no fancy for gossip around the countryside.

One of my underground captains, Tom Goss, was standing near the mine, waiting to see the men away after their long shift. I liked Tom. He was true Cornish, usually reserved, but forthright when necessary, respected by both miners and management. He and his wife Bessie were middle-aged now and childless, which I knew was a sorrow to them. Therefore his main interest apart from home was his work and welfare of the men.

"How are things, Tom?" I asked as he touched his brow in greeting.

"Fair enough, Mr. Cremyllas, surr," came the answer. "At the 'ends' though it's hard going without light."

"Why no light?" I asked sharply. "There are plenty of candles to be had."

"At sixty fathoms below adit candles don' burn unless they'm held upright," Tom told me. "Another thing, candles take air, and with bad ventilation and humidity like you've got down there, air has to be saved, so we snuff 'em out when we can."

We chatted for a bit about ventilation and working conditions, touching on matters that made me feel suddenly very raw and inexperienced. I realized that here was something providing an outlet for my surplus energy; a challenge that might ease domestic tension, and bring its own fulfillment to my life.

Before leaving I held out my hand to Tom, which he grasped firmly.

"I can see that I have a great deal to learn," I said. "You'll be able to teach me a lot, Tom, and if there's anything that can make working conditions better for the men, it shall be done."

As I walked back to Carnecrane I felt lighter in spirit than I had for many a day. Caroline, I supposed, uncomfortably, would expect some sort of apology for my behavior that morning. In my more convivial mood I decided it could be done provided she would meet me halfway. But when I entered the house and saw her coming down the stairs, the sour haughty look on her handsome face made me realize the futility of such a course. I should only lose "face" and be greeted by a slow, grudging acceptance intended to make me feel what a brute I had been. "I hope you've had a pleasant day," I said with a touch of irony. I would have passed her, but she blocked my way.

"Unfortunately my head had been exceedingly painful," she answered.

"Oh, dear. How distressing for you," I murmured. "Your eyes certainly look a trifle heavy."

Her face flushed. "Do you mind talking to me in the drawing room for a minute or two?" she inquired coldly.

"Why should I? Drawing rooms, unlike bedrooms, are the proper places for conversation, are they not?"

She lifted her chin an inch higher, walked up the hall, and was about to enter the room when I stepped quickly in front and held the door wide.

"Allow me," I said.

She swept through, turned, and stood facing me. "Do you mind closing it behind you."

I did so with a slam. "And now, what is it?"

"After what happened today," she said, "I feel in need of a change."

"Do you really? Yes, well, I can see your point. An event of that nature is certainly rare enough to be quite a shock."

"Perhaps we could be practical for once," Caroline said, "without the sarcasm."

"But, my dear Caroline, I *am* being practical. I was merely speaking the truth. I agree with you. You should go away for a change. We've been married for seven months now, too long without a break, for one of your delicately bred constitution. I well know Cornwall is not Cheltenham or Oxford. So make any arrangements you like. When you've done so I'll book with the post chaise for your journey."

She stared at me. "Do you mean you don't mind?"

Mind? I thought, how little she knew! It astonished me that even then she hadn't a glimmering of her own excessive stupidity and egotism. Yes, Caroline was a stupid woman; it was a discouraging thought, because as she grew older it was hardly likely she'd become more resilient or companionable. Clearly the only bearable solution was for her to spend certain months of the year elsewhere.

So I said politely, "If it's what you want, I'm sure it's the right thing to do. I have one condition though."

"What?"

"If by any chance you find yourself in . . . what is it . . . an 'interesting condition' . . . you will return immediately. When I have a son I want him to be born at Carnecrane. So please see you have no foolish ideas of giving birth away from Cornwall. I shall make certain how things are with you, and trust you will keep me informed of your health. If you don't, I'm afraid I shall have to make the tedious journey to bring you back. Understand?"

From her expression I saw that she did.

"There will be no need," she said. "And I hope . . ."

"You hope that when you return, a contrite and reformed husband will be waiting for you," I interrupted. "I'm sorry, Caroline, for your sake. I'm really not that type of man. I was born as I am, and if you'd had any sense you would have troubled to discover before the fatal step was taken just what marriage was all about."

She turned away. "There's no point in going into all that . . ." she said coldly. "I know now . . ."

"But you don't," I thought as she left the room. "That's the whole trouble. You've failed me, and I've hurt you. I didn't mean this to be so. When I saw you first, you seemed the most beautiful thing in the whole world. I meant to give you everything, including myself . . . every bit of me. We should have had ecstasy, fulfillment, and peace together. But we have nothing of importance . . . just a cold union of mistrust and dislike."

I had an impulse to run after her, and speak the words that were in my mind.

But I didn't.

When my wife left with her maid for Oxford at the end of the week, we parted coolly, as strangers making an effort to be polite.

The house seemed empty without her; empty and free.

I realized with a stab of surprise that this was the first time I had ever been on my own as complete master of my estate. The sensation was invigorating.

I did not miss feminine company. I made it my business to visit tenant farms, and attended a lunch at the count house for smelters' agents at Wheal Gulvas, where piles of tin ore were sampled, and found to be rich in quality. As I left that day Joe Cadmin was hovering about the building. He had been retired five years because of a chest infection due to dust. He eyed me warily, thinking back, I guessed, to past events. I went out of my way to be civil.

"I'm sorry about your illness," I said. "I hope you don't go short of anything that could help?"

He paused a moment before replying, "We get along. A manager can save, and my wife's a thrifty woman. It's those poor buggers below that need a bit of help."

"In what way?"

"D'you know the average monthly wage of men that make you rich, Mr. Cremyllas? Two pounds as the highest, mostly less. Have you ever thought what it's like pushing along narrow galleries, hammering, hammering hour on end in a hot bad atmosphere, and then at the end of et having to climb steep slimy ladders and to the main shaft before gettin' to grass? . . . From heat and sweating to a killing gale. That's the way of things for a miner. D'you think et right then, for men like you to have all profit from those who slave and wear themselves sick before their time? . . . Oh, I'm one of the lucky ones. I'm past sixty. But most of the workers are dead or laid off before forty."

"No," I said. "No one should have to die so young. But don't put the blame at *my* door, Cadmin. There was a time when my mother flung herself into the cause of the miners. Look what response she got."

"She was a woman. She didn't understand. Times were bad, and country folk have no other defense except to put blame somewhere. She asked for it, though I did my best to protect her when the time came."

"I don't want to think of it," I said shortly.

"Then don't. But it was you brought it up."

"Yes." I turned to go. "I'll think about what you've told me," I said, "and do what I can."

"It's education's needed," Joe said. "A change of system. With respect to your brother the Lord, he'd rather things stayed as they are."

I had a shrewd idea he was right, but answered evasively, "My brother Thurston has a great deal to occupy him, and probably doesn't know what goes on. In any case . . ." faced him squarely with pride, "I have the largest interest in the two mines. My word has weight."

"There are others," Cadmin pointed out. "But good luck to you. If you can get a fairer deal you'll've done something really worthwhile."

And that was what I intended to do.

But when I rode over to Pengalva the next day, Thurston was noncooperative.

"Why must you stir up unrest?" he asked icily. "You know very little about business affairs, and practically nothing of mining. Remember that Wheal Gulvas is a company, and not entirely *your* possession. Cadmin was a good manager in his time, but if you had any wisdom you'd take what he said with a grain of salt. Of *course* he's on the side of the men. Of *course* he resents our holding what is ours by right. I do wish you'd try to be more adult, Laurence."

This stung me. "I am adult enough to know where responsibility lies," I answered curtly. "I've had a good look at things. I'm of age, married . . ."

"And how's the marriage?" Thurston interrupted. "I hear Caroline's gone away."

"She needed a holiday," I answered, irritated because I knew the unsavory subject of my wife had been pursued to divert me from mining matters.

"I should have thought you would have accompanied her."

"I don't like Oxford, and I don't like her family," I said bluntly.

"Couldn't you try? They're cultured people with influence. You never know when you may need their backing."

"If you're thinking of politics you're wasting your time," I said. "And if I never take another step out of Cornwall it won't worry me. I belong here."

Thurston's glance was enigmatic when he said, "Don't be too sure. There's a restless streak in you . . . from your mother obviously, although our father wasn't entirely . . ."

"What?"

"According to tradition, shall we say?" Thurston replied in his usual ambiguous yet precise way.

"And thank heaven for that," I retorted with my irritation on the verge of boiling over.

I was thankful to be gone. When I reached Carnecrane by late afternoon the fading sky was already settling to early twilight. I did not feel like going indoors, so after leaving my horse to be stabled and fed by the boy I went down to the cove.

The air was calm and quiet, with only the gentle lapping of waves to break the complete silence. I was overwhelmed by a sudden inexplicable sense of loneliness. There seemed no one at that moment I could turn to for understanding or companionship. My wife, a stranger, was away; my brother Jasper had his own inner world which did not really include me. Thurston's life was lived on a completely different plane. Only Mama would have understood.

I started remembering.

Her face, her voice, the wild sweep of her lovely hair, seemed everywhere. I sat on a rock with my head in my hands. I had thought myself self-sufficient; but I wasn't. There was a hungry unfathomable yearning, deep in my being, that might never be fully appeased. I recalled words I had once read in a book: "the dark depths of the soul," and identified myself with the passage. Almost immediately the strange mood began to lift.

I would never be alone; of course not, she was there with me, the lovely Carmella who had given me birth. I could almost feel her hand touching me, and knew with certainty and sense of exaltation that something of me would go on.

My son.

I felt refreshed and unified as I climbed the steep path to Carnecrane. My step was buoyant, my heart quickened to a lusty steady beat.

For once my mother's ancestry had spoken through my blood. Everything would be well with my line. I had not been conceived for nothing. From far back, through my own loins and spirit somehow, somewhere, would rise a personality to imprint the world.

Though my mood might be wild and extravagant, and my confidence a madness, their promise would be proven. I knew it as surely as I knew the hard granite of my land. The certainty made me feel even more kindly toward Caroline. That very night, I decided, I would write a letter sending my good wishes for a pleasant stay, telling her also that when she wished to return I would welcome her, and endeavor to study her wishes in any possible way.

But my wife did not come back until the middle of July, and before that something quite unforeseen arose.

3

In early June I made an effort to call on every farm cottage, small-holding, and miner's dwelling in the district. My journeying one day brought me face to face with Tom Borde's widow. By now fully aware of the circumstances leading to her daughter's death in childbirth, and other miseries which had been so falsely laid at my mother's door, I did not expect a warm welcome. I did not get it, but she asked me into the one downstairs room grudingly.

"Sit down, Mr. Cremyllas," she said, indicating the chimney seat by the stone hearth.

"After you, Mrs. Borde," I said, remembering my manners.

She seated herself on a wooden spindle-backed chair, and after I'd made myself comfortable I asked her how she was doing.

"Doing?" A small harsh sound between a cough and a laugh rattled her thin chest. I thought how wan and old she looked in her drab black dress. But then she must be nearing sixty. Thirteen years had passed since Tom and Maria had gone. "We make out," she continued, watching me from narrowed eyes. "I have one boy down the mine. The rest are dead or away. Why? What es et to you?"

"You're my tenants," I said.

"And aren't we paid up with the rent? Don't you get et without having to come askin' . . . however hard it may be to find it?"

"There's no need to take up that tone, Mrs. Borde," I

said firmly. "I didn't come to make complaints, and I don't handle the rents. My purpose visiting you is to show good-will."

"You? *Her* son?"

"Please don't allude to my mother," I said. "What happened in the past wasn't her doing, and she suffered as much as any of you. I just want you to know that if you're short of anything . . . if you're sick, or in need, to let me know. I want friendship with all my tenants and workers. Is that understood?"

Her eyes bored into mine unblinkingly. "Ef I'm in need then the good Lord will provide," she answered unemotionally. "Trust in the Lord, Mr. Wesley said, and that's what we do."

"It seems to me that the good Lord may need a little help now and again," I retorted, taking four sovereigns from my pocket. "And here's a beginning. There's not an amount of holiness in me, Mrs. Borde, but money, whatever it comes from, counts as much."

As I got up to go I thought for a moment she was going to throw it back in my face. But she thought better of it, and said, "I should thank you; an' I do. We can't afford to lack what's needed because of pride."

"Very sensible," I said. "Good day then, Mrs. Borde."

"Good day."

I could almost feel her eyes boring my back as I closed the door behind me. I realized that it had been hard for her accepting help from the son of Carmella Cremyllas. But I knew I had broken a barrier and that word of it would soon spread to other families.

I rode back by a different route, skirting the village of Tywarren, which lay past a sharp curve in the road beneath Rosemerryn hill. Most of the cottages and houses were concerned with the mining industry, having a few small farms on the outskirts. There was nothing beautiful about the place, but its gray roofs, gray walls and straggling streets had a character peculiarly Cornish which filled me with satisfaction. As I rode along the hillside I saw a preacher in the square with a small crowd of women and men . . . mostly old or young, grouped around. A little later when the tinners had eaten, I guessed the number would swell. Tywarren was a large village, almost a small town, and Methodism, apart from its evangelistic stimulus, also provided entertainment when some erstwhile sinner or drunkard was miraculously saved with a crescendo of "salutations" and "amens."

"God!" I thought. If they could accept a deity who chastened and forgave and made penury and sickness a blessing, then good luck to them. For myself I had recognized no God in all my life, but in the eyes of animals, the warm arms of my own mother, and a glowing feeling sometimes that life was good, and the rich earth full of promise . . . a vital living entity providing tin, and food, and the fine strong thrust of growing things.

As I rounded the curve of the hill, I thought again of the son I hoped might be mine. "When I hold him in my arms," I thought. "I will go to chapel or church and give thanks. Then I shall know God."

I drew my horse to a halt, and stood for some minutes staring down upon the distant roofs and towers of Carnecrane. Then, with a quick jerk to the bridle we started off at a canter that increased to a gallop, soon bringing us back to the house.

When I took the horse to the stables, I sensed immediately that something was afoot. The boy eyed me strangely as though he knew something I didn't, and when I spoke to him he had to jerk himself to attention from thoughts that were elsewhere.

"What is it, Matt?" I asked. "Anything wrong?"

"Oh, no, surr. No, Mr. Cremyllas. At least . . ."

"Yes?"

"Nuthin', surr. Nuthin' of account," he answered, turning away.

I went through the back door to the kitchens. The girls,

too, had a conspiratorial air about them. I decided not to bother questioning them, but to tackle Mrs. Mellyn, who was doubtless in her room upstairs. I met her coming down the front hall.

"Oh, Mr. Cremyllas," she said immediately, "I'm glad you're back. I've not known what to do."

"Why? About what?"

"There's something you should see, upstairs," she said.

"You're very mysterious. What the hell's . . . I beg your pardon, but what the devil's going on? Matt was cagey; the girls have a damned odd look on their faces, and now you're telling me about 'things upstairs.' "

"It's not a *thing*," she said shortly. "It's a child. Not more than a month old if that. A foundling. It was just after tea. I thought I heard something at the front door, and there it was . . . wrapped up in a shawl . . . a shabby thing if ever I saw it, although the baby was clean enough."

"A *baby*," I echoed. "Well, what did you do with it? Where is it?"

"In my room. I thought it best to see it was comfortable."

"But . . ."

The housekeeper's eyes fixed me intently. "There's something else. Something I've kept to myself for your sake. But I think you should not waste time knowing about it."

I followed her upstairs into the room which had formerly belonged to Mrs. Thomas, and as the door closed, a thin wailing sound came from the curtained bed. Mrs. Mellyn pulled the material aside, saying, "There she is. I've fed her with milk, but it's as if she knows she doesn't belong, poor little thing."

I looked down into the small crumpled face which was dark complexioned, and red from whimpering. "A girl," I said. "No beauty either." A moment later the child opened its eyes wide, stopped crying, and looked at me. My heart lurched. Beneath the fuzz of soft dark baby hair strange

slanting eyes peered questioningly into mine . . . eyes with
the glint of green in them, my mother's eyes.

I drew back abruptly. Mrs. Mellyn thrust a piece of paper into my hand. "This was pinned on the shawl. No one
else knows about it, sir. And no one will from me."

I took the paper to the window and read the words
scrawled there in childish illiterate writing.

*"Gorgio dear, hers yors, hopin thee'll do wel for her.
Luv Rosa."*

There was no sound in the room but the ticking of the
clock on the marble mantelshelf. I turned and said in level
tones,

"I'm grateful to you for keeping this matter to yourself.
Take care of the child, Mrs. Mellyn. Get anything for her
you consider necessary. I shall arrange something for her
future. In the meantime I do not wish to see her again."

"Just as you say, sir."

The next day I went to see Tom Goss and his wife, and
made arrangements for them to take the baby into their
home and bring up as their own.

No reference was made concerning the origins of her
birth, and no questions were asked. All I told them was
that she was a foundling child who would have to go to the
poorhouse unless worthy folk could be found to care for
her. I arranged with them to pay well for her unkeep provided she never knew. They probably guessed something of
the truth, but this did not worry me. I was well satisfied
with the turn of events, and my conscience could rest in
the knowledge that in their home she would be a wanted
and much loved child.

In July Caroline returned with the heartening news that
she was pregnant.

4

The knowledge that she was having a child suited Caroline. She relaxed into glowing contentment, blossoming in the security, no doubt, of having lengthy respite from sexual obligations. I had no illusions about her attitude concerning approaching motherhood, and complied without argument with her suggestions for separate rooms.

"Do you mind, Laurence?" she said pleadingly. "I *do* get headaches, and *do* need peace. For the sake of the baby, it's very important . . ."

" . . . Not to be troubled by male proximity," I interrupted.

She pouted. "There's no need to talk like that. I asked the doctor."

"I'm sure you did."

"Well, what are doctors for?"

"My dear Caroline," I said quickly, "there's no need to prove your point. I accept that we live as monk and nun for the time being."

She flushed. "You might be nicer about it. After being so horrid before going away, and you *were* horrid, weren't you, darling . . . ? I do think you could be a bit more gracious."

"I'm not a gracious character," I stated bluntly. "Which you well know. So let things rest. You're back, and you're looking very fit. I'm glad."

"The doctor said that with care I should not have a difficult time," she told me, emphasizing the *care*.

"There's no problem then. At Carnecrane you can do just what you like and have everything you ask for, although I hope you're not going to stay in bed all day. Giving birth is a perfectly natural business; gypsies have children and move on the same day, I've heard, and not a whit the worse for it."

"I'm not a gypsy."

The statement, spoken so coldly in Caroline's well-bred voice, irritated me profoundly. I wanted to say, "Nor could ever be. There's a gypsy I know with eyes of velvet and lips of fire, with warmth and desire and tenderness in her." But the one word that came was, "Quite."

My wife stared at me blankly for a moment before saying with forced gaiety, "Well then, let us be nice to each other, Laurence. It will be so wonderful, won't it, having our own sweet baby, even if it's a girl?"

"Dear God!" I thought, "save me from that . . . from having a second placid, bovine Caroline." The mere suggestion that it could be so, that the son I wanted might turn out to be a female in the Weldon image, filled me with horror. For the first time Caroline's undisputed beauty was itself distasteful to me, and as I walked out of the room sharply, I allowed the thought of that other tempestuous night to blot the present from my mind. I walked to the place where Rosa and I had lain together, remembering with a sense of pain that was alien to me, her youth, her innocence in coming to me without condition or demand, expecting nothing but the mutual pleasure of taking and giving.

I stood for a time by the ruined wall, thinking back, watching the shadows gradually taking the undergrowth into brooding darkness. Her presence seemed everywhere. Her name filled the wind's whisper with a haunted sense of joy gone forever.

I pulled myself up abruptly, chiding myself for such a lapse into sentimentality. Rosa had been a mere incident. I had taken her as one might pluck a wild flower growing gay and beautiful in a bed of thistles and weeds. But life was a practical business, and the future had to be molded and worked for with sense and vision.

So I put the memory behind me and walked back to Carnecrane. My brief venture into the past, however, had taught me one thing: I must never pause to look upon the face of Rosa's child. And if I met her by chance in the years ahead, I would look resolutely the other way. I did not realize at that point how easy it was to make decisions and how difficult sometimes to keep them.

When next I saw Tom Goss, I asked him how things were.

"Oh, fine, surr," he answered. "An' the baby's a real treasure. Made all the difference in the home she has. Didn't realize before how child-starved that Bessie of mine was."

"What are you going to call her?" I inquired.

"We'd thought Bessie, after the wife," Tom said doubtfully. "Then again, et doesn't somehow seem to fit. It'll have to be decided though, because the baptism's a week Sunday."

"What about Rosalind?" I said on impulse.

Tom scratched his head. "Well now . . . I can't say I ever heard tell of a Rosalind hereabouts. Where did it come from then?"

"Shakespeare," I said. "But take no notice of any wild idea of mine. It's not my concern anyway. You go ahead and call her Bessie, Tom."

His shrewd eyes stared at me reflectively for a moment, then he said, almost casually, "Rosalind. That's et. She can be called Rose then for short, or Rosie. The wife always had a weakness for flowering things."

And so, ten days later at the small stone chapel where John Wesley had preached, the little bit of myself that had been conceived in a few moments of irrational sweetness was blessed in the name of Rosalind Goss.

My son was born in December, shortly before Christmas.

Caroline had a hard time, and I was touched when I saw her face marble-white against the pillows. I took her hand, feeling tenderness toward her, mingled with pride and a rush of gratitude for fulfilling my greatest wish.

She opened her rather prominent blue eyes and smiled at me. "It's a boy, Laurence."

"I know." I pressed her hand and went over to the cot for a proper glance at the newly born Cremyllas. The nurse we had engaged came in just then. She was a domineering large woman in a frilled white mobcap and apron.

"The little boy should be left to sleep," she said reprovingly. "He's had a struggle being born into this sorry world."

"There shall be nothing sorry in life for my son," I replied, lifting the coverlet gingerly. When I saw his tiny yellowish face, the thin fist crumpled against his cheek, I experienced a mild shock. I had expected him to be small, but I had also expected some slight indication of a likeness either to my family or Caroline's. There was nothing characteristic of either. He was not my idea of a healthy-looking infant.

I turned away, trying to subdue a feeling of mild repulsion.

The nurse pulled the coverlet possessively about his head. "He'll need care," she said.

"What do you mean?"

"Just that, surr. He's small, with a touch of the jaundice they sometimes get. But it'll clear."

The doctor confirmed it. "It's a complaint quite common in babies," he told me. "No need to worry about that at all."

He was right on this point. But there was something else. As the days passed into weeks, it was quite obvious that the child did not thrive as he should have done. The doctor shook his head anxiously, and eventually agreed that further medical opinion should be sought. Accordingly I sent for a specialist, Sir Humphrey Treffan from Truro.

This was only the beginning of endless consultations
about my son, which eventually culminated six months later, when I was told by Sir Humphrey that I must prepare
myself for what could be "a somewhat . . . difficult . . .
situation."

I braced myself. "Well?"

"I have to tell you the boy has a slight spinal defect.
Also, that your wife, though of fine stature, is not physically equipped for easy childbearing and . . ."

"What the hell are you talking about?" I said. "At one
moment you say he's sick, with something wrong with his
back. Then my wife . . . what's it mean? Are you trying
to say my son's a cripple?"

The doctor's eyes were cold when he said, looking me
very straight in the face, "This is a moment for you to
compose yourself, Mr. Cremyllas. Getting angry will not
help matters. The boy may grow out of what could be an
entirely temporary condition. It's impossible to say yet. As
for your wife, sir, I must warn you that to have any other
child might easily endanger her life. I am extremely sorry.
However . . ." he forced a note of brightness into his
voice, "the fact remains you have a son. We must hope that
with care he will develop normally and become a comfort
to you both."

But he didn't.

As he began to crawl about the floor, and eventually pull
himself to his feet with the aid of a chair, it was all too
obvious that my son William was an ill-formed weakling,
who, though not a cripple, would never be entirely straight-
backed. These physical shortcomings which made him
more dear to his mother only bred in me an intense irritation that increased with the years. Occasionally I was
touched with pity, making overtures of friendship in an attempt to compensate him for what was not his fault; but it
was soon clear my sympathy was not needed. William was
bright mentally, but with the Weldon influence behind him
might easily make his mark some day in a sphere which

did not entail physical prowess or endurance. I knew in
earliest days that we had nothing in common, just as I was
forced to realize the dull future of my marriage. I accepted
both with an impatience at first which gradually turned to
resignation. The unpalatable truth was that as time passed
my desire for Caroline turned sour. She no longer interested me mentally or emotionally. I had what I wanted of
her, which didn't amount to much; indeed, her presence
became increasingly irksome. If she had shown some sign of
response things might have been different; but I no longer
expected any.

For the sake of appearances we stayed together. Caroline's sense of social values would not admit failure. But
shortly after William's sixth birthday, when she suggested
going to Oxford for a month or two, I agreed more than
willingly. It would be a relief to have both her and William
out of sight for a time. In the meantime I would lead a
man's life, and busy myself exclusively with mining matters and affairs of the estate.

During my wife's absence a tragedy occurred which temporarily diverted my mind from domestic shortcomings.

Tom Goss and two of his workers at Wheal Gulvas were
killed when a ladder leading from one level to a higher one
collapsed, sending the men hurtling down the shaft to the
sump. The fuses at the nearby level had already been lit,
and in the explosion which followed the miners had no
chance of escape. Their mangled and burned bodies were
eventually brought to the surface, a sight which sickened
and repelled me, filling me with rage and hot resentment
on behalf of all tinners who worked under such dangerous
and unpleasant conditions for the meager wages they
earned.

I rode over to Pengalva immediately, and confronted
Thurston about the whole system.

"Why don't you stand by me and call a meeting of the
company?" I demanded. "Or don't you care about men like

Tom? . . . Tell me this, would *you* be prepared to work in filthy stinking air underground for what they get . . . ?"

"Of course not," Thurston replied imperturbably. "And again, of course I care. But what do you expect *me* to do about it? . . . Double their pay packets out of my own pocket?"

"Why not?" I said recklessly. "You can afford it."

"So can you, for that matter."

"All right," I said coldly. "We know now where we stand."

I was turning to go when Thurston called me back. "Don't be a young fool, Laurence. If you start financing the workers yourself you'll be bankrupt in no time . . ."

"So can the mines be bankrupt if I take it to the trade club," I pointed out. "No work no pay. That works both ways, Thurston. Without workers the mines can be made defunct."

"Just what are you trying to become?" Thurston asked coldly. "Social Benefactor Extraordinary? Or Blackmailer in Chief?"

"Mrs. Drew has lost her son," I answered. "Mrs. Goss her husband, and Will Paynter was a widower with three young children."

"All right, all right," Thurston agreed. "It's sad. You've made your point. I'll do what I can within reason. But a great deal depends on the accounts at the next meeting, and on the rest of the company."

I had to be satisfied with this compromise, and on the way back to Carnecrane called in to offer my sympathy to Mrs. Goss. There was something stoical about her as she asked me to sit down. Her eyes were red-rimmed from weeping, yet there were no tears in her eyes now, rather a muted suffering as though life could damage her no more.

"I'm sorry," I said, feeling at the same time the helplessness of words. "He was a good man. I valued him; we all did."

"Yes. Good," came the answer.

"If there's anything I can do . . . ?"

She shook her head. "Nothing can bring Tom back, can et? Mr. Wesley said trust in the Lord, and that's what I do try to do, because there be nothin' else. But though my Tom may be in a blessed heaven et's not the same as havin' him here with me, or bein' able to touch his hand when I've a mind to." Her voice broke. "Oh, Mr. Cremyllas surr, take no heed of me. I've the child to be grateful for."

I was about to turn the subject to other matters when the little girl came running in, and then stopped abruptly when she saw me.

"Come here, Lindy," Mrs. Goss said. "Say good mornin' to the gentleman."

She moved forward hesitantly. I tried not to notice her, but when I saw the small hand held out obediently, I had to smile and take it. "Good morning, Lindy," I said, wondering why she had not been called Rose instead. She looked up at me, with a half smile on her lips. From a mass of dark curls faintly tinged with reddish lights, slanting green eyes studied me as though assessing my merits. I perceived then that she had promise of great beauty; a beauty that even then stirred my heart because of its likeness to my mother. At the same time I was resentful that nature could have so endowed this girl with the qualities that my legitimate son was denied.

I turned to go. "I shall see that you receive your husband's wages, each week," I told Mrs. Goss. "Also that any funeral expenses are covered. The allowance for . . . for Rosalind will of course continue. And please if at any time you need extra let me know at once."

"You are very kind," I heard her say. "I'm grateful."

I shook her hand, gave a slight formal bow, and a few moments later without another glance at the little girl was walking from the cottage.

For some days after the interview I was disturbed in spirit. Except for Carnecrane itself there seemed little of

value in my life. I buoyed myself up with the frail hope
that when Caroline returned everything might be different.
She would have changed, and become warmer to me. But I
knew deep down that this was wishful thinking. Caroline
had been set in a certain mold which allowed no divergen-
cies of mood or character. She was entirely predictable,
and I had to accept her as she was, or somehow dismiss her
from my existence . . . which in itself would be an impossible situation.

Of my son I refused to think at all.

Caroline stayed away for six months, during which time
I managed, with Thurston's grudging support, and the fact
that the two mines were providing increasing revenue, to
get a better deal for our tin workers. Although my interest
in political matters was small, I recognized, unlike Thurston, that radical reform would be eventually inevitable in
the country. When the time came I meant to be in good
repute with the working and middle classes, because it was
there that future security would lie. Much as I disliked in
some ways the doctrines of Wesley . . . men like Dod-
ridge, Price, and Joseph Priestley were making an impact
both theologically and intellectually through their dissent-
ing academies. Their freedom from traditional approach to
culture gave weight to their opinions. I was not entirely in
support of their philosophies, which seemed to include, as
well as worthy reform, a certain slavery of the poor when
necessary, to suppress crime. Indeed, I opposed this; but I
knew the unstable reign of George III was going to see
drastic changes in the country; a word here, a murmur
there . . . a sense of increasing unrest all pointed to it. I
was determined that my own lands and responsibilities
should not be jeopardized.

I read at this time more than I had ever done. Unlike
Jasper, who was now studying drama in London where he
had already had a minor part at Drury Lane with Mrs.
Siddons, I had little interest in books. But I had to be fully
occupied. My temporary victory over Thurston and his pol-

icies left a vacuum which I found hard to fill. Riding the countryside was not enough. Brooding over the past was futile. An inner frustration was boiling up in me which I knew only a woman could appease.

In such a mood one day I went down to the cove where a restless sea pounded in a brilliant cascade of foam under a summer sky. With the flying clouds were the flying gulls crying widly above the waves. I knew then what I wanted. I wanted union with the earth and the sea and the harsh thrust of the jutting rocks. So I took off my clothes and plunged into the swirling water. The cold sting against my body felt good. But when I went back to the shore my throbbing flesh was unappeased. The male in me clamored for the dark thrill of possession and being possessed. I dressed with savage haste and went to the house.

How quiet it seemed. How empty; for the first time a shell without a soul. I went upstairs and on the landing saw Mrs. Mellyn coming toward me. Something in my face must have betrayed my mood. Her eyes in the cool strange light of the stained glass window were pools of compassion, holding an inner yearning and comprehension which started my pulses hammering. She was many years older than I; I had never before consciously observed her womanliness. Yet in those few seconds of sex awareness, she was all woman . . . symbolic of everything feminine: mother, lover, and friend. As we stood staring at each other her warmth became a pool of sunlight in which I wanted to drown, at the same time taking her to me, absorbing my loneliness in her encompassing capacity for giving.

I said nothing until she spoke.

"You are lonely, Mr. Cremyllas, surr."

I touched one of her hands gently. "Yes."

"It isn't good for a man such as yourself to be denied his needs."

"I know," I said abruptly. "It can't be helped." I wanted to move, but couldn't drag myself from the gentle, quiet magnetism of her presence. She laid her other hand on top of mine.

"I've been a widow for a long time. I know what it is."

There seemed no more need of words. Simultaneously we began walking toward my room. I pulled the curtains, but the summer sun still penetrated the quietness. As she undid the buttons of her bodice, I started to undress myself. "No one will ever know," I heard her saying presently. "The girls are out. The men are at the stables."

I looked up. She was standing naked with her brown hair tumbled around her shoulders . . . a full-bosomed, large-hipped, cream-skinned woman touched to gold by the filtering light. The harshness and frustration in me melted as I went toward her, touching her gently at first, letting my hands stray lingeringly over the full curve of her breasts, and downward where her thighs pulsed with a long desire. I drew her close, savoring with my eyes shut her earthy sweetness.

Then we lay together, and my being was submerged into the deepest core of hers, where peace took my unrest away, leaving me fulfilled and content.

When she got up a little later and put on her clothes, I noticed from my dreamlike state how quietly she moved, without haste or agitation. With her hair pinned back, she looked what she had been before, Mrs. Mellyn my housekeeper, and I knew with certainty that she would remain so until I wished it otherwise.

At the door she turned and said, "If I've helped, I'm happy, surr. All I wish is to serve you, in any way I can."

A moment later she was gone.

I knew then that I had found my retreat; an oasis where body and spirit could drink and be renewed. I had no conscience. If Caroline had wanted me, it would have been different. But she didn't.

When she eventually returned to Carnecrane, it was all too clear that although she was cringingly willing to fulfill her wifely obligations at certain intervals convenient to herself, sexual proximity was a strain to her and something to be endured rather than enjoyed.

Therefore when I hypocritically suggested to her that her nervous system might benefit without the strain of physical intercourse, she agreed with a rush of relief and gratitude that I found rather pitiful. And so a new plan of life developed. Caroline thrived in her role of elegant hostess and mistress of Carnecrane, and at social gatherings was much admired, commanding respect and envy from both men and women.

No one guessed what lay behind the facade, and I was careful to keep it so. It was not difficult. Caroline was an unsuspecting creature, and was so often away in the years that followed, that she had no occasion to doubt my fidelity. Whether the servants had any inkling of the true state of affairs I never knew. Life was for living and not for worrying. As for William . . . he seemed more like Thurston's child than my own.

By the time he was fourteen, he was a studious boy with a stooping back and a thin figure, finely featured, but with none of the Cremyllas characteristics, except in one thing only . . . a desire to become a barrister. Thurston encouraged it, and I agreed compliantly. He was my son. I wished him well, but I felt no affection for him, and looked forward to the day when he would be away at university.

Before that time, however, something unexpected happened. The widow of Tom Goss died.

5

On a spring morning in 1786, as I was about to ride over to Pengalva, I saw the figure of a girl hurrying from the high moor path toward the house. With the early sunlight streaming against my eyes, I did not recognize her, she could have been anyone. But an urgency about the silhouetted figure, the way she ran, unheeding of stones, brambles, or tearing gorse, arrested my attention. I paused at the gate until she got there.

And then I knew.

There was no mistaking the rich deep glint of blown hair, the golden peach-bloom skin from which the big green eyes stared frightened and distressed. She was breathing hard, and it was moments before the words came tumbling out.

"It's my mother, sir . . . . it's . . ." She swallowed hard as I jumped from my horse and put my hand on her shoulder.

"Take your time," I said. "It's all right, I'm here . . ." I paused before adding, "You're Rosalind, aren't you? Rosalind Goss?"

She nodded. "My mother's very sick. I think she's dying. She sent me to you because . . . because . . ."

"She wants to see me. Is that it?"

"Yes. Hurry, please hurry."

"Wait here," I told her quickly. "I'll send the man to fetch the doctor. Then I'll take you home."

I tried to be impersonal about the sorry business, assur-

ing myself I would have done the same for any of my tenants or workers. This was true; but the image of the slight
figure in her brown cape with the lost lonely look in her
green eyes cut me to the heart. I did not wish to get involved with Rosa's child. I had seen to it that there had
been no contact since she was very small. That I had fa-
thered her had been a trick of nature bred of a wanton
moonlit night, no more. Now, as we rode together over the
desolate moors with a chill wind against us and the knowledge of sadness ahead, I sensed acutely for the first time
an inextricable link which neither time, circumstance, or
the greatest force of human will could ever entirely erase.

Her thin arms were tenacious round my waist; as we
rounded the hill a stronger gust of air sent the soft drift of
her hair against my cheek. I could feel her face pressed
against my back, and a surge of emotion swept through
me . . . a protective instinct to cherish, which I had not
thought I possessed.

It took a full quarter of an hour to reach the Goss cottage, which was superior to those that had been mostly
erected by the tinners themselves near the mines. Gray-
stoned, gray-roofed, it stood on its own, in harmony with
the landscape, partially sheltered from the elements by a
background of massed granite and furze.

There was a small vegetable garden in front and at the
sides, where greens and potatoes struggled in rows that
needed weeding. I realized that the girl herself must have
been caring for it in the best way she knew, since her
mother had been ill. I wondered how long that had been.
As we went through the door Rosalind said, "It's untidy,
sir. I can't help it. . . . There's been a lot to do."

"When was Mrs. Goss taken ill?"

"It just came," she answered simply. "Not much until
. . . first it was a cough, and then . . ." Her voice wavered. "Matty Price says it's consumption."

From the sound of the dry cough upstairs I guessed
Matty Price, whoever he was, might be right. I followed

the girl through the half-open stair door up a narrow flight of steps to the bedroom; and there she was, a thin shell of a woman lying under a patchworked quilt, her eyes enormous in her drawn face where the color burned feverishly in two vivid spots of crimson. Her breathing was labored, tearing at her chest in rasps of pain. It appeared to me that she might very well be dead by the time the doctor arrived.

I went to the bedside. "Why didn't you let me know before, Mrs. Goss?" I asked. "I told you I would do anything for you at any time."

She nodded, making a pathetic attempt to smile. "I know, surr." Her voice was a whisper. "But . . . we've managed, as you can see. It's just . . ."

"Yes?"

Another fit of coughing seized her. Rosalind ran for a bowl from the chest, and mixed with the sputum when it came was a bright flood of red. Pity for the woman was swamped by an instinctive anger on behalf of the girl. This was *my* child; my flesh and blood. What right had anyone, even the woman who had cared for her, to lay upon her young shoulders and heart such an agony of suffering and ugliness.

"I've sent for the doctor," I said, trying to keep the coldness from my voice. "Perhaps you should rest now until he comes."

Mrs. Goss lifted one hand and clutched my wrist. It was as though a skeleton held it. "No," she managed to say. "I want to . . . to talk. Lindy . . ." Her eyes sought the girl's.

There was a whispered "Yes?"

"Leave us."

Dumbly, like some stricken young animal, Rosalind obeyed; and when the door had closed at the foot of the stairs, the feeble voice began again.

"It's . . . the girl." I could hardly hear what she said, so I put my head nearer, though the stench of sickness revolted me.

"I . . . what will happen to her? . . . Bal maiden? . . . Farmer's girl? . . . It's not right for Lindy. She . . . she's been good. She did well at the Dame's school. Here . . ."

From under the pillow Mrs. Goss took a shabby book which she pressed into my hand. "Always readin' et. A real scholar. And sometimes . . . sometimes . . ." The cough started again. When it was over the weak voice continued, "She speaks it aloud like. Makin' music out of the words, she said. I never did understand et . . . because in some way she's so full of life . . . good with animals . . . loves roamin' about the place . . . though, poor soul, she's had little chance of it these last days . . ."

I glanced at the book and said with a kind of wonder, "Shakespeare," adding under my breath, "my poor sweet Rosalind."

Pulling myself from my dream, I heard the tired voice murmur, "Bal maidens work hard. It's not . . . it's not . . . right . . ."

I laid my hand on the thin shoulder. "She shall be no bal maiden or farmer's wench either. You understand, Mrs. Goss? Your . . . your daughter shall have every chance." I almost added, "Because she's *my* daughter too." But I didn't have to. The look in the woman's eyes was enough to tell me she already knew. I would have been surprised had it been otherwise. Tom Goss had been no fool; and any doubts he'd had about the truth must have been dispelled with the child's developing likeness to Carmella, my mother.

After our brief conversation the sick woman closed her eyes, and I left the room to wait with the girl until the doctor arrived.

His examination was brief and negative. A second hemorrhage, he said, would undoubtedly be the end.

Mrs. Goss died that same night, as the cold spring twilight spread a gray shroud over the hills and sea. Rosalind did not cry; but the terror and anguish on her face told far more than any tears could have done. She did not touch the still form of the woman who had been mother to her for fifteen years. She just said, "She's not the same. That's not my mother. It can't be; it can't be."

Instinctively she ran toward me, burying her face against my breast.

My arm tightened around her slim waist. I fumbled in my mind for the right words to say, and all I could think of was, "Try not to think of it. Come along, Rosalind, we'll go home."

"Home?"

"To Carnecrane," I said. "In future you must think of it as your rightful place, and me as your father; because I'm going to look after you from now on. Do you understand?"

She did not, of course; neither did Caroline.

"It seems quite fantastic bringing a *miner's* daughter into our home," she said petulantly when I spoke to her after Mrs. Mellyn had taken my daughter to her bedroom. "I'm sorry for her, of course. But was there any *need*? I mean you can't just go fostering any waif and stray that takes your fancy . . ."

"I can do just what I choose in my own house," I said coldly.

"Don't my wishes count?"

"No. Not in this case."

"What about William?"

"Well, what about him?"

"He's your son. Nearly fifteen. At that age boys are impressionable. And she looks . . . well, she's got a rather . . . bizarre . . . look about her."

"I don't think you need worry about your son," I replied, trying hard to keep my temper under control. "Next term he will be going to Eton. I spoke about it to his tutor, the rector, the other day. He agreed with me that it would be better for him to be with boys of his own age in a normal masculine environment."

Caroline's large presence bridled with indignation. "I

knew nothing of this. Why didn't you tell me? . . . You know very well that William is delicate. He would not be as strong as he is but for my care. I don't agree with it. I will never let him go . . . *never*."

I put my hands on her shoulders, so my thumbs pressed deep into the white flesh which bruised so easily. An unbecoming flush mounted her cheek; her face had broadened with the years and was already faintly pouched beneath the eyes. "My dear Caroline," I said, "you have absolutely no say in the matter. That you gave birth to a weakling was your misfortune. That you gave me no more children was your own fault and responsibility. However, I happen to be the father of this boy, and he is going to have every chance." I dropped my hands, adding more quietly, "I'm sorry we disagree over so many things. I don't wish to bully you, but if I have to, I will. So shall we stop arguing. It's quite pointless."

"I know that very well," I heard my wife say acidly. "You've never shown me the slightest consideration or gone one inch to meet me over any matter concerning our marriage; it's been you . . . you . . . *you!* All the time. And now this . . . this Goss girl. I only hope you won't wish me to sit with her at table."

"That will be your business," I answered shortly. "If you want to take your meals in your room I have no objection. With William and myself she will have company enough."

In the long bitter look which passed between us I felt a sense of shame that two people could live together with such hatred for the other.

Caroline said nothing more on the subject, and the next day, at lunch, she was there at the table, facing me, with William on one side, and Rosalind on the other.

Mrs. Mellyn had equipped my daughter with a simple gray dress of her own which she had taken in and adapted the night before. Rosalind's face was pale, but her eyes were watchful and curious, studying William with intense interest. Against the sober shade of the frock her coloring seemed full of fire and light. Pride stirred in me because I had begotten her. Even her speech was curiously lacking in the strong Cornish burr common to most of the country folk.

"Rosalind is an authority on the works of William Shakespeare. Does that interest you, William?" I inquired, trying to stimulate friendship between the two.

William stared at me as though I were undergoing a temporary aberration.

"Not much," he said in his clear light voice. "I do not care for literature. Law is my subject."

"If you allow yourself to think in only one direction your life will be exceedingly limited," I said dryly.

"But successful," Caroline interposed. "If . . . if William allowed himself to be diverted by things like poetry, and reading plays, his *real* subject, at which he's quite brilliant, as you well know . . . would suffer."

"Oh, but *The Merchant of Venice* is all about the law," Rosalind said quickly. "Didn't you know that?"

"Of course I did. But it's boring to read. Besides, I don't like women who try to do men's things."

I could see from the slight lift of Rosalind's upper lip, the flash of her eyes, that William's remark made him a very poor creature in her estimation.

I was about to offer a placating remark when Lydia, who was a middle-aged woman now, brought in the salmon. I could see Rosalind glancing uncertainly at the variety of cutlery on the table, and to put her mind at rest and spare any embarrassment, I very obviously took up the proper fish knives. I saw with satisfaction that she was quick to learn; even Caroline could not justifiably have complained about her manners.

Later, however, when as a gesture I thanked my wife for being civil to the recently bereaved girl, she said coldly, "You gave me no option. Besides . . . I realize now that you had a reason for bringing her here."

Her eyes, usually rather placid and stupid-looking except when she was scared of any connubial demands, had for once a shrewd look in them.

"What do you mean?" I said. We were both in the conservatory where she had taken me to complain about the gardener's handling of a certain plant. Her face in the light and shade cast by the greenery had a mottled appearance. She really had become a cumbersome woman, I thought distastefully as I waited for her reply.

"I was in your study after lunch . . ." she began.

"Why?" I demanded with irrational anger. "What right had you to go there?"

Her blond almost undistinguishable brows wrinkled above her eyes.

"I do inspect, sometimes, to see that everything is well dusted for you," she answered facetiously. "Besides . . . I wanted to make sure."

"What about?"

"That portrait . . . the one in the alcove by the fireplace . . . it's your mother, isn't it?"

For once I was taken aback by the turn of the conversation.

"You know very well it is."

"Yes." The words came slowly. "I remember you told me so."

"What the devil are you . . ."

"You needn't swear," she interrupted. "I don't like it when William's about."

"William's in the garden with Rosalind, I sent them there. And if you ask me, a little healthy swearing would do the boy a deal of good."

"I'm *not* asking you, Laurence; I'm not asking you anything. I'm *telling* you. And not only about bad language and all the other insults you fling at me. I'm quite sick of it, do you understand? Sick of everything. Of you, and your vulgarity. Of your attitude to my son. Of being deceived. That's another thing. You see it's so obvious. That girl's your child, isn't she? Your bastard. That's why . . ."

I brought my hand hard and quick against Caroline's face. "Mention that word again," I said through my teeth, "and it's more than a slap across the face you'll get, my fine madam. Yes, she's my daughter. And she was conceived before I was ever fool enough to marry you. For your information she will be acknowledged as such from now on, and if you don't like it you can get out, and go and do whatever you damn well please."

"I *don't* like it, and I *shall* get out," Caroline answered. "You say William is shortly going to Eton. Perhaps it is not such a bad idea after all. I shall go with him and join my family at Oxford where I shall be nearer my son."

"Good. But remember this; in the holidays he will come back to Cornwall. I admit he's not my idea of an heir. But he happens to be so, and when I have the opportunity, away from your molly-coddling, I shall do my best to instill a little manliness into him."

Unknown to me, William had come to the garden door of the conservatory which was half open, and was standing there silently listening to my last few words to Caroline. I saw her mouth drop, and a kind of pain flood her eyes. I turned my head. William came forward and clutched his mother's hand. "I hate you," he said in clear precise tones which held a chilling quality. "I always have, and I always will, because I think you're a beast . . ."

Caroline pulled him to her protectingly. "William, don't . . . he didn't mean it, Laurence. . . ."

I threw back my head and laughed.

"*Afraid?*" I said to my wife. "Afraid I might strike a *cripple*? What a fool you are."

I didn't wait for more. I just walked out abruptly and went up to my own room. Although I didn't want to admit it to myself, I knew I had behaved badly. To have spoken to my son in such a way was despicable, even though he had goaded me into it. The idea of an apology occurred to me, but I put it aside, because an apology in this case could never have erased the taunt.

The memory of that unfortunate interlude was with me, at intervals, for the rest of my life. But it did solve one thing: my future at Carnecrane. Caroline, as I had expected, meant what she had said, and when William left for the summer term at Eton, she went with him, never to return, leaving me for the first time free to enjoy the company of my daughter. We had six months together, in which she became the most precious thing I'd ever known.

It was with regret for myself, but with high hopes for Rosalind, that I eventually arranged for her to join my brother Jasper in London, where he agreed to introduce her to the world of the theater.

Carnecrane seemed desolate without her . . . peopled only by ghosts of the past, of my mother, and those of my family I had never known. I could turn to only one other person at that time, Mrs. Mellyn, who gave, and gave generously of all she had, to bring me back to contentment and reality.

III

Rosalind

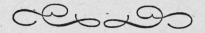

I think I had always sensed since I was a child able to puzzle things out for myself that I did not really belong to my parents Tom and Bessie Goss. I loved them. They were good people, and did all they could, I'm sure, to make me happy. But we were so different. Sometimes I felt chained, because life at the cottage was so bound by routine. None of us was free. Bessie was bound by duty to her husband and to me; Tom, though caring for us at home, was bound to his work at the mine. There was little color in our life, which was mostly as gray as the stone cottages, lumps of granite, and mine-workings of the moor. The only break in the pattern was chapel on Sundays where we went regularly to listen to Pastor Scobell preaching the moral doctrines of John Wesley, delivered with much condemnation and little joy. Occasionally a sinner was saved, after flinging himself on the ground and declaring his unworthiness to God. I did not believe in his god, and I did not believe he was saved. If he was right, then I thought the devil's company would suit me better. Naturally I kept such thoughts to myself, but inwardly I chafed. I had a great longing to wander; to leave the desolate hamlets behind, and take the ribboned paths among the heather and gorse, going on and on to strange new places of beauty and warmth. Sometimes on my rare walks alone I made a wreath of berries for my hair, and pretended I was Titania. I had learned to read early, and at six years old knew all about Shakespeare's *Midsummer Night's Dream*, because at Mrs. Trewhella's

school, which I already attended, I had been taught to re-
cite certain passages even before I knew how to write my
own name. Mrs. Trewhella was a widow who had started a
dame's school when her husband, who had been a printer,
died. There were only six pupils; they came from the larger
farms in the district, and seemed to think it strange that a
miner's child . . . even the daughter of a manager . . .
should be able to have lessons with them.

I didn't mind. I soon made friends, and Mrs. Trewhella
appeared to favor me. She took endless trouble to see that I
learned to speak properly, and to mind my manners. To
have good manners meant listening to what old people said
and not interrupting; to say "thank you", and "please," and
to curtsey to gentry. I thought this business of manners was
silly, and half the time longed to shout and sing, or run
away from lessons. But Mrs. Trewhella had a birch, which
all of us had learned to respect. It was only when I was on
my way home that I felt free.

Over the hill was a secret place . . . a dell where I
could reign in imagination, with tall foxglove flowers growing lush in the bracken, and a thorn tree that in spring was
a froth of white, curving behind me like a throne. It was
not far from the school, which stood in a belt of trees on
the opposite side of the valley, facing Wheal Gulvas. On
the way home I had a walk of half a mile down the lane
and up the moorland track to our cottage. Usually Billy
Paynter, whose father's farm was near, went with me. But
sometimes I escaped from him and went to the dell. I never
stayed long, because my mother would have questioned me,
and I was a very poor liar. So the dell remained my own,
and my retreat.

"If only I could stay here," I often thought. "If only I
could live like Titania for ever and ever, and never see the
ugly mines again, or hear men coughing because of the
dust and work." It was the hard work I mostly resented,
because it seemed to sap all happiness from life. My
mother was always tired with cooking and scrubbing and

washing our clothes. And besides his cough, my father had a bent back and poor eyesight through working so much underground. If we lived in a cave, we could have roamed at will and ate and slept like the animals. I wished sometimes I were a badger with a round hole to go to, or a wild fox able to slip through the undergrowth with the speed of the wild spring wind, coat burnished brown in the sunlight. I dreamed and wished so much those days that when I came back to earth I felt a deep loneliness that was hard to explain. It was then that I realized, deep down, I did not belong to Mr. and Mrs. Goss.

Once, in a fit of confidence, I revealed my suspicions to Mrs. Trewhella.

She looked at me oddly for a moment, then said, "That is a stupid idea for a child to have. Just daydreaming . . . nothing else. You are Rosalind Goss, and your parents are both very worthy and hardworking people. So put such stupid notions out of your head at once, and attend to your lessons."

I knew then that it was useless trying to make adults understand.

Once, when I was seven years old, shortly before my father was killed in the accident at the mine, I couldn't bear to go back from school to the cottage. It was daytime, and round the back of the hill, away from the huddled ugly tin mines and gray buildings, the bluebells glinted thick in the fresh springing bracken.

Billy Paynter was late leaving the classroom, so I darted off, and was soon out of sight around the bend. The air was still and sweet with the scent of flowers, moist earth, and young thrusting grass. A blackbird was singing from a crab apple tree which was a foam of blossom against the blue sky. My heart leapt, and my body became music as I danced there with my arms outflung and such a wild joy in me I thought my lungs would burst. Presently I sat on a rock to rest. From a nearby stone I watched an adder uncoil itself and slither toward me. I had always been warned about snakes and told that this kind could kill. But I felt no aversion or fear. It was so beautiful with its head raised on its elegant neck, small strange glittering eyes watching me.

"Come here, snake," I whispered. "Here I am, lovely one. Do you understand? Do you . . . ? We are both wild ones, aren't we? . . . I wouldn't hurt you, and I know you wouldn't touch me either . . ."

For some moments the silent communion held us enthralled. Then gracefully and quietly, the adder slipped away beneath the stone.

I got up and wandered on, singing quietly to myself, an unknown song that seemed to belong somewhere far away; a distant memory from another life.

I walked further than I knew. When I reached the road leading along the front of the hill back toward the lane up to my home, the sun was already much lower in the sky, sending long shadows streaking like witches over the moors.

I guessed my mother would be worried; and suddenly I was rebellious it should be so. Why must I be bound by duty and affection? When all I wanted was to be free to go my own way until I was so tired I dropped by a ditch to sleep, with the darkening sky above, and the fragrance of grass in my nostrils.

So I didn't take the road. I crossed it and walked toward the coast down a track leading between windblown bushes and straggling trees.

And then I saw it . . . a darkening silhouette touched with gold from the dying rays of the sun. I had seen the house before on the few occasions when we'd gone in the cart along the high road to St. Ives for shopping. But this time was different. Its turrets and chimneys had a significant imaginative quality that made it suddenly intensely important to me . . . a place of secrets and irresistible magic, beckoning me with the enchantment of a dream.

My steps moved forward involuntarily until I came almost to the door. I slipped behind a bush and stared, not

aware, in my youth, of the sham gothic structure which
had been added to the older Elizabethan part, or of the
later Georgian wing. The house was alive for me as an
entity, its eyes of windows burning with living gold, until
suddenly the sun had dipped beyond the horizon, leaving
the air darkened and swiftly chill.

I turned and ran, realizing then how very late I was.
When I reached the cottage, my mother and father were
both there, waiting. I had never seen my mother so angry.
She slapped me hard . . . something she had only done
once before in my life. "Et's sinful of you," she scolded, "to
have us feared like we were. Don't you ever do that again,
Lindy Goss. Haven't we told you time after time to be
straight back after school? Where were you then? You just
be tellin' us. Come along now . . . tell us straight what
happened."

I was shocked, but I didn't cry. "I felt like walking," I
said. "It was all sunny and kind of sweet, and there was a
blackbird singing. So I walked and walked, and I came to
the big house."

My mother was so taken aback her anger seemed to die
like a pricked balloon.

"You . . . *what*?"

"I went to the big house."

"Carnecrane, do you mean? Mr. Cremyllas's?"

I nodded. "I didn't go in. I just looked at it. The windows were burning . . . they were all dancey . . ."

My mother put her hands on my shoulders and shook
me. "Now you just listen to me, Lindy," she began again.
"Don't you ever dare go near that place again, d'ye hear?"

"Why?" I asked.

"Because it's trespassin'," she told me. "Mr. Cremyllas is
a gentleman, and gentlemen don't like . . ."

"Sh! Bessie," I heard my father say quietly. "There's bin
enough scolding for now. Just leave it." He turned to me
and his eyes were kind. "When people own property they
don't want others walkin' there unless they be asked," he

explained. "Et's like havin' a garden, see? You could walk
on somethin' and do damage."

"I didn't though," I answered. "I just stood by a bush."

"Well, that was a funny thing to do, wasn't et? . . . Sup-
posin' you'd have seen somethin' you wasn't supposed to!"

"But I didn't. I didn't see anything but the towers and
the lovely windows. And if *I* had a place like that I'd *want*
it to be seen," I said stubbornly.

"Maybe, maybe," my father said in a resigned way. "But
you see you haven't, Lindy. 'Tisn't your place and that's all
there is to it."

But it wasn't.

After that time I was haunted by the memory of Carnecrane. Being forbidden territory only added to my determination that one day somehow I would walk in through the
front doors and see for myself what it was like inside. Little I dreamed then that when the time came I should be
escorted there by Laurence Cremyllas himself after the
deaths of both my foster parents, and learn, following the
funeral of Mrs. Goss, that I was his natural daughter.

I shall never forget that moment.

The desolation of the funeral was still about me; I had
known during my previous three days at Carnecrane that
something else was wrong, which had not helped. Mrs.
Cremyllas, I knew, did not like me. She made no attempt
to hide it, although her silences and brief conversations
were painfully, condemningly polite. But I could understand her resentment at having me there. I did not belong
to the gentry. I was an outsider who through her husband's
kindness had been forced upon her. This was not what
worried me. It was the suppressed anger of two human
beings that seemed to haunt the shadows and corridors,
echoing at times in subdued whispers through the cracks of
closed doors, at others in bursts of raised voices which
made me hold my hands to my ears and want to run.

William had caught me like that one day in the hall, and said, "What's the matter?"

I didn't answer. But he knew. "Don't worry," he said, in a grown-up way. "They're often like that. My father and mother can't stand each other."

"Don't you mind?"

He shrugged. "I've got used to it. So will you if you stay."

"I shan't," I said. "I'm going tomorrow, I expect."

"Where?"

I couldn't answer. I didn't know. My first thought was that perhaps now I was fifteen, almost grown-up, I could help Mrs. Trewhella at her school. She had eight pupils then, and had complained that she could do with assistance. The next moment I knew how stupid the idea was. I should hate teaching, and all I really knew was about words and poetry, and how to say lines from Shakespeare and Thomas Gray. If I could have been an actress, I thought, I would work night and day if necessary and would never want to run away from that. But of course there was no chance. I supposed for a time I would have to help at a farm or be a bal maiden at a mine. Then, the next time Zachary Andrewarthe the peddler came my way, I would slip off with him, because Zachary liked company, and I knew I could help him at the larger places he went to, by showing off his beads and ribbons, and the trinkets he carried with him. He was getting old, and some said he was getting past it. If he gave up I could carry on. Yes, I'd be a peddler girl and roam as I'd always wished to. The thing to do was to get away as quickly as possible from Carnecrane, where I wasn't wanted.

So it was that after my mother was buried I found Mr. Cremyllas in the library and told him what I intended to do.

It was a dark room lined with books, but a shaft of pale light cut sharply across his face, accentuating its bold lines, the firm thrust of his chin under the dominant nose. He was handsome, I thought, in a way I admired; but I could understand why the fear showed so often in his wife's blue eyes.

"What do you mean, you're going?" he said, frowning.

"Well I must, mustn't I? I don't belong here, I've no . . ."

"Who says you don't?" he interrupted, coming toward me with a forward thrust of his fine head.

"Nobody. There's no need. You've been very kind, sir, but I've got to make out on my own. I don't want charity."

He paused a moment with something in his dark eyes I couldn't understand . . . half curious, half admiring; then he said suddenly, "Good. I like that; you have spirit. But then you would have . . . being my daughter."

At first the implication of the words was lost on me. I thought he was merely trying to make me feel secure. Almost immediately afterward I knew I was mistaken.

"It's true, Rosalind," he said, putting both hands on my shoulders. "Look at me; I'm not lying. You really *are* my own child."

I stared at him while my head spun from the conflict of emotions that left me momentarily speechless and a little frightened as though the earth had opened beneath my feet. This first reaction was followed by a sense of anger and humiliation. Why, if I was his daughter, had he left me neglected for so long?

When I'd regained composure, I said, lifting my head an inch higher, "If I *am* . . . why did you pretend? Why did I have to think my mother and . . . that Mr. and Mrs. Goss were my parents? And what about Mrs. Cremyllas, is she . . . ?"

"Good God, no," he almost shouted. "My dear child, I'm sorry . . . I should speak more gently. I'm afraid . . ." he gave a slight rueful laugh, ". . . gentleness and I aren't always the best company. The last thing I wanted to do was shock or hurt you. You see, Rosalind, your mother was not my wife. You were conceived before I was married."

"Why didn't you marry my mother?" I asked bluntly.

"Because . . ." His voice saddened. "I didn't ask her. And because I'm sure she wouldn't have wanted it."

"Didn't you love her?"

There was a long pause before he spoke. I waited until he said, "I don't know. I might have done, in time. But I wanted her very much. You must believe that. But . . . her ways were not mine. She was a wanderer, Rosalind . . ."

My heart lifted. "A peddler girl, do you mean? Or a . . . a gypsy?"

"Yes, she was a gypsy, and quite the loveliest thing I ever knew . . . wild, shy, sweet, and warm. It's hard to make you understand. I wish I could but . . ."

"But I *do*," I cried. "Now I know, it's all right. Because you see, I'm the same, I'm a wanderer too. I know what it's like to feel trapped and bound down by stupid rules and things. I loved my mother and father, I mean Mr. and Mrs. Goss, but it never seemed right somehow."

"And how do you feel now?" my father asked quietly. "Does *this* seem right? Belonging to me?"

"It seems right that you're my father," I told him truthfully. "But belonging for ever and ever . . . what is 'belonging'? Do you know? Doesn't everyone *really* belong just to themselves?"

"You've done a lot of thinking, I can see," I heard my father say. "Your last remark was personified in the lyrics of Robert Herrick, the poet, over a hundred years ago. 'Gather ye rosebuds while ye may . . .'"

"'Old time is still a-flying . . .'" I interrupted.

"Hm. What else do you know about reading?"

"Shakespeare mostly. I wish . . ."

"Yes?"

"I wish I could be an actress," I said quickly. "If only I

could be Miranda . . . or . . . or Titania . . . or Rosalind, the real Rosalind in *As You Like It* . . . I wouldn't even want to wander."

My father gave me a long hard look. Then he said, in a voice as though he really meant it, "We must see what can be done about it then, mustn't we? I have a brother in London who's an actor, your uncle Jasper. He has been playing with Sarah Siddons, who is a very great actress. If you showed promise for a theatrical career, I'm quite sure he would give you all the help possible. But first of all I should like you to stay with me for a few months . . . just to give me time to get to know my own daughter."

That was how it happened, and how, in the November of that year, I went with my father by post chaise to London for a meeting with Jasper Cremyllas.

2

London quite dazed me at first. It was so large, with so many churches, towers and spires, such a great river, and so many fine hostelries for the gentry to stay in. My uncle Jasper met the chaise when it arrived at the wonderful New Road. He was tall, slight, and fair-haired, extremely elegant, wearing a gray velvet coat with heavy silk breeches and hose, and a lemon-colored waistcoat. There was something noble-looking about him. He had not the powerful features of my father, but could easily have been a poet or artist. I could visualize him as Oberon in *A Midsummer Night's Dream*, or Ferdinand, who loved the beautiful Miranda in *The Tempest*.

For the time of year, the weather was not cold. If it had been I should not have noticed, I was so excited by the carriages and sound of horses' hooves, the twilit streets where candles flickered from windows on every side.

My uncle took us in his own chaise to a select hotel in the West End. We had dinner together in a dining room which was quite the most splendid place I'd ever dreamed of, with a pearl and green ceiling embossed and painted, pearl-gray domes, having green walls beneath, lit by Venetian glass candelabra. The carpet reflected the same shades in deeper tones, and the chairs and tables were elegantly designed in shining walnut, except for one gilt chair and a pouf in an alcove, which were upholstered in gray satin, with gilt legs.

My uncle told me that the hotel had been converted

from a great house and redesigned by a famous architect called Robert Adam, and that he had also been responsible for the screen and gateway to the Admiralty.

Although I must have looked very different from the other diners there, attired as I was in my plain high-necked brown silk dress which Mrs. Mellyn had chosen for me in Penzance when we went shopping, I was too busy listening to my uncle to bother about my appearance just then. He had so much to tell me about the people and buildings of the capital that my head spun. In the middle of the game pie which had followed upon two other courses I suddenly went so giddy that I had to leave the table to go up to my room, which had been reserved for me for the three days my father and I were staying at the hotel.

I felt very ashamed, but my father understood. "Jasper should not have ordered so much wine," he said, "and we should have stayed at a simpler place. It has all been too much for you. But try and get a good night's sleep. In the morning after breakfast we will take a look at the city if you feel like it, and afterward discuss plans with my brother."

I was so excited I thought I would never get to sleep at all. But I did. The mattress under the canopy of the large bed was so soft, and I was so tired, that I dropped off almost immediately.

In the morning I woke slowly, waiting to hear the wild crying of gulls over the Cornish moors. Then, as I opened my eyes, thoughts and events gradually took shape in my mind, and I remembered where I was.

I was suddenly wildly excited, and jumped out of bed, running to the long window covered by wine-shaded brocade curtains. I pulled them wide. In the gray light of the November morning the city looked different. Carriages were already to be seen, but there were fewer. Instead of silhouetted buildings lit to a fairyland of candled windows and towers of fantasy, were endless gray rooftops broken by the spires and domes of the larger but very real places

of history and our eighteenth century. As I watched, a thin
shaft of silvery sunlight broke the cloud, and I was filled
with joy at the prospect of the day ahead. I went to the
chest where my clothes lay . . . not neatly folded as Mrs.
Goss had taught me, but in a careless jumble. I picked the
garments up, one by one, giggling at the thought of the
night before, the wine I'd drunk, and how my uncle Jasper
had reacted, not with scolding or censure, but as though he
was mildly amused. Then I was quickly subdued. My
brown cape, the sober dress, and inelegant shoes were not
right for such a place. I was shy of going downstairs to
breakfast in such attire.

I need not have worried; shortly afterward there was a
knock on my door and breakfast was brought in on a tray;
there was also a note from my father which read:

> Rest as long as you wish, Rosalind, but try to be
> downstairs before noon. A shopping expedition is nec-
> essary before we visit the theater or meet your uncle
> again. You must have clothes befitting your station as
> my daughter.

My senses leaped at the vision of being able to buy clothes
of my own choice. I would have silks and satins and rich
colors instead of the dull shades forced on me by necessity
in Cornwall. I had always wanted pretty things to wear,
even though I'd been taught early that to have such
thoughts was vain and unworthy of a respectable girl.

But I wasn't respectable.

In a flash I saw myself for what I really was: gay, wild,
ambitious, with a sensuous longing for the pleasures that
had been for so long denied. I didn't care. It didn't matter.
It was only when life was gray and hard like it had been
for the Gosses that people had to make a god as dull and
dreary as their own lives. I didn't see why life should be
wasted, I didn't believe that just because so many individu-
als in the world were poor and miserable everyone else had

to be the same. It was right to be happy and extravagant if
the chance came along. Mrs. Goss, I knew, would have
said such thoughts were sinful. But even in the days when
Zachary Andrewarthe the peddler had pushed a ribbon or
trinket in my hand, asking no coin for it, but telling me to
keep it hidden, I had known that sinning could be fun.

I stared at myself through the mirror reflectively. It was
a pretty mirror, with a gilt frame surmounted by a wonderful gilt eagle. I pulled my hair to the top of my head, and
wondered how I would wear it. Not powdered certainly, as
I had seen in a colored print at Carnecrane; no, I would
not let myself be swayed by other women who had not my
striking coloring. I recognized that my dark hair, which
was so often bright with red lights, was unusual, and I
meant to be an unusual person, because quite soon I would
meet the famous Sarah Siddons perhaps, and it was necessary for me to make an impression.

I was downstairs two hours before noon, and my father
was waiting.

"I don't have to ask how you slept," he said with a smile.
"It's quite obvious. You look as fresh as a daisy."

I thanked him for saying so, although his reference to
"daisy" amused me. Daisies were pure and white and hum-
ble, and I didn't feel the description suited me; but then
men didn't know much about flowers generally, I told myself understandingly. One of the things I had noticed about
Carnecrane during my first days there had been the lack of
flowers about the house.

The first full day in London was exhilarating beyond my
wildest anticipation.

First of all my father hired a private chaise which took
us to the most fashionable shops in the West End. I had
determined to choose everything myself from the collection
of silk, satin, and velvet garments. But the costumier suggested that the orange and green brocade of my fancy
might detract from my complexion and hair. My instinct

was to disagree; then I had to admit the sense of what she said, and when she brought out instead a violet silk gown with a small saddle fixed to the underskirt under the waist, I knew the style and shade were perfect for me. What I did *not* enjoy was the special corset to go with it, which had a triangular wire, padded and curved to form what the costumier called the "pigeon's breast."

A handkerchief was crossed over the neckline, knotted like a fichu, and held up so stiffly that it appeared my own breasts must be false.

"I don't like it," I said rebelliously. "I don't see why I have to wear these stupid things."

"It is the fashion, madam," the costumier told me. "Ladies do not go about unequipped and floppy like country and serving maids. And believe me . . . you are so truly elegant and beautiful to dress."

So I gave in.

After my first choice two more dresses were purchased: a green velvet with a long, swinging, fur-trimmed coat to match, and a pale blue silk with embroidered panniers. After that we went to the millinery establishment. I wanted to laugh when I saw the strange feminine creations favored by fashionable women.

"I'd rather have a simple hood," I said to my father. "Just look at that."

The modiste, looking a little prim, took the hat in question from its place and fingered it lovingly. "It is a very beautiful hat, and would suit Madam perfectly."

I restrained my impulse to giggle, and allowed my hair to be pinned up on top to support the ridiculous creation.

I was surprised. When it was on it did not look ridiculous at all. It was boat-shaped, trimmed high with flowers, feathers, and ribbons.

"There. What did I say!" the modiste retorted triumphantly. It went so well with the green velvet that I took it, and one other, a wide-brimmed, very tall-crowned affair in black with three immense feathers curling upward above a cluster of artificial rosy apples and silver leaves. I liked this one the best because of its swinging veil which fell to my waist at the back, and made me feel indeed truly regal.

My father looked astonished. I was not quite sure that he approved. "You certainly look very grown-up," he said, when he saw me fully clad in the velvet outfit with the plumed hat. "But . . ."

"You don't like it? Then I won't wear it," I said quickly. "It's heavy, anyway."

"My dear child, you look beautiful, and you will certainly wear it," he insisted. "At lunch we will see what my brother says."

My uncle Jasper was flattering, and told me I'd made an admirable choice for going about and seeing London. "But when you come to meet my company tomorrow," he said, "and I hope, Mrs. Siddons, I would like you to wear your cape, Rosalind."

My heart sank. "My old *brown* cape? . . . That thing?"

He nodded. "That 'thing.' It may not be the height of fashion, but it's you. In it you're a waif and change-ling . . ."

"A wanderer?" I suggested, suddenly relaxing.

He nodded. "In London we see many fashionable women attired in rich clothing. But so rarely a wood nymph with hair of autumn and mermaid eyes. Do you understand?"

I did in a way. I knew I was going to like my uncle Jasper very much.

"You do say nice things," I remarked.

"My brother is an accomplished actor," I heard my father say with gentle irony. "That doesn't mean he isn't genuine in what he says. You must listen carefully when he advises you; and I must say I agree with him about the cape. The clothes are for formal social occasions, but the cape is more romantic."

I sighed. "I see."

"Before I leave for Cornwall," my father continued after

a pause, "we shall have more things to buy. At the academy you'll need something useful."

"What academy?" I asked sharply.

"Well now, after I've gone you won't be at the theater *all* the time," he explained. "Last night, after you'd gone to bed I discussed things with Jasper, and we agreed that you could spend the mornings getting a little more education . . ."

I stared at him, horrified. "*School,* do you mean?"

"Not school in the ordinary sense," my father said a little uncomfortably, "just . . . well . . ."

"A little painting perhaps," my uncle interposed tactfully, "languages, learning the social assets. . . . Oh nothing very terrible or difficult . . . but things that will help you with your career, Rosalind, if you really want to be an actress. I mean a great one such as Mrs. Siddons."

I didn't know what to say or think. Of course I wanted to be a great actress, but I didn't see how education at an academy was going to help that.

"Miss Pettinger's Academy for Young Ladies is a very pleasant place," I heard my uncle continuing, "and you really won't be there long enough to be bored . . . just two and a half hours each morning. Then in the afternoons you will be watching rehearsals, and other things connected with dramatic work."

"You seem to have planned a lot in such a short time," I said.

"We haven't got very long, remember," my father pointed out.

"Where shall I live?"

"Mrs. Craig, our wardrobe mistress, has agreed to have you with her at her lodgings while you are in London," my uncle said. "It's a comfortable place, and she's a good soul. You'll like her."

"I don't always like good souls," I said pointedly.

My father's expression turned to sternness. "Then you should try."

"Why? Do you?"

"I'm a man," he answered. "It's quite different. And yes . . . I certainly appreciate worthy qualities in people. So just because your head may be turned by this new adventure, don't let it continue, or you may find yourself in trouble."

I flushed. I had never heard him speak in that manner before, and just for a moment or two he was once more Mr. Laurence Cremyllas of Carnecrane, and I was the rebellious daughter of Mr. and Mrs. Goss. His brother broke the tension by saying, "Now, Laurence, don't scold. It doesn't suit you . . . or the occasion. You two haven't long together, and what I suggest is that you go and see the sights this afternoon, then about seven-thirty when you've had your meal you can come along to Drury Lane Theatre. I've got you two box seats for the evening performance, which should give you time for a brief introduction to Mrs. Siddons before the curtain goes up. And don't wear a hat, Rosalind. Any of the dresses will do, provided you have the brown cape over it."

And so it was all arranged.

As we were going back to the hotel for an early dinner, I insisted on wearing the tall plumed hat with the green velvet for sight-seeing, which was a crowded breathtaking business indeed. We went first by chaise to the Royal Botanic Gardens at Kew, and saw the famous Orangery, which my father told me had been opened by the Dowager Princess of Wales in 1759. It had been built by Mr. William Chambers, I learned, also the Pagoda, the Arch, and the Temples.

I did my best to remember the details, because I wanted to appear as educated as possible when I went to the wretched academy which I guessed would be a stuffy, prim kind of place, with young women there who had never had a whiff of the wild Cornish moors, or known what it was like to be a tinner's daughter living in poor circumstances in a gray cottage near the dark mines.

The journey to Kew took quite a time because they were seven miles from the city, and when we returned it was already late afternoon, but my father insisted on showing me the Tower, and Blackfriars Bridge. They were very impressive, but I would rather have seen the true East End near the Port of London. When my father asked me why, I had to think for a moment before I answered, "Because I think there'd be vagabonds there."

"And what would you be doing with vagabonds, dressed like that?" he said.

I didn't know. The truth was my taste of fashion that afternoon had been enough for me. I was a bit tired; the corset affair was bothering me, and I wished being elegant wasn't so uncomfortable, although I had enjoyed being stared at by so many men, especially by one particularly splendid-looking and handsome gallant—I had heard that was the term used—whose glance, from my hair and face, had traveled meaningfully to my uptilted bosom, which had been obvious even beneath the velvet coat.

Many sensations which had been strange to me before now began to awaken in a confusing, thrilling way. But the highlight of the whole day was when we went to Drury Lane after dinner.

Uncle Jasper met us at the stage door, and as we went along a threadwork of corridors to the dressing rooms, he said, "Sarah is already making up as Isabella, so the meeting will be only for a few moments. Then tomorrow, if she agrees, you will be able to watch rehearsals."

He stopped outside a door, knocked, and, hearing a "come in," entered, ushering me before him. Candles flickered on a slender figure sitting before a mirror, with a woman in stiff black silk, dressing her hair.

She turned. "This is my niece, Sarah," I heard Jasper say. "The child who wants to become an actress."

"My dear, you don't know what you're in for," Mrs. Siddons said after a smile and brief glance in my direction. "Unless the theater's in your blood."

"It is," Jasper Cremyllas told her. "Although you may not think much of my own talents . . ."

"Oh, but I do. I do," she said. "You are an excellent Claudio, dear Jasper. But one competent actor in a family does not make it an inherent quality."

"My grandmother was an actress," I said impulsively, forgetting whom I was speaking to. "My father said so. And my great-grandfather. They traveled about and acted all over Cornwall."

Mrs. Siddons and her dresser both turned and for moments said nothing. I suddenly felt rather stupid, and wished the earth could open and swallow me up. Instead Mrs. Siddons said, "That's interesting, and tomorrow you must tell me more about yourself. For the present, child, I haven't time, neither has Claudio. So run away, both of you. And I hope you and your father enjoy the performance tonight."

I did. *Measure for Measure* was not one of Shakespeare's plays that I knew properly, but I could not keep my eyes from the graceful figure of Mrs. Siddons as she moved in her blue panniered dress across the stage, looking quite beautiful, with her fair complexion and golden hair surmounted by the pale blue headpiece and flowing veil. I felt also terribly proud of my uncle, who, as Claudio, seemed to suit the part so well. One passage moved me profoundly, and when I got back to the hotel that night, I took out my book of Shakespeare's plays and read it for myself.

> Why give you me this shame?
> Think you I can a resolution fetch
> From flow'ry tenderness? If I must die,
> I will encounter darkness as a bride,
> And hug it in mine arms.

I thought the verse very sad, so sad that I imagined myself in the part of Isabella and spoke her answer aloud:

> There spake my brother: there my father's grave
> Did utter forth a voice. Yes, thou must die:
> Thou art too noble to conserve a life
> In base appliances.

I was interrupted at that point by a knock on the door, and my father's entrance.

"Well, well," he said. "Practicing already? I thought I heard you. You should be preparing for bed."

"I will in a moment."

I ran toward him and took his hands. They gripped mine hard as I said, "Thank you. I never expected such a wonderful thing to happen. I'm so grateful."

He shook his head. "I want no gratitude," he said a little sadly. "Just . . ."

"Yes?"

He shrugged. "No matter. Nothing; you're my daughter. What you have now you should have had long ago, that's all."

But I knew the word he'd wanted to say, and hadn't, had been *love*. I almost said it myself, told him that indeed I did love him. But at that moment it would not precisely have been true. I was part of him. His blood ran in my own veins, but there was a side of him which was still strange to me, despite our time in Cornwall, and I recognized that in one way I had closer understanding with his brother Jasper, my uncle.

"Why can't you stay in London longer?" I asked, thinking this would give me a chance to get to know him better, and also defer perhaps the unpleasant thought of having to attend the Academy for Young Ladies quite so soon.

He shook his head. "I don't belong here, Rosalind. Carne-crane's my home and needs my attention. I'm a country man, and no actor. When you're free I shall hope to see you back in Cornwall, and it may be I'll come to town occasionally. There's just one thing I want you to remember."

"Yes?"

"If life here irks you, if at any time you begin to feel smothered and caught up into something that isn't you— the *real* you—then give it up and come home to me. A bird in a cage may sometimes sing, but very often its heart can break."

Those were the most serious words I'd heard my father say, and I never forgot them.

Two days later when I'd had my first experience of watching rehearsals at the theater, and also been introduced to Miss Pettinger's Academy, Laurence Cremyllas, my father, boarded the post chaise for his journey back to Cornwall, and a new phase in my life began.

3

The next two months gradually settled into a routine which, being varied, did not irk me too much. The Academy for Young Ladies was not so boring as I'd feared. The other girls who were mostly my juniors, boarded at the establishment, and although they resented my being in a different category, the resentment soon changed to envy and admiration when they knew I was about to train for the stage. I was careful always to look my best, and knew that my appearance impressed them. As I was only there for a certain part of each morning, I wasn't made to study mathematics or geography, but was given lessons in French, etiquette, and tuition in piano playing. I was quick at French, but the piano did not interest me.

"I'd rather dance," I told Miss Pettinger. "Why can't I learn how to dance at balls?"

Miss Pettinger's mouth screwed itself into a button. "Is it only the vain studies that appeal to you, Miss Cremyllas?" (My father had insisted I take his name.)

"Perhaps," I agreed stubbornly. "But if I'm going to be an actress, and I *am*, you know, Miss Pettinger, dancing is very important."

In the end Miss Pettinger agreed I should have lessons in the minuet for half the time, providing I practiced my scales for the other.

And so the days passed.

In the afternoons I went to Drury Lane for rehearsals. At first I'd been disappointed, because I hardly ever saw

Mrs. Siddons. I just sat in front of the stage watching the chief understudies practicing their parts.

My uncle Jasper occasionally came to see me there.

"How are you liking theatrical work?" he asked one day.

"I don't know, do I?" I said sharply. "I never get a chance to try. It's always watching other people. And they're not even the *real* ones."

"That's where you're wrong," he said. "In stage work *everyone* counts . . . stage hands, prompters, understudies . . . even those who walk on without speaking a word. The production of a great play is a united affair. The failure of one small part of it may ruin the whole. Do you understand?"

"I suppose so," I agreed grudgingly. "But it isn't quite what I thought."

"Nothing worthwhile ever is. Oh, I understand that you want the color and excitement of going before an audience, and I'm sure when you're ready to do that you will take everyone's breath away. But you've got a way to go yet, and if you're wise, Rosalind, you'll watch the producer very carefully. Note his manner of grouping the performers . . . his insistence on the right moments of entry, and that every gesture should be natural and convincing."

"I'll try," I said.

"By the way, how are you getting on with Mrs. Craig? Are your quarters comfortable?"

"Mrs. Craig is quite nice," I said. "But she's rather domineering. She makes me go to bed every night at half past nine, and always tries to follow me if I go out on my own."

"Good," came the quick answer. "That's what she's there for. I realize your quarters at her lodgings can't compare with the hotel, but even if your father had afforded to pay for you there, the glamour might have gone to your head. Don't you think so?"

I could feel the hot blood flaming my cheeks. "Why?"

He smiled, and his smile radiated his whole face. He really was extremely handsome.

"Any girl with spirit and looks like you would be the same," he answered. "And that's a compliment."

My resentment faded. "I know. And I'll try and do what you say, Uncle Jasper."

But it wasn't easy.

Every afternoon I longed and longed for the chance to get up on the stage and speak just a few lines. But I wasn't allowed to. The producer was a small, white-haired, rosy-faced man, with a quick temper and a frightening way of shouting and striding about when things weren't to his liking. I would never have defied him in his presence. But one day he was a little late, and so was Mrs. Siddon's understudy.

The rest of the cast present did their bits over and over again, until I could stand it no longer. I jumped up on the stage and with a wildly beating heart spoke the understudy's words as I thought they *should* be said.

> Could great men thunder
> As Jove himself does, Jove would ne'er be quiet,
> For every pelting petty officer
> Would use his heaven for thunder,
> Nothing but thunder, Merciful heaven!
> Thou rather with thy sharp and sulphurous bolt
> Splits the unwedgeable and gnarled oak
> Than the soft myrtle; but man, proud man . . .

I stopped abruptly, aware of figures at the wings. One was the young woman who should have been playing, accompanied by the producer, and beneath the stage, not far from the door, an elderly man who was a complete stranger.

There was a dreadful prolonged pause. Then Mrs. Siddons's understudy rushed forward and stood facing me with hostility wild on her handsome hard face. "How dare you take my place?" she demanded with her breasts rising and falling heavily. "You've wanted this from the start, haven't you? . . . I've seen it, I've noticed, I'm no fool

. . . but you haven't even learned the first rudiments of how the speech should be said . . ."

"No," I cried. "Not from you. Because I don't think you do it properly. My way is best . . ."

Her arm came out and she slapped me hard on my face so my ears and cheeks stung. I had a violent desire to scratch her hard and pull her hair, but I was prevented by the producer, whose hands came on my shoulders, tearing me away. Then he pointed to the floor.

"Get down there!" he said in a furious voice, with his pink face puffed in anger. "And don't dare to take another step on to this stage until I give you permission. To have a scene like this is unthinkable. It has never happened before. Never, *never*. And don't imagine you can yet act, miss. The shocking display I've just witnessed is more in keeping with a gypsy brawl."

I felt so humiliated I rushed out of the theater to the dressing room, with the sting of tears in my eyes. My heart was palpitating wildly, and such a misery of unhappiness filled me that I decided I would not stay there a moment longer than I needed. That very evening, or tomorrow at the latest I would leave London and return to Cornwall. I wasn't an actress after all. I belonged to other things, to the open sky, the wild sweet turf of the moors and gaunt rocks above the sea. Reigning in a Cornish dell was so different from reigning as an actress. I hadn't realized it; but my father had. He had known what he was talking about when he'd said, "A bird in a cage may sometimes sing, but very often its heart can break."

Suddenly, without any warning, the tears began to fall. I sobbed and sobbed, and was still doing so when I heard a cultured male voice saying,

"My dear girl, don't so distress yourself."

I looked up. The tall elderly gentleman who had been watching when the unhappy scene occurred, was standing in the doorway, smiling at me kindly. He was very

distinguished-looking, and dressed elegantly, with a short
cape falling from his shoulders. His hair was gray but unpowdered, caught at the back with a bow. I remembered
these details afterward, but at the time my only impression
was one of very great kindness.

"May I come in?" he said.

I wiped my eyes hastily. "Yes, of course. It's not my
room. It's . . . I shouldn't be here . . ."

I was about to leave when he motioned me back. "You
have every right to rest yourself after what's just happened.
That's what I came to tell you."

I stared at him, puzzled.

"I don't understand, sir."

"Of course you don't. He was very terrifying, our friend
the producer. But, believe me, he has to be. If he wasn't,
he'd get no order, or nothing done to his liking." He
paused, adding after a moment, "And of course your action
was quite . . . unprecedented, shall we say?"

"I know. I'm sorry. Anyhow, I'm not going to be an actress after all."

"Oh? Who says so?"

"I've decided," I told him bluntly.

"Then you're making a great mistake, my dear. Believe
me, I know what I'm talking about. You see, you were
good. *Very* good. You showed considerable dramatic talent,
and took the lines with an original approach that I found
stimulating. You were too quick of course, and a little over-
enthusiastic, but these are things that can be overcome,
with patience. I know what I'm talking about. I'm . . . Sir
Charles Cranmere, if that means anything to you, which I
don't suppose it does." There was a pause, until he added,
"Why should it? Anyway, forget the 'sir.' The important
thing is that I know the theater and have influence."

After that, everything changed.

Sir Charles must have spoken to the producer, because
the following week I was given private tuition and audi-

tions in a variety of parts each day, which kept me in a daze of learning and reading and practicing voice production.

When a month had passed in this way, I was told that with determination and self-discipline I might even rise to the heights of Sarah Siddons in dramatic achievement. "I'm not saying you *will*," the producer told me, "but that you *could*. There will be no copying though, you understand? No modeling on other actresses anymore. You have first to learn to be more completely yourself . . . then how to shed your personality wholeheartedly, so you can assume the skin and character of the individual you are interpreting. Do you know what I mean?"

"No," I answered truthfully. "But I will try."

"You're lucky that Sir Charles takes such an interest in you," I heard the usually irate voice saying quietly and consideringly. "He is extremely rich, a patron of the theater, and can do a very great deal for anyone he thinks worth it. He knows more about stage work than most of us producers, and I have never known him wrong in assessing the possibilities of an aspiring actor or actress."

"And do you believe he's right *this* time?" I questioned.

The bushy brows came together in a frown. Finger and thumb held the pointed chin reflectively, and then the answer came, with a beam of a smile that completely transfigured the peppery face. "Yes, I do, so long as you do as you're told, young lady. If you behave well you'll be off on tour in no time."

"On *tour*?" I gasped.

"That's what Sir Charles has in mind. You must keep it as a little secret for the time being, but he told me only the other day that he was ready to finance a company for traveling the provinces." He paused, adding significantly, "Your name was mentioned, incidentally, as a possible female lead."

"*Me?*" I gasped.

"Don't count on it though," he little man said more brusquely, "but bearing such things in mind you should study hard, in the time left, at different types of acting. There are other plays besides Shakespeare's . . . excellent comedies such as Oliver Goldsmith's *Good Natur'd Man*, which was staged at Covent Garden. Ever heard of it? You haven't? . . . Well, no matter. *She Stoops to Conquer* is another, and well suited to provincial audiences. It's possible Sir Charles could easily decide to put on the latter. On the other hand you might find yourself launched as Portia. I don't want to frighten you, but you must be prepared to tackle anything that is offered."

"Oh I am, I *am*," I cried. "And I'll do all that you say, I really will."

He patted my shoulder. "Good."

So a new routine started. As the protégée of Sir Charles Cranmere I was treated with more respect, though strictly, being taken time after time through different roles in different plays at hours when nobody but Sir Charles and the producer were present. I was sometimes frustrated and tired; there were times when I longed to shout or scream and rush off the stage in tears. But I never did, because I knew how much was at stake.

Then, in August, my patron asked me out to dinner at his establishment in the West End. Even now my memory is bemused by the occasion . . . the wine, the candlelight, the cut crystal, and shining silver on the table . . . the pale blue hangings and rosewood furnishing, the delicious food served by a butler and footman. I wore my blue silk with the embroidered panniers and I couldn't help being aware of Sir Charles's admiration.

When the meal was over, and we were seated in the drawing room by a leaping fire which touched the crystal candelabra to rainbow-flame, Sir Charles said, "You know of course that I have great faith in you, don't you, Rosalind?"

Guessing what was coming, and endeavoring to keep the color staining my face, I answered, "Yes, and I'm very grateful. I never expected you to be so kind . . ." My voice wavered, and died into silence. He smiled. His smile was the kind that took the years away, and I knew in that instant what he must have looked like when he was really young . . . handsome and noble, with his finely cut features and penetrating deeply set eyes. There was something else too . . . a quality that set him apart from anyone else I had known . . . a pride and compassion. A rare quality that gave meaning and reality to living. He must have had his faults; he was only human. But I never found any; perhaps even then, as he was speaking, I was realizing how warmly I felt to him. I was only in my seventeenth year, and he must have been nearing sixty, but the communion between us was an instinctive thing. The barriers of age, culture, and experience were nonexistent in those moments of awareness. I hardly knew what he was saying, until a few words caught my attention. "So from tomorrow, my dear, you will have a new producer, and start rehearsing for Katherine in *The Taming of the Shrew*. The touring facilities will be as comfortable as possible, and extend through the west country, including Bristol and Bath . . . possibly Plymouth. I have my home in Devonshire, and will accompany you for much of the time."

He paused, eyeing me anxiously. I tried to speak, but couldn't find the words until he said, "That is, if you agree?"

"*Agree?*" I echoed stupidly. "Oh . . . Sir Charles . . ."

I ran to him, half laughing, half crying, sank onto my knees by his chair and said, "You are the most wonderful of men. I never imagined anyone could be so . . . so . . . so inspiring and good. I . . . I mean . . ."

The whole thing became a dream, and in the magic of it I felt his hands close over mine, vaguely noted the break in his voice when he said half sadly, with emotion, "Rosalind, my darling child . . ."

I shook my head so the earrings tinkled like tiny bells, and my hair fell from its ribbons to my shoulders. "No," I said quietly, "I'm not a child. My mother was a gypsy, did you know? And my great-great-grandmother. Gypsies mature young. I am a woman; I hope you don't mind the gypsy part?"

He shook his head. "Who could mind? You're quite adorable. But you're only at the beginning of life, Rosalind, and I am approaching the end of mine. . . . Oh, yes, it's true. That's why we can talk perhaps. It's the years between that can become dull and confused. But morning glory and the sunset . . . those are the beautiful times. Do you know what I mean?"

"Yes. That's how I feel too."

There was a long silence filled with a golden contentment that had no need of words. All the same I knew that a time would come when unspoken thoughts would be said. It had to be so; I knew it as surely as spring must follow winter and pass into summer's high noon. Our relationship held no doubt for me. I not only admired and respected him, I loved him. It didn't matter to me that he was a widower with a grown-up son. Years . . . time . . . circumstance . . . they were the merest illusions. Whatever the cynics might say later—and they said plenty—the truth was in our hearts. The truth would endure.

It did.

Six months later, during a Shakespearean season at Bristol, Sir Charles Cranmere and I were married, and as a brief respite went to his home Lyncastle in Devon before continuing with the company to Bath.

4

In the next few years it seemed I had everything; my career, a growing reputation as an actress, my youth, travel, and most of all . . . my love. It was a perfect era of my life.

When people say that it is impossible for youth and maturity to find happiness together, they are wrong. Charles gave me all I could wish for at that time: physical peace, mental stimulus, and wonderful companionship. When I was with him, everything shone. The sky was more blue; the sun had a deeper glow; success mattered, chiefly because he wished me success.

In our most intimate moments as man and wife his gentleness enveloped me as the warm earth a seed, so that I opened to happiness like a flower opening to the spring.

No words can adequately describe how I felt.

Before, I had been rebellious and ambitious, fundamentally an untamed spirit. But Charles, just through being himself, revealed God to me; not the pagan god of my secret childhood, or the god of the church . . . but the truth of enduring love. It was as simple as that.

He seldom missed a performance during those years of touring, and his holidays were spent with me, either abroad in Italy or France, Lyncastle, or occasionally with my father. But we did not go to Carnecrane much. Although he did his best to be pleasant, I could not help sensing an underlying resentment in my father's attitude, a secret jeal-

ousy that discomforted me. I had thought he wanted only
my happiness, and did all I could to show how happy I
was. When this didn't please him I was mildly annoyed.

Once, during a brief visit, he said, "You have lost your
wildness, Rosalind. But I suppose being Lady Cranmere
puts demands on you."

Being Lady Cranmere had never affected me at all. At
first I had enoyed having bows and respect when my husband and I went into society, then, after a time, I never
noticed it. The only thing that warmed me except for
Charles's love was the response I got from audiences where
I played.

"You must not worry about Laurence," my uncle Thurston said one day when I had been hurt by my father's
manner in a slight difference of opinion with my husband.
"He has a bitter streak in him, which is why he lost his
wife in the first place. You are all he's got except a son he
doesn't care about. Treat his little peccadilloes with contempt. I know my brother."

I wondered. It had seemed to me that Lord Pengalva
had little contact with Laurence, my father. I thought it a
pity, because although my uncle was elderly-looking for his
years; he was the same age as my husband. I could tell that
he was often lonely, and would have liked to think of Laurence as a son. He had no children of his own, and Helena,
his wife, though friendly enough, was a cool, remote kind
of woman, with a vague manner and air of a wilting
snowdrop. She was also forgetful and repeated her remarks
from time to time, which made her husband chary of any
conversation with her.

"Marrying stupid women seems to be a foible of the
family," my father remarked once when we were alone
together. "Pengalva married one, so did I."

His dark eyes were suddenly upon me with a half-
apologetic, half-searching look. "I should have chosen your
mother and to hell with respectability."

"Having me wasn't respectable, was it?" I said lightly.

"No. And see how well you've done. You're welcomed everywhere, aren't you? But as I said . . . being Lady Cranmere is a help."

"You bother too much about that sort of thing," I said quickly. "If you're happy everyone likes you. If you're not . . . well, it shows."

"Meaning me?"

"In a way. Why . . . ?"

"Yes?"

"Why don't you see William more often? He's done well, hasn't he? He's a barrister, he seems to be thought well of . . ."

"Who told you?"

"Charles. And once we met when we were in Glouces-ter. Quite by chance. He was on some sort of a case and we happened to run into him at a hotel. Charles knew him quite well. I was so surprised."

"I see." His voice was grim. "And what did you think of your . . . half brother, my respected son?"

"He seemed nice. Rather quiet, you know, shy. But very gentlemanly."

"Oh, yes. His mother saw to it that he learned all the assets of the perfect social prig."

How sad, I thought, that a loveless marriage could breed such bitterness.

"I think you should be friends all the same," I insisted stubbornly.

"My dear Rosalind, whenever we meet we are extremely civil to each other," my father said quickly. "He is heir to Carnecrane, remember . . . although of course you will be provided for . . . not that you need it. But the truth is . . . well, I cannot stand the sight of him."

"You *what*?"

"It's true. The way he stoops . . . with his head pushed a bit to one side . . . offends me; his manner irritates me and his smug legal mind bores me to death. So don't sing his praises. I'm well acquainted with them. If he was less virtuous no doubt we should get on better."

I realized there was no point in pursuing the matter. Laurence in his middle years had hardened perceptibly in character. His bold eyes under the fierce graying brows held now a cold glint. For the first time I glimpsed the cruel streak in him which must at times have hurt his wife.

I had seen her only once since she left Carnecrane, when I had been playing at Oxford in *As You Like It*.

I was brought face to face with her by Charles, at a university gathering.

"I realize, Mrs. Cremyllas, that you two knew each other in the past," he said half pleadingly. "But much water has run under the mill since then, and I hope you may both get acquainted all over again and learn to like each other." He paused. "You should have more in common now; my wife is always anxious to talk of the theater, and I know you have a very sound knowledge of it."

To my surprise the large, handsome face softened as a dull color mottled the ample shoulders and cheeks. She held out her hand, which was strangely small for her size, and replied, "Naturally I am pleased to meet Lady Cranmere. . . . That she is also Rosalind Cremyllas the actress makes it a double pleasure."

We chatted of this and that for some time; Caroline was certainly well versed in current cultural and theatrical affairs, and had attended the opening of the new Drury Lane Theatre in 1794, which had been enlarged by Richard Sheridan, the playwright. I had already played in his *A Trip to Scarborough*, a fact which gave us a starting point in conversation. But I was relieved when a chance came to get away. Her amiability was oppressive, and behind the polite facade I could not help sensing an undercurrent of restrained hostility.

We were only in Oxford for the next week, and the following Sunday were leaving for Bristol, taking some days on the journey. This was my last touring season of Shakespeare before opening with a new play in London. In between we had arranged for a respite at Lyncastle. For the first time Charles seemed drained of energy. I realized with a stab of foreboding that he had reached a time of life when he should be able to relax in peace without the continual business of travel and theatrical activities. I noticed the tired lines of strain about his eyes and mouth, the way his hand trembled sometimes for no obvious reason. I was suddenly frightened. If I lost him, how could I go on? I realized in those few dreadful moments of comprehension that the spiritual part of our union had been the mainstay of our devotion. The physical side of a necessity had been curtailed in recent years, but it had not consciously bothered me, because I had *him* . . . the best part, the enduring part. Now this quick awareness of inevitable parting some time ahead filled me with black depression.

"Charles . . ." I said, as we unpacked in the Bristol hotel, "I've been thinking . . ."

"What about? Any problem?"

"Yes," I told him bluntly. "It's time we had a life of our own. After the season, and it's not long, is it? . . . I think we should put off the London productions."

He stared at me. "But, my love, *why*? . . . It's meant so much to you . . . planning and dreaming all these years for the chance. Now tell me, what's the reason?"

"Just what I said. I think we're both tired."

He smiled, shook his head, and said gently, "Not you, Rosalind. You've never looked more vital or lovely. I admit I don't feel like a twenty-year-old anymore, but the idea of curtailing any plans is not only ridiculous but quite unnecessary. Now stop worrying your head about me. I'm quite all right."

I had to give in, realizing that any insistence on the matter of his health would only emphasize the sad but true fact of age difference. And so I forced my apprehension away, and gave my mind to the forthcoming Bristol opening.

An hour before the curtain went up for *As You Like It* on the Monday, something happened.

Victor Adams, who was playing Orlando to my Rosalind, was taken suddenly ill and his understudy called to take his place. I had met him occasionally at rehearsals, and though I had always admired his looks—he was tall, young, dark-haired with very striking blue eyes, and an arrogant sensuous mouth—something about him had from the first instinctively annoyed me. He was too sure of himself, too calculated in the art of charming. Therefore when the producer ushered him backstage, saying, "Rosalind, my dear girl . . . it *could* be a calamity, but it mustn't be. Victor's collapsed with some . . . with some . . . oh never mind . . . what it is. But he won't be appearing tonight, so you'll have to make do with Roderick." My first instinct was to think, "Good. I'll make him toe the line." Just as quickly I switched my attention to the realities. All that mattered was for Roderick Carew to feel sufficiently at ease to undertake the role competently.

So after a quick run-through of vital speeches, I flattered and soothed him, inwardly complimenting myself on my achievement, not realizing until later that the reverse was true. His own confidence had enthused into me.

The evening was a success, and the many other evenings following. I enjoyed playing with Roderick, forgetting to worry over Charles, who assured me he was well, and appeared to share in the warmth and appreciation shown by audiences each night.

I felt younger, revitalized, filled with mounting excitement, not realizing that I was falling in love, with the instinctive response of youth to youth.

And then, one evening, everything changed.

Charles, feeling a little tired, had excused himself from the performance. I was later than usual at the theater, owing to some hitch concerning my dresser, who had left early owing to an attack of migraine. I did not mind. There

were times when I preferred to be on my own; I was about
to slip off my gown when there was a knock on the door of
my dressing room, and Roderick entered. My pulses ham-
mered. But my voice was intentionally cold when I said
calmly enough, "What do you want, Roderick?"

He smiled, closed the door, and ambled casually toward
the stool where I sat in front of the mirror. Then he said
quite simply, "You."

My spine froze, but the hot blood melted the ice to fire,
as his lips touched first my neck and the bare shoulder
where my dress had tumbled. Then he swung my head
around, and his mouth was on mine. For a delirious moment desire for him obscured everything else; the room
spun, until I remembered.

Charles.

I pushed Roderick away wildly, catching his face with
my nail. I had not meant to hurt him, but he thought I did.
His hand went to his cheek where a thin red line already
showed.

"You little . . . fool," he said softly, almost in a whisper. "I don't take that from any woman. And don't tell me
you haven't wanted me; you've lusted in your heart for
weeks . . ."

"Get out!" I cried, trying to keep my voice down. "And
don't ever touch me again, do you hear?"

He shrugged. "I'll get out. But next time—and there'll
be one—I'll have you and you'll like it. You'll like it so
much, my darling . . . you'll be on your knees for
more . . ."

I picked up a pot of cream and flung it at his head. It
just missed, falling to the floor with a thud. I heard him
laughing quietly as the door closed, leaving me shaking,
with knees trembling and a dreadful unhappiness in my
heart. My world had collapsed, because there had been
truth in what he'd said. I *had* wanted him, although I
hadn't accepted it until then; I had been false in my
thoughts to myself, and to Charles, who was still so dear to

death was horrible to me; especially when it was faced with such fortitude by the man who had given me so much, and of whom I was still so deeply fond. If I was going to die, I thought frequently, I could not bear to sit there day by day watching it hour by hour drawing a little closer; I would want to run away and find a ditch somewhere, where I could lie with my face pressed close in the thick grass, smelling the earth smells and the tangy scent of damp leaves.

"It isn't fair . . . it isn't fair," my heart cried in lowest moments. But I made sure that Charles never knew. It wasn't easy. I was only twenty-seven, and my youth was already seared by an inner agony I couldn't suppress.

Once my husband said, as he sipped the tea I had just given him, "Rosalind my love . . ."

"Yes, darling?"

"When I'm gone . . . Oh yes, now don't try to stop me saying what has to be said. We both know how things are, and there's nothing unnatural about it. It's the pattern of existence, my dear, something I'm sad you have to learn so soon . . ."

"Please don't."

"I must. For your sake. You see it couldn't be otherwise, neither can I expect you to go through life unloved as a wife."

"Charles . . ."

"One day you will find someone who loves you," my husband continued firmly, "someone of your own age, who can give you what I have not . . . children, and emotional security for the future. So I want you to remember that this is my wish. Go forward to meet what is offered, Rosalind. Will you promise?"

I could not answer because of the blur of tears in my eyes and at the back of my throat. But when he insisted I nodded blindly.

He took my hand. "Good."

There was a silence between us, silence so complete that

every small stir in the garden held intensity and meaning . . . the flutter of birds' wings in the grass, of a chestnut dropping from a nearby tree, and the distant murmur of the stream trickling into the lily pool. Presently I heard the quiet voice continue, "I have made ample provision for you, of course. Frederick naturally will inherit this place, and he will be executor of the estate. But I should like to think of you being happy, and that is why I suggest your returning to Carnecrane for a time when . . . when I shuffle off this mortal coil. You'll get things into perspective there with your father, and I'm sure you'll take up your career again, unless you choose to settle down to domesticity . . ."

"Stop! *Stop*," I interrupted. "Don't say these things. Don't leave me, Charles . . . you mustn't, you can't. If you do . . . if . . . if . . . don't you see? I shall die too . . ."

But I didn't.

Death, except for the old, is not as easy as that. All that happens after the loss of a loved one is a dreadful anguish slowly turning to a mechanical capacity for endurance. When Charles died peacefully in his sleep one day in November, I did not faint, or even cry at first. The tears only came later; and by then I had learned that hearts don't break: they just ache with a pain worse than any physical hurt . . . something that can go on and on, until one day life starts up again, like a shoot long frozen in icy ground forced to growth by light and sun.

I was standing in the winter sunshine on a cold December day shortly before leaving for Carnecrane, when Roderick appeared at Lyncastle. I had been wandering around, staring unhappily with a kind of wonder at the first green shoots which were already pushing bravely with pointed tips through the dark earth. A few snowdrops were clustered near the roots of a tree, their greenish-white buds bowed as though shamed by their audacity at arriving too soon. Without thinking, I bent down to touch them; and then I heard his voice.

"Rosalind."

I jumped up and turned around quickly. He stood tall and strong in the clear light, his eyes burning in his handsome face, a half smile on his lips.

My reaction was of shock, followed by a steely determination to keep control of myself.

"What are you doing here?"

He took my arm. "I'm so sorry," he said.

His sympathy touched me, bringing in spite of everything the sting of salt to my eyes. I turned away abruptly. The last thing I wanted was for him to see me in my grief, which was my own personal affair. I did not recognize then and would not have admitted that Roderick Carew was already a disturbing factor in my life. My sadness held pain, but was something to be expected. I was afraid, though, of exposing more of my inner self.

"Thank you," I said coldly. "But please don't talk about it."

"Very well." As I started to walk back in the direction of the house, he went with me. "About you then, shall we?"

"Why?"

"Are you coming back to the company?"

I stopped, facing him with anger quickening my heart. Anger and something else . . . a longing I would not admit. "I don't know how you *can!*" I said. "You follow me here . . . find out where I am . . ."

"I knew where you were. Everyone knows the whereabouts of Lady Cranmere."

"Well then, I should have thought you'd have more . . ."

"Tact?"

"Decency, than to force yourself on me at a time like this."

"I've no wish to force anything," he said. "As for decency . . . is there anything not decent in trying to . . ." He waited a moment before continuing heatedly, "Damn it, Rosalind. Why have you got to think the worst? If you must know, it wasn't just to see you or to offer sympathy.

It was . . . to apologize for what happened at our last meeting."

"I see."

"No, you don't. You haven't the first idea. I'm not even apologizing for what was said or done . . . but for the manner of it. I should have been more gentle, more . . . considerate. But you must have known I was in love with you?"

"In *love*? What do *you* know about love?" I said irrationally, wanting to hurt him.

"As much as you, I think," he said meaningfully, "perhaps more."

"How dare you . . ."

"For God's sake, spare me the outrage and indignation," he said. "Keep it for the stage . . ." I hurried ahead of him, with my chin up and my heart pounding. But his hand caught my arm and pulled me back.

"I shouldn't have said that at a time like this. But I've done it. I know you cared for . . . for your husband. But he was an old man, Rosalind . . . when he died, when you married him; and you were a child at the time. I don't doubt your sincerity, but there's something more than dreams and hero worship for a woman like you. Look at me . . . *Look at me*."

I tried not to, but his hands were pressing into my shoulders so hard I glanced up involuntarily. My eyes for a brief few moments were transfixed by his, more blue than the deepest blue of the Cornish sea.

"Since we parted you've never been out of my mind for a single moment," he said. "And it's the same with you; I know it. It's in your eyes . . . your wild leaping heart . . . and eyes don't lie . . ."

I tore myself away, and as if from a distant dream heard myself saying, very loudly and clearly. "Go away please. You must be mad. Apart from the impertinence of intruding at such a time, you are nothing to me, nothing at all. I never want to see you again."

And that, perhaps, was the greatest lie of my life.

I did not watch him as he walked away, just stood there under the bare branches of the great chestnut from which a single last leaf drifted slowly past my face to the ground.

When I looked around, he had gone.

Later, I cried.

I went to Carnecrane for Christmas, and could not help noticing a change in my father. His eyes seemed to hold a brighter gleam, his walk had a boldness about it . . . almost a swagger, which could not be entirely explained by the festivities of the season.

I wondered at first if there was a woman concerned, but decided there wasn't, as he was so insistent on my remaining with him for as long as possible. "I'm alone a great deal," he said one day, "not that I'm lonely. I have the estate, the mines . . . which entail a good deal more work now, because of Pengalva's age. But the companionship of a woman . . . of my own daughter . . . would mean a great deal to me. I hope you'll agree to stay, Rosalind."

"I've made no plans," I said sadly. "I'll stay, of course, until . . ."

"Until what?"

I shrugged. "I really don't know. It's impossible to look too far ahead, isn't it?"

"You mean you may go back to the stage?"

"I may."

"Hm. Well, that will be for you to decide, of course. I wouldn't stand in your way. I didn't before, when you were a girl, and I certainly shan't play the clinging father now."

"It wouldn't be much use, would it?" I said dryly.

"No. I really have no claims on you."

Beneath the stilted tones I sensed that he was hurt.

"Oh, but you have; of blood . . . of being my father. Only . . . I'm not the type of woman to be chained."

He threw up his hands. "What an expression."

"I'm not sure you know what I mean."

"What about Cranmere? Were there no chains there?"

I shook my head. "None. Only of my own making. I loved him."

He looked slightly embarrassed, and I knew that my meaning of the word *love* had little, if any, significance for him. I wished I understood him better. In some ways he was a withdrawn character, and when we were together he would frequently look at me speculatively, as though I were some enigma beyond his comprehension. This was not hard to understand. Until my arrival back at Carnecrane most of his time had obviously been spent with men discussing male affairs and matters of business. I could not help noticing that although he professed interest in the theater, the subject was quickly turned to mining and tenancies when an opportune moment arose. Both mines on the estate had now been equipped with Watt engines instead of the Newcomen type, and although I was not interested in the smaller amount of coal necessary for pumping a certain quantity of water by the newer method, I tried to appear interested, finding even this mental effort took my mind slightly away from sadder things.

There was something else too.

The house.

At nights, when I frequently lay sleepless, trying not to remember, the house seemed to be whispering, especially on still evenings, when there was no breath of wind, no soughing of trees or rattle of windows and doors; only the occasional high crying of a seabird outside. There was no actual sound, and yet I could sense movement and undercurrents of voices . . . disturbances of the atmosphere which told me the silence was not real, but a shroud to unseen activities, as the mist was a shroud to the coast. I asked my maid—the girl I had brought with me from Lyncastle—if she slept well in her new surroundings. The answer was in the affirmative, and as her room was only three doors from mine, nearer the back stairs, I told myself my imagination must have been playing me tricks.

But the whispering went on.

One night in early February it became more than that. I heard distinctly the soft padding of footsteps which vibrated in a queer manner through the floorboards. I opened my bedroom door and looked out, listening. For some moments there was complete silence. Then, further down the landing, facing my maid Anne's room, I saw in the filtered wan light from a window, the door of Mrs. Mellyn's room opening slowly. I waited, tensed up and hardly breathing for fear of betraying my presence. The next moment the figure of a man slipped out in front of a woman's, and with pantherlike stealth sped to the stairs and disappeared. I didn't move at first. The shock had me temporarily paralyzed, because despite the gloom and the fact that I had not seen his face, I would have known his gait and manner anywhere . . . even though it was just a blurred shape temporarily visible in a fitful beam of watery moonlight.

My father.

I turned quickly and caught the door with my foot. The housekeeper looked around. How long we faced each other almost unseeingly I do not know. But presently the landing was swallowed up in complete darkness. I heard the creak of a door, and the furtive sound of a key turning. Then, except for the shrill crying of birds disturbed, all was silent.

I went to my window and peered out. There was no light, no sign of anything afoot, until the mist temporarily lifted for a few brief seconds, revealing the indistinct silhouettes of three or four men hurrying down the path toward the cove, and to my right the tall shape of something that could have been a mast reaching from the creek.

I slept little that night, and in the morning got up early impelled by a mixture of apprehension and curiosity.

As I thought she would be, Mrs. Mellyn was already dressed and about the house, although she generally did not rise until nine o'clock.

I met her at the foot of the stairs.

"About last night . . ." she began.

"You'd better come in here," I interrupted, going toward the dining room.

When the door was closed and I had made certain no one was hovering about, I said coldly, "What is it, Mrs. Mellyn?"

I thought at first she was going to find some stupid excuse which I could have accepted with a show of belief; but she didn't; this made me respect her more. Indeed, there was a certain dignity and comeliness about her still, though she must have been nearing sixty that I realized might well appeal to my father.

"Miss Rosalind . . . Lady Cranmere," she said. "I'm not going to explain things without the master being present. What you saw, you saw. I'm not denying facts, and there's been no harm done to you. If you want to ask Mr. Cremyllas about his relationship with me, you are at liberty to do so. I've done what I could for him in providing a little . . . companionship . . . when he needed it, and companionship is about all it is now, because I'm not a young woman . . ."

"I thought you weren't going to explain," I said quickly.

She smiled. "Well now, that doesn't need it, does it? It's clear. But the rest . . . that's for the master. But if you take my advice, you'll not harry him about his little excitements. He's a man who has to have action. How else could he live here without family for most of the time? It isn't as if he's a real society type. The gentry don't interest him. And the mines . . ." She broke off and was about to go when I said quickly, "What about the mines, Mrs. Mellyn?"

She shook her head. "Nothing. Forget what I said, my dear . . . and forgive me for calling you that, but I can't help remembering you when you were a frightened child after poor Mrs. Goss died . . ." Her eyes were so troubled in her broad kind face that any resentment or distaste I'd felt about her relationship to my father immediately vanished.

I smiled. "Thank you for being frank with me. What my father does with his life isn't really my affair, and I'm sure you must have been a comfort to him. I shan't say anything about last night. And I shan't try to spoil whatever it is . . . he's about."

After she'd gone I tried to make sense out of what I'd just heard. Her own part was obvious; she hadn't tried to deny she was his mistress; it was her reference to the mines and "little excitements" that intrigued me. Especially the "excitements." Clearly Laurence Cremyllas was involved with smuggling of some kind, although if challenged he would probably have a ready answer, as he considered any activities adjoining or on his own property were legal. Only a day or two before he had affirmed that he held the wreck rights from the creek to the opposite side of the cove.

"What do you mean by that?" I'd asked with a stab of distaste.

His bushy eyebrows had shot up, and he'd looked mildly amused.

"My dear girl, not *murdering*, if that's what you're thinking. In fact when men of substance hold their rights it means greater protection for crews of abandoned vessels. Men like myself, landowners, gentry, can claim cargo and assets if a ship founders on their shores; whereas if it was left to laborers and tinners and the like . . . there'd be the devil to pay in fighting and drowning, and loss of life."

"I see." But I didn't really. Always I had held my own views about land, which was that in reality it could be owned by nobody. I had chafed at the forbidden territory of Carnecrane when I was Rosalind Goss, and been punished for trespassing. And although I was now Lady Cranmere, the theory of possession still irritated me. In this I differed much from my father. The estate, the land, the mines, the house . . . had value for him because they were *his*. Not because the gorse flamed gold in summer or the earth smelled sweet from heather and brine, not because the four winds chased about the headland in winter gales, or the primroses and bluebells grew thick in the spring bracken. He had *rights*. The word was repulsive to me. I had heard it all through my childhood . . . Mr. Cremyllas has "rights." The rights of ownership . . . of having men toil in the mines to fill his pockets. The mines. I remembered Mrs. Mellyn's half-spoken allusion, and wondered what it meant.

On the first opportunity I brought the subject up to my father.

"You were talking about the Watt engine the other day," I said casually. "I'm afraid I couldn't have sounded very interested. Well, I don't understand about such things. But how are the mines going these days? . . . Do they still pay well?"

Laurence did not answer at once, then he said, "They will . . . they will. We've had a few technical difficulties lately, but they'll pass. You see, lodes don't last forever, and there's a limit to the tin obtainable. Even with the best and newest facilities in the world you can't mine what's not there."

"Do you mean they're running out?" I asked. "The mines, I mean . . . of tin?"

"No, no," he said irritably. "I said nothing of the sort. It's just that . . . at the moment things aren't too good."

"Do you mean you're short of money?"

"Good God, no."

But his tone was too confident to be true.

"If you ever are," I said, trying to speak casually, "you must let me help. Charles left me quite comfortable, and I've nothing to spend my money on."

"But you will have sometime," Laurence said more gently. "You've got your life ahead."

"Have I? For what? Charles said that," I answered. "What good is anything if it has no purpose?"

My father put both hands on my shoulders, and looked intently into my eyes.

"What's the matter, Rosalind? Is anything wrong?"

I shook my head, thinking, "Yes, I'm empty of love. If only I had a husband to love me." But it was not of Charles I thought just then. I remembered how I'd sent Roderick away from Lyncastle on the cold December day when he'd told me he was in love. I had been cruel and bitter, and he had not troubled to realize that the bitterness was only shame of myself for wanting him so. The picture of the parting was suddenly so clear and painful in my mind that I had to drag myself, as though from a great distance, to hear what my father was saying.

"I believe you've been fretting."

"Of course I have."

"Then it's got to stop," he said firmly, "and no more talk of money or expense. I've all I want, and to spare. Perhaps you'd like to take a holiday somewhere . . . Bath? Bristol?"

"*No*," I said on a sudden impulse. "I don't want to go away. I just want to share what you do here."

He frowned. There was a long pause before he spoke. "What do you mean?"

His bewilderment made him look quickly younger, as though he'd been caught out in some monstrous misdeed.

"I know all about you, father dear," I said. "The smuggling . . . the little night jaunts . . . the . . ."

His mouth fell open. "You *know* . . . How?"

"Observation," I said. "I'm not blind, you know."

"But . . ."

"And don't tell me you have the right," I remarked pointedly. "You know very well you haven't. Smuggling's illegal. But that doesn't worry me really . . ."

"You are the most *amazing* girl," he said when he'd recovered. "To think that . . ."

"To think that the respected Lady Cranmere and actress Rosalind Cremyllas should sink to a desire for dark dealings?" I prompted. "Oh, but . . ."

"Yes?"

"You're forgetting one thing. My mother."

He shook his head. "No. I shall never forget her. And by God, Rosalind . . . I'll take you in. You shall be the boy I wanted, as much as the daughter I love."

And so a week later I went by chaise into Penzance, where I purchased clothing for a youth of my measurements, which would be admirable for the new and exciting part I was to undertake in real life.

6

During the next two months I had practical experience of my father's "little excitements," which did a good deal to take my mind from other unhappy matters. In some ways my role was similar to the many stage parts I had played. I had to live it, shedding my own personality completely. It was an audacious, thrilling escapade, touched with danger that brought me closer to Laurence than I had been before. The two "runs" were undertaken on moonless nights, in which the trickiest business was the conveyance of the contraband . . . on each occasion kegs of brandy and a quantity of silk from France . . . from the boats to safe storage for disposal on land.

There were a dozen in our shore party, including five from the house; my father, myself, the two men, and a boy. The rest were tinners and a tenant farmer and his workers. The activities were carefully planned and carried out with incredible secrecy and speed. After unloading by the French crew, I assisted in rolling the barrels across the narrow strip of sand to an apparently harmless-looking cave, which was deep nevertheless . . . opening into a passage leading directly underground to the cellars of Carnecrane. A door had been made overhead in the rock, which served for immediate escape if necessary. But the usual practice was for the goods to be hidden in the ground, behind jutting masses of rock, for disposal at a later time. The men were well paid, either in kind or cash, and I knew Lau-

rence made a tidy sum on each enterprise. But I think the
main interest for my father was the challenge. It was the
same with me. I became on such occasions a character as
far removed from Rosalind Cranmere as night from day.
Against a savage stage set of dark elemental force, I was a
male lawbreaker taking pleasure in it for the joy of defiance . . . something that stimulated and filled me with
wild irrational triumph. In the guise of youth or man, my
loneliness died. It was only afterward when I lay in bed
thinking over events, that I realized it was indeed, just a
game, a superficial little drama, which, once my youth's
clothes were shed, left me still with heart raw and bleeding.

And then, despite myself, sometimes I wept.

I wept for Charles, for myself, and for my womb un-
filled. And I wept for the love I might have had from Roderick; most of all, perhaps, for that. Deep within me I knew
that a barren woman was a woman bereft of purpose. I had
not been destined for a life of sterile mourning. My breasts
pricked firm and ripe toward the sun. My thighs ached for
a man's caress. The worship I had felt for Charles had now
become an earthy longing for physical consummation. "I
must have love," I thought. "I must have . . . or wither
into an empty and degrading old age."

But how? Where? When I glanced at my father in qui-
eter moments, I almost disliked him because of his secret
life which was denied to me. I had merely the paltry adventures without the passion. I had soon discovered that
Mrs. Mellyn was not his only refuge. He had others. There
was a strong smell about him of perfume mingled with
spirits when he returned from his jaunts to Penzance or
Falmouth, which told their own tale all too clearly.

Yet it didn't seem to occur to him that I was without
such comfort; and when I mentioned returning to the stage
he seemed outraged and hurt. I looked around for male
company, but those who came to Carnecrane as guests
were either portly and old, or boringly genteel. Only one
man on the estate had any interest for me . . . a large

fair-haired dark-eyed tenant farmer who had been besieged by most of the local girls looking for marriage.

I had caught his eyes on me covetously whenever we met; but circumstance did not often bring us together, and any serious thoughts I had just then were solely for Roderick.

As it happened, Roderick and I were soon to meet.

One day in early May I heard by chance that he was appearing in *A School for Scandal* at a theater in Truro. I knew suddenly that I must go. I could travel with Annie by chaise, and eat at the Red Lion, where we could put up for the night. This would give me ample time for doing a little shopping, taking a walk around, and seeing the show in the evening.

When I told my father, he said, "Well, if you must, you must. I thought by now . . . or rather hoped . . . that playacting and theatergoing were things of the past."

"I never said that," I reminded him. "And please . . . don't try and chain me. It won't work. I told you before."

"Oh, you and your chains," he retorted. "When have I ever tried to stop you doing what you wanted?"

I smiled. "Plenty of times. And you've also forced a number of distasteful things on me. Do you remember the Academy for Young Ladies?"

"Are you suggesting I've been a tyrant, Rosalind?"

I shook my head. "You easily could be, though. I wouldn't like to be your wife."

As soon as the words had slipped out, I realized my blunder. He did not look at me, just walked to the window, stood there a few seconds, then turned facing me, and said, "I'd rather you didn't remind me of distasteful matters. Caroline and I were completely unsuitable and that's all there is to it."

"Please don't be so touchy. I didn't mean anything."

"Touchy?" He forced a laugh. "Oh, all right, all right. Take the chaise and Trevaskiss shall drive you. When are you thinking of going?"

"Tomorrow," I said quickly. "I shall stay overnight, naturally, and start back early on Friday morning."

The following day was bright, with a faint haze filming the rocks and hills which predicted the weather would hold. We set off early, and were soon traveling briskly along the main road, past hamlets, fields, and cottages crouched gray against the moors where mine-works stood, briefly tipped with smoky gold by the climbing sun. From the distance their half-veiled starkness was picturesque in the quivering light; but to me they remained a symbol of bitterness and hardship which even if I lived to be a hundred I would never forget. And so I turned my mind to pleasanter things, and thought of Roderick. Roderick! . . . When was it I had first realized I loved him? On that day in the garden following Charles's death? Or earlier? . . . Yes. When I was honest with myself, I knew that at our very first meeting a spark had been struck between us that nothing could ever eradicate. I had not wanted to admit it at the time because I loved Charles Cranmere sincerely, and respected him. But the love a young girl could feel for an elderly man was different indeed from the passionate yearnings of youth for youth. I knew it now. Knew it with the whole of my being. I did not regret my time with Charles, who had shown such gentleness and understanding. He had taught me what goodness was; become the emblem of all that was fine and noble and as far above me as the stars from the earth. But I had never wanted to run my fingers through his hair, or feel his hands warm and demanding about my body. I had given him all I could, at the time. But now I had more, so much more to give, and to be given, in return. I wanted the pain of love as well as the pleasure. I wanted Roderick; to feel the hot pure flame of his blue eyes burning my senses and spirit . . . to abandon myself completely in the union of soul and flesh. To be his wife. "Oh, God . . ." I prayed, "let it be so."

Perhaps Annie was subtly aware of my mounting excitement, which must have charged the silence between us with a restless tension that stiffened my spine in anticipation, bringing a stinging warmth to my cheeks. I remember her saying once, "We shan't be long now, shall we, my lady? Are you tired, ma'am?"

I turned sharply, smiling. "Of course not. What makes you think that?"

"Oh, nothing," she answered, adding after a moment, "is the Red Lion a big place, ma'am?"

"Quite large," I told her. "The finest coaching house in the district."

"I've never been in anywhere like that," Annie commented.

"Then it will be an experience for you."

"It's only for gentry, I s'pose?" she asked tentatively.

"Mostly. And their servants."

"Oh."

I took her hand impulsively. "But you're not just a servant, Annie, you're my friend. You'll be eating with me at table; and don't be nervous . . . you know how to behave. And you really are looking very pretty today."

She sat back, pleased, allowing me once more to think about Roderick.

By the time we reached Truro the midday meal was already being served at the hostelry. I realized I should have had rooms reserved in advance. The new theatrical show had already brought considerable crowds to the town; the hall was busy with travelers, and echoing with laughter and chatter from the tap room. However, when I gave my name, "Lady Cranmere," I was received politely, almost with honor, and taken upstairs to a room which though not elegant had an air of dignity, being furnished with sturdy mahogany furniture, and well carpeted. As I went along the landing with Annie behind me, a bucolic-looking gentleman flamboyantly attired in purple and gold came from the opposite direction, almost bumping into us. He stopped, bowed briefly over his stout stomach as we passed, with

that look of surprise and covetous admiration in his eyes
which I had learned to know well in my theater days. I was
not displeased. There was security in knowing my attrac-
tions still remained; for if other men wanted me, then how
much more would Roderick!

When Annie had left me and gone to her smaller room
adjoining mine, I took off my cloak and waited for hot
water to be brought. A girl presently appeared with a can
which she took to the washstand and placed beside the
ewer and basin. "Shall I pour it, m'lady?" she asked. "It's
real hot."

"No, thank you," I said. "I can manage."

She gave a brief curtsey and withdrew. I poured water
into the bowl, slipped my bodice down, and washed. When
I saw my reflection in the mirror, I was grateful for my
cream skin and firm breasts that showed no sign of aging. I
was a little plumper perhaps than when I'd first met Roderick, but slender where I should be, and with a riper glow
about my body, which no man had touched since Charles
died. I was glad now I had kept myself chaste for Roderick . . . thankful that I had not squandered passion as in
my loneliness I might have done, had not respect and hon-
or for Charles's memory sustained me.

Ten minutes later I was seated in the dining room with
my maid, suddenly hungry, in spite of my excitement. We
had broth, game, apple pie with cream, and very excellent
cheese, which with the good wine enhanced our high spirits. Once or twice I caught male eyes upon us. I was not
surprised. Annie seemed bemused and elated, not only by
her surroundings, but by the knowledge that she was to
accompany me to the theater later. Her childlike enthusiasm made her almost beautiful, with her fresh rosy and
white skin, dark almond-shaped Cornish eyes, and wealth
of black hair.

It was past three o'clock when the meal was over. As
there were hours to spare before the play, we went out
later, inspected the shops, bought a few trifles, had a pleas-

ant interval in a coffee shop, then walked back to the Red
Lion in time to change comfortably for dinner.

The performance started at eight o'clock, and we had
already been in our box ten minutes when the curtain went
up.

I don't remember much about the play, except that its
social airs and graces irritated me profoundly. The plot
seemed to me naive, and although it was considered Mr.
Sheridan's masterpiece, I preferred his *Duenna*, and *A
Trip to Scarborough*, in which I had once played. Annie
caused attention through being over-enthusiastic in her applause. But it didn't worry me. My one thought was of
Roderick. The way he spoke and looked, his voice, his fine
profile and easy charm. "I'm here," my heart cried. "It's
Rosalind. I *want* you . . . give me one glance . . ."

At that very moment he seemed to look briefly in my
direction. A second later it was over. There had been no
answering recognition, no sign that he had seen me. But of
course, he was a "professional," I told myself stoically. A
"professional" could not allow his thoughts to stray from
the part in hand.

After the final curtain, when the applause had died and
the company taken its bow, I told Annie to wait for me in
the vestibule, and made my way to the dressing rooms. A
card had been placed above Roderick's door, saying MR.
CAREW. The very sight of his name made me tremble so
violently I had to pause a moment before giving a sharp
tap.

"Who is it?"

"Rosalind," I managed to say clearly, pulling myself together. "Rosalind . . . Cranmere."

There was a short pause before the door opened, and I
saw Roderick, half dressed, with a cloth to his face, wiping
away makeup.

"Do come in, Lady Cranmere," he said with an inflection in his voice which I could not quite understand. "I had

no idea you were present. The company would have felt honored."

I swept past him into the darkish cubbyhole of a room lit by a single small oil lamp and two candles. He motioned me to a stool, and as I sat I heard him turn the key in the lock. "I'm sure you'll forgive me attempting to make myself presentable," he continued, pretending to ignore me. "While I do so, I'd be pleased to know your reason for coming here. Surely not to congratulate me on my performance."

"No," I said bluntly, trying to keep my voice steady, though my heart was pounding. "I don't think the part suited you."

He swung around. "No?"

"No. Too civilized . . . too paltry."

"Paltry? *Sheridan*?"

"That's my opinion only. I can be wrong."

"What an admission. Rosalind Cremyllas *wrong*?"

I got up. "Oh, Roderick . . . *must* we?" I said, holding out my arms, longing for him to hold me, give me release from my deep need of him, which at that moment was acute pain.

But he didn't smile. His hand gripped my shoulder. "What the devil are you playing at?" he demanded, shaking me so the film of chiffon fell from my head leaving my hair tumbled from its pinned curls to my shoulders. I was shocked, but not entirely surprised. Of *course* he was angry, I told myself, of course; after the manner I'd sent him away.

I lifted my face to his. "I'm not playing," I said simply. "Don't you know? . . . Can't you *see*?"

He didn't answer, just stared at me until his warm sensuous lips were on mine, while my body strained and flowered to his touch. He lifted me in his arms, and carried me to a corner of the room, where a few cushions were tumbled against a wall. All the torture of the last weeks seemed resolved then. The long look between us was in itself consummation. I forgot the world, the past, the stuffy room and circumstances of this meeting, aware only of Roderick's face . . . his sudden thrusting force taking me to darkness, with hands and caresses urgent and fevered upon my body.

Afterward I had a few brief seconds of complete content, a sense of appeasement and purification, before he asked bluntly, "Was that what you wanted?"

I was taken aback. His voice sounded strange to me, different, holding a kind of shamefulness which I didn't understand. At last I replied, "Yes . . . I wanted it. I . . . you . . . you know I love you . . ."

"Do you? You didn't appear to the last time we met."

"Oh, but, Roderick, I did. It was before . . . it was too soon. Charles had only just died. I couldn't . . ."

"*Charles!*" he said derisively. He jumped up quickly. "For God's sake, dress yourself," he cried. "If anyone comes along it's going to be awkward . . ."

I was suddenly colder than I had ever been in my life. As I adjusted my clothes, fumbling with the fastening because my fingers trembled so, I asked mechanically, "What do you mean? . . . If anyone comes? Who? . . . Does it matter?"

"Of course it matters. My wife for instance . . ."

The ground seemed to sway and I had to steady myself against the dressing shelf to keep from falling. Through a blur of faintness I heard my voice echo, "Your wife?"

"Since a month gone. Why? Does it interest you? I shouldn't have thought so. You were so painfully clear that day at Lyncastle . . ."

"But . . ."

"All you wanted was a doormat, wasn't it? . . . Something to snub and treat like the lowest worm that crawled the earth. Then, when it suited you, you thought, 'He's waiting. There's always Roderick if I need a man.' Servile, faithful Roderick. Well, I'm not that kind, Rosalind. I'd have gone to hell for you once, I worshiped you so. But not anymore, my darling. So, if you don't mind, just go, will you? And I hope you feel better for the experience."

He held the door wide, and I rushed through, with my heart pounding so hard I thought I would die from shock and shame . . . the dreadful humiliation of being treated like any common whore. I ran blindly, almost knocking Annie over in the vestibule. I did not see her face, my vision was blurred; but I heard her saying, "My lady . . . what is it? . . . Is there something wrong? . . . Oh, ma'am . . ."

"Yes," I answered chokingly. "I'm ill. Take this . . ." I handed her my purse-bag with coins in it for payment at the hostelry. "Pay them for tonight and the rest . . . food, accommodation, everything we owe. Bring the bag, then get Trevaskiss to have the chaise here. We're going home."

"*Tonight?* But, ma'am . . ."

"Go. *Go*," I shrieked wildly.

Like a terrified hare she disappeared into the fitful light, leaving me standing by the door, propped up against a wall. How long it was before the chaise appeared I have no idea. It could have been seconds, minutes, or hours. Probably it was not long, because I was not aware of anyone passing me while I waited. When at last the carriage appeared, I had recovered sufficiently to speak calmly to Trevaskiss, though my body was still trembling.

"Drive back to Carnecrane," I said, "and drive fast."

In the wan oil lighting the man's face looked mottled, a little puffed, as though he had drunk and eaten too well.

"On a night like this?" he said, "with a mist coming? There'll be fog on the moors Camborne way . . ."

"You heard what I said . . . drive hard."

I sat rigidly in the chaise with Annie by my side as the horses started up, cantering at first, then a little quicker, stimulated by the crack of the whip and the harsh voice of Trevaskiss. Outside the town we slowed again because of the steep climb toward the moors.

"Hurry," I shrieked. "Faster . . . faster . . ." I struggled toward the figure of the driver, with my maid pulling me back. Reason had deserted me. All I wanted was to be away from the nightmare, to find oblivion of past events . . . even if the oblivion meant death.

When we reached the high moors and more level ground, our pace increased again, taking us into curling waves of deepening mist. There was no light and no dark for me anymore; only the sound of hooves in the wild air, with the blurred shapes of rocks and bushes flying past like demons curdled from the pits of hell. At times I dimly recognized Annie screaming; but her screams mingled with others . . . the rush of wind, and a moaning and hooting that could have been driven from Carn Kenidzek itself, the hooting carn.

When the horses reared, and Trevaskiss would have slowed, I would not allow it, but forced him with tormented frenzy to increase speed.

Why we did not all perish on that terrible night, I never knew.

But at last it was over. We were back at Carnecrane, with Annie lying on the floor of the carriage in a faint, the horses bathed in a foam of steam and sweat, and Trevaskiss slumped in his seat as though dead. I found the brandy bottle I always carried with me on such occasions in case of mishap, gave some first to Annie, then Trevaskiss, and when they had both recovered sufficiently, the man took the horses and carriage to the stables, and I helped Annie to the door. I did not wish to disturb the household, but was just about to do so, when Mrs. Mellyn's head appeared at a window above, looking like a specter's in the flickering gleam of candlelight.

A minute later the bolts were pulled from within with a grinding rattle, and the housekeeper's hand came out and took my arm. "What is it? What's the matter? Lady Cranmere . . . my dear love, is it an accident?"

"I was taken ill," I said. "So we drove back."

"In this? . . . But you could've been . . ."

"We weren't," I said sharply, on the verge of screaming. "We're all right, and my sickness has passed. But I couldn't have eaten at the hostelry . . . Now please, Mrs. Mellyn, not a word of this to anyone. Understand?"

She nodded doubtfully.

"We'd better not talk anymore," I said, with my tension relaxing into overpowering exhaustion, "or my father may hear."

"Oh no. He's out for the night."

"I see." And vaguely through my weakness, I thought, "With one of his women I suppose."

It didn't matter. Nothing mattered. I stood against the banisters with my head on the cold rail, and heavy sobs shook my lungs, sobs which tore my body with a terrible, physical pain. A comforting plump arm came around my shoulders.

"There, there. My poor love . . . my poor Miss Rosalind, what is it, then? My dear life, I never thought to see you in such a state."

I let her help me upstairs, take the clothes from my body, and see me into bed. Then she fetched the warming pan and a hot brick wrapped in wool, just as Mrs. Goss had done when I was a child, and pulled the quilt around me. "I don't suppose you want to tell me about it," she said presently, "because it's not my business, and you're a woman grown. But if you ever do . . . remember I'm here, my love, and I can keep silence."

I knew that. I touched her hand gratefully, gave it a little squeeze, and gradually began to feel better.

"Now I'm going to get you some hot milk," she said, "and after that maybe you'll sleep."

I did. I slept until noon the next day, and when I went downstairs my father had just ridden back on his horse from a jaunt around the estate.

"Mrs. Mellyn tells me you returned last night after all,"

he said perfunctorily. "I knew because the chaise was here."

"Yes," I answered. "I was tired, the play was rather boring, and something I ate disagreed with me."

"Hm." Whether he believed me or not I couldn't tell. He gave me a quizzical look, then said abruptly, "Glad to see you anyway. We have a run tonight."

"I'm afraid I shan't be with you," I answered. "I'm sorry, I don't feel well enough."

As it happened, I was never to indulge in smuggling again. In July I found I was with child.

On a wild February day in 1800 I gave birth to twins, a boy and a girl. Laurence was delighted. Although I had refused to name the father, the fact that his blood ran in their veins was the important factor in his eyes. The boy was strong and lusty, fair-skinned but with a thatch of hair so red, the likeness to his great-grandmother in the portrait by Joshua Reynolds was already obvious. "Just look at it . . . red," Laurence cried exultantly, "and that's what we'll call him. Reddin, so he can be Red for short. Reddin Cremyllas."

"And the girl?" I asked, revealing the second tiny bundle of humanity.

My father peered at the minute baby, olive-skinned, with perfectly formed features under a mere drift of black hair. One crumpled small fist was curled by her cheek. Just then her eyes opened, soft as velvet, black as sloes. Laurence held his breath for a moment, then touched the child's forehead gently. "A real little Romany," he said almost in a whisper. "And that shall be her name. Romany. Roma if you like . . ."

"I think they're both nice names," I agreed.

The children were registered as Reddin and Romany Cremyllas, and a month later baptized in Penzance. Laurence saw that their surname was properly legalized, which as matters turned out, was as well; because in the summer of that year, his son William died from enteric fever, leaving Reddin as sole heir to Carnecrane.

During the next three years my father was content to forgo many of his former dubious activities although he took a jaunt into Penzance whenever enforced celibacy proved too frustrating. His relationship to Mrs. Mellyn had now become no more than an amicable understanding between employer and housekeeper, an arrangement I sensed that was a relief to her. We had little company to the house. The only women I met were the wives of tenants or occasional contact with the gentry. The latter were rare. Laurence, like myself, was now considered beyond the pale of social respectability, something that mildly amused me. Entertaining, apart from theatrical affairs, had always irritated and tired me. Besides, there was now the matter of expense. The mines were at low ebb. Penbreen was producing a minimum of tin, and Wheal Gulvas had suffered not only from a diminishing value of the lodes, but from a fire started by a lighted candle which had ignited the roof timbers and spread to the large stull. A great section of the mine was destroyed, and when after weeks of burning the fire was finally extinguished, the falls of earth made future working impossible without a great deal of capital to sink a new main shaft. Lord Pengalva, whose interest in tin had never been of vital importance to him, was wary of investing more of his own capital. Laurence had not sufficient to do so, and shareholders with minor holdings preferred to face their losses rather than throw good money after bad.

"We have the land," my father said. "There's ground to be salvaged on Carnecrane . . . the future of the countryside lies in agriculture. Everywhere ground's being enclosed and brought into cultivation. And with the new Board of Agriculture at our backs we have a lot to gain. New machines, new drainage . . . fertilizers . . . it all makes sense. If I invest anything it will be for threshing machines and a wheeled plow. The future's there, Rosalind . . . for Red, and those that come after him."

I sensed he might be right, and I wanted it to be so. My youth had taught me the grim side of Cornish mining, and the sooner it was eradicated from my own personal concerns, the better.

Laurence's increasing obsession with land development brought me more into contact with Lewis Baragwanath, the tenant whose homestead was half a mile away on the western side of Carnecrane land. The ground was poor, but in the last few years he had reclaimed ten acres, with the help of a boy, breaking much of it by hand, removing stones and turf, building "hedges" from the former, and using the burned dried turf eventually for manure. Barley, wheat, oats, and hay were cultivated, much to my father's gratification.

"Congratulations," he said, when we called on him and his sister one day. "You've been a man ignored these many years, Baragwanath. In future you shall have help, and together we'll make this a thriving estate."

"Will 'ee have a taste of saffron cake, ma'am . . . surr?" Miss Baragwanath said, coming from the kitchen to the parlor. "And a sip of elder wine?"

Intimidated by her glance, which dared me to refuse, I took a little of both. Judith must have been quite ten years her brother's senior, and in appearance did not resemble him at all, being hawk-nosed, sallow-skinned, with shrewd dark beady eyes that scrutinized me appraisingly. I judged her to be fifty or over, and could understand why Lewis had remained unmarried for so long. A young girl would have to be daring indeed to snatch Baragwanath from under her nose. And yet he had a desirous glance, and I sensed was not without experience. His fair hair was thick and virile, waving back from a wide forehead, which had heavy brows over deeply set eyes. I had imagined his eyes to be brown, but when a beam of light caught them I discovered that though dark, they had a bluish tinge, flecked with darting specks of gold. They were discomforting, but in a way which I did not find unpleasing. And he had pride; I liked that. Pride in the manner of holding his head, the straight way he looked at me and did not attempt to hide the work-scarred hands which were blunt-fingered and strong. I knew with a guilty stirring of my blood that Lewis Baragwanath and I might have much in common.

There were times during those years at Carnecrane when I thought longingly of the stage, of the career which had started with such promise and success, and been disrupted so abruptly by the death of Charles. Occasionally I had to face the fact that but for the agonizing meeting with Roderick in Truro I might now have been commanding large audiences in London.

Victor Adams wrote to me suggesting we do a season together at Covent Garden.

My Dear Rosalind,

Is it necessary to bury yourself completely in the wilds of Cornwall? Your public is still waiting for your return . . . as of course am I and others who played with you . . . but audiences do not languish unrewarded for too long. They can be fickle, and forget, should another compelling star appear in the firmament. I well understand the fascination of solitude, I have frequently longed for it myself. But is there need, dear girl, to remain so completely cut off? . . . It seems such a waste.

Do think over things carefully, and if possible decide to make a timely comeback. Comebacks, as you know, can be delayed until they are no longer a practical undertaking, and I should be distressed for it to happen to you.

As ever,
Victor

I wrote back immediately, explaining that as I now had two children to consider, there was unfortunately no chance of the season he proposed. I did not elaborate on matters. However frustrated my ambitions might be, I knew that my first duties now, and my love, were for Red and Romany.

The children were as different to look at as two of the same age could be. At four years old Romany was still slight, small-featured, with a petal mouth, brilliant brown eyes shaded by black lashes, and a wealth of curling intensely black hair. She was quick and lithe in her movements . . . secretive sometimes, and inclined to wander on her own. Red, on the other hand, was tall and strong, with a boldness in his walk and manner that endeared him to my father.

"Look at him," he said, "A real Cremyllas. He'll run this place one day as it *should* be run. He has his grandmother's spirit, and Cremyllas bearing."

His interest in the boy, amounting almost to infatuation, irritated me frequently. The rebel in me knew that being a Cremyllas was not all that important. I didn't want my son to grow up a "family fanatic." I wanted him to learn real values of ordinary people, to be able to mix, and mix happily.

Once I said to Laurence impatiently, "You spoil Red. You're putting ideas of grandeur into his head which are making him conceited."

"*Red*? Conceited? Nonsense. And if he is, what about it? He's something to be conceited about. All I have will be his one day."

"And what about Roma?" I asked coldly. "She's your grandchild too."

"Roma will be provided for of course," he answered in more subdued tones. "But girls are more the business of womenfolk."

"Do you believe that?" I said. "Look at her." Romany had just crept up behind me and was peering around at him from her fabulous dark eyes.

"Hm. Yes . . . she's a pretty girl, aren't you, my love?" he said, bending down to pat her head.

The child did not smile. It was as though she sensed his attitude, knowing that in comparison with Red she had but a small share of his affection.

One day in the autumn of 1804 my little girl slipped off just before Zenoby the nursemaid was about to give the children their tea. We called and searched to no avail for almost an hour. I had the dreadful premonition of approaching disaster, which always beset me before a thunderstorm or any unexpected happening.

Blind instinct or intuition must eventually have taken me to a ruined barn some distance from the house, where I found her sitting on a stone behind a tangle of brambles and undergrowth, looking upward into the face of a woman huddled in a black shawl. When they heard me, they both turned. I shall remember that moment always . . . the yellow light, the dead-leaf smells, the encroaching mist mingling with distant woodsmoke, and the lean dark face of the woman with the burning brilliant eyes so like Romany's. The child had a tentative smile on her lips, and from the touch of the brown thin wrist reaching from the shawl to caress the little girl's hair, I knew no harm had been intended.

I knew something else. Knew in a moment of awareness between the three of us that the meeting was no chance affair. Kinship, unrecognized yet deep in ancestry and blood, struggled to life, and held us silent for seconds until I said, "Who are you? What's brought you here?"

The woman stood up. She could not have been more than fifty, but rough living had carved deep lines into her face. Once she must have been beautiful; now her bloom had gone, leaving only a rugged kind of dignity and defiance in the set of lips and lift of chin. Yet when she shook her head at me and said quietly, "Is she yours then? The bebee?" Her expression was soft.

"Mine; yes."

"And you? . . . Thee's no gorgio surely?"

"I'm . . ."

She raised her hand and said something in a language that sounded like doggerel to me, but had a flavor of wildness and beauty about it. Then, after another long last look, she added, "That's Romany for luck. But beware the sea for thee and thine. Good-bye daughter; good-bye, bebee."

A moment later she had slipped into the shadows, darting speedily down the narrow path between clumps of furze and gorse, until she was lost from sight, leaving me standing there in a dream, with Roma's hand in mine.

I said nothing of the incident to anyone. But the encounter haunted me. She had wished us luck, but had also given a warning. Yet how could the sea hurt us, when Laurence was no longer engaged in smuggling, and none at Carnecrane was of an age for naval service in the renewed war against France? Would there be an invasion? I wondered often. Seamen and politicians were convinced that Napoleon's one dream was to take England. He had the ships and the men. But Laurence said he was a prevaricator . . . a dictator without the temperament to take undue risks.

As it happened he proved to be right. But war, however remote from personal involvement, nevertheless could not fail to be a distrupting influence. My father's faith in Admiral Nelson was a sturdy and perhaps as bigoted as his faith in himself. I did not feel so safe. Charles's death had shaken my world. Roderick had smashed it; my future lay with my children, and now had come this warning bred from past impulses which had begotten me, though I myself had had no part in them. I tried to shake off the anxiety which, though suppressed, still haunted me. I saw to it that the children were not taken to the cove, and was only really content when they were safely in bed or somewhere about the house. "The sea," I thought, "beware the sea for thee and thine." And I wondered which was threatened—Red or Roma.

It was neither.

In December a Dutch ship was driven ashore to the rocks beneath Carnecrane cliffs. I woke up about midnight, disturbed by the gale which drove its lash of fury against windows, rattling doors in fitful gusts, with torrential rain which made one sound undistinguishable from others. Feeling restless, and knowing I should not get to sleep again, I got up and went to the window. Behind the clouds a watery moon glimmered intermittently, and at first I thought the tumbled blackened shapes against the rim of cliff and sky were merely massed clouds blown by the wind and storm. Then I heard my father's voice. I ran to my door and opened it. He had his boots on and a storm cape about his shoulders.

"Get back, Rosalind," he shouted when he saw me. "There's a wreck. And on such a night those poor devils, whoever they are, won't have a chance."

I didn't wait to hear more. I dressed quickly in my youth's clothes, and rushed after him, though when I got to the cliffs he was already out of sight, followed by the two men and the boy, who were just disappearing down the path to the cove. The wind and torrential rain tore at my lungs, catching my breath and blinding me as I struggled on, hearing vaguely a confusion of shouts and screams issuing from the rocks below. I scrambled down, and when I reached the shore the sea was a swirling mass of blackened timber and broken cargo . . . of men's arms grasping at the air . . . clawing for anything that was at hand to keep them afloat in the hungry, sucking swirl of that evil tide. When the moon broke clear of the hurtling cloud, splashing pale and silvered over the turbulent scene, I could see the white faces of drowning men, and the drowned floating uselessly on the water. And as I wondered helplessly what to do, dark shapes scrambled down the cliffs from every side . . . eager like hungry vultures for cargo. There was no mercy shown for the wretched crew. Time after time I saw men who would have scrambled to safety pushed back

mercilessly as plunderers struggled for anything that could
be taken . . . kegs . . . hogsheads of wine . . . bundles
that could have been silk . . . even timber of the vessel
itself. It did not seem possible that such a crowd of country
men could have heard so quickly of the sinking ship; it
only proved the full horror of the wrecking system, and I
realized how futile was my father's claim to "wreck
rights," when he could be outnumbered by so many in such
a short time.

I ran to the water's edge, where the waves pounded,
sucking flounderers back again into the fury of darkness
and breaking foam. I reached for a hand clawing for rescue, but before I could grasp it, it had disappeared. I stood
up, steeling myself against the wind, and it was then I saw
one poor mariner being most viciously assaulted by a plun-
derer. The next moment in a vivid streak of pale light my
father's figure was momentarily starkly clear. I saw him
strike out toward the attacker, in an effort to rescue the
unfortunate victim. It was no use; he was attacked from
behind and was suddenly submerged himself and no more
seen. I waded through a wave, screaming for help. But
there was no help that night. All decency and respect for
human life was obliterated by the greed of poor men out
for a little gain.

How I myself did not perish, I never knew. All I remembered when I came to myself was a confusion of sound and
water sucking and choking me, of trying to breathe and
then falling.

I opened my eyes and gradually everything came into focus . . . the strained blood-streaked face of Trevaskiss
looking down on me; the gray sky lifting to morning. The
tide had receded, leaving only bodies and timber scattered
on the sand. I could feel my teeth chattering in my head as
the man said, "Thank God, ma'am, I've got you around.
You seemed a goner sure 'nuff. But the Lord willed otherwise."

"My father," I managed to say. "He . . . he . . ."

Trevaskiss did not reply. "Tes yourself you've to be thinking of now. And the little ones." He did not have to say more, but added quietly, "Don't fret too hard. It's the way he'd have wanted. Now I'll be getting back to the house. It was hours before I could find 'ee, being cut as I was . . ."

"Cut?" I said sharply.

"Just the leg. It'll heal. But for longer than I liked you was dead to the world, ma'am."

"The others?" I asked.

"Tom's taken the boy back . . . a piece of flesh torn out of his thigh. But he'll be down unless we be going. Come on now, ma'am, a sorry sight I may be, but quite capable of handling things."

Despite my protests he lifted me into his strong arms like a child, and hard as it must have been for him, he managed somehow to get me back to Carnecrane.

For the first time in my life I really hated the sea. The horror of that night was to remain with me all my life, as were the words "Beware the sea for thee and thine."

In the months that followed I was on the point many times of packing up and taking the children as far as possible from Carnecrane—London, Oxford, anywhere. But as the days passed, my fears began to recede. The place would be Red's when he was of age. Laurence had entrusted it to me for him, and to fail would be to betray him. There was also something else. At Carnecrane there was little chance of meeting with Roderick. I could not have borne that.

So life went on as before, except that I was lonely, and for that reason began to see more and more of Lewis Baragwanath.

7

Lord Pengalva arrived unexpectedly one afternoon in late October to inquire about myself and the children. It was very seldom that he called at Carnccrane, although despite his seventy-six years, he was nimble except for an occasional touch of the gout.

I asked him into the drawing room, and gave him tea with some of the gingerbread biscuits which I knew were his favorites. He was still an extremely elegant-looking man, and was wearing a bottle-green velvet coat with cream breeches and the pointed shapely boots of the period. An extra touch of fashion was the lemon brocade waistcoat, and the knotted scarf-cravat overlapping his chin. His eyes were thoughtful. I was not usually discomforted by men of quality, but Thurston Cremyllas had the capacity of reducing my self-confidence to a minimum.

"I have been wondering how you are placed financially, Rosalind," he said, following the usual polite formalities. "I am, after all, your uncle, or half-uncle, to be precise, however deviously the relationship emerged."

"It sounds so complicated," I said. "And I haven't a mathematical mind. But you needn't worry, Uncle Thurston. As you know, my husband left me provided for, apart from my father, so please don't give my circumstances another thought."

I did not mention that most of my capital had been sunk in my father's agricultural enterprises, leaving me only the income from Carnecrane estate, the capital being held in trust for Red.

"I hope you're being quite frank about it," Lord Pengalva said. "I shouldn't like any of you to be without the things you are used to. As you know, Laurence and I did not see eye to eye on many matters. Otherwise he might have made me his executor instead of that bourgeois little solicitor in Penzance. This would have made it easier for me to advise you on any problem."

"There aren't any problems," I told him. "And even if there were . . ." I smiled, adding a moment later, " . . . I could always go back to the stage."

"Oh, no, no, no," Thurston said, with a wave of his hand. "With two young children it wouldn't be practical. Or would it?"

I thought for a moment, trying to subdue an irrational longing which I knew would never entirely leave me. Then I remembered Roderick, and said firmly, "No, it wouldn't be practical."

"I'm glad you see it," he said, his eyes half-veiled, inscrutable. "For a moment I thought . . . you're very like your grandmother sometimes, you know."

"I can hardly help that," I said lightly.

"I didn't mean it derogatorily, my dear girl. She was a beautiful creature. Quite the loveliest thing I ever knew. Wayward, fey, and yet full of fire and courage."

I wondered curiously if he had been in love with her. The answer came without its question.

"Once I thought I might even marry her," he said with a hint of regret. "But it wouldn't have worked, and my father got in first. They were well suited."

"She loved him very much, didn't she?" I remarked.

"Too much," my uncle replied abruptly. "When he died her love destroyed her."

"Love? *Destroy*?"

"She turned fanatical," he stated bluntly. "Like a tree thwarted so its roots turn in and go sour. Remember that,

Rosalind. The bitterness of lost love can break and kill.
Carmella couldn't endure without my father."

"I can understand," I told him.

"Yes, I thought you would, which is why I mentioned it.
You were young to be left a widow so soon, and though
you may think me a pedantic old prig, I never blamed you
for having Red and Romany. I am not fundamentally a
conventional man. But, my dear, try not to let any other
human being affect you too deeply." He paused. "I hope
you'll forgive me for touching on such personal matters."
He got up, steadying himself on the arm of the chair.

I gave him my hand and kissed him lightly on the cheek.
"I'm grateful for your interest, Uncle Thurston. And you're
not to have another doubt about our welfare. We're all
right, I assure you."

"Well," he said, "when I'm gone you will have a reasonable legacy. But of course, with no legal heirs, the title will
die, and naturally my wife will inherit the assets of Pengalva and my major capital."

"I wouldn't expect anything else," I told him. "I hadn't
even thought of anything like that."

He patted my shoulder. "No. You were never merce-
nary. But I thought I should tell you. Have you given any
thought to the children's education?"

"Not really," I admitted. "It's a bit soon, and obviously
Eton is out of the question now, funds wouldn't quite run
to it; in any case I somehow don't see Red fitting in."

"Why?"

"Because he belongs to the out-of-doors," I answered. "I
don't think he's fitted for a studious life. I know it's early
days to say, but I *feel* it. What I had thought of doing was
to have a tutor perhaps . . . someone who could teach
both children . . ."

"Would that equip him for mixing with others of his
own station?" my uncle inquired dubiously.

I gave him a very direct look. "What *is* his station, Uncle Thurston? My mother was a gypsy, and my grand-

mother had gypsy blood. I was born out of wedlock; so were Red and Romany. It doesn't worry me, but it doesn't exactly make us acceptable to conventional society, does it?"

He looked discomforted, then said consideringly, "You made a good marriage, and I am sure that when Charles married you no stones were thrown."

"But Charles is dead," I said, with sadness reviving like the pain of an old wound, "and things have happened since. If I went back to the stage . . . well, the theater's different. It has its own morality. But, as I said, that's out of the question. So I shall stay here and do the best for Carnecrane as my father would have wished, and of course for the twins."

He gave me one of his engaging smiles that took years off his age, and said gently, "I am not in the habit of flinging compliments about, my dear, but believe me I am genuine when I say how I admire you."

I was astonished. *"Me?"*

He nodded. "Out of all our brood, you seem to me the only completely virtuous one to emerge. I know that the children were conceived when you were in great anguish . . . I'm no fool. I know people. I've never wanted to pry, and I don't now. But don't starve yourself of love, Rosalind. And don't expect too much of men. Charles was one in a thousand. But then . . . he was old."

"He was *good*," I said simply. "And he made everyone else feel the same. That was his great gift."

"And a danger," my uncle remarked. "Light and shade reflect life as it is in the world, Rosalind. Something you've learned now. My dear girl . . ."

"Yes?"

"Don't run from the shadows. Or you'll never get through to reality."

I was still staring at him silently when he added, "That sounds like a poet's stuff, doesn't it? It's funny, you know, that was what I once wanted to be. In the days when I first

met your grandmother. She was standing on the seashore in
the mist. . . . I was Ferdinand, and she was Miranda."

"You make it sound as if it were only yesterday."

"Memory can make time short," he said. "The years
that change us . . . stiffen a woman into a dominating
character, and shapen a man's sensibilities into business
and political acumen . . . can be so easily bridged . . ."

"Yes."

"But it doesn't do. Life is the present. And now, if you'll
forgive me, I must leave. Good-bye, Rosalind. If you ever
want advice you have only to let me know."

"Thank you."

He picked up his cane and with a slight limp went to the
door. A minute later I was alone.

Alone. And I couldn't bear it. I busied myself about the
house, and turned my thoughts consciously to the children.
But they weren't enough. They had fulfilled a part of me,
but only a part. I loved them because they were mine—and
Roderick's. But I was no placid self-effacing creature dedi-
cated to the role of motherhood for motherhood's sake. Underneath I was restless. Despite my protestations to Lord
Pengalva, there was a great deal missing in my life, and he
had known it. I wanted to be needed as a woman. I was
only in my thirties, but middle age lay ahead, and it was
distasteful to envisage myself as a crabbed spinsterish creature growing each year more thwarted and perhaps possessive of my children.

In such a mood I met Lewis Baragwanath one afternoon
in early November to discuss the future of Carnecrane's
agricultural policy. As we walked around the estate, taking
note of the land he had enclosed on his farm, which he
held on a life lease—the moorland that could still be
brought under the plow, and the rough soil on the seaside
which was nevertheless workable given time, interest, and
sufficient labor—I said on impulse, "Can you see any future here, Baragwanath?"

"Future?" he echoed. "What do you mean?" His curious

dark-blue speckled eyes traveled to the distant mine-works and huddled cottages on the hillside above Tywarren. "There?"

I shook my head. "You know very well that Wheal Gulvas needs great wealth to get it started again, which I haven't got, and Penbreen has become a liability."

"Yes, I know that. And because of it, destitution's driving the workers away. Soon Tywarren will be a dead place."

"You mean I should shoulder responsibility for their poverty? Support them? How could I?"

"I'm not saying that," he answered. "These days you've got to be realistic. Men have to live where there's a living to be got. There are other mines . . . Falmouth way, they're needing men. Sometime maybe some man with initiative and the gold in his pocket will open up Gulvas again. There's plenty of tin right under, I'd stake my life on it. But it'll not be in *your* day, Mistress Cremyllas."

"My name's Cranmere," I reminded him.

"Sorry, *Lady* Cranmere." There was irony in his voice. "I forgot. When you're talking business to a woman she becomes like any other."

I was mildly irritated. "I see."

He laughed. "I doubt it. Besides . . ." Though I didn't look at him, I could feel the intent gaze of his eyes on me. ". . . I wasn't speaking the exact truth. It seems to me you're one on your own. Willful."

Ignoring the implication of his remark, I said quickly to disguise my discomfiture, "Since the mines went, my father staked everything on the land; for farming I mean."

"Yes. But he was no farmer. To make farming pay properly you have to be born to the job. That's the trouble in this country. They want corn. They want this and that . . . special produce needing specialized labor; but the laborers themselves are treated little better than cattle, while the rich landowners make themselves richer through their workers' sweat and skill."

"It was the same with mining."

"And still is. The haves and have-nots. But it'll change one day . . . it's coming."

I glanced up at him. His profile was set, strongly carved against the dying light of the fading winter afternoon. He had not married. Why? His strength, the relentless quality that I had sensed earlier, had in itself a sexual appeal. Was it that he found no woman sufficiently desirable? Or was his shrew of a sister the stronger?

Either cause was a challenge, stimulating me to say impulsively, "What about being my agent, Lewis?" Involuntarily his name slipped out.

He stood quite still, and I hurried on. "I mean, my farm manager . . . to take over the whole lot? Arrange what labor's necessary, the machinery, and going ahead? You say corn is needed. Well, we could grow more. I've faith in you. You'd want a good salary, naturally. We could arrange that . . ."

I waited for him to say something; it was minutes before he replied.

"Is that all you have in mind then? Growing corn?"

It seemed to me there was faint derision in his tone, though I couldn't be sure.

I hesitated. "Well . . . not necessarily *only* corn; there are other things to cultivate, aren't there?"

"Plenty," he agreed, staring down at me from narrowed lids. "Plenty, if you've a mind for it." He took his pipe from his pocket, lit it, and sucked at the stem thoughtfully. I was suddenly irrationally confused and annoyed.

"If you want time to think it over, you can have till next Monday," I said coldly. "Otherwise I shall take it you're not interested." I started to walk away quickly, but he caught me up almost immediately.

"What an impatient woman you are. That comes of being 'my lady,' I s'ppose. Of course I'm interested. Only don't expect me to go jumping into something before I know what it is, and don't expect any bowing and scraping, because I'm not that kind. Just so long as we understand each other?"

I stood facing him with my chin raised only slightly higher than the level of his shouder; the communication between us was swift and instinctive. "I think we do," I said.

He relaxed, and smiled. "Good."

But I wondered. Generally I was fairly competent at assessing character. There was something about Lewis Baragwanath, however, that eluded me. He attracted me in a purely physical way; that he was hardworking and competent at his job was obvious. But there was no telling what secret depths lay hidden behind the male exterior. Was he kind and understanding? Or merely possessive and insensitive like his hard-faced sister Judith? No, not that. I had seen him with animals, and his touch had been gentle. He was probably just undemonstrative and secretive, as the Cornish so often were. Living with the witchlike Miss Baragwanath must have been intimidating enough to drive any normal man into a shell.

Following that exploratory meeting I did not see him again for three days. Then he arrived at the house, and told me bluntly that it seemed a good "deal" to him, providing the money was right.

"But there are other things too," he said finally. "Points to get settled for the future."

"Such as?"

"I want that life lease on the farm altered. I want something signed and witnessed saying none of my family will ever be ejected from my home. As facts are at the moment, Judith could be turned out if I died or went away. Now it's not likely . . . she's a dozen years older than me, but things happen sometimes, and a man likes to feel he's done the right thing."

I didn't hesitate. His proposal seemed to me quite fair.

"Of course. I'll have my laywer over, and get the thing settled. Your salary can be discussed too."

"Not with any outsider," he stated bluntly. "Not the salary. That shall be between you and me. But the farm . . . yes. All clear and legal. That's what Judith wants."

Judith! I thought, with a stab of anger. It was nothing to do with her. What she wanted or didn't want was of no concern to me. I almost said so, but thought better of it. I needed someone like Lewis about me, and a little mental blackmailing on his part wasn't going to affect the issue.

So it was arranged; a month later Lewis Baragwanath took over complete administration of Carnecrane lands. I did not realize at the time how completely he was also taking over me.

From the first Red did not like him, although there seemed no reason for it. Lewis made determined efforts to be friendly, always telling my little boy when a ewe had given birth to a lamb, or a mare to a foal, offering to take the child along where he could see the newly born animals for himself. But Red shook his head and walked away.

"*Why?*" I asked him once, when Lewis had shrugged and given up. "You're so fond of animals, Red. Mr. Baragwanath was only being friendly. You should be more polite. Do you understand? I don't like you being rude."

Red's chin came out aggressively. "I don't like him."

"But *why* don't you like him?" I asked again. "Has he ever said or done anything to hurt you?"

Red gave me a long uncompromising look before replying. When he did, his words took me unaware, bringing a flush to my face.

"He *looks* at you."

"And what is that supposed to mean?" I demanded sharply. "Of course he looks at me. So do you; so does anyone look at a person they're talking to."

My son hung his head and said in sulky tones, "That's different."

"You're a silly boy," I told him lightly. "Now next time Mr. Baragwanath offers to show you anything, please let him . . . for my sake."

But he didn't. And one day Lewis said, "That boy of yours has character, but it needs a bit of shaping."

"What do you mean?" I asked sharply.

"He needs a man about him."

"He'll have one after Christmas," I said shortly. "I've already arranged for a young graduate from Cambridge to come to Carnecrane as tutor for Red and Romany. As he is the nephew of the rector of Tywarren, it will work out very well. He'll come daily to the house, and go back to the rectory each evening."

Lewis shrugged. "Red's *your* son."

"Exactly."

I sensed that Lewis was not pleased by the news, and could not think why, until that same evening when I met him by chance walking along the field path from the farm leading to Carnecrane. I had been for my usual stroll before turning in for the night, and was surprised to see him walking with such urgency. Usually his step was unhurried and deliberate, and at first I wondered if anything had happened, if Judith was ill or had had an accident.

Then he said, planting himself squarely in front of me, "This man . . . this learned chap . . . is he courting you or something?"

The suggestion was so ridiculous I forgot his insolence and laughed in his face. The next moment I realized my mistake. Lewis took me by the shoulders and, with his face bent close down to mine, said in a tense strained voice, "Don't play with me, woman. I'm not that kind. And don't mock. For weeks now I've kept myself under, because I've respected you . . . although many wouldn't, bringing those children into the world without a real and proper father . . ."

"It isn't your place to . . ." I struggled to free myself but he held me.

"That doesn't mean to say I haven't wanted you," he went on, ignoring my protests. "I've wanted you so much I've walked at nights instead of slept. I've stood looking up at that great house wondering which bed you were lying in, wondering why a fine woman like you hadn't been snapped up all legal so soon as she was widowed. And I've thought what it would be like to have you as wife. Well, that's been my burden, and it's none of yours. But if you've got any man on a string . . . any man who's likely to get what I haven't of you, then tell me and have done with it. I'll know where I stand then, and can act accordingly."

The warmth from his body was strong in the winter air. I was shocked and bewildered; so troubled by a tumult of feeling that I couldn't speak.

His hands dropped to his sides. "I see," he said. "So that's how things are."

"You don't see at all," I cried. "You know nothing of my affairs. And you've no right to presume that just because there's to be a man in the house he's a potential lover or husband. You forget yourself, Mr. Baragwanath. What I said was true, though I have no need to explain to you. There is to be a tutor for the children, which means someone to *teach* them. And that is all. Can you take it in?"

The silence between us seemed endless. I shrugged and was about to walk away when he pulled me back abruptly. "Marry me," he said, drawing me close, so close I could detect the male strength and freshness of his body through the rough coat. "Marry me, my lovely. I know what a woman wants. I'll be good to you; I'll take care of things. I've no fancy way of talking, but it's lonesome for a man my age living with a spinster sister."

"Is that why you want to marry me? To get away from her?" I managed to say tartly.

His grasp tightened around my body, one hand slipped possessively around the thighs, where my deepest pulse leaped in response to his.

Sensing it, he laughed and said, "I could have had any woman around here I wanted, and you know that. But none of them mattered. None . . . till now."

He was so sure of me. With no mention of love between

us, no tender word or promise of fidelity even—the starved physical need in me proved stronger than reason, discrimination, or common sense, responding to his will with the unquestioning compliance of fate aleady resolved.

"All right," I said, from a cloud of darkness. "I'll marry you."

"You won't regret it," he told me. It'll be a *real* marriage . . . so long as you know your place . . ."

"My . . ."

"As my woman. Understand?"

I understood. And I should have taken warning.

But I didn't.

In January Lewis Baragwanath and I were married.

8

At first everything was all right. Or if it wasn't, I was too submerged physically to realize it. Lewis was a competent lover, able to awaken and fulfill desire in a manner strangely exciting. It was as though the life stream in me, long suppressed, was suddenly released in a torrent of passion which submerged all other facets of my life, obscuring in its dark demands the painful memories of the past.

Even Roma and Red became secondary images, duties demanding temporary attention and care. I hardly noticed them. When Lewis went out each morning, the day became merely a waiting period for his return, and the evening but an interim for the night.

The fact that he still had his midday meal at the farm with his sister only made me the more restless for his presence, keeping our relationship highly charged and self-sufficient. One day, however, it was different.

The weather was chilly, but oppressive, with low, yellowing clouds hugging the rim of land and sky. I felt tired, with a mild headache, and was longing for Lewis to return, not with passion, but to have him there . . . someone to talk to as companion and friend. There was something faintly menacing in the air . . . a lonely morbid quality that put me on edge and ill-at-ease. It was unfortunate that he was late. We usually had our evening meal at seven, but as he had not arrived I told the girl to delay serving until he got back. Half an hour passed, then an hour. So I decided to eat on my own. He did not get back until a quarter to nine, and by then anxiety had sharpened my temper.

"Why are you so late, Lewis?" I demanded. "I was beginning to imagine all sorts of things."

He did not kiss me, or even smile. Just said shortly, "Judith's ill. I'm going back now."

"What do you mean by ill? Is it anything serious?"

He paused for a moment before answering. The look of his eyes under their narrowed lids was reflective, a little furtive when he said, "Who's to know? She's sick. Many folks around here have been ill lately."

"Well . . . it's the time of year, isn't it?" I said reasonably. "Colds and fevers get about in the winter."

"Hm."

"Would you like me to come along?" I asked impulsively, although the idea was unpleasant to me.

"No. She wouldn't like it. I'll be back now and stay the night."

"The *night?*" I echoed. "But why? She's got Dolly Craze there . . ."

"That's different. Judith wants me."

"And me?" I queried, unable to keep the bitterness out of my voice.

His lips curled derisively as he said, *"You?* . . . Can't you do for once without . . ."

Before the obscene word was properly out, I gave him a violent push, screaming, "Go on. Go on then . . . to your precious sister. And don't ever talk to me like that again . . ."

His hand came smartly across my face. "And don't you ever come the fine madame on me either. I warned you, didn't I? And you just remember it. I'll do what I like *when* I like. And you'll behave proper to me and mine or I'll beat the devil out of you . . ."

I was so shocked I didn't see him go. I sat back in a chair while the room revolved around me in a black vortex of fear and shame. It had been a frightful, a degrading scene. I had never imagined any man could look so ugly or speak with such venom. For the first time I had been witness to the violent undercurrents of my husband's nature. He had been a stranger . . . frightening and coarse; the merest travesty of the man I had thought I'd married.

When the pounding of my heart had ceased, I was shivering. Red came in just then, wearing his nightclothes. "What is it, Mama?" he asked. "What's the matter?"

I drew him to me. "Nothing," I assured him. "I have a headache, that's all. And why aren't you in bed?"

"I heard him," he said.

"What do you mean? . . . Who? You were dreaming."

"No I wasn't. It was him, wasn't it? I hate him. He's nasty and cruel. If he hurts you I'll kill him."

"Red," I said, trying to soothe him, "you mustn't say or even think such things. Your . . . your stepfather was worried. If he said anything you didn't like, you must forget it or at least try to forgive. He's very worried about his sister, your aunt Judith; she's not well."

"She's not my aunt. She does nasty things. She's a witch."

"*Red* . . ."

He stamped his foot. "She is. She *is* . . . she lays spells and things. Ellen saw her roasting a toad, and Ellen said . . ."

"The servants have no right to speak like that," I said with a strange chill running down my spine.

"But it's true," the little boy persisted. "She has little dolls too, and sticks pins in them."

"Well, if she does," I said lightly, "it's just a game."

But he would not be convinced, and later, when I'd sat by him and waited until he went to sleep, neither was I.

After that Judith Baragwanath became the symbol of all that was threatening and dark in my life.

Lewis stayed at the farm for three days. When he returned it was as though nothing had changed between us. The glance of his eyes was warm and speculative, holding the well-known look of desire. If he had made one gesture of apology or at least some slight show of tenderness, I might have responded and gone halfway to meet him. But he didn't. And although I did not, that night, withhold my body, my spirit was revolted and turned away.

I tried not to show it, and Lewis probably never noticed. Superficially our lives continued in the same pattern. But inwardly all was different. It was as though I had woken from a wild all-absorbing dream to reality which showed ruthlessly the bitter differences between mere passion and love. I noticed things I had not been aware of before: the way my husband ate, with his head bent low toward the plate, the quick avaricious manner in which he swallowed his tea, rubbing his hand across his mouth afterward. His remarks at times concerning the servants verged on vulgarity—especially his allusions to a new girl I'd engaged to help Ellen about the house. I did not expect him to be unfaithful; I'm sure he never was. But his attitude to women savored of that of a farmer to cattle. In short, as the days passed, his earthiness began to revolt me, and I looked back nostalgically to my gentle Charles, who had brought such graciousness into my life, longing at the same time for Roderick, and only him.

I did not admit it at the time, but Lewis frequently frightened me. Perhaps he sensed my inner rejection, and resented it. He could not tolerate my speaking to another man, even if it chanced to be a farm worker. He became watchful, and sometimes when I took a stroll on my own, I would be startled by the snapping of a twig or movement of a bird through the undergrowth, thinking he was behind me.

Once he said, when I'd been in conversation alone with the children's new tutor, Robert James, a bespectacled quiet youth, "Fancy him, do you?"

I turned away impatiently. "Don't be ridiculous."

"I said, *fancy* him?" he repeated.

Goaded beyond endurance, I answered angrily, "And if I do?"

"He'd better look out," he said, "and you . . ." He lifted his large outspread hand in the air threateningly. "Understand?"

"Don't you dare touch me," I said loudly and clearly.

Lewis threw back his head and laughed. "If I ever catch you out, I'll do more than that, woman, so don't go getting ideas."

I began to hate him. The physical need which had brought us together now shamed me with a sort of terror. He knew it and was cruel. I thought wildly sometimes of running away with the children to Pengalva. But my uncle was old; he had not agreed with the marriage in the first place. I knew I had somehow to work things out on my own. Carnecrane too was mine. If I left, Lewis would retain it as his. I was not quite clear about the law concerning such matters, but he had said more than once, "Remember when I married you I took on what was yours. Don't think you'll get rid of me by your tantrums. I'm here to stay."

In such moments I knew how a woman must feel when she was driven to murder. But, for the sake of Red and Romany, I kept myself under control. The land was thriving. My husband was an excellent organizer, worker, and administrator, stimulated partially no doubt by the excess of energy which began to make my personal life impossible.

One night after a desperate emotional scene when I refused his physical demands, he took himself off to his sister's and stayed there for a week.

It was a blessed relief, until I discovered at the end of it that I was with child.

On the night of his return, Lewis appeared in the bedroom as usual, with the demanding look on his face which I had learned so to dread and loathe. It was always the same. He would approach me slowly and deliberately; disrobe me with a covetous half smile around his lips, then draw me suffocatingly close until my will was subjugated utterly to his.

"No," I cried. "Not now. Leave me alone."

He stood there, momentarily nonplussed.

"What have I done? I've not so much as touched you."

"Neither must you," I told him harshly. "I'm having a child."

His jaw dropped. "What?"

"A child. *Yours*," I told him. "What did you expect?"

"Are you sure?"

"Of course."

"That it's mine, I mean?"

"What sort of man are you?" I cried. "To suggest it could be any other's?"

"Well, it happened before, didn't it? . . . You bred them without marriage lines."

I was too sick at heart to argue or even revile him. I turned away, and the next moment his hand touched my shoulder tentatively. "All right," he said, "I believe you." There was a pause, while I stood stiffly, my spine rigid. Then he added, "*Mine*. That's what I wanted. A son. I won't harm you, why would I? So long as it's a Baragwanath in your womb."

Disgusted, I left him. I didn't want his child. I didn't want anything of his. I was dreading the day when the baby was born.

That day never came.

On a warm day in July when I was returning from a walk down to the cove, I tripped on a stone, and fell several feet back down the steep path. I was four months pregnant, and the twisted muscles brought severe pain which kept me lying there for some time. Overhead, the yellow-black sky was charged with approaching thunder, and presently the first few drops of spattering rain fell on my forehead. I drew myself to a sitting position and as I did so could feel the warm trickle of blood between my thighs. The pains became excruciating agony. Whether it was my own scream I heard, or that of the gulls overhead, I never knew. I fell back into a well of blackness, and when I recovered consciousness it was over. The child Lewis had so wanted was already dead before it had been properly brought to life. I lay there for a timeless period with the heavy rain washing the anguish away into a negation of forgetfulness and peace. When at last I had the strength, I struggled to my feet and in a semistate of oblivion somehow found my way back to the house. Ellen saw me as I stumbled through the door. After that I knew no more until one afternoon I opened my eyes and found the doctor looking down at me.

"You've had a bad time, my dear," I heard him saying, as though from a distance. "Fever from getting so cold and wet, on top of the miscarriage. But you'll do; you'll do. You're strong."

"How long has it been?" I managed to say.

"A week."

I closed my eyes, trying to remember, trying to piece facts together in my mind. When the picture formed, I shuddered. "The children?"

"They're all right. Miss Baragwanath took charge."

I sat up with the sweat running from me in a stream of weakness and fear. "You mean they're with her? They're . . ."

"Oh, no, no, no. She moved up to the house here. It seemed an admirable arrangement . . ."

From the bewilderment in his voice I knew he did not understand. There was no reason why he should. "Of course," I agreed compliantly. "But I would like to see them."

"Tomorrow," the doctor promised. "Tonight you must rest."

Lewis came in later. He stood by the bed, a rough, handsome intruder, looking awkward and ill-at-ease, fumbling for words which came gruffly from his lips. "How're you feeling?"

"I shall be all right," I answered, trying not to look at him.

"You lost my son," he said. "Next time it'll be different. Next time you won't go crawling about cliffs acting as though you wanted it to happen."

"Oh, God," I thought. "Let there be no next time. Never again."

I waited for him to go. But he still stood watching me. I closed my eyes against him.

"It's no good looking like that," he said. "I know what's in your mind. I know what you tried for that day . . ."

I sat up, forcing myself to speak more loudly and clearly.

"I'm tired, Lewis. Do you mind going now?"

He shrugged. "If you say so."

He turned and went to the door. Then with his hand on the knob he said, "The doctor says you should be fit as a fiddle in next to no time. All you've got to do is feed yourself up and not brood. Judith'll take care of that. The fancy stuff these girls cook's no good for man or woman. One of them's gone already."

"*What?*" I gasped. "One of the servants?"

"That woman Ellen. Full of cheek she was. Naturally Judith wasn't having it."

"Do you mean . . . do you mean your sister sent one of *my maids* away?"

"That's right. Good riddance too. Spoiling the children . . . interfering when I tried to discipline them, whispering to that namby-pamby tutor fellow . . . Oh everything's sorted out proper now. I've seen to that. Everything and everybody in their right places. I'm master from now on."

I was overcome by a wave of anger which left me faint and frightened. Carnecrane was my own home, and yet in it I was now caged and helpless. Weakness streamed over me in a clammy tide. If only my father was alive, or Charles . . . someone who really cared about me sufficiently to act on my behalf. But there was no one. Until I was up and about again, I was at the mercy of the Baragwanaths . . . not only myself but my children. Their presence now had become a nightmare; but as a kind of stupor took me into troubled sleep, something rational told me that because of past events my judgment was contorted. Lewis was not all that bad; he couldn't be. I had married him. It had been all right at first . . . until that scene concerning his sister Judith. It was Judith who had worked the evil. I had to get better quickly, so I could send her away. The memory of her hard witchlike face with its black button eyes made me want to scream. I hated her. *Hated* her.

But when I woke hours later, she was there, staring down at me, with a bowl in her hand. "Broth," she said shortly. "I didn't want to wake you, but you have to have something."

I drew away instinctively. "I'm not . . ."

"You take it," she said. "It's not poisoned. I'm not like some; I wouldn't hurt a body, however much I had cause."

I allowed her to feed me from a spoon, and when I'd finished it I felt stronger.

"It's what I said," she remarked smugly, taking the bowl away. "You need nourishing stuff inside you. Perhaps after this you'll heed what I say. And don't think I want to bide here an hour longer than I have to. There's my own place waiting, and those twins of yours are a handful. If they were mine I'd have seen they were better disciplined. So just pull yourself together now and try to be the wife a man needs."

She may have done what she could to help at that time. But her helpfulness was a one-sided affair concentrated only to one end . . . regaining complete influence over Lewis and his affairs.

Although I struggled hard to regain my health, I was not fully recuperated until the end of September, and even then I was tired, with my spirits at a low ebb. There were times when I had to use every device and trick in my power to keep Lewis from my bed. When I failed, he showed no mercy, though afterward he was shamefaced and for a period there would be an uneasy calm between us.

"How long are we going on in this way then?" he asked frequently. "Isn't it about time you did your duty and gave me a child?"

"Duty!" I thought. As though he *owned me*. Fierce pride stiffened in me, strengthening the battle between us. However he might ill-use my body, my spirit he could not touch. Physical contact with him had now become abhorrent, something endured with mind and senses steeled against him. I tried not to show it, for the sake of the children, but I think they knew something was not right. I frequently caught Roma looking at me in a puzzled way as though waiting for me to explain. Red was watchful and on the defensive. He had never tried to disguise his attitude to Lewis, and I knew would have welcomed an open break. I was worried about it, because I wanted the twins to have a happy uncomplicated childhood in a normal environment. But the atmosphere at that time was far from normal. I had no housekeeper; the servants, either resentful of Lewis and what went on, or tittering and whispering behind my back, were forever leaving or having to be discharged. I struggled to retain outward dignity, suffering in secret the ignominy of frequent brutality, my only prayer being that the children should not know. But walls have ears, and though I moved my room as far as possible from others in the house, contact could not entirely be severed.

"How are the children getting on with their studies?" I asked Robert James one day. "Is the routine working out?"

The young man gave me a very straight piercing look.

Though mild in appearance he was nevertheless an astute judge of human character.

"They are both intelligent children," he said. "Roma is an engaging little girl, and extremely clever artistically. Yes. I would say she is happy. The boy . . ." He paused, adding suddenly, "He could be aggressive and resentful. I've not found it personally, but later I think he should go to school."

"I see."

"Do you?" Robert smiled. "It isn't always easy for a mother to understand a son. And although I shouldn't say so, it seems sometimes he thinks too much of you. Oh, I don't mean he doesn't *work*. As I said, they're both bright children, but a boy needs contact with his own sex. If he had brothers, or his own father . . ."

"I have no relations at all," I said, "except one very old uncle, and my uncle Jasper . . . Jasper Cremyllas the actor; since I left the stage we've lost contact. I wouldn't want to bother him with Red's problems."

"There's no problem yet," the young man assured me. "But think about school."

I thanked him, and with a sinking feeling at heart, slipped on a wrap and went outside for air and to get my thoughts into order.

The men were all busy harvesting in the fields on the far side of the Baragwanath farm, where the land lay patch-worked green, brown, and gold under the quiet sky. The sight was satisfying, and a credit to Lewis. If he had remained my farm manager only, I knew we could still have been friends. The disastrous emotional situation between us had arisen simply because I had married him, and for the wrong reason. Sex alone was not a sufficient basis for a lifetime together, and sex thwarted could turn a man sour.

I should have listened to Uncle Thurston when he'd said, "Think well, Rosalind. Lewis Baragwanath may be a worthy enough man . . . but he's a rough diamond, not bred to the ways of gentry."

Yes, I should have listened. But I hadn't wanted to, because my wild longing for bodily fulfillment had resulted largely from despair and the need to forget Roderick.

So I had used Lewis.

Lewis had been merely an antidote and second best.

The truth was not pleasant, but facing it revived a faint hope in me that marriage might become tolerable. Surely, if we could both admit mistakes and a portion of blame, something of it could be salvaged decently?

As I walked the moors that afternoon I had almost made up my mind to lay my cards on the table when I returned, to say to my husband that night, "I should not have married you so quickly, Lewis, but I did, because I needed a refuge. I have failed you in some ways—I realize it—and you have done things I didn't expect. But if you still want me I'm willing to try again. Only be gentle if you can. Otherwise it's no good."

Would he understand? I wondered. Would he know what I was talking about?

He didn't have the chance; because when I was coming down the hill path skirting Tywarren, I saw Roderick coming toward me along the lane below.

It was a shock.

Although so long had passed since our last anguished meeting, he had not really changed. I would have known him anywhere . . . the lift of his head, his lithe figure, a certain way he had of walking; and when we drew close . . . the lips curved in a well-remembered half-smile . . . pleading now, as though asking understanding . . . the probing warm glance of his eyes under their thick lashes. He was a little older looking, slightly graying, that was all. "Oh, Roderick, Roderick . . ." my heart cried, "why did it happen? . . . Why? Why?" There was no resentment anymore; all bitterness had faded in the years between.

I tried to speak, but no words left my mouth. I just waited on the brown hillside where the bracken now was crisp and withered, yet already spattered with pale new growth beneath the decay.

He took my hands. "Rosalind."

Before I could stop him, even had I tried, his lips were on mine. Then as we fell apart, I said, "Why have you come?"

"To see you," he said simply. "We've just finished a run of Shakespeare at Plymouth, so I took the opportunity of looking you up. I'm staying at the inn—the Tinner's Rest."

"At Tywarren?"

He nodded. "Till Monday, that's all."

"But are you comfortable there? I mean . . . isn't it rather primitive?"

He shrugged. "I'm an actor, Rosalind. Forgotten?"

"Oh no," I said sadly. "How could I?"

His hand reached for mine, holding my fingers gently, with affection.

"If you knew how I've regretted what happened. If . . . I rather thought . . . I hoped . . . but I hear you're married . . . ?"

"Yes."

"I see."

"So are you," I reminded him.

"That's true. If you can call it a marriage."

My heart leaped, trembled with irrational joy, until reality touched me with its cold hand. "My husband's a farmer," I told him.

"Yes, I heard that too. Are you happy?"

I looked at him, and didn't have to answer.

"Oh, God! . . ." he said. "Why were we such fools? . . . Why was I such a stubborn, thick-headed, bloody fool . . . ?"

"Sh . . . sh," I said, trying to keep the tears from flooding my eyes. "Don't, Roderick . . . please, I can't stand it. It's done. It's all so long ago. The children are seven now . . ."

"Children?"

There was a sudden silence. Silence so complete it seemed even the frail wind held its breath, leaving the world motionless and we two its only living creatures, held by a bond irrevocable which no time or circumstance could sever. Then he echoed, "Children? . . . Do you mean . . . ?"

"Yours, of course," I said. "Is it so surprising?"

He would have taken me in his arms, but I resisted.

"Please . . . it's no use."

"No use? What do you mean? Why didn't I know? You could have told me . . . you could surely have . . ."

"After what happened?" I reminded him, with a touch of remembered pain. "The things you said, when I'd done all I could to show you . . . to make you understand how I loved you? . . . Do you think it was easy for me making that journey to Truro that time, with all I had in my heart? . . . I would have gone to the ends of the earth with you then, Roderick. No one, nothing else mattered but you. And then afterward . . . the look on your face when you told me of your marriage . . . how could you expect me to tell you anything again?"

He wiped his forehead with his hand; his face was tortured when he looked up. "We can make a fresh start," he said slowly. "We can take off somewhere with the children . . . and have our own theater company. I have a little put by. And you're still beautiful, it would be simple to make a comeback . . ."

Even while the prospect tempted me, I was aware of its futility. The name of Rosalind Cremyllas was now a half-forgotten word in the theater. My reputation had burned brightly for a brief time, but as quickly faded. Had I been free I might have risked the chance; but I was not free. I had Red and Romany—and Lewis.

Lewis! The thought of him jerked me to the truth with a stab of newly awoken apprehension.

"I must go," I said urgently. "My husband may be . . . he may be waiting for me . . ."

"Then let him wait."

"No . . . you don't understand. He . . ."

Roderick grasped my arm, swinging me around to face him. "What do you mean? Is he cruel to you? By God if he is, I'll . . ."

"No, *no*," I lied. "Of course not. I can't explain now, but . . ."

"Then when?" Roderick demanded. "When can we talk? And the children . . . when can I see them?"

"I don't know. It's so difficult . . ."

"Then I'm coming back with you now," Roderick insisted. "No one could object to you seeing an old friend, surely?"

If only he knew, I thought miserably. If he could only understand one little bit of the situation at Carnecrane, he would realize the impossibility, even danger, of such a suggestion.

I worked things out feverishly, searching for an adequate excuse. My only resort was to lie. "I have friends coming presently," I managed to say with reasonable calm. "I have to change and prepare. Today is no use, Roderick."

"When then?"

His insistence, and my own longing to see him again, eventually overcame discretion, and I promised to meet him the following afternoon, bringing the twins with me if weather permitted, on the pretext of blackberrying. I indicated a certain spot behind the curve of the hill, not far from the little dell I had visited in childhood. Then, without further contact . . . not even a touch of the hand, I turned and left him, running lightly across the lane past the patches of furze and stone-walled fields until I reached the house.

As I got there I saw Judith standing at the gates with a basket in her hand. Her face was watchful, hostile with an inscrutable look in her narrowed eyes under the black bonnet. Everything about her was depressing and dark. Her very mind seemed to project disapproval and resentment. "I've brought you these . . ." she said, handing me the basket. "Mushrooms. I thought you'd be in at this hour."

I thanked her for the mushrooms, adding, "I thought a little exercise would do me good. Are you coming in?"

She shook her head. "I won't inflict myself. Lewis is back."

"So early?" I exclaimed sharply.

"Why not? He's master, isn't he? What's the matter with you?"

"Nothing's the matter."

"Oh." Judith's voice was smug. "For a moment I wondered if you'd been up to something."

"What *could* I be up to?" I swept past her and went into the house. The girl I'd taken on in Ellen's place was coming down the corridor from the kitchens with a cloth in her hands. "Is my husband about?" I asked, disturbed by his sister's insinuations, wondering if it was possible she had seen my meeting with Roderick and conveyed the news to Lewis. But it was hardly likely; we had been standing at an angle not visible from Carnecrane, and Judith no longer walked quickly; she could not have covered such a distance in the time allowed. Steadying my nerves, I heard the girl saying, "He's in his gun room. Going out rabbiting, I believe, ma'am."

I found him in his particular place, a cubbyhole of a sanctum where he stored a few private possessions and shooting equipment. It was a dusty, essentially male retreat which I seldom visited.

I opened the door. He was polishing the butt end of a gun and, when he heard me, looked up.

"Judith told me you were back," I said. "If I'd known I'd not have stayed out so late. Do you want a meal now?"

His face was expressionless when he replied. "No, later. I'm off to take a rabbit or two and that devil of a vixen if she's about. Too many birds going. Last night four hens."

"Isn't the light rather bad for that?"

"Time to get her," he said briefly. "Off guard. That's the only way to deal with sly ones like her."

I shivered, sensing undercurrents in his brief statement which could have had basis, or have been merely the results of my keyed-up imagination.

He arrived back an hour later with a satisfied look on his face, which told me he had been successful with the fox. I was sickened. Although poultry had to be protected, the thought of any wild creature being deliberately killed always upset me, especially when it was a mother with hungry little ones waiting.

I went to bed early, and was about to turn the key in the lock of the door when Lewis entered. From his face I knew what he wanted. I clutched the wrap tightly about my neck and walked quickly away from him to the other side of the bed where I pretended to straighten the quilt.

He followed me.

"What's the matter?" I heard him say behind me, with his breath warm on my neck. "Still tired?"

I turned sharply. "Yes, *yes*. I'm tired. I'm sorry, Lewis, I'm not . . ."

"Not ready? Then why did you go walking so far then? It seems to me a woman who can go tripping about like that should be able to give a man what's lawfully his."

I tried to evade him, thinking wildly, if I could get out of the room downstairs he wouldn't dare follow me. The servants were still about: he was a proud man in his way; he wouldn't want his dignity harmed.

But I had no chance.

He was relentless, and he was strong. He took me in lust, as implacably as he'd taken the life of the vixen. In ten minutes he had gone, leaving me shamed and hurt, and wishing him dead.

The next day it was raining. All morning I hoped it would clear, watching the gray sky anxiously for a sign of the clouds lifting. But though the downpour died, it left a drizzling mist which hugged the moors and hills into somber uniformity. By afternoon I knew the blackberrying project was off. I blamed myself for having told Red about it when I'd said good night in the usual way to the children. "But why can't we go," he said after I'd delivered the news. "It's not raining much. We could wear boots . . ."

"No," I said firmly, knowing that Lewis would suspect something if I took the children out in such weather. "Another day."

"Tomorrow?"

"Perhaps," I said. "If it's cleared up."

I knew how bitterly disappointed he was, and although he had to accept my decision, resentment showed in every line of his sturdy small figure as he walked away. I should have worried about his mood more, if I had not had Roderick on my mind. How was I going to meet him now without causing comment? On such a day Lewis would probably be in and out of the house. What excuse could I have for taking a moorland walk?

It was with relief that I heard him say after a cup of tea at three thirty that he was off with one of the men for Penzance in the wagon to fetch fertilizer for the ground. I saw him stride down the fields a little later, and afterward caught a glimpse of the wagon and oxen taking the track toward the lane.

Red and Romany were with Robert James when I slipped out cautiously into the deepening afternoon light. It must have been almost half past four, and the mist was a thin gray shroud over the hills, giving an ethereal quality to the humped bushes and rocks where the path wound pale and silvered, twisting this way and that through the undergrowth.

When I reached the curve of the hill, I thought I heard something behind me. I stopped, standing quite still, listening, with my heart hammering against my ribs. But there was nothing; no more sound, no sight of any living creature save the winged shape of a bird flying upward into the gray sky. Below, to the right, the dim desolate outline of Tywarren village emerged ghostlike beneath its huddle of ruined cottages and relics of mine-workings. Memories filled me with sudden, sad nostalgia . . . of kindly people who had worked so hard and given me many small kindnesses. Those who had suffered and died tragically either from accident or sickness. And other things . . . days of happiness and childhood discoveries, of finding my bluebell dell and reigning there as Titania with a foxglove scepter in my hand. Nobody had known about this except old Zachary Andrewarthe the peddler who had so enjoyed telling me his stories and giving me cheap trinkets from his tray.

I had dreamed so much then; perhaps I had never stopped dreaming. For was it not some wild dream now that was driving me to meet the man I still loved, who, if I had not rejected him those years ago out of mistaken loyalty to Charles Cranmere, could well have been my husband? *Could* have been? . . . Oh, *was*, surely. Marriage was not a matter of vows unthinkingly taken, but a tie of deepest love. Only such a love could possibly have survived the scars of mutual wounds inflicted from our hearts' anguish. Yes, I was his, and he was mine; the father of my children. It was unthinkable that the past which had divided us could not now be erased leaving us to find happiness together.

Unthinkable, but true.

I knew it as he appeared around a twist of the path, was aware, even through my joy, of my own self-deception; conscious of a doomlike quality in the very air. "This cannot last," I thought, as I went trembling to meet him. "This is too beautiful to endure."

With only a few feet between us, I saw the look on his face, as though he were seeing sunlight for the first time; and yet there was no sun. Nothing but gray sky and brown earth . . . a great solitude holding only the hidden subtle crackles and disturbances of nature's domain.

"Roderick?" I cried, and ran into his arms. Then, suddenly, there was a scream, high and shrill, that could have been a bird's or a child's. We both turned, and saw a man's shape looming from the furze by a rock . . . a man startled into movement by the cry, with a gun in his hand. Lewis. He half slipped, tried to steady himself, and fell. There was a sharp report, and the next moment I saw my small son scrambling through the bracken toward us.

"He was trying to kill you, Mama," he gasped breathlessly. "I saw you . . . He had the gun. I followed him. That's why I shouted. Oh, Mama . . . Mama . . ."

"Hush!" I managed to whisper, taking him into my arms. "It's all right. Don't look, darling . . . don't look."

I held him to me as Roderick went over to where Lewis lay, badly hurt yet still living, his face contorted with pain and condemnation. My first instinct was of repulsion then of pity. But he had no pity for me.

"I'll see you pay for this for the rest of your life," he said with such concentrated hatred that I almost swooned. "I'll live, and I'll make you suffer as I'm suffering. You'll not leave me now. I've got you . . . for good."

"He's raving," Roderick said. "I'll go and get help."

"No," I told him. "Let me go; I'll take Red."

"Very well."

Red and I walked down the hill together, through the thorns and furze and dripping gorse. "Raving," Roderick had said, but I knew it wasn't so. Lewis had been wildly, completely clear in his mind. He meant to live, even though his life might be that of only half a man. Perhaps he would recover absolutely, but deep down something told me it wasn't possible. In a vivid flash of intuition I saw my life ahead, administering to a sadistic invalid. I could leave him of course, but I knew I wouldn't, because the memory of the incident would be with me always, spoiling any chance of happiness with Roderick. My son's shrill cry had caused the accident. What the alternative might have been didn't count. Neither would anyone believe that Lewis Baragwanath had set out that evening with the intention of murder, and I, for one, would be thankful. The worst possibility of all to me was to have Red involved, for my young son to be questioned in court, and harried by legal proceedings.

The matter never arose. Lewis's explanation to the doctor later was perfectly reasonable. He had been out rabbiting and fallen on his gun.

The story was accepted.

Roderick left two days later. I did not see him alone again before he went. Later I thought sadly how ironic it was that his one and only meeting with his son had meant nothing to either.

Meanwhile I forced myself to face the future, which was starkly clear, and as I had imagined, Lewis would survive, but the lower spinal bones were shattered, and would leave him paralyzed from the waist down for the rest of his life.

He had spoken truly when he'd said, "I've got you . . . for good."

However much I wanted freedom, I had not the capacity to desert a man in such a state. And so I put the past behind me, and concentrated my love and hopes in Romany and Red.

9

Eight years passed, in which time I did what I could for Lewis, usually mechanically from a sense of duty, sometimes stirred by compassion. At first he sat all day in his chair, staring broodingly and watchfully out of the window or moodily noting every movement I made in the room. Later one of the men pushed him around the lanes in his wheeled chair, so he could see what was going on, advising and criticizing, chiefly the latter. He was critical of everything: the way the men worked, the way the house was run . . . especially since I had taken on another servant to help deal with the extra work. The future of the country appeared as bleak to him as the future of his life. With his body incapacitated, his mind had become increasingly active; he resented Parliament's recent passing of the Corn Law, which he said was a panic measure destined to bring distress to many farmers. His hatred, from me, had turned to Red, whom he saw as the instigator of his misfortune. Luckily I had taken Robert James's advice, and sent my son away to a minor public school when he was eight; so there was no contact except for holidays when Red kept out of his stepfather's way. For Roma I had engaged a governess, a quiet understanding girl from an impoverished cultured family.

Somehow the estate was kept together, though I had to economize in any way I could. It was not easy. But when Uncle Thurston died in 1816, I inherited a legacy which though not large was sufficient to dispel any immediate worries.

It was shortly after Thurston's death that Lewis said surprisingly one spring afternoon, "I didn't mean what I said, you know . . . about making you pay. You've done a lot for me. I'm content to forget how it came about."

I was distressed. "Don't think about it, Lewis. It was so long ago. Like another life."

"Yes. When you were my wife and I could be a real man for you," he remarked broodingly. "Don't you ever want it now?"

"No," I answered truthfully. "I'm forty-five. No longer young."

"If you did, I couldn't stop you," he said with the watchful look on his face again. "That's what she's always saying . . . 'How do you know what's going on? She's the kind who wants certain things. Why don't you have me there to see to your needs? Someday she may take off and where'll you be then? I may not be here to care for you. You think about it.' That's what she says."

"Who? Your sister I suppose?" I said sharply, unable to keep the dislike out of my voice.

"That's right."

I didn't answer.

"I don't listen though," he went on, as though trying to convince himself. "She's an old vixen these days. One day I'll get shut of her for good. You see."

His description was apt. Judith, now approaching seventy, had become a withered, malicious creature always wanting to make mischief . . . always furtively looking in on Lewis when she thought I wasn't about. It was rumored by country folk and the villagers of Tywarren that Judith Baragwanath was a witch indulging in orgies with the devil. Her four cats, one old native alleged, had been heard talking together in human voice at night. On another occasion a youth who kept pigs with his mother on a patch of land above the sea had passed her cottage on a dark night and seen a deformed half-clad ancient figure performing leapfrog with a goat over a burning chamber pot. When he reached his hovel, his wits had gone, though the garbled tale had been received as truth. Naturally these stories bred others. However ignorantly they had arisen, I could not help being discomforted, remembering Red's allegations as a little boy that she roasted toads and worked spells.

Whatever the truth, the fact remained that Judith Baragwanath had an evil influence wherever she was. I did all I could to keep her away from the house, telling her openly her presence was not wanted.

"Not by *you*," she said once. "I know full well what *you* want . . . to have him to yourself so you can get rid of him properly this time. Oh, I know what went on by the moor that day. And you'll not get a second chance. When I leave my brother, it'll be him that sends me."

It was.

One sultry evening I returned from the garden and found her there in the dining room where the table was laid ready for the meal. Lewis was sitting in his chair nearby, looking down on his sister, who lay on the floor in a pool of blood, with a knife in her back. For seconds he did not move; neither did I. I just stood there, paralyzed with horror, until he turned his face toward me and said, "I've done it . . . I've got rid of the old vixen as I said I would. She was always on at me . . . on and on, whispering, saying things . . . twisting my mind so I couldn't see straight. Well, it's over now. She'll not bother you anymore, or me."

"Oh, Lewis," I cried, when the first terror had passed. "How could you? You've . . . you've . . ."

"I've killed her, and good riddance," he said with no trace of emotion. "Now go and send one of the men for the doctor. Then the law."

But the law was not needed until later. I was halfway down the hall when I heard the sharp report of a gun. I rushed back into the room. My husband was slumped over in his chair, with a trickle of crimson coursing down one cheek. I knew, without having to be told, that he was dead; realized with a flash of intuition that it had been premeditated, and that he must have taken the weapon from his collection earlier in the day, and hidden it somewhere— perhaps under the rug—for a suitable moment. Judith's entry and malicious nagging had been the last straw and driven him to his last desperate deed with the breadknife before taking his own life.

Later, when the doctor had been, and all the necessary formalities completed, I was surprised to find, following the first initial shock, how remote and detached I felt. It was as though suddenly an unpleasant dark period had been swept ruthlessly from the house, leaving me free at last, cleansed of a long shame.

That same night I opened all the windows of Carnecrane, letting the summer air into the passages and rooms. The scent of roses and heather, mingling with a faint tang of brine, brought temporary healing and peace.

I went upstairs to the study which had been my father's. From the wall, where the fitful light caught it, a portrait looked down at me, almost yearningly, it seemed for a moment. I stood staring, and suddenly the ice in me thawed. Under the proud lovely face of Carmella Cremyllas, my grandmother, I cried for the first time in many years. Then, with a silent "thank you," I went upstairs and sat a long time by Roma's bed where she lay sleeping peacefully, one hand curled beneath her glowing cheek.

IV
Red

I was seventeen when I left school and went back to my home, Carnecrane. I was glad to be there. I had never liked studying; lessons had bored me except for drawing and painting, which wasn't the kind the masters liked. I'd been good at sports because I was big for my age . . . six feet, and strong. This had given me an advantage over the other boys, and I could easily have bullied anyone I liked into fagging. But that kind of thing had always sickened me, perhaps because I had seen too much of cruelty in my early youth, when my stepfather had been so beastly to my mother. I had heard her whimpering more than once at night, and though she'd denied the truth when I questioned her, I knew he'd beaten her. One terrible evening I'd crept along to her bedroom and I'd seen it through a crack in the door which hadn't been closed properly. I was going to scream and fight him, but suddenly he stopped and pushed her down on the bed. I ran away quickly because he'd had a belt in his hand, and I knew if he'd found me there he'd have used it on me too. When I was grown up, I told myself, as I lay trembling in my own bed, I would pay him out. I would half kill him for what he'd done to my mother. But I'd not been able to because of the accident. I wished he'd died; suffering had seemed far too good for him. I had never understood how Mama could bear to look after him the way she did. But she had always been soft over wounded things.

"You must try and understand about your stepfather . . . about Lewis," she'd said one day in the holidays, when I was about thirteen. "Being an invalid is harder for him than most people, because he was once so strong. When I married him, I did not really love him. I thought I did, but it was something quite different, which I should have realized. He found out. That's why he . . . why he tried to hurt me sometimes. . . ."

"He *did* hurt you."

"That's over now. You must try to forget unpleasant things. Otherwise you may grow up with wrong ideas, and I don't want that. So for my sake, Red, as well as your own, will you please do your best to be a little friendly to a man who will never be able to walk again. It's very terrible for him, you know."

I had not answered her, but because of her plea I'd made tentative efforts to be polite. It hadn't worked. Lewis Baragwanath had always hated me. This had made it much easier to go on hating him.

Now all that was over. I was home and looking forward to the day when I could take over the estate. In the meantime I spent much of my time with Jed Paynter, the new manager of Carnecrane, who took me around the ground and property whenever possible, introducing me to the land workers, including the women who helped with potato crops, radish pulling, and in other ways when necessary. Most of the men earned about seven shillings a week, women four pence a day, and children, when they were needed, about three pence, working from six in the morning till six at night.

Jed told me that oxen were more adaptable than horses for plowing, as they instinctively took a straight line, however steep the slope of the field in question. When the double-furrow plows were in use, they were each pulled by four pairs of oxen. At that time there were two dozen working in our fields.

I liked animals, and was more interested in their habits

than their economic value. The fact that oxen worked better when they were sung to by the boys and men fascinated me, and I could have listened for hours as the friendly intelligent beasts toiled early and late to the accompaniment of male voices humming and droning a reiterated chorus of the animals' names. They were strange names for such great creatures . . . like Portly, Lively, Beauty, Winsome, Bravely, Gentle, and Speedy. The same pairs were always yoked together, and would come obediently when called to be harnessed.

The saddening part to me was that at a certain age they were often put out to grass for fattening as beef.

"A farmer can afford to be kind to his animals," Jed Paynter told me." "He has to be, to get a fair deal out of them. But when the time comes there's no room for sentiment."

Although I recognized what he said was sound, I couldn't feel like him, and knew I never would. However much I had to conform practically, I had a soft spot in me for dumb things which was as much a part of me as my dislike of bullying and men of Baragwanath's type . . . whom I would have fought with pleasure any day.

I tried not to show it, knowing that only women were supposed to have weaknesses of this kind, and in appearance I looked far more mature and developed than my age. When I was fourteen, girls much older had been after me, but I'd thought them silly creatures; my one sexual experience had been with a serving maid at a cake shop near my school, more because it was the expected thing than from desire. Most of the senior boys had had her, and the affair had been deadly disappointing, and left me cold. No one had understood my lack of interest in women, mostly I suppose because of my build and flaming red hair. Certain offensive suggestions had been made to me by other boys of my own age, which I had rejected with contempt. The truth was I liked sport and open air, and anything to do with nature. I was not clever, but I liked making things

with my hands, and during that autumn of 1817, inspired
by an old seachest which had been washed up with half its
lid torn away, into the cove, I took a penknife and carved a
mouse from a piece of cherry wood lying in our woodshed.

The carving inside the chest was quite different . . .
ornate rose-leaf patterns and floral designs cut intricately
in the numerous small shelves and surfaces of drawers. My
skill was too limited for such work, and I would not have
had the patience to labor so hard at such tough wood, teak.
Animals were a different matter. After my first effort I
searched for the best wood I could find, and put it to dry
thoroughly before attempting anything else.

Roma, whose governess Eva Lane was remaining at
Carnecrane until after Christmas, was enthusiastic when she
saw my first three carvings . . . the mouse, a gull, and a
small creature of my imagination inspired by a piece of
driftwood I'd found in the cove.

"But they're good, Red," she said with a kind of wonder
in her voice. "You ought to be a proper sculptor and go to
London."

Her slanting dark eyes were brilliant in her heart-shaped
face, which was spritelike under her tangled black curls.

"London?" I said with scorn. "I'd hate it. This is only a
hobby. I'm going to do what my mother wants and what *I*
want . . . farm Carnecrane."

Roma shrugged. "I don't blame you. But . . ."

"Yes?"

"You won't ever be rich, will you? I mean we're always
having to economize over something."

"Jed says that's because of price fluctuation or something," I told her. "It started with the Industrial Revolution. If the mines were working, we *would* be wealthy. But
it'll take a fortune to start Wheal Gulvas off again . . .
and anyway I'd hate mining."

When she didn't say anything, I looked up at her curiously. "Do you want to be rich, then?"

Roma shrugged. "I'd like new clothes. I've only got two

dresses, and Eva Lane says waists are lower now instead of these pushed-up things."

Eva Lane was her new governess and companion.

"Why don't you get Mama to go with you into Penzance, then, or Falmouth?" I suggested. "If fashion's so important to you."

"It isn't. It's just . . . well, I'm grown up, Red. I'm as old as you, and yet I still have to have a governess, and be treated like a child."

I laughed. "Eva's only for what they call 'finishing' purposes, isn't she? . . . You know, to learn French properly, and manners, all that sort of thing."

Roma scowled, looking for a moment half wild, like a gypsy girl.

"I don't want to be finished. I want to be *me*. Why should I have to learn things from Eva? . . . She's only five years older than me. And she's so *quiet*."

"Oh, cheer up," I said. "Next time I go into St. Ives we'll ride there, and I'll introduce you to Nick Goyne."

"Who's he?"

"A fisherman," I answered. "He speaks Breton, and has lots of yarns about the sea."

My sister's face brightened. "I'd like that."

Afterward I almost wished I'd not said anything about Nick. He was my one retreat, my one male contact from Carnecrane, and we'd enjoyed a drink together at the old inn on the wharf. Roma's presence would change things, because a girl, especially a sister, meant having to be careful what was talked about, and never swearing or acting except in a gentlemanly way; still, it would only be for once. After that she'd have to put up with Eva Lane and Mama until she was old enough to be "launched" or whatever it was they did with girls when they were expected to find husbands. I couldn't see Mama doing that either. Since Baragwanath's death my mother hardly went into society. Then what kind of life or opportunities would Roma have? Eva had only been taken on for a year, and when she left, Roma would be at a loss for something to do. Eva. It was true what Roma said about her . . . she was very quiet. So quiet I'd hardly noticed her.

.But that evening at dinner, I did. And what I saw gave me a slow, warm, pleasant kind of shock. She was so gentle-looking and subdued, wearing a brown high-necked dress, the same shade as her eyes, and brown smoothly dressed hair. Her skin was pale, and her smile shy. She reminded me of a young fawn, or even of the small mouse that had first impelled me to carve from wood. Gentle Eva. I had never seen any girl remotely like her. Although I was five years her junior, she seemed young to me, and in need of protection. I wanted to touch the shining hair and trace my hand down the soft lines of her face.

Roma noticed. "Why were you looking at Eva like that?" she asked later.

"Like what?"

"As if she was beautiful or something."

"I think she is," I answered promptly.

"You *do*?" Her voice was incredulous.

"Yes."

"But she's *insipid*. There's nothing about her."

"That's because you haven't looked," I replied sharply.

"Oh, *you*," Romany exclaimed. "You're sorry for her, that's all."

"Why should I be sorry?"

"Because she's an orphan and has to work for her living. Don't tell me you didn't know."

"I didn't know she was an orphan. Anyway . . . having to work doesn't matter. I admire her for it. She's clever and courageous."

"And much older than you, don't forget," Roma added quickly. "Oh, I know she's nice and all that. But don't . . . don't go romantic about her, Red. Mama wouldn't like it, neither would I."

"If I wanted to be romantic it wouldn't matter what either of you liked," I said sharply.

And it didn't.

By Christmas I knew that I was in love with Eva Lane.

I could not bear the thought of her leaving after festivities were over, and on the last day of December I asked her to marry me.

We had gone down the path to the cove for a walk. It was a quiet afternoon; the sea was calm, rippled only by a mild breeze from the west, which shimmered the small green pools left between the rocks from the receding tide.

Eva had a thin brown shawl over her hair, which gave her the appearance somehow of an old painting. "I've so liked being at Carnecrane," she said reminiscently, with a half smile on her lips. "You've all been so good to me. Your mother is a very wonderful person."

"And Roma?"

"Romany is unusual and very clever," she answered. "It's a pity she doesn't see more young people."

I touched one small hand tentatively. "She will. I shall ask John Fortescue down in the spring. He's at Oxford now. We were friends at school . . . he's going in for law or something, but he writes poetry too, and can paint. Most girls run after him. He looks like Lord Byron."

"Oh."

"Don't you approve, Eva? . . . You don't mind me calling you Eva, do you?"

"Of course I don't. And how could it matter to me whether your friend looks like Byron or not? Anyway, I'm rather sorry for him. Byron, I mean. I don't believe those unkind things people say about his sister Augusta and him."

I held her hand more tightly. "I can't imagine you thinking ill of anyone," I said warmly.

She turned her head away, but not before I'd seen the warm flush staining her pale cheeks.

"You shouldn't say things like that, Red," she remarked.

"What things?"

"Well . . . as though I haven't any faults. Ask Roma."

"I don't need to ask Roma anything," I said bluntly. "She can be willful and overbearing, and difficult. You must have had to put up with a lot sometimes."

"Oh, no. I've been grateful. I don't suppose my next place will be half so nice. It's in a large house in London, with three girls who've been spoiled and need disciplining. . . . That's what their mother told me . . ."

I swung her around, looking down into her startled face, which was below the level of my shoulder. "Then the idea's ridiculous," I said. "You couldn't possibly go there."

"Oh, but I am. It's all arranged."

"No it isn't," I told her impetuously. "You're staying here."

"What do you mean? I'm not needed anymore. Roma has learned all I have to teach her. I can't just remain as though . . ."

"It was your home? But that's what I want it to be," I said, putting one arm around her and drawing her close. "I want you to marry me, Eva."

She stiffened and drew herself away, looking at me for a moment as though I were mad. "But . . . oh, Red . . . you don't know what you're saying. I know you're kind and considerate, and you may be sorry for me, but . . ."

"Don't say I'm a boy," I interrupted. "Look at me. I'm a man grown, and I know what I want. I *love* you, do you understand? Oh, Eva . . . Eva darling, do marry me . . . please, please marry me. I'll take care of you, I swear it. If only you could . . ." I waited then continued, "If only you could learn to like me too . . ."

As I spoke the shawl fell from her face, revealing clearly the widely set velvet brown eyes under the smooth forehead, where a few tendrils of silky hair had escaped from their modest coils. Her lips parted as though to speak. But she didn't. I took her into my arms and pressed my mouth on hers, and the response was not cool, but warm and sweet, and filled with tenderness. When I released her, she said simply, "I'm twenty-two, Red. How can you want to marry a woman as old as that?"

"*You'll* never be old," I told her. "You're the youngest and loveliest thing I've ever known. Look at me, Eva . . . look hard, can't you see it's true?"

She studied me in silence while the very world seemed to pause and wait for her answer. Then she replied almost in a whisper. "Yes, I see."

"And you?"

"I think I do love you," she said, "I'm sure I do. But . . . what's the use? Your mother won't like it, you *are* young, Red—in years, anyway, and I couldn't bear to make trouble. Everything would be spoiled . . ."

"Nothing will spoil it, and my mother will make no trouble," I assured her. "I shall tell her tonight."

I did.

After Roma had gone to bed with a book, and Eva had tactfully disappeared, I followed Mama into the drawing room, and informed her about my plans. She didn't say anything at first, just went over to the fire and stood for a few minutes with her back to me, hands outspread to the flames. Then she turned and said gently, "You're very young, Red. Marriage is a responsibility. Don't you think it would be better to wait a year or two until you've met other girls? Eva Lane's attractive in a quiet way, and clever. I've nothing against her personally, but she is considerably older than you."

"Five years is nothing," I said stubbornly. "And if you must know, she's very young for her age. I feel it's the other way about. I'm not a child anyway. Of course if you're going to go against us I shall marry her just the same. I'm nearly eighteen . . ."

"Eighteen isn't twenty-one," Mama reminded me a bit sharply. "But I wouldn't try to stop you legally, not if I was sure you really loved each other . . ."

"We *do*," I interrupted quickly. "I've never been so sure of anything in my life . . . and it's such a wonderful thing,

Mama . . . don't you see? I want to look after her and protect her, and have her children. I want everything to be
perfect for her . . . and I don't want a moment wasted. I
want us to *belong*, properly, before anything happens to
prevent it. . . ."

Suddenly my mother came toward me and put her arm
around me.

"Red, darling, I understand. If you feel like that, of
course you should marry her. Life's too short to miss one
day of real beauty. I did . . . because I was wild and
headstrong and too impatient to know the truth from the
false. But I can see you're not like that. Perfection though
. . ." She sighed, adding after a brief second or two, "Perfection can be transient, Red. Real life doesn't always give
us as much as we expect . . ."

"I don't expect if for myself," I said. "But for Eva, yes;
I want it for her. I want things so she never has a single
worry or shadow anywhere in her life. She *needs* looking
after, Mama. She's so little and helpless."

My mother bit her lip, which was trembling, and smiled.

"Go and tell Eva it's all right," she said. "Bring her in
here, and we'll have a glass of wine to celebrate."

I wondered as I left the room why she had tears in her
eyes.

When my mother suggested we waited until May for the
wedding, I agreed, because she had been so understanding
about the whole thing. In the meantime I worked hard
about the farms, knowing that with a wife and a possible
family later, the more I knew about the fundamental prin-
ciples of management and what it entailed in physical hard
labor the more competent I'd be to make a success and
improve Carnecrane, for the benefit of my wife and children.

Roma was a little scathing at first. "It seems so silly,"
she said when I told her the news. "Why do you want to
get married so soon anyway? And to Eva! She isn't even

good-looking. I should have thought you could have found someone more colorful."

"Not all men like black hair and red lips," I said bluntly.

"Meaning me?" she said sharply with narrowed eyes.

I shrugged. "Not necessarily. But you *have* got an untamed look sometimes."

"And sometimes I feel it," she told me with a flash of temper. "I want to run and dance, and scream round the cromlechs. Perhaps I'm a witch."

"Perhaps you are."

She stamped her foot. "Can't you ever say or do anything except argue in that smug voice?" she demanded. "Oh . . . you bore me. That's what my life is . . . just one long bore."

She ran from the room, and I thought a little guiltily that I might have been remiss in my preoccupation with Eva. Roma certainly needed distraction of some kind. So that night I wrote to John Fortescue and invited him to Carnecrane. "I'd like you to be my best man," I told him in the letter. "It will be a simple affair at Tywarren church; but if you could forsake your studies for a bit and come earlier we'd be glad to have you. My sister's at a loose end . . . in fact she's damned difficult. Please, old chap, do try and come. You could help by taking her off my hands for a bit." John replied quickly and told me he'd be delighted, and would somehow manage to get away by the beginning of April.

Roma brightened up a little when I told her, although as she pointed out April was still three months away. "And you said you'd take me into St. Ives to see that man—what was his name—Nick something?"

"Nick Goyne. Yes I did. All right, we'll ride over tomorrow afternoon," I told her.

"With Eva?"

"No. You know very well Eva doesn't ride."

"Good. I mean . . . it'll be nice for us to be together for once," my sister said almost placatingly. "It isn't that I

don't like Eva really, I know she's nice, but we *are* twins.
Twins are supposed to be close, aren't they?"

"Supposed to be," I agreed. "But you're too quick for me
by half. I can't keep up with your moods."

She smiled quickly, a smile that transformed her face
into that of some lovely changeling.

The next afternoon we rode over the moorland road into
St. Ives. It was a sharp day, with a bright cold sky and a
nip of frost in the air. As we came to the top of the hill
above the town, we saw a family of gypsies by the wayside
camped with their wagon beneath Rosewall hill. A wood
fire was burning in the crisp air; there were several children, two or three adults, and an ancient-looking crone
smoking a long clay pipe. Roma drew her mare to a halt,
pausing for a moment or two. The crone stared at her from
dark pebblelike eyes without moving or speaking; unseeingly it could have been, yet as though she saw everything.
The children too were suddenly still, as if spellbound at the
sight of Roma in her green velvet riding clothes. The next
moment a man came from the back of the wagon with a
bundle of sticks under his arm. He was dark, wearing a
leather jerkin, with a feather in his peaked cap, a torn
white shirt, and crimson stockings. His eyes were wild and
knowing under his tangle of black curls; and his gaze was
for Roma. There was something about him that made me
eager for a fight or wrestle, but sensing my sister's interest
and resenting it, I said sharply, "Come along. If you want
to meet Nick there's no time to waste."

As we rode away, a woman darted across the road,
swarthy-faced and angry-looking with a basket in one
hand, a baby under the other arm. She glared at Roma,
and when I turned my head, had put the baby down, and
was tirading the man like a wild thing. He was laughing.

"Why did you stop to notice people like that? Tinkers?" I
said sharply. Roma did not look at me, just answered
coldly with her chin up.

"I liked them. The look of them, I mean."

"You wouldn't like their habits," I said.

"I don't *have* to," she retorted. "And I don't suppose they like us either."

"The man did," I said. "And you know it. You had your eye on him. It's undignified."

"I don't see why."

"Because you're a Cremyllas, and they're what they are. Besides he had a woman."

"Oh, don't be so smug," Roma shouted. "Come on . . . let's ride . . ."

From cantering she broke into a gallop, and did not slow down until we reached the blacksmith's at the crossroad. From there we went at an easy trot into the town, and had our horses stabled at an inn near the marketplace.

When we reached the harbor, a group of fishermen were having a service before setting out in their boats. The strong smell of salt and fish—the hundreds of masts stretching to the sky—always excited me. This was a man's world, a world where women were content to serve menfolk not only in the home as wives and mothers but in hawking "catches," and salting for winter use.

"It's early yet for the mackerel," I told Roma as we walked along toward Smeaton's Pier. "March and April are the best months, but you always get a few setting off earlier."

"Oh yes. But what a smell," my sister said, wrinkling her nose.

"What do you expect in a fishing place! . . . Anyway, here's Nick."

Nick Goyne lifted his large hand in greeting, and came to meet us. He was a ruddy-face, dark-eyed, black-haired man somewhere in his early forties. His grandfather had been a Breton who had married a St. Ives woman. But with the close intermingling of the Bretons and Cornish, the Goynes still spoke bilingually. He was good-looking in a hearty way, but Roma did not respond with the friendliness I'd hoped.

"He's *old*," she said on our way back to Carnecrane, "and he doesn't even speak proper French. I thought you said he was interesting."

"So he is . . . to me," I replied crossly. "The fact is you're not a bit concerned about other people. All you want is to be admired."

"That's not fair."

"Well, isn't it true?"

Roma smiled suddenly in the engaging way she had and admitted, "Of course I want to be admired. All girls do . . . even your Eva. Only she's too modest to show it."

Thinking of Eva softened me toward Roma. "John Fortescue will please you better," I said. "You just be patient and see."

To Roma, possibly, the months before his promised arrival seemed endless. But to me the days flashed by. Spring came early, and though I worked hard, my leisure moments were rich, golden times, filled with happiness and my increasing love for the girl so soon to be my wife. Whenever possible we wandered off into the hills above Tywarren, where, in solitude and free from prying eyes, we lay in some sheltered place, luscious with the scent of young growing bracken and primroses, close in each other's arms, lips desirous but tender, knowing our love to be the one reason for being born.

I worshiped Eva, with my body and my heart. And I knew she felt the same for me. At times I longed for her so much it was all I could do to restrain from taking her. But I didn't, although I knew if I'd asked she'd have come to me without demur.

"We'll keep it," I told her. "That's how I want you, my love . . . my only love . . . so much that it will wait until we're properly married."

She understood, and was grateful.

Once early evening when the pale spring sunlight filtered low through the fresh undergrowth near a cromlech on the other side of Tywarren hill, I said, with a queer trembling sensation about my loins, "Eva . . ."

"Yes?"

"Let me see you, just once," I begged. "Without your clothes. I won't touch you . . . I swear it. I just want to look at you."

She smiled, and undressed without question. In the dying Cornish light her body was all pale fire and beauty. I wanted her with a longing that was pain, but I loved her more, and bent to her feet, kissing each in turn, with a kind of reverence. When I stood up, she came toward me and stretched her arms to my neck. "I love you, Red," she whispered. "For ever and ever . . . eternally."

"And I too," I said. I drew her close, then took her hand, staring in wonder. Her small breasts, pale and pink as unopened lily buds, seemed waiting on the verge of full flowering, for the sun to warm them. I stroked her fallen silken hair, and let my fingers trace the delicate outlines of her immature slim thighs. At that moment it was as though I knew God for the first time. Then a breath of wind trembled around the hillside, and she shivered. I put my coat around her while she dressed. The compassion in me was strong and glowing. As we walked down the hill, I made a vow that never during our life together would I consciously wound or discredit her in any way. And, to my knowledge, I never did.

2

Although John Fortescue had agreed to visit Carnecrane for April, he never came, owing to illness, which meant that I had to fall back upon Nick Goyne for best man, and for the rector's nephew to give Eva away. Roma therefore was left to her own devices in the meantime, and did a good deal of riding around the countryside. Often she came back with a flushed look about her, and a gleam in her eye once or twice. But when she shrugged off my curiosity with a laugh and, "What do you think? Who is there to know around here? Tell me that. . . ." I let the matter drop being too preoccupied with Eva to wish my thoughts diverted by my sister's uncertain activities.

Sometimes Eva and I walked through the fields in the evenings, taking the path that eventually wound past the Baragwanath farm. Since the dreadful tragedy of Judith's and her brother's deaths, no one had lived there. Judith's reputation for witchcraft still hovered in the minds of local folk, imbuing the building with an evil aura. We used it on the estate for storing potatoes and hay, and although the exterior of the house was mostly intact, the inside was completely derelict.

"It seems a pity," Eva remarked one warm evening in mid-April. "I mean, it could be made such a pretty place, and cottages are so needed, aren't they?"

"Not so much now," I told her. "At one time it would have been a godsend to a mining family; but since Wheal

Gulvas had to close, lots of cottages are falling into ruin. Besides, who'd want this house after what happened?"

Eva paused, staring at the sightless windows thoughtfully. "It wouldn't worry me," she said calmly.

"What? . . . But what do you mean? Don't you want to live at Carnecrane with Mama and Roma?"

Her small hand tightened on mine. "Of course I do. I just don't think you should let yourself believe in bad atmospheres and things like that. Anyway your stepfather and Judith didn't die *here*."

"No. But / . ."

"Yes?" she insisted.

I hurried her along. "I don't like remembering," I said abruptly, with a queer intangible tug of fear at my heart as a frail cloud passed the fading sun, leaving for a few moments only gray light and a shiver of chill air. "Judith was *evil*, darling, and I couldn't bear anything about her to touch you."

"Well it won't," Eva said. She turned her head suddenly. "Look!"

I waited reluctantly, as the sun briefly flamed again, touching the outlines of the farm with gold before setting quickly below the rim of earth and sky.

"You see?" Eva said, leaning close against me. "It's all gone now . . . all the darkness. We've exorcised it, Red, by love."

I tightened my arm around her protectingly, and we walked on, with the heady scent of may blossom and bluebells rich and fragrant in the evening air. She was right of course. No old hag of a dead Baragwanath had the power to touch Eva's innocence of heart; our love for each other was in itself a cloak against evil. All the same I could not quite dispel what I had seen for a brief moment before going on: a shadowy witchlike shape at the corner of the building, which could have been a low cloud, or a wisp of mist driven from the sea. It could have been, but was it . . . when the evening was so still and free from real wind?

"What's the matter, Red? What is it?" I heard Eva say presently. "Why are you so quiet?"

I looked down at her, and her face, pale as a flower in the spring dusk, drove all other thoughts from my mind.

"I love you," I said gently. "Never forget that, Eva . . . I love you so very much . . ."

Eva's voice was tender as she remarked musingly, "I wonder how many times we've said that to each other. It must be hundreds, or more. I wonder if we shall ever get tired . . ."

"No," I told her. "That's one thing I'm sure of. All my life and yours, Eva, I'll go on saying it—I love you, I love you . . ."

It was as though I sensed deep down, without recognizing it, how short that time could be.

In the few weeks before our marriage, my mother and Eva were busy preparing a wing of the old house for our private use.

"I don't believe in mothers-in-law being in close proximity with the younger ones," Mama said determinedly. "We'll always be pleased if you want to have meals with us, but the kitchens are large, so I think one of them should be Eva's private domain. The small one will be large enough; that won't interfere with Zenobia."

Zenobia Phillips had been at Carnecrane for a year to shoulder the duties of cook-housekeeper. She was a plain, worthy, middle-aged woman extremely capable in handling the two younger girls. Because of economy, we'd had to get rid of the houseman, retaining just a boy for the heavier work such as chopping wood and attending to the stoke-hole. My mother hadn't minded the decrease in staff. She was active herself, despite her forty-seven years, and when she put on man's clothes for gardening she could have been a youth in a stage play.

I was curious about the clothes. "Where did they come from, Mama? Whose were they?" I asked one day.

She paused before replying, and when she did her lips and eyes were alight with mischief, emphasizing somehow the reddish lights in her black hair, which was still hardly touched by gray.

"Ah. That would be telling. These clothes are quite precious to me. They represent a Rosalind Cremyllas you never knew."

"You mean when you were on the stage."

She shook her head. "No. Although of course I played a boy's part in Shakespeare many times."

"Why didn't you go on acting?" I asked curiously. "Didn't you enjoy it?"

A shadow crossed her face. "Never mind. It was . . . shall we say . . . the pattern of life."

I knew then that she would never tell me.

A month before Eva and I were married, we were surprised when Roma appeared at teatime with a stranger; a tall, handsome, fierce-looking man wearing the clothes of a preacher.

"This is Mr. Gwarvas, Mama," she said with a fiery challenge in her dark eyes which clearly indicated *Like him or there'll be trouble*. "Richard Gwarvas."

Mama invited him to join us, and we learned that he had been in the vicinity of St. Ives for a month, preaching Methodism on the harbor and in the surrounding moorland parishes. He was not very forthcoming, but from the square jaw and flash of eyes I realized that he could be. Roma was obviously enthralled, which struck me as extremely odd. She was the last person I'd have thought to have an interest in religion. But then perhaps it was not the gospel but the man, I told myself dryly.

It was.

Before Mr. Gwarvas left, he asked Mama for permission to marry Roma. Eva and I had left the three of them together, but the door had been left ajar, and I listened without a pang of conscience.

"Marry?" I heard my mother echo loudly. "But Mr. Gwarvas, I hardly know you, and I'm sure neither does Roma."

"Oh, yes, I do," my sister said. "Where do you suppose I've been while you've all been so busy with Red's affairs? I've ridden to every service there's been. It's been marvelous. I'm converted, truly I am. I want to serve God all my life . . ."

I turned away. I felt mildly sick. At heart Roma was a wild girl. I remembered the look on her face when the gypsy eyed her that winter day when we'd gone riding to St. Ives to meet Nick Goyne. I hadn't liked to admit it then, but they had been two of a kind. Deep in her heart Roma wanted an earthy love, not psalm-singing and prayers. If my mother gave consent to her marriage with a preacher, disaster was inevitable. But when I saw Roma later I knew she'd won.

"Of *course* I'm going to marry him," she said, after Gwarvas had left. "I love him. He's wild and strong and full of fire. He makes me feel *wonderful*. And if Mama had tried to stop me, I'd have run away just the same. I don't want a *quiet* life, here in Cornwall all my life . . . I want to *travel*, Red. I always have. And Richard will take me all over the world. We shall see strange places and convert Indians, and have a church in America . . ."

"America?"

"Oh, yes. Wisconsin. There are farms and mines there, and heathen people waiting to be told about God. Richard says if I'm good and learn to obey the Bible properly, I may become a deaconess in time. Imagine it."

I couldn't. The whole thing seemed quite mad to me. But obviously there was no point in arguing. Roma had made up her mind, and as Mama pointed out, Richard Gwarvas was at least a man of strong will who would doubtless keep her in order as effectively as anyone would. Roma and her preacher planned to be married the week after Eva and I. Mama would have preferred them to wait another month, but as the immigrant ship was due to sail in the third week of May, she agreed, though reluctantly.

May was a splendid blossoming month that year, as though nature intended to be its best for the two weddings. Eva and I, as planned, were married on the seventh at Tywarren church, and Roma and Richard Gwarvas at the Methodist chapel which stood at the other end of the village. The days preceding the two events were a daze of feminine chatter about fashion and bridal cakes . . . whether Eva would be bridesmaid or matron of honor . . . what clothes Roma should have for the long journey into the wilds of America. . . . Sometimes I wished the whole business was over. All I wanted was to have Eva to myself and get on with life quietly at Carnecrane.

My mother was very understanding. "The ceremony of marriage is always more important to a woman," she said one day. "And with Roma going so far away it's natural she should take the stage."

She did of course. Although, as befitting the bride of a preacher, she dressed soberly in pale gray at her wedding, she managed somehow to look all the more vivid with her brilliant eyes, dark hair, and flushed bright cheeks. Eva, my wife of one week, delicate-looking and flowerlike in blue, said almost enviously after the ceremony, "How lovely she is. And did you see how fierce her husband looked when she spoke to your friend Nick Goyne afterward?"

"Yes I did," I answered.

"Not at all like a preacher, just then."

"A good thing too," I answered dryly. "Roma will need more than religion to make her dutiful."

"Dutiful. What a word!" Eva said. "Is that what you expect of me?"

I smiled and kissed her. "No. Just you as you are. Just for you to go on loving me as you do now," I told her.

She didn't answer; she didn't have to. We were so close there was no longer the need for words between us.

We had all expected to go and see Roma and Richard set sail from Falmouth. But Roma would not have it. "I hate good-byes," she said on the day before. "I'd probably cry, and Richard would be cross."

Mama glanced at Richard inquiringly, saying a little sharply, "I'm quite sure he wouldn't. Any girl has a right to a few tears when she's leaving home for the first time."

Gwarvas faced my mother squarely. "My wife is quite right," he said uncompromisingly. "I have explained to her what is expected of a preacher's wife. Tears would be unbecoming. With the love of God in her heart why should she weep?"

I was suddenly resentful of him, and fearful for my sister's happiness.

"Because she's human," I said with anger. "Or hadn't you thought of that?"

Eva touched my hand. "Red . . ."

"No," I said, "I must say it, darling. Roma's my sister. And I'm the only man she's ever known properly until now."

"Until *now*. Yes."

"I have a feeling," I went on, "that you've not considered Roma in any way except your own. Well, you'd better start. If she's unhappy I'll fetch her back, Gwarvas, so help me God."

Roma ran foward and clutched my arms. "You mustn't say such things," she cried. "He's my husband. I love him. I want to be the kind of wife he desires, and please him in any way I can."

Despite the high flush on my brother-in-law's strongly carved face, he did not betray his temper. "I appreciate your brotherly concern," he said smugly. "But Roma's welfare is now my business. You need have no fears about her future life. What dangers we face we shall face together. She knows full well what is expected of her, and will conform in any way required."

I was about to speak again when my mother interrupted

placatingly, "Quite enough has been said on the subject. Roma and Richard wish to set off without emotional stress, which I can quite understand. So tomorrow we shall be sensible and say our farewells from Carnecrane."

And that's how it was.

But the tears were there; bright in Roma's eyes as the single-horse carriage took my sister and her preacher husband down the drive from our home for the last time . . . bright on the grass and lilac bush, where the rain fell softly and quietly from the gray sky. Bright on my mother's cheeks when she turned and went into the house. I put my arm around her.

"Never mind," I said. "It's what she wanted."

"Now, yes," Mama agreed. "But in a year's time?"

"You've said yourself so often it's the present that counts," I reminded her.

"I know. I'm a silly woman. You're quite right, Red. I was just thinking, that for a girl newly married . . . a girl like Roma who so loves pretty gay things . . . how strange it was to set off on a long journey with practically no possessions and no really becoming clothes."

She may have been thinking all that, but I did not have to be told that her true sadness was because she knew she might never see her daughter again.

She never did.

3

Two years passed, which were the happiest of my life. The estate, though its agricultural development kept us, if not rich, at least free from worry, Eva and I were completely happy, living in perfect harmony with my mother.

Despite her quiet exterior, my wife had a lively mind, and was by no means the conservative, compliant character her gentleness suggested. She was interested in all types of people, and all kinds of conditions in other countries, having sympathy with those who worked to improve the lives of primitive folk. Slavery of any kind was abhorrent to her; she was an ardent supporter of the Abolition Society headed by Buxton and Zachary Macauley which urged the banning of slavery itself—a natural outcome, it seemed to her, to James Fox's success in getting the slave trade abolished within the British Empire.

"We have no right to colonies at all," she said one day, "if we use such inhumane methods of labor. One day everyone will be free, you see. Then those wretched planters will have to find their level with other ordinary people."

"How do you know so much about politics and world affairs?" my mother asked curiously.

Eva smiled. "I don't, really. I suppose it was with my father being so much of a scholar . . . and a radical too of course. He always had more interest in the poor and unprivileged people; that's why he wrote those books that made him so unpopular."

"I haven't read any," my mother confessed. "But I've heard they were very forthright."

"He was a courageous man," my wife said with a smile of pride. "Or he'd never have married my mother."

"Why? I'm sure she must have been a charming person."

"Yes. I remember that; but not much more, because I was only six when she died. I didn't mean she wasn't nice . . . I meant . . . well, it was difficult for my father. She was just a lady's maid, you see, and the family turned against her. They became sort of social outcasts."

"How very snobbish and ridiculous."

"Not to my grandfather. Social differences meant a great deal to him. He practically cut my father out of his will; after that he had to leave Oxford, he'd been hoping for a fellowship . . . but there wasn't enough to keep him there, so we went traveling about, managing to get through on the little we had. That's why I had to earn my living."

"Well, I'm sure you must have had a more interesting life than being cooped up in stuffy society," Mama remarked promptly.

Eva smiled. "Of course. I wouldn't have had it any different. My father was a wonderful person; he taught me all I know. But it wasn't easy for him *or* my mother. If things had been more comfortable, I'm sure they wouldn't have got the fever. That was the awful part."

"Don't let us dwell on sad things," my mother said. "The important thing is the present. Red is lucky to have found such an intelligent wife. But don't make him jealous, my dear, men like to *think* they're superior, even if they're not."

"Oh, I don't want to be *superior*," Eva said quickly. "You make me sound like a schoolmistress; it's just that I can't bear cruelty . . . like slaving, I mean, and keeping simple people down. . . ."

"You're a born mother," Mama said with a warm look in her eyes. "Until you have a family of your own you'll not

change, and if no children come along you'll go looking
and finding some."

Eva flushed. I knew the words had stirred her deepest
longings. What I did not know was that she was already
with child.

She told me that night.

"I wanted to make *quite* sure before I said anything,"
she said with her face pressed close against my shoulder. "I
know you've wanted a son, Red, and I've wanted to give
you one. Now it will come true."

I was shaken by emotion. At first I could not speak, only
stroked her hair gently, then pressed my lips on her own,
until suddenly the impact of her words registered. "Oh,
Eva . . . darling, darling Eva," I whispered, easing myself
up in bed so I could look down upon her face . . . the
starry wide-eyed glow of her . . . lips slightly parted, skin
pale yet translucent, holding the faint pink luster of some
delicate seashell.

"It may not be a boy," I said at last. "Have you thought
of that?"

She shook her head. "No. I'm *sure* it will be a son."

"It doesn't matter which," I told her. "I shall love him
just the same . . . or her."

In the days that followed there seemed no cloud anywhere. Although so slight and small, Eva blossomed, showing none of the usual unpleasant symptoms which are
usually connected with approaching motherhood.

The baby was expected the following May, and up to the
month before, my wife was active, making clothes for the
child, supervising the arrangements for the conversion of a
room next to our own, as a nursery.

A nurse, approved of by both Eva and Mama, was engaged, and the doctor said he was entirely satisfied with
Eva's condition. She was a healthy young woman, he de-
clared, and would probably have an easy time when the
baby was born.

But he was wrong.

At the end of April my wife suddenly seemed to sink into a state of apathy, although she tried to convince me that all was well. "It often happens," she said one evening when I sat on the side of the bed staring anxiously into her shadowed eyes, noting with a clutch of fear her rapid breathing, the laborious way she moved her body, which had become cumbrous in the past few weeks.

"What do you mean, often?" I demanded.

"To women, Red. They get tired at the end."

Tired! I thought, she looked more than that. She looked completely exhausted.

I got the doctor to come over that same evening, but he did not seem unduly concerned.

"Mrs. Cremyllas has a healthy constitution," he said when he'd examined her. "She is not, of course, the peasant type. She is delicately formed, and her time is nearly due. I'll see she has a sedative, however, and get the midwife to come a week earlier. That will ensure complete safety."

But the midwife was no use. No one was.

On a day early in May when a blackbird was singing from a hawthorn, and the bluebells were thick among the gorse and young bracken, my son William was born. He was a lusty strong child, with a healthy voice which could not however disguise the screams of my wife. She screamed, until it seemed to me that the whole world was nothing but a cry of pain. I knelt beside her and took her hands; I prayed to God as I had never prayed in my life. For one brief second it seemed I was heard. Eva's torn body relaxed; she opened her eyes, and smiled. I think she spoke. Her lips formed the word *Red*. Then just as quickly her head fell to one side, and all was still. There was no sound, nothing but the wail of the newly born. No breath of wind to stir the curtains . . . no breath from the slight figure I had loved so much.

Presently, after the doctor had been, the midwife pulled

the sheet quietly over Eva's face. I couldn't bear it. It was horrible. They tried to move me away, but I wouldn't leave her.

"Get out!" I shouted. "Get *out*."

They left, and I buried my face into the quilt, crying as I had never cried when a child, long, terrible male cries of despair that went on until I had no strength left.

How long it was before my mother came in I do not know. But at last I allowed her to help me up and take me to her own room. She gave me brandy and made me lie down. Then she said, "One day it will pass, Red. Everything does. I can't expect you to believe it now. But there's a pattern to life. It can hurt unendurably, and in the moment of giving can take away. Where love is, though, something always remains. You have a son. Eva's."

I wanted to shriek, "I don't want him; he's murdered her. If it wasn't for him she'd still be alive." But the words didn't come. Even then, in my hour of utmost agony, I sensed that such an outburst would have been desecration, a betrayal of all that had been most precious in my life.

After the first shock I refused for days to accept Eva's death, allowing nothing of hers to be touched, not even her cup and saucer to be removed from her bedside.

Then, after the funeral, after seeing the small coffin lowered into the ground at Tywarren churchyard, I knew it was true.

The day was still and gray and fragrant, damp with thin rain which sweetened the scent of flowers and summer undergrowth. I remembered with pain Eva's words only a week before, when she'd said, "Soon it will be over, Red darling, we'll have our baby and it will be a wonderful summer."

Summer. The word was a mockery. The perfume of the early roses in the garden was torture. I did not know how to bear it. When Mama said anxiously, "Please try and grieve less, Red . . ." I simply said with ice in my voice, "Eva is not dead. How could she be? She's everywhere."

"Red . . . you're only young. You'll . . ."

Then I broke down. "What has this to do with youth, except make it worse? I loved her . . . loved her . . . and I don't want you to speak of it again."

I rushed out of the room, and from the house over the moors beyond Tywarren to Castle Tol, where I stood breathless and faint, with my face pressed to the cold granite. All was quiet and lonely, with the gray sky hugging the gray hills, a ghost place of forgotten people and civilization into which I was drawn and became one . . . a relic, as the grouped stones were, of something gone never to return.

I stood there a long time, until my anguish froze and became unified with the harsh strength of the rock. When I went down, hours later, there were no tears left to cry, no warmth left for suffering. There was no past and no future. Only the hours to be endured, and work to be done.

It was like that for a year. I worked as I had never worked before, driving myself, goading the men.

One afternoon after a battle with Jed Paynter, my mother was waiting for me when I went into the house. I was pushing past her to go to change when she stopped me at the foot of the stairs.

"Look, Red," she said, "I've got to talk to you. It's time you got a grip on yourself."

"What do you mean?"

"Just this." She had a fiery look about her as she stood there; her eyes flashed with a wildness I had never seen before. "All my life," she continued, "I've tried to do my best for you and Roma. I gave up my whole career for you. But perhaps you never thought of that. . . . It has never occurred to you, has it, that acting was once my life, and that it could well have been again. No. Well, think of it now. Do you imagine for one moment I would have been content to bury myself at Carnecrane if I hadn't thought it was for your good? . . . Look at me. I'm not yet old. But I soon will be if we go on like this. Fretting won't bring

Eva back; ignoring your child and leaving him to others will breed nothing but bitterness . . . bullying the men will send them away and mean ruin for the land. You are destroying yourself, Red, and all you contact. But you will not destroy me, or your son. And I mean that. So take a good look at yourself, and get rid of that thing . . . the canker in your heart, before it's too late."

She turned and swept past me, a living fury in her purple silk.

That night I thought of many things. And the next morning, which was the anniversary of Eva's death, I knew what I had to do.

I waited until dusk, then went down to the Baragwanath farm. In the dim light its twisted chimney looked like a crooked finger from the dark roof, and as I drew nearer, the empty windows had a sightless mocking glow which seemed to linger in the shadows like a knowing smile on the face of an evil crone. This was the canker, I thought, and always had been. Somewhere, over that bad patch of land, the dark spirit of Judith Baragwanath still hovered, casting an evil darkness over everything I loved. And so it must be destroyed; destroyed so thoroughly that nothing of the house or its haunting remained. Then, I knew, I would be free.

I went down the path, into the derelict parlor which now was filled with dry hay. I took the matches from my pocket and lit many, one after the other, thrusting them into the quickly ignited brown grass. As I got outside again, the flames were already leaping in streaks of orange and crimson, catching the woodwork until black smoke mingled with the rest. At the gate I stood and watched. In a few minutes the farm was a blazing inferno, curdling into the night sky where a few frightened and screaming birds wheeled into the distance. But it was not their screams I heard, or their shapes I noticed. There was something else . . . a haglike contour of cloud and smoke blown wildly toward the sea, accompanied by a high-pitched shriek which I knew as the death of something intensely vile.

As the flames began to ebb, I hurried away, knowing that the men would soon be on the scene. I went to the stables and saddled my horse. Then I rode away. I rode and rode, heady with triumph and elation, feeling Eva's death to be avenged. When I arrived eventually in Penzance, the inns were not yet closed. I went into the first, and drank heavily until they pushed me out. Then, at a kiddleywink near the moors somewhere, I drank still more.

I remember vaguely being helped onto my horse later and sent off with much ribaldry and laughter, of falling forward and clinging helplessly to the horse's neck. We were galloping and swerving, rearing and pitching together. The blood thudded dark in my head, and in my ears. There was stampeding and blackness, and a flash of fire, as I plunged ahead into a world of pain and clutching undergrowth.

Then, mercifully, all was dark. I knew no more until the dim light of morning streaked the sky, bringing a blur of gray shapes that wavered and died and were eventually resolved into the humped outlines of bushes and rocks. I tried to move, but could not.

"Rest, brother," I heard a voice say, as though from a long way off.

At first I thought it must be illusion. Then presently a figure emerged from the grayness and bent down with a cloth for my forehead. A woman.

"You've had a bad time," she said. "And it was a mercy I found you. But there'll be pain for you for many a day."

I remembered then.

"Where is my horse?"

She shook her head. "Gone, brother." She had a rich voice, and when my eyes could focus I saw that she was young. A strange-looking woman with a brown face and long yellow hair.

"Where am I?" I asked.

"The hill behind is Trencrom," she said. "I was pitched with my cart and tent there for the night. Peaceful, I thought, until you came along, with the blood dripping from your head, and your feet caught in the stirrups. It's through God's mercy you lived, brother."

I closed my eyes, trying to piece events together, finding their sequence difficult, though I had recollection of the fire and riding to Penzance. I looked up with a further question, but the woman had disappeared. When she came back, she had a bowl of something hot for me.

"Drink this," she said. "It's my own brew, and will help you to recovery."

With her assistance I eased myself up and tasted the liquid. It was like nothing I'd had in my life.

"What is it?" I asked.

"Herbs, brother," she told me.

"And why do you call me brother?"

"It's our way."

"You mean you're a gypsy?"

She shook her head. "No. Though I've belonged with them all my life. Now don't you question. Just bide and sleep if you can. Then maybe when you wake again the sprains and cuts will hurt less."

"I can't stay here," I cried, suddenly realizing everything that had happened. "They'll be looking for me. My mother will be worried. There was a fire. I . . ."

"I saw it," she said. "A red glow to the east."

"What is your name?"

"Esther," she said.

"Then will you help me walk home, Esther?" I asked.

"I will not, brother," she answered firmly. "You will not walk far for some time yet. But when you are well enough Sheba shall take us both in my cart wherever it is you want to go."

"Sheba?"

"My donkey. My very old and faithful friend. We are

both looking for a home; I for steady work and a place to eat and sleep. All Sheba needs now is a patch of ground . . . a very small patch would do, brother . . . just to graze and lie and nibble and dream."

She smiled. And the smile lit up her strange face, with its radiance. She was remarkable to look at. I had never seen such heavy hair of so bright a gold before.

"So it's a home you're looking for?" I remarked.

"Work," she said. "No charity. And I'm not asking for yours or any gorgio's. So just stop bothering me, will you, and let me cleanse those cuts again."

She had a determined way with her, and although I was not used to being managed by any woman, I had to give way, because not a limb of my body was free from cuts or bruises, and it felt as though one ankle was broken.

When I was properly washed and rebandaged, Esther made me as comfortable as possible with a blanket over me and something soft under my head. "Do as you're told now," she said, "and sleep."

I did.

I slept until the afternoon; the sky was still gray, with a thin summer mist veiling the landscape. I lay for some time without moving, thinking back until the details of preceding events were quite clear. My head still ached, and my body was sore, but my mind was no longer confused. I eased myself up, feeling the bandages on legs, arm, and forehead. The strange woman was a competent nurse whatever else she was, I thought wonderingly, recalling the thin honey-brown face and bright yellow hair. Just then she appeared with a mug of something that had a strong bitter smell.

"What's this?" I asked. "Another gypsy concoction?"

"Drink it," she said. "It'll ease the fever from your blood."

"Fever? I've no fever," I said.

"Maybe not; but you *had*."

I drank the stuff, which had an unpleasant acrid flavor. After that she brought me a bowl filled with water, a cloth and a comb. "You'd better clean your face and straighten yourself up," she said practically, "if you want to get to your place this night."

"You don't waste words," I said cryptically.

She shrugged. "Nor anything," she said. "All I've had is there in the cart."

"Oh?"

"A few sticks of this and that . . . my shawl and crystal, and things I used at the fairs."

"You mean you were a performer?" I asked.

"A kind of one. Since the gypsies had me, I learned their arts and went with them from the tip of Wales right down the breadth and length of Cornwall."

"What do you mean by 'when the gypsies had you'?" I said.

"It was when I was little. Four perhaps, five . . . I don't know. There was my father as well at the start. He was a painter, and we joined the travelers . . . he got work doing portraits at the fairs and places . . . you know." She shrugged. I waited. "Then," she continued slowly, "he got consumption, and after his death I just stayed with them."

"What about your mother?"

Esther shook her head. "She died when I was a baby. I can't remember her; only through a locket I had with her picture on it. It disappeared somewhere. But she came from a good respectable family . . . whatever that means."

The irony in her voice did not escape me.

"Haven't you seen any one of them since? Your Grandparents or relations? Surely you must have some . . . ?"

"And if I have what of it?" she interrupted fiercely. "They're nothing to me. They were against my father from the start. That was the trouble. If it hadn't been for them she might not have died. So don't ever talk of them. The

only family I had were the travelers, because they minded
and cared for me. I liked being with them, they made a
great fuss of me. When we went to doors in the cities sell-
ing brooms and mats and posies of cowslips, everyone said,
'What a pretty little girl.' So you see I was old enough to
know the meaning of words."

There was silence between us then. I watched her walk
to the patch of grass where the donkey was grazing, unteth-
ered, and bring it nearer the cart and primitive tent where
I was lying. Then she took the harness from the wagon and
slipped it on. Esther was a graceful creature, hardy, with the
sinuous movement of a young lioness.

"Why are you alone now?" I asked presently.

"The way of things," she answered. "In the last year our
folks have separated, some taken by the law, others—
Pyramus and Jason—settled with gorgio women. And people die, brother. The old woman, Leonora, the Queen, was
taken with typhus only six months ago. She left me all she
had—the cart, the crystal, and Sheba. That's why I'm alone
and for settling down."

I could not help smiling, although the movement made
me wince.

"Are you sure you're ready for that?"

"I'm sure."

Obviously she did not wish to talk much about herself,
but I couldn't help asking, "And what's your other name,
Esther? Esther what?" She shook her head so the yellow
hair floated in a golden cloud around her shoulders.

"Who knows? Rose. That's what my father called me
. . . because Rose was my mother's name."

"Esther Rose," I echoed. "Pretty."

"Good enough," she said, "though there's not much of
the rose about me."

I didn't contradict her; did not say, "No, you're far too
feline." Though I thought it.

"When you've lived quiet and wild for so long," I heard
her saying half dreamily, "you come to wanting nothing

else except country places. And that's it, you see . . . all I need's a small patch somewhere where I can work the land or weave the mats, and watch the days come and go, with Sheba comfortable in her last years."

"Don't you want a husband and children?" I couldn't help asking.

For a moment she did not reply. Then she said tartly, "You want to know too much. I could ask the same. Maybe I have a right to know, seeing that I've taken and nursed you, and done what I could for a poor wretch of a heedless gorgio man sick with drink, and wounds probably of his own making."

"I can't speak of it," I said shortly, remembering with sudden clarity the burning of the farm and the misery that had driven me to set it alight.

"All right then," Esther remarked. "So we understand each other."

She did not speak again before we set off, except to tirade when I tried to walk on my own.

"You've no more strength yet than a two-year-old," she said, as I was forced to lean my weight on her. "And not half as much sense."

Somehow she managed to get me into the cart, where I lay between the pieces of household crockery and the equipment of her trade, including the crystal ball, propped up by cushions on a pile of shawls. Over my body, which had begun to ache again, she laid her own gaily striped blanket.

"What about you?" I managed to say as Sheba brayed impatiently.

She gave a short laugh and turned around before jerking the donkey's reins.

"Me? . . . I need no cape. This is how I like it, with the fine rain on my face. So don't start worrying. Just tell me the way and we'll be off."

I directed her as well as I could, and the journey back to Carnecrane began. It was the strangest journey I'd ever

made . . . down a threadwork of twisting tracks and lanes
cross-country, past mine-works and scattered gray cottages,
coming at times to patches of woodland rich with shrubs,
and lush dark green rhododendron bushes aflame through
the gray air with crimson blooms. Then the scene would as
suddenly thin out into stark desolation, yawning with derelict pits and scattered rocks of wasteland. We passed no
one; or if we did, I did not see. It was like traveling
through a dream world. At one point I wondered if I had
died and was searching for Eva. A wave of giddiness
claimed me, and I wished it was so. Then I heard the
woman Esther saying, "Are you all right then?" And I
knew I still lived.

"I can still feel pain," I answered.

The cart drew up at a crossroads. "Where do we go
now?" Esther inquired.

I propped myself up. The rain was turning back to mist,
and under the lowering cloud the lanes were no more than
pale threads of light through the gathering gloom. I managed to turn my head, seeing far behind the looming shape
of Trencrom hill blotting out the sky.

"Straight ahead," I answered. "We have to reach the far
coast."

I knew very well it was not really such a distance and
that on my horse and in my proper senses I could have
covered the ground in a reasonably short time, but the ab-
normal circumstances made the journey laborious, and by
the time we reached Carnecrane it was already quite dark.

Despite the rain the air was still faintly pungent from
the fire. When I realized what I'd done, I was shocked, for
the first time, but not sorry. My action had been that of a
madman, perhaps, but it had been justified, and I knew
anyone who guessed the truth would not blame me.

Mama guessed.

"It was you, Red, wasn't it?" she asked, when Esther, who
refused to be parted that night from Sheba, had been com-

fortably bedded down with her in the kitchen of the harness room. "*You* put a light to the farm. Am I right?"

"Yes, and I'd do it again," I told her, without compunction. I was lying in bed following the doctor's visit and my mother, satisfied that my injuries were not so bad as she had feared—mostly cuts and sprains—was in a sharp mood.

"Then it's a good thing you don't have to," she said. "Arson is a crime, son, according to the law; I suppose you realize that?"

"They can't prove it," I said stubbornly.

"Perhaps not. But you'd better be careful. There's been enough gossip as it is, with you riding away as you did." She paused, adding thoughtfully with her eyes intent on my face, "She seems an unusual character, this . . . this Esther you found."

"She found *me*," I pointed out. "I owe a lot to her."

"I know that," Mama said quickly. "And any debts will be paid in full, Red. Whatever the girl wants, in reason, she shall have."

Esther had already told me what she wanted, and it proved to be true. A job of work, a place to sleep and eat, and rest for Sheba.

Mama let her take the harness room, and saw that it was simply but comfortably equipped. She was given work on the land with the men, and the donkey had his patch of grazing ground.

I hardly saw her until the winter. Then it was different. The weather turned cold, and with the harvesting over there was not so much to do outside. So Esther came in to help with the house, but surprisingly it was my son William who claimed her. From the first moment, his eyes followed her wherever she went; and she was good with the child, knowing with uncanny insight what his needs were, and how to charm him into being good.

"She has a strange aptitude with young things," my

mother said. "But in William's case perhaps it's not so strange."

"Why?" I said. "What do you mean?"

"Haven't you noticed how bright he is?" Mama said. "He has great character too . . . Eva's intelligence, and my father's looks. Yes, in appearance he's a Cremyllas. But . . . he has a very warm heart, Red. It's time you realized it. You owe a duty to your son. For his mother's sake as well as his."

Her words were a rebuke as well as a plea, and I no longer had the heart to ignore either.

After that I took more interest in the little boy, and life became once more endurable.

4

In the summer of 1823, we had a visitor. I had just returned from a ride around the estate with Jed, when Mama met me in the hall with great excitement on her face. "Go up quickly and change," she said. "There is someone here very anxious to meet you."

"Why change?" I said rebelliously. "I'm weary from work around the farms. After a bite of food I shall be out again. . . ."

"No, you won't," my mother said with the peremptory note in her voice which brooked no denial. "Tonight you'll be sociable and look as much a gentleman as possible."

I went upstairs, changed my coat and breeches, tied a clean scarf at my neck, attended to my hair, and went down. "We're in here . . ." I heard my mother call from the conservatory. "Come along, Red."

I went through the dining room into the large glass annex place which opened out onto one side of the house. I have never cared for it, because its pungent smell and close atmosphere which could be overpowering although the light itself was cool and green from trailing ferns and climbing plants in pots. Mama was showing the visitor a newly cultivated type of geranium when I went in. She was looking her best in silver gray, with a white flower placed like a star in her hair. The visitor wore a plum-colored coat over fawn breeches. When he turned, I saw that he was not young. His hair, luxuriant but unpowdered, was graying at the temples. There were finely chiseled lines running from the nostrils of the aquiline nose to his well-cut mouth above the cleft chin. A distinguished-looking man, with a cape slung over his arm.

I knew him immediately. And with recognition something uncomfortable stirred in me, something I wanted to forget from the past.

"This is a very dear friend of mine, Red," I heard my mother saying, almost pleadingly. "Roderick Carew. A long time ago we acted together; Roderick . . ." She smiled at her companion. "This is . . . is my son."

The man held out his hand; I took it automatically, struggling against the desire to cry, "Out with it. What's the mystery? I've seen you before."

But I was silent. There was a long pause while his eyes burned into mine. Then he said, "You remember, don't you? The day of the shooting?"

"Yes," I said abruptly. "It wasn't the sort of thing anyone would forget. Even a child."

"I'm sorry," he said gravely. "It was a shocking business. The last thing I wanted . . ."

"What *did* you want, Mr. Carew?" I asked pointedly. "I think I've a right to know."

"Red . . ." My mother's hand came out to me imploringly, but Carew took it in his own. "No, Rosalind," he said. "We must tell him."

My mother's lips opened to speak, but he got in first.

"I'm your father, Red," he said very clearly. "Your mother and I loved each other. We should have been married if things had been different."

I was not really surprised, but the knowledge did not impress me; I had no sudden instinctive feeling toward this stranger who had deserted us for so long.

"Oh, well . . . I'm pleased to meet you," I said awkwardly, feeling a hypocrite.

He laughed. "There's no reason to pretend affection. But it gives me pleasure to see what you are."

"But you don't know what I am, do you?" I said. "You

don't know a thing about me, except what Mama told you. For instance, would it shock you to know I set fire to a farmhouse? I did, you know, and not so long ago either. In a way that was because of you."

"*Red!*" My mother's voice was shocked. "How *can* you say such a thing . . . ?"

I could feel my lip curl as I answered, "It's true. If he loved you so much why did he let you have me and Roma and do nothing about it? If he'd not left you in the lurch you'd never have married Baragwanath and we'd not have been cursed by that dreadful thing."

"*Stop* it," Mama cried furiously.

"No. Let him go on," Roderick said quietly. "He's a man and has a right to his opinion."

"Well, you've had it," I said abruptly.

Roderick shrugged. "I can't see where the farmhouse comes in, I'm afraid, but I fully understand your resentment, Red. Still, now you've got it off your chest, perhaps you'll be able to see things a little more kindly."

"I don't see why," I told him, wishing he would lose his temper so we could face each other on equal ground.

"Well then, I'll tell you something," Mama said with heightened color staining her cheeks, her eyes darting fiery sparks from their darkness. "Your father and I were not married, because I was very cruel to him at a time he came to comfort me. This made him . . . thoughtless to me. Cruelty and misunderstanding were on both sides. I'm not going to say any more, because it really is not your business. But it *is* my business to see that the evening is not spoiled by jealousies or recriminations of the past. So shall we have a drink now, before dinner?"

Realizing that I had no course but to agree, I nodded, and said, "All right, yes. What will you have . . . Father?" If irony underlay the word, Roderick did not appear to notice it.

"A whiskey I think," he said equably, "with just a tot of soda."

"Sherry for me," Mama said, as I turned to the door. "But not here. Come along, Roderick . . . the drawing room's more comfortable."

I held the door for them, and as they went through could not help thinking what a handsome pair they made, although it was hard to imagine them lost in passion so wild and demanding that Roma and I had been the result of it.

However, the evening passed off politely and pleasantly enough. I learned that Carew was playing in Truro the following week, and had taken the opportunity of making a brief visit to Carnecrane before rehearsing at the weekend. Mama had persuaded him to stay the night, although I guessed he had intended to do so. I tried to hide my disgruntlement for her sake, but jealousy and resentment boiled up in me again. Having him visit us for an hour or two was one thing, putting up with him under the same roof for a whole night quite another. I didn't want Mama to get involved again. He had done enough to her in the past. The decent thing would have been for him to leave without the risk of further distress.

I was not tired that night, and sat for some time in the library when they had both gone up to bed . . . presumably to separate rooms, though I had no proof that they would end so. The thought irked and troubled me. What right had the man to come back just as though he'd been away for a short time, expecting his relationship with my mother to be the same? And how could she tolerate such a position? Was she still in love with him? She must be, or the glance of her eye would not have been so warm. I could not understand her. I had thought her to be a woman of pride. What pride was there in allowing anyone to treat her so casually?

The questions were running through my mind in a miserable circle when I heard the door opening quietly. I looked around. Mama was there, still dressed, with a lamp in her hand. She came toward me, and put her hand on my shoulder. "Why are you sitting here, Red?"

"Oh, nothing," I answered. "I was just thinking."

"Obviously," she paused, adding a moment later, "about your father?"

"Well, it's natural, isn't it?"

"I suppose it is," she agreed. "So long as your thoughts are pleasant. Didn't you like him?"

"Oh, yes. He seemed all right. Quite attractive to women still, I suppose."

"He's that kind of person," she said. "Like your uncle Jasper. By the way, Red, that is one of the things Roderick came about . . ."

"Oh?"

"He brought a letter for me from my uncle—written before he died in January."

"I didn't know he was dead," I said. "But he must have been old, and he never came, did he? He was another who let you down."

"Neither of them let me down. Your great-uncle fell on hard times. That's why he didn't contact us. He married a woman who thought she could act and couldn't. She insisted on appearing with him in every production . . . consequently his career was completely ruined. That's how it is in the theater. He became ill, poor Uncle Jasper. He was so charming, Red. He did so much for me at the beginning, when I first went to London. I met the great Mrs. Siddons, you know, and at that time the name of Jasper Cremyllas was quite famous on the stage. If I'd known about him—how sick he was, I should certainly have had him at Carnecrane."

"And his wife, I suppose, and all the lame ducks you could collect?"

"What a thing to say."

"True though. You've got a soft heart, Mama."

"Maybe. But my head is quite clear," she remarked with a shrewd look at me. "That's why I've come down to set your mind at rest."

I was startled. "Whatever do you mean?"

"*You* know," she said. "Don't deny you've been picturing your father and I under . . . connubial circumstances . . . isn't that the way they put it?"

Her forthrightness confused me. "I don't see why . . ."

"Oh, yes, you do. And understand, Red, if I wanted to sleep with Roderick I should do so, and have every right to. But I have no intention of it. I'm fifty-two. I may love him still, I always shall. But that's different from being in love. At my age emotions change, and love becomes more . . . warm friendship, if you life. I have my life with you and William, which is all I desire. Roderick has a wife, and his stage career. Our ways don't meet anymore, except to touch briefly, like tonight. The contact has meant a great deal to me, but nothing else. I want it to mean something to you. So go to bed now, my dear, and sleep well. In the morning be nice to your father, for my sake and his. Will you try?"

I felt suddenly ashamed. "Of *course*. I'm sorry, Mama. I've been a bit of a prig and a boor. I started remembering things."

"Going over the past is no good . . . unless it's the best part. Remember that."

She left me then. A little later I went upstairs, realizing that my son had not been mentioned throughout the whole evening. Tomorrow, I thought with pride, I would introduce him to his grandfather. The idea mildly amused me, and set me thinking as well of Esther . . . the strange girl who had taken such command of the child, and was so content to remain in the background, attending to little William's needs, working in the house or outside, and spending her leisure moments talking to the old donkey in a foreign language I did not understand.

5

During the next two years my memories of Eva gradually became less painful. The hard physical and mental work involved in managing the estate combined with a growing interest in my young son kept me more concerned with the present and future than with the past. Occasionally I caught my mother's fine eyes turned upon me speculatively, and one late afternoon in the autumn of 1825 she said over our evening meal, "You have no social life, Red. Do you find work with the men sufficient?"

"What do you mean?"

"Exactly what I said. You're young. Most men of your age need other things than just work. The new people at Pengalva Court seem very pleasant. Worthy retired folk connected with shipping, from Plymouth, I believe. . . . They have a son and a daughter. The son is about to leave Cambridge, the daughter's at home at the moment, attractive girl. The rector introduced her and her mother when I was in Penzance the other day. We've been invited over."

"Good God!" I said.

Mama laughed. "What's wrong? Does it sound so ridiculous for me to have an invitation out?"

"Of course not," I told her. "The ridiculous part seems the 'worthy people.' I'm not sure I like the sound of them."

"No," she agreed. "I thought you mightn't. However, I think we should go. It will be a change."

I knew she had made up her mind, and on the evening

in question we set off at seven o'clock in the carriage to meet the Thomas family.

I had not been to Pengalva since I was a very young child when Great-uncle Thurston and his wife Helena were alive, and my memories, which had become a legendary impression in my mind of harmonious taste and elegant gentility, received a shock when we entered the gracious building. Obviously the house had been completely refurnished and decorated in a sham gothic manner that, although colorful and ornate, verged upon vulgarity. The whole place reeked of money. Footmen and servants emerged on every conceivable opportunity. Wilson Harvey-Thomas—the hyphen alone conveyed his ambitious and successful personality—was a portly, convivial, shrewd-eyed man in the late middle-aged category, with an impressive knowledge of wines, political matters, and an ebullient cigar-smoking manner which had doubtless got him to where he was. His wife, more cultured, but timidly under her husband's influence, was pleasant enough in a colorless way—"worthy," as my mother had said.

Their daughter, Olivia, was different.

I had never seen a more striking girl. Except for her nose, which was a little too formidable, she was beautiful, with fine china-blue eyes under very thick dark lashes, masses of chestnut hair ringletted about her face, against which the flawless cream skin glowed with vitality and health. She was fashionably attired in green silk cut low on the shoulders to reveal her fine neck and suggestion of swelling breasts beneath the fitted bodice.

She was provocative and alluring. I wanted her.

I was fully aware that she was conscious of her effect on me, just as I knew it was what she had wanted and had intended. I pretended indifference, and later, when we'd left, Mama said, "You weren't very friendly to Olivia, Red. Why? Didn't you like her?"

"No," I said, which was true.

"But why ever not? She's well educated and extremely good-looking. I thought you'd get on well together."

"She's not my type," I answered abruptly.

"If you're thinking of Eva," Mama said tactlessly, "I know they're very different. But . . . oh, well." She shrugged. "No one can arrange these things."

"Quite," I agreed. What I did not tell her was that I had not been thinking of Eva at all just then, and that although Olivia annoyed me intensely, she had disturbed me profoundly sexually, and for the first time since my wife's death I consciously longed for a woman.

After that first meeting, we had many. They were chance affairs at the beginning—or cleverly contrived to seem so—when Olivia lost her way riding the moors and appeared conveniently near my doorstep. Later we discarded the pretense, and arranged to see each other usually in the evenings at remote spots where we could be together undisturbed by prying eyes. She confused me.

The first time I kissed her she appeared taken aback like any shy, inexperienced young girl, and yet there was something about her that suggested the contrary—a faint mockery in the sidelong glance of her eyes, and curve of her full lips—a "knowingness" which far from putting me off, only increased my interest. *Interest*, of course, was not the word. I was not really concerned about her mind, what she thought, her history, the mode of fashionable life in Plymouth, or the dances she'd been to, her father's indulgences, or her mother's connections with a titled family. None of it registered except in a negative way. Women liked to boast sometimes, I knew that. Let her prattle on. Her prattling meant nothing; she hardly knew what she was saying half the time. I could tell from the flush in her cheeks, the brilliance of her eyes, that she felt as I did. The rest was facade. Before October was out, I knew I had to have Olivia Harvey-Thomas either in wedlock or out of it. The former would have drawbacks, including the endless dull business conversations with her father. On the other hand she would not come to me empty-handed, which could be a help and ensure little William's future. If she'd been as poor as the proverbial church mouse, however, my feelings would have been the same. Providing she'd have me, I would marry her.

My ardor shocked me. I tried not to think of Eva, and didn't just then.

Olivia became an obsession. My work slackened off considerably, and when Esther stopped me on the drive one day to tell me that Sheba had died, I did not, at first, take in what she'd said. I was walking on, but her hand pulled at my coat forcibly.

"Did you hear what I said?"

Startled by her shrill voice, I turned and saw the tears brimming in her eyes.

"I'm sorry . . ." I answered. "I . . . you said something about Sheba."

"She's dead."

"Oh. Oh, Esther . . . that's bad. I really *am* sorry."

Misery made her almost plain. She stood rolling her handkerchief in one hand, swallowing in an effort to hide her emotion. Then she asked harshly, "Will you help me bury her?"

"Can't the boy do it for you, Esther? I'm . . ."

"You're off out, I suppose. That's all right then. I just thought . . ."

"Look," I said, feeling mean, "I'm not unsympathetic. I liked the old donkey. But me burying her isn't going to bring her to life again. Get the boy and Jed. They'll do it more thoroughly than me."

"All right." She turned abruptly and walked away with her yellow hair tumbled about her downcast face as though in a veil of mourning for her dumb friend. I was momentarily depressed, and irritated because of it. It was a wonderful autumn afternoon, and no one had a right to be sad, least of all myself, who was off to meet Olivia. So I shook the thought of Esther aside, saddled my horse, and was presently cantering up the lane over the road and around the hill, past Tywarren, skirting Castle Tol on my right, taking the track beyond mine-workings to a group of stones immediately below the cromlech. The air was heady and pungent with the seductive earthy smell of damp dead leaves and distant scent of dying bonfires.

I felt strong and excited, filled with the longing to hold Olivia in my arms.

She arrived soon after, looking radiant, in dark blue velvet riding clothes that only added to the brilliant blue of her eyes.

When I'd tethered the horses to a thorn tree below, I went back and took her in my arms. Her lips were warm and passionate as we kissed. I could feel the soft tip of her tongue against mine. "Olivia," I whispered, unable to stop my voice trembling. "I want you so. Oh, darling . . . love me . . . please love me . . ." Her chestnut hair brushed my cheek as she looked up at me, her lips red and full and inviting.

"Dearest Red," she murmured. "How strong you are."

"Oh, God, Olivia . . . don't tease me . . ."

A ripple of laughter came from her throat. "Why would I tease you?"

A fire ran through me as she strained against me, her breasts, firm and taut beneath the velvet coat. I unfastened it and slipped it off, the frilly thing beneath, and the long full skirt. She stood there looking absurdly young . . . but with the allure of all the feminine beauty there had ever been, or could be. I laid her down in the brown ferns and dead bracken, and took her into a thrill of forgetfulness not once, but twice, until passion was allayed for the time being, and I could look at her passively in peace. I laid my cheek against her. "You're so beautiful," I murmured presently. She touched my hair lightly.

"And you can love very well, Red," she said. "But I

must dress." She jumped up, reaching for her skirt. "Oh look," she cried. "My hat . . . my lovely hat . . . all squashed as flat as a pancake."

"Who minds about that?" I said, trying to pull her back to me.

She shook herself free. "*I* do. It cost a lot. It's the very latest style. We got it in Paris in the summer when we were there."

"I'll get you another just as good," I said, thinking she was just teasing. "We'll go to London and buy as many hats as you like."

She frowned. "What on earth do you mean? Go to London with *you*? Why should I?"

I stood up, facing her in bewilderment, wondering what I'd said that was wrong.

"Haven't we just . . . I mean, it was all right, wasn't it?"

"What? . . . Oh, *that*. Yes, of course. I said . . . you were quite good."

"I don't understand. I thought . . ."

"What? That you were the first? That it was an enduring grand passion?"

I still couldn't believe she wasn't putting on an act. "Yes," I said. "I was thinking we could make a trip when . . . Oh, God, Olivia . . . don't look like that. What I'm trying to say is . . . marry me. Will you be my wife, darling? I love you, you know I do. We love each other, don't we?"

I broke off, shocked by the sudden scorn on her face.

"Marry *you*?" she cried. "*Love*? What on earth do you mean? Do you really imagine I'd marry a *working farmer*?" The inflection in her voice was that of a queen talking to the lowest scum of her kingdom.

I stared at her while dull anger mounted in me until it became rage. But I kept my tones calm while I said, "Just what do you mean by that?"

She shrugged contemptuously. "Just what I say. I'm no bourgeois pauper governess like the scheming spinster who grabbed you from the cradle. I've heard about her. On the shelf, wasn't she, poor thing? But she must have known a thing or two . . . and I wouldn't dream of taking her leavings." While I struggled to control myself, she continued casually, "If you must know, I'm practically engaged to Sir Clive Redell."

She got no further. The sneer against Eva, on top of the other insults, was too much for me. I brought my hand sharp and hard against her face. She stepped back, lifting her own hand to her cheek. As she did so the skirt, which was not fastened properly, fell to her feet again.

"How *dare* you," she cried.

I swept her over my knee, delivered a number of smart slaps, and then pushed her away, flinging the skirt after her. "Now get out," I cried. "And don't ever come sniffing around me again . . . I don't like trollops, and you're the first of your kind I've met."

Aflame with indignation, she pulled her clothes on, shouting, "You'll hear more about this. You're nothing but a vulgar oaf. I hate you, hate you. I'll tell my father. I'll see the whole district knows . . ."

I laughed. "Good. They'll enjoy it. You'll be the laughing-stock of the district. Why don't you have it inscribed on this stone. 'It was here that . . .'"

I didn't finish. There was no need. Olivia Harvey-Thomas, looking wild and disarrayed without her hat, was already untethering her mare from the tree, and a minute later was cantering away in the direction of Pengalva.

I picked up the hat, staring at its absurdity, before flinging it as far as possible after her. It stuck on a bush and remained there, looking like something dropped by a clown.

As I rode back to Carnecrane, a kind of shame filled me. Shame not only for having lost my temper so violently, but most of all for having dreamed of putting Olivia in

Eva's place. Well, it was over now. Olivia Harvey-Thomas was out of my blood for good. I had been played upon and seduced by a promiscuous girl like any callow youth. In future I was done with women.

But I wasn't.

Mama must have sensed that something had happened that day. After dinner the same night she said overcasually, "Did you enjoy your ride this evening?"

"It was all right."

"You went to meet Olivia, I suppose?"

"Yes."

"Hm. Do you want to talk about it?"

"Why should I?" I said with a scowl.

"No reason of course. But it sometimes helps when . . . when things go wrong, as I presume they have. You've been very glum. What happened, son? Did she turn you down?"

"Why do you think there was anything to . . ."

"Oh, come come. I've eyes in my head. For the past few weeks you've had no thought in your head but Olivia. I didn't say anything because it wasn't my business. But I couldn't see much happiness for you in that direction. Since our visit to Pengalva I've heard a number of things about Miss Harvey-Thomas. For one thing . . ."

"You needn't tell me," I said. "She's going to marry Sir something-or-other-Redell. She likes men. *Any* man. I know that too."

"Oh, Red."

"I could have put up with it . . ." I said bitterly. "I suppose I should have had the sense to know she was out for bigger fish to fry. But when she sneered at Eva . . ."

"She . . . *what?*"

"What she said was cheap. All I'd done was to ask her to marry me . . ."

"*All,* Red?"

"Well . . . anyhow," I said, brushing her question aside. "She mocked and threw it back in my face as though

I were dirt. It was that about Eva, though . . . I wasn't taking it from any woman. So I . . ."

"Yes?"

"I just let fly; I put her over my knee and she got what she deserved, right there, under the cromlech. And I'm glad. Damned glad. I'd do it again; so if you hear any tales . . ." ·

I broke off because my mother was laughing. She laughed until the tears ran from her eyes. "Oh, Red, I think that's the funniest thing I've heard for years. Olivia Harvey-Thomas, and under the cromlech. Imagine it."

She went on laughing, and suddenly I saw the humor of it and joined in. After that I felt better, although I guessed my mother might not have treated the business quite so lightly if I'd told her everything.

How much Esther had guessed about my relationship with Olivia I did not know. For over a week I managed to avoid her, passing her only occasionally on the stairs or landing as she left the nursery. The avoidance, I think, was mutual. Since Sheba's death Esther had seemed unconcerned with everyone but little William, speaking only when she was questioned, and answering then in monosyllables, her strange eyes remote and cold.

Then one morning when I went to the stables I saw her coming from the harness room with the colored blanket slung over her shoulder, and loaded obviously with her few belongings. She would have passed me, but I planted myself in front of her squarely and said, "Where are you going with all that, Esther?"

"Where the will takes me," she answered shortly and enigmatically. "It's my business, isn't it?"

Her odd-looking yet attractive face was haughty and cold.

"Not entirely," I said. "There's William and Mama, and me."

"*You!*" Her voice held scorn. "You don't need me, neither does your mother."

"And my son?"

Her eyes softened but only momentarily. "As you say . . . he's *your* son. I only hope when you . . . when you bring this proud Miss What's-her-name back as your wife, she'll be kind to him."

"Who said I was bringing anyone back as my wife?"

"If you don't then I should say you ought to," she remarked. "People talk, you know. I hear things, and I've eyes in my head."

"Well, if you must know . . ."

"I don't want to know anything," Esther said, pushing past me. "But watch out, Reddin Cremyllas. Before you know it you'll be drawn into something that isn't of your making."

She walked on, down the drive, to the gate.

"For heaven's sake, Esther," I shouted, going after her. "You can't just walk out like this. Does my mother know?"

"Of course."

"Didn't she say anything? Try to stop you?"

"At first. Not when she saw my mind was made up."

She waited a moment, then held out her hand. "Goodbye, Red . . . this is for the best. I've served my purpose. And don't fret about me. I'm no gorgio fool. I have my craft. Since Sheba went there's not been much for me here. When something you love goes, a bit of your heart goes with it."

She smiled briefly, heaved her load further over her shoulder, and in a few minutes her thin form had disappeared around a bend of the lane.

I felt suddenly and inexplicably bereft, remembering how we'd first met, how she'd cared for me and brought me back after the burning of the Baragwanath farm. Since then she'd become part of the household; I'd been used to seeing her about the fields and in the nursery, always willing to take on any job that was necessary, not speaking much or inflicting herself in any way. A remote, proud girl, moving quietly about her work with the instinctive grace of some wild creature untainted by the ways of society.

The house seemed empty without her. I had never imagined her to be so vital a part of Carnecrane. William became troublesome too, flying into tempers for no reason, which put my own nerves as well as Mama's on edge.

"We'll have to get another girl," my mother said when Esther had been gone a week. "It shouldn't be too difficult to find someone suitable. I'll go into Penzance tomorrow, and if I have no luck there we can take a trip into Falmouth."

"All right," I agreed. "But it's Esther he wants."

"She's gone and that's that," Mama said tartly. "I can't blame her. She got precious little, living here."

"What do you mean by that?"

"What I say. You never spoke to her, or hardly ever. Even when Sheba died and she was needing sympathy, you left her to find Jed to bury the poor old thing. The truth is, Red, you lost your head. And believe me, though you may not think it, I have a feeling we haven't heard the last of Olivia Harvey-Thomas yet."

"Why?"

"Because rumor has it her engagement—if it was ever fact—to the Redell man is off."

"Good for him."

Mama eyed me shrewdly. "There's no chance, I suppose," she said, "that the girl could be pregnant?"

Under the straight fiery gaze of her eyes, my own faltered, while the blood crept in a hot wave under my cravat. "How do I know? She's had men. She admitted it. Besides it's too early . . ."

"Babies can be born conveniently prematurely," my mother remarked coolly. "And you've put yourself in an extremely vulnerable position. Still, we shall have to see."

I could not imagine Olivia showing her face again at Carnecrane after what had happened. But a niggle of fear persisted. Fear mingled with something else . . . of desperate longing for Esther. That evening I rode around the countryside, searching for her. It was a cold moon-bright night of frost and fiery stars, of wind and flying shadows that gave the wild landscape an eerie quality, peopled only by the ghosts of things long gone and forgotten. Loneliness engulfed me. My eyes searched the pale light desperately for a glimpse of a girl with long blown hair and a bundle on her back. I rode all the miles to Trencrom hill, pausing at intervals to put my hand to my mouth, calling "Esther . . . Esther . . ." but there was no reply. No sign of the slight strange creature who had slipped into my life and out again like a phantom creature of my imagination. Why had I let it happen? Why? I had been blind, and a fool. She had been rare, and beautiful, with something of her very self to give, which I had rejected.

As I rode back, taking another route which brought me eventually on the far side of Tywarren, I thought at one point that the legendary dark horseman of the Gump, from below Carn Kenidzek the Hooting Carn, was ahead of me with a thunder of galloping hooves. I turned back. But when I looked around there was nothing but streaking moonlight and driven clouds chasing across the sky. I cut down toward Carnecrane. I was surprised how late it was—twelve thirty.

My mother was up. "Wherever have you been, son?" she asked. "You should tell me when you're away for the night. What was I to think? What *could* I think but that you were out on some drunken brawl again?"

I felt completely exhausted. "You know it isn't my habit," I answered. "I was looking for Esther."

She looked contrite. "Oh. I'm sorry. But . . . Esther is a girl of her word. Don't expect her to return. Why should she?"

And I thought, "Why indeed?"

A few days after that Wilson Harvey-Thomas arrived unexpectedly at Carnecrane. I was out in the fields where liming was in process, and attired as I was, did not feel at all disposed to speak to the ambitious tycoon. I wished nothing to do with him in any case, but Jed, who'd brought the message, was insistent. "Go on," he said. "Your mother was determined. Get it over with. Nothing to worry about, he's all geniality and swagger."

Felling thoroughly truculent and aggrieved, I went back to the house, washed my hands, brushed the mud from my clothes, and went into the library where Olivia's father was examining the hunting prints on the walls. Mama was standing by him. She turned and glanced at me warningly when I went in.

"Here he is," she said to the visitor. "Mr. Harvey-Thomas wants a few words with you, Red. So I'll leave you."

She went out, and Harvey-Thomas and I faced each other.

"Well, lad," he said, smiling broadly, "nice to see you."

"Oh?"

"Yes. Cigar?" He flashed one before my nose but I refused. "No thanks. I don't smoke much."

"Hm. Economy, eh?"

"Not at all."

"Oh, no offense. I just thought . . . well, running a place like this isn't all jam these days, is it?"

His familiarity jarred me. "I don't see . . ."

"What it is to do with me? No, maybe not. But I've been looking over the place . . . the ground I mean, and it's quite impressive, or could be with a bit of money spent on it. That mine, for instance . . ."

My irritation turned to hot resentment and anger. "Do you mind telling me what right you have to come prying into my affairs, Mr. Thomas?"

His blandness still remained, though the shrewd eyes narrowed.

"Of course I don't. It's what I've come about. I want us to be friends, Red. That's what they call you, isn't it, Red? Not hard to see why. Hot coloring, hot blood, and none the worse for it. I was hot-blooded when I was young myself, still got a touch of it when it's needed. So's my daughter . . . that girl you've been escorting around the country-side." The smile had left his face, leaving only the bullying quality I'd known was there, underneath the aplomb.

"Well?"

He paused before continuing. "She's missed you. Now I know young people have lovers' quarrels, and what yours was about I don't know. But don't let it go on too long, boy She's willing to forgive and forget. And so are you; if you're the sensible young man I think."

"I still don't see what my relationship with Olivia has to do with you," I said coldly, though I was beginning to.

"Now, now, don't take that tone with me. I can make things good or bad for you, and you know it, lad. This visit is a token of goodwill, with a message from Olivia to say she's sorry if she acted hastily. Can I tell her you feel the same way?"

"No."

"What's that?"

"There's nothing between your daughter and myself," I said pointedly and very clearly. "We were friendly for a bit, but it's over. I'm sorry, but that's how it is."

"So you're going to be difficult, are you? After seducing that girl of mine you're trying to get out of it like any . . ."

"*Seduce?*" I shouted. "What the devil are you talking about? You ought to know your own daughter by now . . ."

"I know you assaulted her," Harvey-Thomas said, purple-faced, his voice shaken with fury. "I know you treated her like any common whore and then took off to other amusements, no doubt . . ."

"If that's what you really think," I said, "and I don't think you could be so shortsighted—just make a few in-quiries around the district, and you may be surprised. Now, if you don't mind, I've work to do . . ."

I walked to the door, opened it, and waited for him to move. When he did not, I said as insultingly as I could manage, "I have no intention of marrying Olivia, even to give any bastard she produces a name, because I hardly think it will be mine, sir."

He took up his cane, marched toward me, and brought it sharply against my cheek. "My God," he said, "you'll pay for this. I'll see you hounded from the district and branded as the cur you are, if it's the last thing I ever do."

"I don't think so," I said, mopping my face with my handkerchief. "And now if you don't mind . . . get out!"

His fury was so great he walked the wrong way to the kitchens. I was about to call him back when I had a shock.

There, coming toward us, with her hair loose on her shoulders, her face woebegone, and eyes imploring, was Esther.

My relief was so great I could have cried. I went forward and took her hands, forgetting momentarily the hulk of the portly figure beside me. Then I remembered and, before he could escape, said impulsively with my arm around the girl's waist.

"This is Esther, sir. My wife-to-be. We are getting married shortly."

I thought at first he was about to suffer a stroke. Then, drawing himself up to his full height, he said, "This is not the last you will hear from me." The words were aggressive, but no more, I guessed, than an idle threat.

He would have gone through the kitchens, but I took his arm, bowed sarcastically, and said with a wave of my hand, "You are taking the wrong direction. Gentry use the front door."

I watched him walk heavily and impressively back along the corridor. When the door had banged behind him, I turned to Esther.

"I'm so glad you're back," I said awkwardly. "It was lonely without you. William fretted . . . but not as much as me."

She shrugged. "You're a funny one. And what was all that about your wife-to-be? It's the first I'd heard of it."

"I know. And me. It was just an idea. But . . ."

"To get you out of trouble. Yes?"

I looked into her clear hazel eyes, and found I could not lie.

"Yes. Partly. But not all . . ." I broke off.

She shrugged. "Oh, well, I'm always willing to help a friend in difficulty, and I must say you're a quick one with words, Red. But don't try and use me like that again. *Never*."

A flash of unmanly shame flamed through my whole body.

"I didn't mean to use you, Esther."

"No? Then what was it?"

"The truth," I answered. "I really *want* you to marry me. I really *have* missed you. I know it's quick, but . . ."

"Much *too* quick," she said tartly. "You haven't given me a thought, all these months and months. For all *you* care I mightn't have been there at all. So stop the nonsense. Fool yourself if you like, but not me. I'm not that kind; and I'll certainly take no other woman's leavings."

She turned to walk away. I caught her and swung her around, with my fingers hard on her thin brown arms. Her strange eyes shone bright and cold in her pointed set face.

"Esther . . ." I began desperately.

"Yes?"

Her voice, so hard and unrelenting, chilled me. I released her. "Very well, if that's how you feel." I waited for a moment before adding, "As you've come back I suppose you'll be staying for a time anyway."

"If William still needs me, and your mother doesn't mind."

"*You* should know the answer to that," I said.

"Yes."

And so Esther stayed. Her presence, which I'd accepted so unquestioningly when she first came to Carnecrane, now put me frequently on edge. Although she spoke to me only when necessary, and then merely on matters concerning little William, her personality seemed to dominate the house. Her very silence was a challenge and an irritation. Although I tried to break the wall between us, it was useless. I could neither goad nor move her. Once I said, coming face to face with her in the hall, "Is there any need to be like this?"

"Like what? Have you any complaints?"

"Plenty," I said angrily. "You never speak to me, never smile . . ."

"I was never one to pretend or laugh at nothing," she retorted, with her chin raised an inch higher.

"I hear you sometimes, with William."

"William's different, a child. We understand each other."

"Yes, I know. That's the point. You can fuss and bother about my son, yet treat me like dirt. Is it reasonable?"

For a moment the light in her eyes softened. Then her lips hardened as she said, "There's more to life than reason, Reddin Cremyllas. And now let me get on with what I have to do."

I stood mutely as she pushed past, and went on from the passage into the kitchen.

I was baffled, angered, and had a sudden urge to work off my bad mood; so I saddled my horse, and unthinkingly took the moorland track around the hill skirting Tywarren . . . a way I'd been careful to avoid since my last encounter with Olivia.

The air was cold and sharp, the autumn bracken and foliage already withered into the fading brown and gray of encroaching winter. I remembered with distaste Olivia's taunts, which had culminated in such a violent and undignified scene, and began to think of her, not with desire, but the idle curiosity of a man released from an unsavory obsession.

I wondered if what my mother and the irate parent had implied was true . . . that she was expecting a child, which despite my denial could easily be my own. The possibility alarmed and even revolted me now, because I knew I would never marry her. The memory of her revived no more than a kind of lustful shame which the last weeks had resolved into true proportion.

Then, just as I was turning a bend in the hill, I saw her cantering toward me, erect on her mount, wearing a blue habit and blue plumed hat. It was too late for me to turn and go the other way, so I went on, and when we were face to face both halted. She stared at me, hesitated, then suddenly laughed and said, "Hello, darling. Don't be scared. I won't eat you."

"Hello, Olivia," I replied casually. "Glad to see you looking so well."

"Oh, I am," she assured me. "In spite of what my devoted father may have implied."

I was taken aback, and when I said nothing she went on gaily, "He was trying to entrap you, of course. But as you must know, I wouldn't have had you on a plate, darling. Not after what you did. Wife-beaters aren't in my line at all. Neither are bastards."

I must have flushed. She laughed again, showing a flash of perfect ivory teeth. "So don't worry; I'm carrying no by-blow of yours, Red . . . I wouldn't be such a fool. But it was only right for you to sweat a bit, wasn't it? . . . Bye bye then. Thanks for the fun."

Before I could answer, she had flicked her mare to a sharp canter, and had galloped away to be lost quickly against the shadows of rocks and moor.

A fortnight later I heard that she had left her home to live under the protection of Sir Hawtrey-Venna, a middle-aged bucolic shipping tycoon, who spent most of his time at his estate near Falmouth. His wealth, no doubt, adequately compensated Olivia for the disadvantages entailed by the highly born but plain and aging wife he occasionally visited at his town establishment.

I was thankful to be rid, for good, of the problem of Olivia Harvey-Thomas.

But my longing for Esther was intensified. I cursed myself for the fool I'd been; tried in every way to soften her, but it was no use. As Christmas drew nearer, my loneliness, which I hid under a sullen veneer, increased. My only refuge was in remembering Eva—her gentleness and compassion—and this brought pain which was hard to bear.

In such a mood I wandered off one afternoon, taking a way Eva and I had often gone together. The sun had already slipped beyond the rim of hills, leaving a faint rosy flush below a greenish clear sky. Twilight would fall quickly, swallowing the tones of the landscape into cool uniformity. Just for a few seconds I sensed acutely the inevitable passing of time with foreboding which was alien to me. I rested my head against the cool, firm trunk of a tree, and in my isolation gave way to emotions subdued for so long.

Tears had never come easily to me; but for that brief period I could feel their salt sting my eyes and trickle through my fingers. I wiped my cheek with a grimed hand, and the next moment heard the crackle of twigs and a voice saying, "What's the matter, Red?"

Astonished, I turned to see Esther standing there, with a brown cape around her shoulders. She looked wan in the pale light, and not strictly beautiful . . . just strange, and "different," and the most desirable woman in the world to me.

"Esther . . ." I said, and made an involuntary gesture toward her.

She did not move.

"I said, 'what's the matter' . . . brother?"

At first the gist of the *brother*—which meant so much more than that—did not register. Then, in a flash, I knew; could sense rather than see the quiver of a smile about her mouth. I needed no more. A moment later I had her head against my chest, with my lips buried in her hair, murmuring all the foolish words of endearment known to man.

A little later, when we'd both got our breath back, I said, "Why so long, Esther? Why *now*? . . . Seeing me weak and broken, like any . . ."

"Sh . . . sh . . ." she said. "It would have happened anyway, someday. I never could bear to see a defenseless thing hurt."

"Defenseless? *Me?*"

She laughed then, a happy sound, sweet as the trilling of a blackbird in spring. "Well . . . not *quite*, perhaps. You've got hard strong hands, Reddin Cremyllas. My arm will be black and blue tomorrow for sure."

I was all compassion and concern, and lifted the shawl so my lips could travel once more the soft firm flesh.

"I love you," I said simply. "Will you marry me, please, Esther Rose?"

She didn't prevaricate; just said, "Of course I will, Reddin Cremyllas."

And that was how it was.

When we walked back to the house later, my mother guessed, even before we said anything.

"So you've come to your senses at last," she said.

I held Esther close to me with my arm strong about her waist.

"I've asked Esther to marry me," I replied, "because I love her, and she loves me. Well, have we your blessing?"

Mama hugged us both warmly. "I've never been more pleased about anything in my life," she said. "God bless you, my children."

During the next ten years, Esther bore me three daughters: Ann, Elizabeth, and Carmella. Then surprisingly, after another decade, our son Jason came along. William, my eldest son, was then twenty-four: a true Cremyllas to look at, but with Eva's sensitive intelligence. We couldn't afford to send him to university, but he studied at home and loved the land. His heart was with growing crops, wheat and fine barley rather than cattle. He had great ambition for the preservation of wildlife, and wrote many books on the subject. I would think of Eva sometimes, and knew she would be proud of the child she'd given me, just as she'd have approved of my lovely Esther.

Elizabeth was the first of my children to marry . . . a seaman in the merchant navy, which meant that she made her home at Carnecrane, where he joined her when he was on leave.

Ann followed the next year, taking a prosperous farmer, Falmouth way, for her husband. Carmella, a wayward girl of high spirits and great beauty, left home to marry an impoverished artist, who led her a devil of a life in London, but apparently made her happy, and was responsible for her stage debut. Although she made no great name, her impact on society was considerable though perhaps not entirely worthy, since two great personalities of social distinction were rumored to be her lovers. And rumor I suspect, was firmly based on fact.

Jason, the pride of his mother's heart and of mine, after sowing a few youthful wild oats, joined William in running Carnecrane. He married the daughter of a mining engineer from St. Just, a strapping handsome girl who gave him twins, a girl and a boy with the reddest hair of any Cremyllas in history.

And that year, at the age of ninety-six, my mother died.

Queen Victoria had been on the throne for thirty years. With Lord Palmerston's death in 1865, followed by Bismarck's victory in 1866 over Austria, the pattern of British politics and Europe was changing. William already foresaw the depression of British agriculture in the years ahead. But Mama was no longer concerned with the future. Her thoughts mostly lay in the past, and although she was by no means afflicted mentally, it was obvious to us all that she was quickly failing. She made an effort to get down each day for an hour or two, looking with a kind of wonder about the house, frequently reminiscing over days I had never known. "I shall never forget the day my father fetched me," she said not once but many times. "Mrs. Goss had died, and I was all alone. He was an extraordinary character. I loved him dearly. Do you know . . . I once went smuggling with him dressed like a boy. . . . That was after the mines closed. The mines . . ." Her thoughts would usually wander at this point into another channel. "I wonder how Roma is? . . . It seems a long time since I heard. She had sons, didn't he? . . . They went to California or somewhere, from . . . what was the place . . . Wis . . . Wis . . . ?"

"Wisconsin, Mama," I told her. "Mining."

"I should have liked to hear from her again once. She was a wild lovely little thing. She should never have married that preacher. What was his name?"

"Richard Gwarvas."

"Hm. Domineering." Her reaction never varied. "I disliked him on sight; but she always got her own way. Same as me."

When I thought of Roma then it was strange to imagine her as a woman of sixty-six with a family of middle-aged children. We had heard from her only very briefly through the long years of her married life in America. Her letters, though colorful, had been impersonal, telling stoically of the privations and disasters they'd overcome rather than details of family life. Their home in the early days had been a log cabin from where Gwarvas had gone about preaching the gospel fervently to believers and "pagans" alike among the lead regions of Galena. Arrows and tomahawks from Indians had been a constant menace, and in one lurid account Roma had described scalpings and burnings so vividly that Mama had threatened to take herself off and bring her daughter back. She began to refer to

Richard Gwarvas as "that savage" until I reminded her that it was savagery he had gone to combat.

Roma had never commented on her husband except as a fine courageous man, which he undoubtedly must have been. But a suggestion of warmth and affection would have pleased us better. We knew she had had five sons and a daughter during the first twelve years of her marriage, and that the eldest had served in the Black Hawk War.

"Wars and fighting . . . burning and preaching and breeding," my mother used to say. "Roma was born for better things than that."

In retrospect she saw my sister as a sly, intriguing child with large eyes and winning ways. But I knew Roma had been well equipped to face a hard life, which was unquestionably what she'd had.

"It's a pity your mother and Roma can't meet once more," Esther said to me one day in that summer of 1867. "I'm sure she's fretting. All her thoughts seem to be with your sister now."

"Only because she's the missing one," I told her. "The prodigal son kind of thing."

"Well, the prodigal daughter could surely find time to drop a few lines to such an old mother," Esther remarked.

I thought so too; but there was nothing I could do.

July passed into August, and on a warm day following a night of thin rain which had left the hedges and undergrowth fragrant and cob-webbed in the steamy air, Mama suggested going out for a short walk. I was surprised. It was weeks since she had set foot outside.

"Are you sure you feel strong enough?" I asked.

"With your arm and my stick I shall manage perfectly," she answered.

So we set off, and to my amazement she insisted on taking a path to a patch of furze where a derelict barn had once stood. We went slowly, but she was gasping when we got there.

I supported her while she recovered her breath, laid my
coat upon a rock, then eased her into a sitting position.
"Why here?" I asked.

There was a pause before she replied. "It was here she
saw Roma when she was a tiny child."

"She? Who, Mama?"

"My mother."

"But I thought you never . . ."

"Oh, yes. I saw her once," Mama went on reminiscently.
"She was wearing a shawl, and was no longer young. But
she blessed me, Red, and told me 'beware the sea.' She
had the sight, son. And it's her voice in me speaking now."

She lifted her face to me, and her eyes, staring from the
aged flesh drawn tight over the highly modeled cheekbones, were dark and wise with a secret knowledge that I
had sensed in myself during rare dramatic moments in my
life.

"I have not long to live now, Red," she went on half
dreamily. "That's as well. I'm tired; and grateful for what
I've had—all of it, the good and the bad, because that's the
only way we learn."

"I wish you wouldn't say such things," I said, putting my
arm around her shoulders. "You've got time ahead of you
yet. You're sad because the walk's tired you."

"Oh, no, son. And I'm not sad at all. You see . . .
before I go I shall have word from Roma."

And she did.

The next day a letter arrived. It was addressed from a
place at Mineral Point, and though intended primarily for
my mother, included all of us.

Dear Mama, Red, and family,

It is a long time since I last wrote to you, and I hope
all goes well. Through the years I have wished many
times that I could make a trip to the old country, but
lack of funds and duty have prevented it. My husband

died last year, and since then I have been living with
my eldest son Jasper and his wife. Jasper is still in
mining, but his son William has gone into the lumber-
ing business and is making a great success of it. I wish
you could have met all my children and their children, Mama. You would be proud. And this is the
news I have to tell you. You have a great-grandson.
He is the finest baby I ever saw in my life . . . red-
haired but dark-eyed . . . a very strange combina-
tion. *Striking* is the word.

I know you did not want me to marry Richard Gwarvas, but it has worked out well. My life has been a fight,
but then I wouldn't have liked things to be too easy.
And this land is a place full of promise, the future of
the world lies here I am sure. There are many many
Cornish folk around us . . . "Cousin Jacks," they
call them, and a fine Methodist church, which Richard
worked for with all his heart. He remained reli-
gious to the very end. I respected him for his beliefs,
and saw that the children did, but I think he suspected
sometimes that I was far below him in godliness, and I
feel often that when I die—always supposing there is
another life—I shall be wandering about the Red Indians' Happy Hunting Ground, while Richard plays his
harp and prays for me from his Heavenly Choir.

I must confess, though my admiration for him never
faded, my passion for him did. But then, I was blessed
with my wonderful children.

Oh, Mama, I had such a vivid dream of you the other
night. Give my love to the family, and be assured, all
goes well with your descendants here.

Love,
Roma

When I had finished reading the letter aloud to her, my
mother put a scrap of lace handkerchief to her eyes.

"I'm sure I'm a very lucky woman," she said tremulously. "To think of it . . . little Roma spreading the population of that wild, faraway great place . . . and you, Red, and your children; you've been a good boy to me . . ."

"Boy!" I thought, catching a glimpse of my reflection in the gilt-framed mirror on the opposite wall. . . . Whoever saw a "boy" of such tremendous stature and girth and bristling grayish hair? . . . The idea amused me, until I saw the look in Mama's eyes. I really *was* that to her . . . just the beloved son she'd had of Roderick Carew those sixty-seven years ago.

I squeezed her hand, and planted a kiss on her forehead.

"Why don't you go and have a little rest now, Mama?" I suggested. "This news from Roma's excited you."

"Yes, Red, dear, I think I will," she agreed.

And that night, as the summer dusk came gently down over the moors and sea, my mother died.

I went up to say good night to her before turning in myself, and thought how faintly, almost imperceptibly, she was breathing. Her skin too, was paler than usual, ivory-white in the lamplight. "Mama," I said softly. She opened her eyes, and smiled.

"Rod," she whispered. I tried to believe she meant "Red," but I knew just then it was not me she was seeing, but my father. I didn't mind. There was happiness on her face, and the smile was still there, even when the doctor, later, pulled the sheet over her face.

At first I couldn't believe it. She had lived so long and been so integral a part of our lives that her presence had become a living legend. I stood a long while in the darkened bedroom until Esther came and took me in her arms. Then I cried.

"Hush, love," my wife said. "It was a good way to go. The way she wanted."

I remembered something Esther had once said a long time ago.

"Once you told me after Sheba died, that when something you loved went, a bit of your heart went with it," I reminded her. "You spoke the truth."

She drew my head close against her breast.

"This is truth," she said. "You and I . . . the children, and our children's children. Good things don't die. All that happens is change, and who would have it otherwise?"

I looked at her in wonder, realizing fully for the first time, perhaps, the deep wisdom of her womanly heart.

Presently we got up, and hand in hand left the room.

Despite the sadness a great peace seemed to flood the house. Downstairs we went to the front door, opened it, and stood there a few moments looking out into the evening. A solitary bird rose from the west and spread its wings against the sky as the last glow of twilight faded to night.

Like a benediction, quiet descended. Then silently, we turned and went in.

Carnecrane was at rest.